Crucible of Cultures

Anglophone Drama at the Dawn of a New Millennium

P.I.E.-Peter Lang

Bruxelles · Bern · Berlin · Frankfurt/M · New York · Oxford · Wien

Dramaturgies

Texts, Cultures and Performances

Series Editor

Marc Maufort, *Université Libre de Bruxelles*

Editorial Board

Christopher Balme, *University of Mainz*
Judith E. Barlow, *State University of New York-Albany*
Johan Callens, *Vrije Universiteit Brussel*
Jean Chothia, *Cambridge University*
Harry J. Elam, *Stanford University*
Albert-Reiner Glaap, *University of Düsseldorf*
André Helbo, *Université Libre de Bruxelles*
Ric Knowles, *University of Guelph*
Alain Piette, *École d'interprètes internationaux-Mons/*
  Université Catholique de Louvain
John Stokes, *King's College, University of London*
Joanne Tompkins, *University of Queensland-Brisbane*

Editorial Assistant

Franca Bellarsi, *Université Libre de Bruxelles*

Marc MAUFORT & Franca BELLARSI (eds.)

Crucible of Cultures

Anglophone Drama at the Dawn of a New Millennium

Dramaturgies
No.4

© P.I.E.-Peter Lang S.A.
PRESSES INTERUNIVERSITAIRES EUROPÉENNES
Brussels, 2002 – Second printing 2003
1 avenue Maurice, 1050 Brussels, Belgium
info@peterlang.com; www.peterlang.net

ISSN 1376-3202
ISBN 90-5201-982-7
D/2002/5678/18
Printed in Germany

CIP available from the British Library, GB
and the Library of Congress, USA.
ISBN   0-8204-4686-6

Die Deutsche Bibliothek – CIP-Einheitsaufnahme

Crucible of Cultures: Anglophone drama at the dawn of a new millennium. /
Marc Maufort & Franca Bellarsi (ed.). – Bruxelles; Bern; Berlin; Frankfurt/M.;
New York; Oxford; Wien : PIE Lang, 2002 (Dramaturgies; No.4)
ISBN   90-5201-982-7

Acknowledgements

This collection of essays originated in an international conference on contemporary Anglophone drama entitled "Crucible of Cultures," which took place in May 2001 at the University of Brussels. This initial project owed much to the enthusiasm and energy of those who helped me shape it. In particular, I express all my gratitude to Franca Bellarsi, who shared with me the actual burden of programming the conference. Likewise, she participated in the edition of this volume of proceedings as an associate editor, advising me on both scholarly and copy-editing matters. Her meticulous and thoughtful collaboration deserves the highest praise. In my work as a convenor, I was also seconded by Evelyne Haberfeld, who took it upon herself to organize the dramaturgical part of the conference. Thanks to her diligence, the delegates enjoyed readings from contemporary Canadian plays by a talented graduate student of our English Department, Neele Dehoux. In addition, Ms Haberfeld invited in Brussels the London-based Blue Tongue Theatre Company, which performed Australian playwright Michael Gow's *Sweet Phoebe*, a play rarely produced outside Australia. Ms Haberfeld's efforts clearly sparked a fascinating debate between university scholars and theatre practitioners.

The conference proper and this book of proceedings received major funding from various sources. In this respect, I wholeheartedly wish to thank the School of Liberal Arts of the University of Brussels—especially Dean Gilbert Debusscher—, the English Department of the University of Brussels, the Center for Canadian Studies of the University of Brussels—in particular its President and Director, Professors Kurgan and Jaumain—, The Canadian Embassy in Brussels, The British Council, The Australian Embassy in Brussels, the Embassy of the United States in Brussels, The National Fund for Scientific Research-Belgium as well as the Belgian Ministry of Higher Education and Research. I owe a special debt to Mrs Closson, the Senior Editor at P.I.E.-Peter Lang in Brussels, who supported the project both in its conference and book format. I am very also very grateful to Mrs Dassy for her dedicated care during the production process.

Perhaps most importantly, my sincere thanks go to all those participants, too numerous to be represented in this volume, who significantly contributed to the success of the conference, coming as they did from Europe, North America, Asia and Australia. I can only hope that this book will serve as a lasting testimony of the scholarly, theatrical, and friendly "Crucible of Cultures" that marked the birth of the new millennium at the University of Brussels.

Marc Maufort
Brussels, February 2002

Table of Contents

Contemporary Anglophone Drama
as Crucible of Cultures

Marc MAUFORT

Université Libre de Bruxelles

The dawn of a new millennium naturally offers an adequate, if somewhat arbitrary, opportunity to reappraise the political, social, and literary world in which we live. This collection of essays, which gathers essays presented at an eponymous conference organized by the University of Brussels in May 2001, follows a similar agenda, albeit on the more modest scale of English-language theatre and drama studies. The Brussels conference indeed sought to reassess the achievements of twentieth century drama in English, in an age which has increasingly become multicultural. The essays published here will hopefully provide a broad survey of recent developments in the field, thus pointing towards future potentialities in the twenty-first century. This project can be regarded as the third phase of a trilogy devoted to contemporary Anglophone drama and multiculturalism, initiated with *Staging Difference: Cultural Pluralism in American Theatre and Drama* (1995), and prolonged more recently with *Siting the Other: Re-visions of Marginality in Australian and English-Canadian Drama* (2001).

The Anglophone drama of the past two decades has been characterized primarily by a series of major cross-cultural transformations. In this regard, Timberlake Wertenbaker's essay, "Dancing with History," which opens the collection, also provides its guiding metaphor. Wertenbaker's internationalism, coupled with a relativizing historical perspective, underlines the benefits of intercultural hybridization. Entering the dance of history as English, we might get out as American, she concludes. Through the "dance" of Anglophone drama at the turn of this century, playwrights are indeed invited to reconsider their identities in a cross-cultural perspective. New multicultural voices are increasingly gaining access to the international English stage, which more than ever is becoming a crucible of cultures. This new mosaic-like pattern is reflected in the contributions collected in this book. The term "Anglophone" has been chosen to designate the broadening of the geographical boundaries traditionally assigned to English-speaking playwriting. While the dominance of British and American drama may still be felt, the postcolonial talents of the countries of the former British Empire are slowly acquiring worldwide recognition. Within these national boundaries, this phenomenon is further complicated by various multicultural sub-groups, as the section devoted to contemporary American drama, for instance, makes abundantly clear. This survey of present-day Anglophone drama brings to mind Bakhtin's notion of dialogic interaction between cultures, leading to such extremes as the carnivalization of established early twentieth century dramatic conventions (Bakhtin 263).

The structure of the book is in itself dialogic, inviting us to "dance" with, to engage with sometimes widely divergent, contemporary theatrical practices in a journey that encompasses Europe, America, Africa, and Australasia. The book comprises different angles of vision: the artists'—the two opening essays are written by playwrights—the scholars', and the pedagogue's—Helen Gilbert's concluding essay deals with the postcolonial classroom. Within this general framework, narrower divisions can be made. First of all, the introductory opposition of Timberlake Wertenbaker's essay with Drew Hayden Taylor's illustrates the "crucible" theme, the dissonant musical motif, that runs throughout the collection. While Wertenbaker's work illuminates recent developments in contemporary British drama, Taylor's dramaturgy exemplifies the extraordinary emergence of First Nations drama in Canada.

Taking its cue from this "prologue," the first major section of the book deals with British and American theatre and drama. An initial cluster of articles concentrates on new developments on the British stage. Drew Milne's essay explores the much-debated hiatus between drama as text and drama as performance with examples drawn from recent British works. De Vos', Kritzer's, Soto-Morettini's, and Roth's contributions, on the other hand, explore the multiplicities of aesthetic forms characterizing the contemporary English stage. De Vos highlights Ravenhill's postmodern re-visioning of the works of Oscar Wilde; Amelia Kritzer makes us discover the political vision of Caryl Churchill's later works; Donna Soto-Morettini offers an insightful analysis of Michael Frayn's fascination with science, while Maya Roth reintroduces the diasporic cultural theme unifying the volume in her examination of Timberlake Wertenbaker's "willful internationalism" in *The Break of Day*. The second cluster of essays, devoted to American drama, opens with Alain Piette's reconsideration of David Mamet's by now canonical *American Buffalo* in the light of innovative research methods; likewise, Barbara Ozieblo discusses the relationship between an old master like Arthur Miller and the more typically multicultural dramatist Maria Irene Fornes. The three subsequent essays, authored by Harry Elam, Eriko Hara, and Robert Vorlicky, analyze aspects of the post-multicultural in U.S. dramaturgies, focusing respectively on Cherrie Moraga and Susan-Lori Parks, Asian American playwrights, and contemporary hip-hop solo performance pieces.

The second major part of the book deals with postcolonial drama in English. This division opens with an article by Thierry Dubost reminding us that postcolonial drama also finds its representatives in Europe. Indeed, the works of Irish playwright Thomas Kilroy re-vision Ibsen's dramatic output. The next few articles hone in on the extraordinary growth of English-Canadian drama in the past few decades. They clearly demonstrate that Canadian drama now deserves to be considered on a par with its British and American counterparts. Jerry Wasserman's essay centers on the multicultural voices that have emerged in recent Canadian dramaturgies, and in this process have hybridized the very notion of Canadian identity, while Anne Nothof analyzes how Canada's dramatists have questioned the anti-humanist assumptions of postmodernism. The three following articles are more clearly focused on specific First Nations dramatists: Ric Knowles explores in detail Daniel David Moses' strategies of artistic resistance; Robert Appleford concentrates on a lesser known aspect of Moses' work, i.e. his conflation of the popular genre of science fiction with the mode of the history play; finally, Robert Nunn examines Drew Hayden Taylor's controversial *alterNatives*, which challenges all forms of Western or First nations cultural stereotypes. Alan Filewod's more theoretically-oriented essay highlights the cultural assumptions of power underpinning recent Toronto productions of *The Lion King*. Subsequent articles deal with theatre in other regions of the former British Empire. Valérie Bada addresses Derek Walcott's rewriting of *The Odyssey* as a marker of cross-culturality; Erol Acar and Martina Stange pinpoint Wole Soyinka's questioning of widely-held conceptions of gender in *The Lion and the Jewel*; Geoffrey Davis and Marcia Blumberg, in their respective contributions, chart the state of present-day South African drama, in a post-apartheid era that lends itself to reconciliation and testimony; the Australian multicultural scene is analyzed in my own contribution on Jane Harrison's dramatization of the forced adoption of aboriginal children, as well as in Tom Burvill's performance analysis of multicultural works by Asian playwright Meme Thorne and by a Greek Australian collective. Christopher Balme convincingly argues that New Zealand drama is firmly moving beyond the *Pakeha*/Maori dualism in his analysis of the work of Lynda Chanwai-Earle and other multicultural artists. As a recapitulation of the many themes developed in the course of the volume, Helen Gilbert's essay investigates the too often neglected pedagogical implications of these new postcolonial dramaturgies. In considering examples drawn from South African and Australian texts, she echoes Maufort's and

Blumberg's earlier essays, thus providing an apt coda to the book as a whole.

Taken together, the essays of this volume shed light on the mosaic-like facets of Anglophone drama in an era of transition, in a state of "in-betweenness" reminiscent of Homi Bhabha's concept of hybridity (Bhabha 85-92; 102-22). The variety of viewpoints assembled here suggests that in its present tendency towards hybridization of traditional forms and ideas, Anglophone drama will contribute to a redefinition of the boundaries of postmodernism and postcolonialism in the twenty-first century.

Works Cited

Bakhtin, M. M. *The Dialogic Imagination. Four Essays*, ed. and trans. Caryl Emerson and Michael Holquist. Austin: U of Texas P, 1981.

Bhabha, Homi K. *The Location of Culture*. London: Routledge, 1994.

Maufort, Marc, ed. *Staging Difference. Cultural Pluralism in American Theatre and Drama*. New York: Peter Lang, 1995.

Maufort, Marc & Franca Bellarsi, eds. *Siting the Other. Re-visions of Marginality in Australian and English-Canadian Drama*. Brussels: P.I.E.-Peter Lang, 2001.

Dancing with History[*]

Timberlake WERTENBAKER

Tonight I want to talk about the playwright's involvement with and relation to history, his—or I should say her, because I will often be speaking personally—dance with history. I would like to preface this talk with a warning that this is a only a preview of some thoughts I am still working on (being a theatre writer, I need rehearsals and public previews to get things right). As with theatrical previews, I would ask for your indulgence at times, for your effort, and for your feedback. Plays change radically during previews.

I will make some sweeping generalisations and also speak personally. You're welcome to find exceptions to the generalisations; as to the personal, well, you'll have to take my word for it.

So this is an exploration. The query is: is there a defined relationship between the playwright and history, a contract every playwright signs? And has that contract changed? And if the contract has changed, is this because of the playwrights or because of the other signatory, history itself?

Those of you who know me a little will remember that I always go back to the Greeks, both for my plays and my thoughts—*c'est là que je me repère*—they are our starting place. The Greek verb *istereo* means to enquire: I enquire, I observe, I examine. It has a strong scientific association—and yet, ask anyone of us what we think of history and I think most of us will say it is a narrative of events, a narrative of events that happened—but the narrative is important. "Scientific" begins to mean "true": the inquiry becomes account. I'll come back to this later, but note a slippage here.

Now let's look very briefly at the Greek playwrights and their relation to history. Basically, here's a huge sweeping generalisation: they all wrote about the Trojan War at the time of the Athens/Spartan war. One tragedy illustrated and commented on another tragedy. This is particularly true of Euripides, the first man to question war and the hypocrisy of democracy. It's very clear in *Hecuba*, which I know quite well,

---

[*] © 2002 Timberlake Wertenbaker.

because I translated it. The action centres around the sacrifice of Hecuba's daughter Polyxena to the ghost of Achilles. It's a human sacrifice and Hecuba, a barbarian, argues that it is barbaric. No one needs to sacrifice human beings to appease ghosts. Odysseus, who is portrayed here as a kind of Alistair Campbell, our ruthless and wily media manipulator in England, says: "Achilles died for Greece and deserves the highest honours"—and then he adds something revealing about himself: "look at me," he says, "I don't need much, but I want to see my grave covered with honours. I want to be remembered forever." That is: "I want to go down in history." In other words, the honour conferred by history chips away at the grief, the silence of death.

Later, there is another argument: Polymestor, who has killed Hecuba's son (this is tragedy: everything keeps getting worse and worse), justifies it by saying to Agamemnon that Polydorus would have posed a threat to Greece and that he, Polymestor, did it to help the Greeks. Hecuba answers: "I will not allow you a false place in history— No whitewash for you—ever." She demands the truth and proceeds to demonstrate he was only after gold, a dishonest greedy man who deserves no place in history at all. The last line of the play, slightly stretched by me, has the Women of Troy saying, as they go down to the boats: "Down to the shores friends, to endure the bitterness of slavery. History has no compassion."

So there we have the lines drawn by the playwright: the makers of history—the importance of accurate historical memory—and even the voice of the victims of history—this was the great thing about the chorus in Greek tragedy, they gave us the passive victims' accounts, something later plays forgot.

For the Greeks, then, History is metaphor, and history is also, as it was for Carlisle: "nothing but the biography of great men." Within this, we have a doubt, a query about accuracy, truth.

No Greek play, by the way, that I know of, stands outside an historical context or ignores it.

I'll come to the ahistorical play later. Look for the sofa, I say. When you see a sofa on stage, or its modern equivalent, the urban doorstep, you know you're in the ahistorical play. The sealed room. Nothing noticed outside.

Remind me later about the sofa.

So back to the Greeks. They gave the next hundreds of generations of playwrights the blueprint: history through the great men making it, history, that is, as the biography or tragedy of great men and—very rarely— women. It prompted Jane Austen's complaint many centuries later: "real solemn history I cannot be interested in," says a character in *Northanger Abbey*, "the quarrels of popes and kings with wars and pestilences in every page, the men all so good for nothing, and hardly any women at all ..."

There go Shakespeare, Calderón de la Barca, and Schiller ... But there is quite a lot of truth in her comment, and it is true of almost all historical plays down to the present, down to films like *Ghandi*, *Lawrence of Arabia*, anything to do with Churchill.

I think even the playwrights felt too many plays about great men could be too much of a great thing, so that parallel to the historical plays there began to develop the ahistorical plays, outside history, sometimes fanciful, sometimes tragic. And of course, there were the plays that were about the victims of history: this might start with the Greeks, the suppliant women, the women of Troy etc., but it was remarkably continued in Italy in little known plays by writers like Ruzzante, a sixteenth century Paduan who wrote about the down and out, the victims of famines, wars, and pestilences. There, history is this massive cruel force the ordinary person must suffer. So that we have the makers of history, the heroes, and the victims, the sufferers of history. Nothing in between.

Then, something changes. It changes in this century, it changes now. And since we are here at the beginning of this new millennium wondering why we are here, this is what I want to explore. What changes and when?

Let's start with Chekhov at the very beginning of the twentieth century and Vershinin's famous speech, so beautiful and mad: "It seems to me," he says, "how can I put it, that everything in this world must gradually change—two or three hundred years hence—a new and happy life will dawn—we are living for it now." And later in the play, still hoping, as he contemplates the disaster of his own life, he exclaims: "what a life it's going to be!—there will rise people who are better than you." This is the cry of the beginning of the twentieth century: history will be resolved, end happily, history is progressive.

We find this sense of history as a perfectible future in Ibsen and Shaw, and of course in Brecht. In the middle of the century, after the war, you still find this sense of history as a future, but without the great men. All of Beckett's characters wait for the future, no longer with enthusiasm, but with infinite patience. There is still a sense of history as a narrative, rolling forward.

But to now.

In my play *The Break of Day*, I tried to have a dialogue with Vershinin and that twentieth-century view of history. In the play, three women are in Moscow—well, actually, they're in London—and they have work, independence, intelligent people to talk to, but happiness has eluded them. The play then showed women's desperate desire for children—why? Perhaps because, curiously, they do not feel they are working for the future. At the end of the twentieth century, the future feels uncertain, if not bleak. At the end of the twentieth century, it seems, history is not progressive, it is not certain, and I would suggest it is no longer even a narrative.

Many male playwrights have dealt with that doubt by saying that there is no history and that, anyway, it is not important. The modern male playwright explores what was once the domain of women novelists: the domestic, the personal, the ahistorical—there are remarkable exceptions, but few, and fewer and fewer of them.

Women playwrights have on the whole taken another view. This view, certainly my view, is that we have made the wrong model of history and that we are now discovering it is not a narrative rolling inexorably forward, pushed or flagged by great men: it is more complex, several models can exist at once, different voices tell different stories and enquire in different places.

And there is a reason for this gender divergence.

With feminism, women began to look at history, history as the biography of great men, and to feel frustrated and unrepresented. I remember feeling it myself very strongly. I always liked historical plays: who was I to write about? Churchill? Mrs Churchill? So we did one of two things, either looked at women who had been conveniently forgotten by history, or invented them in historical contexts. I remember that when I decided to write *The Grace of Mary Traverse*, I wanted to write about a woman on a quest. Well, there were no models at all. Even in literature: Faust, Peer Gynt etc.—all men with male adventures and male longings—Margarita, you know, that sort of thing. And I wanted a woman in history. I was using history as metaphor, the 1780s for the 1980s (the parallels in Britain were uncanny: we had a summer of riots, of burning streets, reminiscent of the 1780s riots, where parts of London went up in flames and fear of the mob was an excuse for more repressive measures).

Well, to find a woman of historical significance, I had to invent her and then place her with some minor historical figures like Lord Gordon, responsible for the riots of the 1780s. I had slightly better luck with Isabelle Eberhardt, an actual and remarkable historical figure—nonetheless, a minor one. And, of course, biographers started unearthing fascinating women: Mrs Jordan, Mary Queen of Scots became very popular; but really, the fact is not many women did make history except on their backs—excuse the expression—and therefore another thought crept in, what if history is not the history of great men, but more messy? And what about *the middle managers* of history, the women? Dorothy Hodgkin, the third of Crick and Watson, Sophia, the fourth of the Trinity, these women airbrushed out of history. This was certainly true of literary history. When Virago was formed to publish the forgotten writings of women, they unearthed masterpieces—note the word—Olive Shreiner, Elizabeth Bowen, and so on.

Now, if there was a different history lived and witnessed by women, there was also a different history lived and witnessed by the non-dominant cultures, people who were not even celebrated as victims. I encountered this for the first time when I was writing *Our Country's Good*. Men in the eighteenth century all wrote history, by keeping extensive and precise diaries. The founding of the first colony in Australia is unbelievably well documented. I had at hand five different diaries of the same years. Plus history books, modern and not.

Open a book, you get history. But not the alternative history. The first fleet was witnessed by the Aborigines as it sailed into Botany Bay. When finally, thanks to Tom Keneally's help, I tracked down the one account written from verbal hand-me-downs, I encountered a totally different history: the Aborigines had as good a sense of history as the English. They too tried to make sense of events, turn them into a narrative: the aboriginal narrative of the first fleet is—well it's a nightmare. I mean it describes a nightmare. And it was accurate and prescient. I'll read from my own play, if you don't mind: "A giant canoe drifts onto the sea, clouds billowing from upright oars. This is a dream which has lost its way." Later: "This is a dream no one wants. Crowded, hungry, disturbed." For the Aborigines, the boats were giant canoes and the sails clouds—they believed unappeased ancestors had fallen through the cracks in the sky—and if they could only do the right thing, they would go away. This is as good a definition of modern history as any, I think: a dream that has lost its way.

The speeches of the Aborigines were originally much longer. But it's hard in a dramatic piece to recount an alternative history. And because aboriginal history is not the biography of great men, it was impossible to dramatise it in a conventional way.

So suddenly, one finds not one history, but at least three, in fact many. And also, history is not the *Deus ex Machina*, fine if you're godlike, *ex Machina* if you're the victim, but something changeable, depending on what language you use to address it. Conventional or unconventional. Female. Aboriginal. Other ... And now it seems to me the playwrights have another task, and this is the task of the twenty-first century.

It seems to me Michael Frayn tackled the uncertainty of history in *Copenhagen*, Caryl Churchill the collapse of history maybe in *Far Away*. For me, my area of interest has been to try to see what history is and what it does actively to people. I brought it not on stage, but very much as an offstage, almost as a character, in my most recent play

Credible Witness. The question of history dominates *Credible Witness.* It is a play set in a refugee asylum centre, in which a Greek Macedonian seeks refuge in England and disappears. His mother comes looking for him, unable to understand his lack of communication. What has happened to him is that he has lost his history, or his faith in his history, that history being his mother's history: the Macedonians trying to survive among Greeks, Macedonians trying not to be subsumed by Greek history. In a long confrontation scene, mother and son challenge each other. The mother affirming history is solid, the son sceptical and refusing to be bound by his history—which basically is asking him to die or at least be badly beaten in his own country. The conflict destroys them both, and the hope is in the last words of a young Bosnian who decides she will forge a new theory of history: history will no longer be the agreed narrative of certain countries, but some general principles, scientific ones that can be examined. It's not meant to be a serious proposition, but her desire is serious: to forge a new understanding of history—away from cultural and nationalistic boundaries, the boundaries that have made this century so bloody. So history is no longer an agreed narrative of heroes, with undisputed facts, but open to scrutiny, to be looked at again and, curiously, to be chosen. In *Credible Witness*, there is this possibility, which is the common experience of immigrants and the source of much family conflict: you can keep the history you came from, you can adopt another, you can have none. You can, in other words, choose your dancing partner, you don't have to wait, to be asked for a dance. You can find your partner, you can dance parallel, you can keep changing and dance with several partners.

And if that is so, the partner, the human partner, the playwright also changes radically. Human beings are no longer sleeping beauties, waiting for the prince charming of history to tap them on the shoulder and invite them to greatness, as in *Henry the Fourth, Part Two*, when the crown comes down upon Prince Hal's head and he becomes Henry the Fifth. Nor are we the servants of the castle, trailing in the wake of the great men.

We are not heroes or victims. We are amazingly free in our intellects, we are undefined. We are in dialogue with history—with histories, I should say—we intermingle and different histories bump into each other on crowded streets.

At this crossroads of centuries and cultures, represented here tonight in Brussels, I would say we must not turn away in confusion; on the contrary, we must join the dance, because that's the more interesting place to be. In other words, let's not be ahistorical and sit on sofas in plays about adultery and sibling rivalry. Let's not write these plays, however tempting. History is complex, challenging. And so, let's dance with history, because, well, that's where the action is. And what happens to us when we go into the dance is a new mystery. Do we go in as French and come out as English? Do we go in weighted by the anger of one history and in the pleasure of the dance throw it off?

I think that's what the playwrights of the twenty-first century are discovering. It is an invitation to a new dance.

Canoeing the Rivers of Canadian Aboriginal Theatre: The Portages and the Pitfalls

Drew Hayden TAYLOR

First of all, let me begin by saying I am not an academic. I do not know the meaning of the words "post-modernism" or "hyper-realism," though I have no doubt they are important and noteworthy words. The closest I ever came to going to University was when I painted the residences at Trent University when I was sixteen. In reality, I am just a poor, humble playwright of Ojibway extraction, who often finds himself in situations like this, talking about the unique and special world of Native theatre. Not from studying it, mind you, but by experiencing it.

In the fifteen years I have been lucky enough to be a willing participant in the roller coaster ride that is the re-emergence of the Aboriginal theatrical voice, I have noticed a few things. First of all, there is a belief that Native theatre took centre stage somewhere around November 1986, with the première production of Tomson Highway's play, *The Rez Sisters*. This was one of the first—if not *the* first play by a Native playwright (Highway is Cree from Northern Manitoba)—to send significant shockwaves throughout the Canadian theatrical community. This sometimes humorous, sometimes poignant portrayal of seven Ojibway women from Manitoulin Island and their yearning to play at the world's biggest bingo in Toronto quickly grabbed the attention of the Canadian artistic population at large.

Within two years of its original production, the play was remounted and toured most of the larger cities of Canada to rave reviews, and the following year it made its way to the Edinborough Festival in Scotland. While this indeed marked the watershed for the coming onslaught of Native plays, it was by no means the Genesis. Native theatre had existed in several forms in Canada since Time Immemorial. It predates the political structure that currently runs Canada. Native theatre is as old as the stories still being told by its original inhabitants. It is merely the presentation that has changed.

While the proscenium stage may be new to the North American continent, the art of telling stories by using just the voice and physical mannerisms is certainly old hat amongst the Aboriginal people. For example, the Nuu-chah-nulth of the West Coast have for centuries used such elaborate theatrical devices as trap doors, masks, smoke effects, and props to help illustrate their ceremonial dramas.

With all that said, Native theatre in the new millennium is finally out of its infancy and into its teen years—rebellious and trying to find its voice. Writers such as Daniel David Moses, Marie Clements, Darrel Dennis, and Ian Ross have all made fabulous inroads into mainstream Canadian theatre, culminating with Ross's winning of the Prestigious Governor General's Award for his play, *fareWEL*. What once was the exception is now part of the rule.

However, in our zeal to tell our own stories and in our own way, it is my opinion that sometimes a certain myopia develops in the process. That is to say, those of us who follow the expanding world of Aboriginal theatre have noticed the emergence of certain trends in the growing cannon of Native plays—tendencies and inclinations that may limit the potential growth of this distinctive art form.

I personally remember my introduction to Native theatre. I was the Playwright-In-Residence for Canada's premier Native theatre company, Native Earth Performing Arts, during the rehearsal of Highway's follow-up to *The Rez Sisters*, called *Drylips Oughta Move to Kapuskasing*. That 1989 play includes a rather brutal rape of a pregnant woman with a crucifix. During that same period of time, I happened to see a production of George Ryga's *Ecstasy of Rita Joe*, which also ends with a brutal rape of the main character. It was then I noticed a peculiar trend. Rape seemed to be developing as the significant and dominant metaphor for Native expression in the theatre.

Plays like *Now Look What You Made Me Do*, *The Rez Sisters*, *Princess Pocahontas and the Blue Spots*, *Path with No Moccasins*, *fareWEL*, *Jessica*, *Moonlodge*—to name just a few—all exhibited some form of sexual abuse against women. I began to think that if I wanted to be a Native playwright, I would have to include a rape in every one of my plays, and needless to say, I was reluctant to do that.

The more I thought about this unique trend, the more it made sense in a twisted way. Looked at it historically, most of the Aboriginal cultures in Canada were either totally or partially matriarchal, while the invading European government and Church were completely patriarchal, and so the best metaphor for what happened to the Native people and its culture in Canada became rape. When an oppressed people get their voice back, they will usually talk/write about being oppressed. It makes sense.

But as Columpa Bobb, a renowned Salish actress, once told me, as a performer, "it's kinda hard getting raped seven times a week, twice on

Wednesdays." Pretty understandable. It also highlights another limitation developing within the First Nations theatre community, a kind of potential stagnation in the creation of new and interesting character types. In other words, we tend to repeat ourselves.

Several years ago, I wrote a play titled *Someday*. It was about a family that had lost a daughter to the Children's Aid Society thirty-five years earlier and which finds out its long lost daughter is coming home. After the first production, I received an influx of requests from many different actresses to play the returning daughter, should the play ever be remounted. This confused me, because there were three juicy and plum roles for women in that play, but everybody seemed fixated on the Janice character and I couldn't figure out why. Especially since she didn't appear until the last ten seconds of the first act.

It finally occurred to me to ask why the fondness for that one particular character. And then it became quite obvious. Janice makes her appearance driving a Saabe, wearing a full length fur coat, and is a successful lawyer in the city. Yet, at that same time, most of the roles available to Native actresses on the stage could be broken down into any combination of three classifications: victim of some sort of physical or sexual abuse, some poor mother of several children struggling it out on the Reserve, or a bingo player. The concept of playing somebody who was well off and fairly successful appealed to the sense of novelty of most actresses. Many were just happy to try on the coat. I should also add that this was a concern for male performers too.

Like a light from Heaven, this led me on a personal crusade to develop more interesting and varied characters in my plays, for I too had been somewhat guilty of that brand of stereotyping. And while these characters do exist in the Native community, it is important to note that theatre should represent a cross-cut of a culture or society. And I felt there was a lot more out there in the Native community that wasn't being represented by our writers. We needed more varied representations to show the public at large, to show that we all weren't oppressed, depressed, or suppressed. I feel variety is the spice of life and theatre.

My later play, *alterNatives*, featured a trio of academic young Native rebels, who are just as comfortable discussing Sartre and Star Trek ethics as Lame Deer and Chief Dan George. It was great fun to do. However, when you tread on new ground, you sometimes fall through the ice. This play takes place during a dinner party between an interracial couple—he's Ojibway, she's Jewish—and it is a meeting place of ideas and issues. The end result being that during the Vancouver production, the theatre received a bomb threat. Somebody felt the play was racist against White people and told the theatre something to the effect of "if you're going to continue producing plays that make fun of White

people, don't be surprised at what people leave in the theatre." My first
bomb threat. I felt like such an adult playwright.

During the première production of Brecht/Weill's *The Rise and Fall
of Mahagonny* in 1930s Germany, reaction to the play included riots in
the streets. So I felt right at home with my next project. I was busy
working away on writing a musical in the tradition of Bertolt Brecht and
Kurt Weill called *Sucker Falls: A Musical about Demons of the Forest
and the Soul*, an unusual blend of politics, music, sorcery, and extravaganza. Performed in three different Vancouver parks, it raised a fair
amount of controversy by invoking some unusual native characters. In
fact, one review said that it was a good thing I was Native or I could be
accused of being racist, because one character I created was, shall we
say, less then charitable. The idea of a corrupt Native person taking
advantage of her people and the land claims procedure seemed unthink-
able to this critic. Alas, I am sad to report, Native people are just as
human as in any other culture.

The use of spirituality is often a strong theme in Native arts. Starting
with Highway's two plays, and continuing with other works like Darrel
Dennis's *The Trickster of Third Avenue East* and Alanis King's *If Jesus
Met Nanabush ...* , the ubiquitous character known as the Trickster—but
formally known by many other names depending on which part of the
country you come from (Napi, Old Man, Coyote, Raven, Gloosecap
etc.)—has frequently been the focus of many plays, novels, and other
artistic expressions. It had gotten to the point where Daniel David
Moses coined a unique term for academics who seem fixated on analyzing Trickster imagery in Aboriginal literature: he calls it "the Spot The
Trickster Syndrome."

It is my belief that all the things I have mentioned are merely the
settling-in of an industry. They are not meant as criticisms, merely as
guideposts for this new expression. There is so much more out there
waiting to be written and said, and as the cliché goes, the sky's the limit.
Native theatre, in this new Millennium, now has so many different
directions to travel. That is the true joy in revitalizing an art form—the
ability to explore new grounds and new forms. And what's even more
fabulous, the rest of the world is taking interest in this uniquely
Canadian endeavor. Americans are finally acknowledging to themselves
that Native people do have something interesting to say (though if the
truth be told, they are still importing Native playwrights from Canada
and producing them, much like our home-grown comics).

A few years back, I wrote a comedy called *The Baby Blues*; it was
produced several times in the States, and even an Italian translated
version appeared in—of all places—a theatre in Venice, Italy! As
previously mentioned, Ross's *fareWEL* will be seen in Scotland, and

there are constant discussions about co-productions with Indigenous theatres in Australia, New Zealand, and South Africa. Not bad for a Renascence that started with the words from a Cree playwright's creation: "I wanna go to Toronto."

The Anxiety of Print:
Recent Fashions in British Drama

Drew MILNE

Cambridge University

A moment in Samuel Beckett's play *Footfalls* captures an unspoken tension in contemporary anglophone drama. This moment can serve to illuminate some recent fashions in British drama. In the play's final section, in the midst of a narration whose significance is overdetermined by the apparent repetition of earlier parts, May or M says: "Old Mrs Winter, whom the reader will remember, old Mrs. Winter ..." (402).[1] This phrasing recurs moments later in May's narration: "But finally, raising her head and fixing Amy—the daughter's given name, as the reader will remember..." (403).[2] The giving of the name Amy by May is uncertainly fictional, as is the identity of the rememberer. There is something awkwardly literal in the way these names echo each other as letters, letters visible to a reader but heard differently, when said, as a two-syllable and a one-syllable word respectively. Heard in a theatre, the phrase—*as the reader will remember*—is arresting and then troubling. Is the reader in the audience or in the mind of the performer? Is the performer recalling their own act of reading prior to performance? As spoken words, the phrase prompts an audience to imagine being readers, as though listening were analogous to reading, as though performed speech could be understood as writing and as an anxiety about writing felt within dramatic speech. The voice that calls upon the reader appears caught in the movement between the imagined performance of language-making and the imagined recollection of the dramatic author.

---

[1] The French text in Beckett's translation is: "La vieille Mme Winter, dont le lecteur se souviendra, ..." (*Stücke und Bruchstücke* 81); and the German translation, on which Beckett collaborated, reads: "Die alte Frau Winter, an die der Leser sich erinnern wird,..." (*Stücke und Bruchstücke* 73 [this edition credits Erika and Elmar Tophoven with the German translation]).

[2] "comme le lecteur s'en souviendra"/"wie der Leser sich erinnern wird" (*Stücke und Bruchstücke* 73).

There is a curious interruption in dramatic logic here which traverses the different acts of attention involved in reading as opposed being an audience. The assumption that readers behave differently from audiences seems, momentarily, less than self-evident. A deep-seated assumption of theatres calls on audiences to pretend to abandon the protocols of reading which condition texts in performance. A taint of suspicion attaches to speakers or performers who do not somehow break free of the anterior text. The lecturer who merely reads somehow denies the fiction of being involved in an improvised and fluid audience dialogue. Audiences, however, like actors and lecturers, are also readers. With Beckett's plays, perhaps more than any other recent playwright, theatrical realisation and imaginative reading work as shared practices, mutually informing parameters of the imaginative performance horizons extended by Beckett's work. Indeed, the audience for Beckett's plays often come to the theatre with a high degree of textual familiarity as part of their expectation, almost to the point of being too familiar with the text, too difficult to surprise. The 1999 Beckett Festival at the Barbican Theatre, London—one of the most important festivals in recent British drama—took this development of Beckettian familiarity to new levels. The audience remembered remembering. In the process they have begun to sense the textual and theatrical ghosts of Beckett's work in performance. A number of the productions of the 1999 Beckett Festival went on to be memorialised in a series of films. These films play out the curiously diminishing returns of Beckett's play-texts. It would be possible to hear May's evocation of the reader as a quotation internal to her narrative, something she both remembers and invents, as though May were talking to herself, to her own reader rather than to the audience. However heard, the imagined reader is a ghostly presence both in the theatre and for readers of the printed text, suggesting something like a trace of the play's intimate relation with theatrical performance. The staging of writing as reading-in-performance is also explicit in Beckett's play *Ohio Impromptu*, in which the reader and the listener are perilously close to merging into each other. In *Footfalls*, ironies multiply if pressure is put on the force of "will" in the phrase "the reader *will* remember." What if the actor forgets? The actor's fear of forgetting their words, or of corpsing, lives on in any performance in which the actor successfully remembers: performance remembers writing.

The hope that the reader will remember some aspect of what has been read or performed is a literary courtesy, an apology for repetition or reiteration of the over-familiar, and a statement of the pious hope of most play-texts. The printed text not only pre-exists most forms of theatrical speech, but survives theatrical realisation as a printed form of remembrance. A theatregoer startled by this moment in *Footfalls* might wonder if they had misheard and the text is there to assure some measure of memorial fidelity. Actors are also readers and their collaborative cooperation with audiences involves recognition of shared experiences of those texts which support and extend theatrical event-hood. This recognition, the sense that drama is also for readers, whether the readers are actors, directors, critics or textual analysts, seems increasingly perilous in contemporary British drama. The reader may remember what drama might be, but the drama itself seems eager to forget the reader, to free performance from its textual production and reception. Contemporary British drama more often seems anxious to avoid the inauthenticity perceived in dramatic writing and in the modalities of drama as print. It is as if the screen on which contemporary performance is imagined wishes to efface its textual ghosts.

Some of the forces at work threatening the readerly community of dramatic interpretation are sufficiently familiar to seem like journalistic clichés. The impact of new media has weakened the authority of print culture in general. Much of twentieth century British drama is preoccupied with renegotiating the meaning of drama across the media of theatre, film, radio, and television. Hypertext, email and internet communication, along with numerous information technologies and practices, have been widely touted as shifts in the "landscape" of drama as we know it. Patrick Marber's play, *Closer* (Royal National Theatre, 1997) provides a notable instance of the attempt to integrate the potential anonymity of computer chat-room culture into theatrical form, including simulated textual orgasm. In Marber's play the virtual space of electronic "dialogue" is projected onto a screen, but the printed text also includes a version of the scene in an appendix, with the note: "In a production of *Closer* where budget or theatre sightlines won't allow for a projected version of this scene it may be possible for the actors to speak their lines whilst 'typing.'" (Marber 117). In either version, the stage offers an image of characters engaged in typing out an electronic flirtation through fictional identities. The stage action dramatises a "dialogue" of writers writing. Lindsay Posner's production of Shakespeare's *Taming of the Shrew* (Royal Shakespeare Company, 1999-2000) also used screen projections to suggest ways in which information technology might provide new perspectives on Shakespeare. In this production, the play, framed by the opening and closing scenes, was staged as taking place within Christopher Sly's cyber-porn imaginary, as though he were on-line in the mindscape of virtual misogyny. Despite much hype and media interest, however, most recent technological "innovations" are not so much radically new as intensifications of long-standing conflicts between theatre and other media. As Marber's two versions of the same scene imply, the impact of new technology is still somewhat superficial even when it is explicitly dramatised. There is some recognition offered, however, of the way the scale of audience

involvement in film, television, and information technology puts traditional stage-plays under pressure to innovate. But for the past forty years
or so British drama has moved through and between different dramatic
media rather than being divided into separate histories (see Milne). The
flexibility of the stage to gesture towards a range of media articulations—from using film projections as back-drops to increasingly elaborate and layered uses of recorded sound or technologically mediated
environments—means that the long-term shifts in dramatic conventions
can still be understood as compensations for the loss of the layered
registers of speech and writing once possible in dramatic poetry. It
would be possible to trace a history of English drama in print culture
from the bold gesture of Ben Jonson's 1616 folio edition of his works,
echoed in the 1623 folio of Shakespeare's works, to Samuel Beckett's
collection *The Complete Dramatic Works* (1986). The significance of
this history for contemporary playwrights now appears less pressing
than the synchronic conditions of what Raymond Williams called
"drama in a dramatised society" (see *Writing in Society*).

Beckett's dramatic works exemplify the avant-garde response to new
media. An important feature of Beckett's innovative theatricality is the
development of new textual idioms for drama, offering plays that sustain
the interest of theatre audiences and readers alike. Much has been made
of attempts, not least in modern European theatre, to liberate theatre's
theatricality from its literariness, most notably in the often confused
emphasis placed on the significance of "live" theatre in the wake of
Artaud.[3] English-speaking drama, inspired but burdened by its powerful
Shakespearean heritage, has often been more determinedly literary, if
not poetic and word-based. T.S. Eliot remains the most notable figure in
the failed attempt to revive poetic drama, not least because of Eliot's
many acute diagnoses of the difficulties involved (see Williams, *Drama
from Ibsen to Eliot*). British drama has often been accused of being
static, speechified, and visually or physically uninteresting. Beckett's
emphasis on the integrity of theatrical articulation as a scene of writing
is then a salutary and helpful emphasis, and yet curiously difficult to
reproduce or move beyond. Beckett remains unassimilated, a dramatist
whose importance is widely thought canonical by almost all recent
traditions of British drama and yet his influence and example appears

---

[3]   The most interesting deconstruction of Artaud's desire to abolish textuality to
establish a metaphysics of stage presence is provided by Jacques Derrida in his two
essays on Artaud collected in *L'écriture et la différence* (translated in English by
Alan Bass). See also, Philip Auslander. While sympathetic to Derrida's conception of
writing as a way of conceiving speech-writing relations in drama, the drift of the argument offered in this essay is more concerned with the mediations of print as a dynamic of the dramatic imagination.

marginal. A sense of the impasse can be gleaned from Harold Pinter's *Moonlight* (1993).

As well as being a theatre of the dramatic word, Beckett's theatre is also physical, a dimension highlighted by plays such as *Act Without Words* and *Quad*. An important tendency in British drama of the 1990s emphasised performance to the exclusion of dramatic textuality. Perhaps the most public representation of this is the work of Theatre de Complicite, part of a reaffirmation of physical theatre against the supposed dominance of the literary text. Physical theatre in the 1990s was concerned with the attempt to assimilate conceptions of performance that might loosely be associated with Jacques Lecoq in Paris, Tadeusz Kantor in Poland, and Pina Bausch in Germany, along with the work of Robert Lepage, Robert Wilson, and the Wooster Group. Performance art has a largely unwritten history in British culture (see Etchells). Beyond the relative familiarity of names such as Shared Experience, Forced Entertainment, Pip Simmons, Rose English, and Bobby Baker, the paradigm of performance has never quite settled in Britain with the energy and academic vigour of American performance. Performance writing poetics developed in Britain by figures such as Bob Cobbing, Chris Cheek, Caroline Bergvall, Aaron Williamson, and Brian Catling are relatively unknown internationally compared with work produced in north America.[4] Much of the impact of more physically-based theatre in recent British drama has come through the Edinburgh Festival and LIFT, along with the assimilation of work from Eastern Europe since 1989.[5]

The success of Theatre de Complicite appeared to falter in the second half of the 1990s, but their work popularised a more physical conception of theatre among audiences and theatre practitioners. The interest generated by physical theatre has also been redirected back into more physical realisations of Shakespeare, dance or music theatre, but physical theatre aesthetics have also been resisted or criticised for lack of intellectual content. Part of Theatre de Complicite's difficulty appears to be their relation to existing non-dramatic and dramatic texts, and an inability to generate new kinds of performance texts to substantiate the interest of their theatricality. Dominic Dromgoole, artistic director at the Bush Theatre for much of the 1990s, suggests how those concerned to develop new stage writing resisted the claims of physical theatre:

---

[4]   Critical discussion of British work remains fugitive. On Catling, however, see Perril. Analogous American concerns can be gleaned from Bernstein.

[5]   The range of the theatre productions associated with the Edinburgh Festival, and especially the Fringe, is too extensive to survey, but see Eileen Miller. On LIFT, see Armitstead.

Much of this was and is exquisite, formally inventive and brave; much of it is meaningless gesture, pure affectation without content. Some of it has expanded the boundaries of what we think is possible in the theatre; some of it has allowed Oxbridge graduates to show off how good they are at pretending to be chickens. Because of its substance-less nature, it proved highly popular for sponsors and the ruling ideology. Money and Conservatives never minded theatricality, or expressionism, or shock: what terrified them was life. (quoted in Bradwell 72)

Such formulations are representative in their slipperiness. Polemic against vaguely left-wing or political drama has been a staple of new writing tendencies in recent British drama, almost to the extent that political comment has to be rendered through human anecdote for fear of seeming boring. One might call this the unfinished exorcism of Brecht. Dromgoole is himself fond of dismissing political "tracts," but here the political criticism *as if* from the left is turned against physical theatre in the name of "life." The success of shows such as *The Lion King* and the range of large-scale music theatre in recent British theatre suggest that theatricality's claims for an inherently radical relation to dramatic tradition deserve scepticism. What seems new, however, is the extent to which new writing for the stage negotiates the challenge of physical theatre. Underlying difficulties remain significant in the ongoing hostility of British theatre traditions to formal experiments and critical theory, and this hostility seems to distinguish British drama from developments evidently central to the history of European drama and theatre.

Against this background, Dromgoole goes on to claim that the 1990s saw: "the most profound explosion of new dramatic talent that we have seen for many a long decade. The profusion of mid-twenty-somethings who have burst on to our stages have revitalised our theatre" (Bradwell 74). Writing from the perspective of the mid-1990s, Dromgoole mentions Jonathan Harvey, Billy Roche, Sebastian Barry, Roy MacGregor, Catherine Johnson, Philip Ridley, Chris Hannan, Richard Cameron, and James Stock to exemplify the explosion he has in mind.[6] This could be described as the new writing tendency promoted by the Bush theatre, though these writers have a more diverse geographical background and range of approaches than association with the Bush alone would suggest. The Royal Court's range of new writing generates a further list of names in conjunction with Out of Joint and Max Stafford-Clark, a list that might include Mark Ravenhill, Sarah Kane, Sarah Daniels, Clare MacIntyre, Winsome Pinnock, Martin Crimp, Jez Butterworth, and Martin McDonagh, to name but a few.

---

[6] For a flirtatious polemic outlining Dominic Dromgoole's tastes, see his book *The Full Room: An A-Z of Contemporary Playwrighting.*

For anyone unfamiliar with the range of new writing for the stage being produced in Britain, such lists can seem bewilderingly diffuse. These lists represent a surface whose underlying substance is a culture in which the writing of plays is probably more widely practised than at any previous point in British history. Scripts by many of these new writers are readily available, though sometimes quickly out of print. Despite the energetic promotion of this new generation, there is little consensus as to which plays matter or which plays have qualities that redefine the contemporary sense of what is possible. One of the most important features of the contemporary scene is its democratic plurality. Those who like to reduce theatre culture to a small number of titles and proper names have found it difficult to cope. Theatre historians of Elizabethan and Jacobean drama often comment on the quantity and range of plays rapidly produced for an eager audience of theatregoers. The quantity of play-writing in contemporary Britain, often written for relatively small theatres, reflects a culture of theatregoing that is often obscured by the focus on work produced in larger theatres. The plays that have generated most scandal or hype, such as Mark Ravenhill's *Shopping and Fucking*, Irvine Welsh's *Trainspotting*, or Sarah Kane's *Blasted*, have been slow to win acceptance among more critical readers. There is a persistent academic audience for the plays of writers such as Edward Bond, Trevor Griffiths, Caryl Churchill, Howard Brenton, and Tom Stoppard, writers who established their reputations in earlier phases. More recent work faces a different critical climate and has yet to attract comparable critical attention. This new type of stage-play seems more intimate with the rhythms of media publicity than with a culture of analytic interpretation. These plays seem closer to phenomena such as pop music or advertising, which are part of the reflexive formation of British culture more generally, rather than articulate as drama per se. The sensation tendencies of recent British art, much of which is performatively self-advertising, have also attracted more sensational journalism than developed critique.[7]

Earlier relations between artistic practice and intellectual argument or academic study appear to have broken down or found a new dynamic within theatre studies that are less concerned with literary-critical discussion. In the absence of emergent canons or modes of dissemination, much new writing appears to have a short intellectual after-life. What emerges is a diversity of new writing which sees itself as media-savvy and theatrical, distinct from "physical" theatre to the extent of being predominantly about the relation between word and gesture, but with a theatricality anxious to avoid seeming "literary" or comfortable with

---

[7] For an illuminating and provocative cultural diagnosis, with interesting parallels in recent British drama culture, see Stallabrass.

print-culture. Beyond exploiting media sensationalism around sex, violence, drugs and the f-word, the anxiety of print in much new writing suggests that the quality aspired to is a "cool" resistance to text and print-culture in favour of mediatic cynicism, clipped colloquialism, and idioms intimate with the sound-bite.[8] The effect is to generate spoken word drama that is provocative through the display of attitude. The performance of attitude also requires an intimate relation between actors and the parts they play. The craft of acting appears to generate suspicion when its artifice attempts to go beyond the image-postures and speech mannerisms of existing social attitudes. Much new writing remains theatrical because the attitudes struck are unacceptable for British TV drama at the level of language and "adult" content.

The ambition of British television drama remains notable, however. Stephen Poliakoff's recent television series *Perfect Strangers* (2000/published 2001) illustrates an approach very different from what has been called "In-yer-face" theatre (see Sierz), although some allowance has to be made for the comparatively large budgets which allow Poliakoff to work with longer scenes, large sets, and historical flashbacks. In a wider view, a case could be made for the qualities of British television comedies such as *Absolutely Fabulous*, *Blackadder*, and *Father Ted*, as well as series such as *This Life*, *Our Friends in the North*, and *Queer as Folk*, in conjunction with crime dramas such as *A Touch of Frost*, *Jonathan Creek*, and *Cracker*, as being the most lively forms of contemporary British drama. The awkward negotiation of Jonathan Harvey's work from *Beautiful Thing* (1993) to his flawed television situation comedy *Gimme Gimme Gimme* suggests the difficulties that new writers face when given the resources and audience of television. The underlying question for almost all the writers currently writing for the stage is their orientation to the opportunities and difficulties of television and film, not least as a potential source of economic security. Beyond the sensationalism of sex, obscenity, and violence in theatre writing, a number of plays suggest shared idioms across television and cinema, developing a new kind of dialogue with an artifice of direct and, occasionally, more fantastical urban speech-forms. This has had an effect on the printed forms of the published play-script. Indirectly, the presiding influence appears to be Harold Pinter, who has himself expressed enthusiasm for the work of Sarah Kane in particular. Pinter's idiom has found its way into many forms of contemporary drama, through Joe Orton's mediation of Pinteresque comedies of menace, for example, or through David Mamet's cinematic variations on

---

[8]   The recent cultural climate of cynicism can be approached through Sloterdijk and Bewes.

a style recognisably derived from Pinter, a derivation which has in turn influenced contemporary British playwrights.

At the level of the printed playscript, there are intriguing shifts in the conventions used to represent the theatricality of implied performance styles. Underlying some superficial shifts in the conventions of the playscript, more profound anxieties about the significance of print culture can be discerned. Where Pinter's plays characteristically work with conversational implicature, textually represented by the rhetoric of the pause, long pause and silence, the more common marker of implication in many recent plays is the word "beat." This indicates a moment of brief stasis, a moment of verbal stasis and, to a lesser extent, physical stasis, forms of stasis which nevertheless fall short of a "freeze" or frozen tableau. This kind of stasis seems to have become a shared idiom among contemporary theatre practitioners, though less recognisable to audiences unfamiliar with the jargon of the rehearsal room and theatre production culture. The direction "beat" suggests an additional heart-beat, a percussively marked shift, but the thought that "pause" might have served a similar function highlights a specific, if minor sign of resistance to the literary pregnancy of the dramatic pause. "Beat" suggests theatrical temporality rather than the texture of time passing or of menace, the drama associated respectively with the pauses of Beckett and Pinter. The now conventional use of "beat" in many contemporary dramatic texts marks a practice less concerned to offer an experience for readers. On display is something closer to a theatrical technicality assumed to be integral to performance rhythms. The textual idiom marks a shift from rehearsal jargon to print form that implies an assumed theatrical competence rather than literary attention.

Another shift in the textual idiom of recent play-texts is the use of the forward slash to indicate overlapping speeches. Against the artifice of complete sentences alternating through clearly divided speech moments, the desire to overlap speeches indicates an ambition to lend naturalist polyphony to the way actors speak. This might once have been worked out in rehearsal, but the printed instruction that two voices should speak simultaneously presents a dilemma for readers. The device of overlapping speech was probably first popularised by Caryl Churchill's play *Top Girls* (1982), in which the device indicated sisterly cacophony in the opening dinner-party. Once speech overlaps become a convention of printed drama, however, the effect can suggest a fussy sense of theatrical speech. Such indications of performance parameters gesture towards levels of detail lost in the fluidity of performance. Part of the effect on readers is to highlight the secondary quality of printed forms as compared with the more primary authenticity of speech in performance. Ordinary speech competence indicates that native speakers can usually hear and follow two voices that overlap. The imagination of such effects by a reader is less comfortable. A suspicion emerges that the printed rhetoric of overlapping speech indicates a constitutive alienation from the interpretative act of reading and a mildly disingenuous emphasis on theatrical realisation. The "beat" and the forward slash are print conventions easily grasped through familiarity with the implications, but the underlying drift reveals deeper anxieties about print culture.

Put differently, it is difficult to grasp the excitement of much new writing through the artifice of the playscript. Many of these plays require socially resonant acting skills to animate the prosaic surface texture of colloquial speech. This is part of a sociality of public performance that dislocates the autonomy of the text. Characters in many of the plays that seem most evidently contemporary are verbally truncated. An earlier generation of playwrights oscillated between quick-fire dialogue and extended monologues and tirades. The most recognisable tropes in new writing eschew speeches that indicate a speaker's literariness or ease with extended periods. Speech-making and oratory have moved beyond sceptical dramatisation into positions that seem dramatically taboo. The naturalist critique of dramatic poetry extends the reach of prose dynamics further into the available range of dramatic idioms. The effects bear comparison with modes of Hollywood dialogue which prize pace and monosyllabic brevity. There are counter-genres written for both stage and film that offer grotesques in which the artifice of brutalist speech generates new kinds of urban baroque. This tendency is most widely recognised in Quentin Tarantino's *Pulp Fiction*, which, along with *Trainspotting*, exemplifies the sensibilities influential on a number of new dramatic modes. These different tendencies are anxious not to represent characters who speak like books. This reflects anxieties around print culture also evident in the collapse of political rhetoric into the commonsensical sound-bite. Political speech, tabloid and television journalism converge on a rhetoric of platitude in which the performance is designed to avoid any impression of intellectualism. The opprobrium heaped on Gordon Brown's reference to neoclassical macro-economic endogenous growth theory might serve as an example of the pressures on speech competence. Bookish talk falls victim to a general taboo on jargon imposed in the name of populism. Similar kinds of anti-intellectualism animate the discourse of recent British art and music.

If it is a truism of drama that texts should be read through performance history, the anxiety of print culture within contemporary British drama presents a paradox. Performance remains the acid test of these new plays, and yet performances are still disseminated to a significant degree by the print culture of reviews, playscripts and educational discourse. Despite the apparent indifference to traditional conceptions of literariness, many playscripts are published to coincide with performance. What the multitude of new plays has yet to actualise, however, is a critical culture of reading. The priority of performance dynamics even seems motivated by a suspicion of intellectual analysis and literary interpretation.

A notable exception to the dominant relation between performance and the playscript is provided by Howard Barker. A number of Barker's plays have appeared in print before performance. Although the theatre company called The Wrestling School is devoted to theatrical actualisation of Barker's work, it seems likely that Barker is concerned to develop an audience of readers, and that he intends his drama for an audience of intellectually self-critical readers. A recent play, *He Stumbled*, was given its world premiere at the Gardner Arts Centre, Brighton, in 2000, but was first published in Barker's *Collected Plays*, volume 4, in 1998. A significant portion of Barker's audience have read his plays before they see them. An intensity of textuality is also evident in the idiom of his printed playscripts. Barker is fond of alternating bold and normal type-faces as well as providing poetically exaggerated stage directions. In the text of *He Stumbled*, for example, the play begins with the direction: "A high wall. The grieving of masses. A rising sun fingers the top ..." (251). Later, the directions state that the audience, "drained of utterance, falls silent" (315). These disturbances in the pragmatic integrity of the playscript represent the inverse of the ghostly trace of the reader in Beckett's *Footfalls*. Barker's playscripts come closer to a condition of imaginative theatrical possibility which, along lines suggested by Ibsen's *Peer Gynt*, seeks to radicalise readers for new kinds of theatre. Indeed, the theatre of readers imagined by Barker seems closer in intention to the text and performance relations of Ibsen's dramatic oeuvre, working towards a public culture of play-reading and theatre-making with critical and intellectual purpose. In Barker's playscripts, then, the prolegomena provided more often take the form of literary epigraphs than details of first performance. In some respects, Barker's is a strategy for survival in a theatre culture resistant to his work, a strategy that depends on the support of his publisher. Along with a surprisingly large number of British playwrights, Barker's work is more actively read and performed in continental Europe than in Britain, though the status of the theatrical and literary translations involved is hard to assess. Anecdotal evidence suggests that some productions of Barker's plays in Europe use his texts as frameworks for styles of production very different from productions seen in Britain. This suggests an interesting contrast with Beckett's direction of his own plays in European productions. These productions more firmly set the terms of Beckett's dramatic intentions than otherwise possible for texts, even texts as precisely set out as Beckett's. Whatever the fate of Barker's work in European productions, his position in British theatre culture appears isolated. Comparison could be made with the angry autonomy of Edward Bond, who has produced a range of increasingly extended essays and prefatory material to accompany his plays. The decisive feature of Barker's oeuvre is that its avant-garde literariness appears historical and unfashionable. Although Barker's plays and the critical essays collected in his book *Arguments for a Theatre* polemicise on behalf of theatre for future readers and audiences, his trajectory has been received more as the last gasp of drama's older affinity with print culture. Barker's attempt to revive a neo-Jacobean poetics of drama has thus suffered from seeming too anxious to reproduce an earlier kind of drama-print relation. In this sense, Barker's work is the exception that exemplifies contemporary theatre culture's anxious desire to bypass print culture.

For reasons difficult to focus, the most sustained recent tendency in "British" drama to embody a self-consciously literary sense of tradition is represented by playwrights from Ireland and, to a lesser degree, Scotland. Such work has been important in London's recent theatre history. It is almost as if a space for knowingly literary plays is licensed so long as the poetics of lyrical dramatic idioms can be romanticised and affectionately limited to the Celtic fringe. Conor McPherson's play *The Weir* (1997) and Sebastian Barry's *Our Lady of Sligo* (1998) occupy this space with some elegance and have achieved both critical and commercial success as examples of "fine" writing. If the urban baroque and pseudo-cynical dialogue of much London drama cuts sentimental and extended periods into short fragments, many London-Irish plays allow themselves to expand story-telling through longer narrative speeches. The ur-form of this tendency is Brian Friel's *Faith Healer* (1979). If *Faith Healer* dramatises the mystification of public speech as a critique of faith and of the power of oratory, plays such as those of Conor McPherson are less evidently public or knowingly theatrical, almost to the point of being static. Robert Shore's review of McPherson's recent play *Port Authority* sketches a widely perceived limitation in this tendency:

> Does Conor McPherson's new play need a stage? Would it be equally effective if it were performed on the radio or left on the page? It is not hard to see why questions about the work's "theatricality" should have been asked [...] McPherson appears to have regressed, returning to the intertwined monologue format of his 1995 hit, *This Lime Tree Bower*. He is undoubtedly a fine writer, critics agree, but if his thing is monologues, can he really be a "man of the theatre"? (19)

This highlights the way in which traditional criteria of fine writing are in conflict with theatrical qualities. While the plays of McPherson are reader-friendly, their dramatic limitations work as the mirror image of the knowingly anti-literary qualities of plays such as *Shopping and Fucking*. The writer who brings what might be called the London-Irish tendency in recent British drama to its sharpest focus is Martin McDonagh. His fictional fantasy Irelands collapse and satirise some of the sustaining romanticism of Irish writing's position within London theatre. The key here, as in the acute moments of McPherson's play *The Weir*, is that the anxiety of Irish literariness is staged so as to deconstruct an assumed identification between dramatic texture and staged Irishness.

Beyond the fashion for urban baroque speech idioms in the most hyped plays, the work of McPherson, Sebastian Barry, and Martin McDonagh reveals a persistent desire among London theatre audiences for plays with traditional literary qualities. These plays are new in a number of subtle ways, not least in the reflexive critique of generational and historical conflicts which go beyond the immediate impact of theatre made by a generation of twenty-somethings who are now in their thirties. Much hope for the vitality of London theatre has been invested in the possibility of attracting younger audiences. The larger subsidised theatres, such as the Royal National Theatre and the Royal Shakespeare Company, have made attempts to tap into the energies of new writing sketched here. Many recent plays seem better suited, however, to intimate, chamber theatres rather than as developments of the project of civic self-representation so much a feature of 1970s and 1980s British drama. The Royal Court has succeeded in reinventing itself as a place in which new writing is developed and showcased. The economic future of playwrighting as a career in Britain necessarily directs the energies of writers towards television and film. Larger plays attempting public representation are in danger of disappearing. Rumours suggest that the cupboards of Channel 4, the BBC, the RSC, and the RNT are full of large, ambitious plays whose cast-size and uncertain literary quality have proved too anxiety-inducing in the minds of producers to be given the chance of finding their way into production. Michael Kustow's book *Theatre@risk* charts the difficulties faced in putting on John Barton's series of plays entitled *Tantalus*, a project that proved too ambitious for the RSC to stage out of its own resources, despite Peter Hall's status as a director. Kustow charts the anxieties of adapting Barton's plays. Barton's sense that his script was distorted by Hall's production points to further levels of anxiety animating the contemporary playscript and the fragility of authorial integrity within theatre production. Such conflicts are a familiar feature of the way television and film culture appropriate the work of playwrights. Although *Tantalus* is an important landmark in recent British drama, the collaboration necessary to realise *Tantalus* suggests a precarious future for such ambitious projects. *Tantalus* is another exception that exemplifies the limitations of contemporary British theatre. There is a widespread sense, moreover, that the larger subsidised theatres, above all the RSC and the RNT, have lost their way and have failed in their role as fora for national or public drama. Both organisations have produced innovative and commercially successful musicals, while continuing to produce "classic" plays, above all the works of Shakespeare. Viewed from the perspective of hopes for a national and critical theatre culture, these theatres currently seem unsuccessful or secondary as ways of mediating new writing. Public subsidy for a greater diversity of theatre culture would make a difference, but a key difficulty is the lack of intellectual or social excitement associated with the larger theatres, and the sense that this is a theatre culture with a precarious future.

As the reader will remember, however, there are many exceptions to the generalised picture sketched here. Perhaps it is unsurprising that some of the most successful work in recent British drama has taken the form of productions of plays by established playwrights. Michael Frayn's *Copenhagen* (1998) and Tom Stoppard's *Arcadia* (1993) have shown that there is a large audience for plays which theatricalise arguments about probability and science. The success of Lee Hall's work, perhaps most visibly in Stephen Daldry's film *Billy Elliot* (2000), suggests the ongoing interest in intelligent but sentimental populist drama, a tendency which might loosely cover the work of Mike Leigh and Alan Bennett. Although many socialist playwrights, such as Edward Bond, David Edgar, and Trevor Griffiths, are still active in new ways, their work currently appears rather marginal.

Perhaps it is appropriate to conclude by noting that the two most widely respected British playwrights, Harold Pinter and Caryl Churchill, have produced some of their most interesting and surprising work in the last ten years. Pinter's *Ashes to Ashes* (1996) and Churchill's *Blue Heart* (1997) and *Far Away* (2000) in particular, are among the most innovative and suggestive plays of recent years. As if to confirm the drift of the argument sketched here, the play-scripts of these plays reveal new anxieties about the status of literariness and print-culture. All three plays generate dramatic idioms that overlap physicality and tortured speech fragments in new ways. Curiously, all three plays dramatise anxieties around children and parental concern, politicising the trope of the lost or buried child which is one of the most persistent motifs in modern drama, reaching back to Ibsen's *The Wild Duck*. The fashion show which forms the centre-piece of Churchill's play *Far Away* might serve as an eloquent allegory of the anxiety and troubled state of what is fashionable in British drama, being at once defiantly theatrical and stylish, but sandwiched within an anxious textuality of political unrest.

Works Cited

Armitstead, Claire. "LIFTing the Theatre: The London International Festival of Theatre." *Contemporary British Theatre*. Ed. Theodore Shank. London: Macmillan, 1996. 152-65.

Auslander, Philip. *Liveness: Performances in a Mediatized Culture*. London: Routledge, 1999.

Barker, Howard. *Arguments for a Theatre*. 3rd ed. Manchester: Manchester UP, 1997.

_____. *He Stumbled. Collected Plays*. Vol. 4. London: John Calder, 1998. 249-317

Beckett, Samuel. *Stücke und Bruchstücke: englische und französische Original-fassungen*. Frankfurt am Main: Suhrkamp Verlag, 1978.

_____. *Footfalls. The Complete Dramatic Works*. London: Faber and Faber, 1986. 397-403

Bernstein, Charles, ed. *Close Listening: Poetry and the Performed Word* (New York: Oxford UP, 1998.

Bewes, Timothy. *Cynicism and Postmodernity*. London: Verso, 1997.

Bradwell, Mike, ed. *The Bush Theatre Book*. London: Methuen, 1997.

Derrida, Jacques. *L'écriture et la différence*. Paris: Éditions du Seuil, 1967.

_____. *Writing and Difference*. Trans. Alan Bass. London: Routledge, 1978.

Dromgoole, Dominic. *The Full Room: An A-Z of Contemporary Playwrighting*. London: Methuen, 2000.

Etchells, Tim. "Diverse Assembly: Some Trends in Recent Performance." *Contemporary British Theatre*. Ed. Theodore Shank. London: Macmillan, 1996. 107-22.

Kustow, Michael. *Theatre@risk*.London: Methuen, 2001

Marber, Patrick. *Closer*. London: Methuen, 1997.

Miller, Eileen. *Edinburgh International Festival, 1947-1996*. Aldershot: Scolar, 1996.

Milne, Drew. "Drama in the Culture Industry: British Theatre after 1945." *British Culture of the Postwar: an Introduction to Literature and Society 1945-1999*. Ed. Alistair Davies and Alan Sinfield. London and New York: Routledge, 2000. 169-91.

Perril, Simon, ed. *Tending the Vortex: the Works of Brian Catling*. Cambridge: CCCP Books, 2001.

Shore, Robert. Review of *Port Authority. Times Literary Supplement* March 16 2001: 19.

Sierz, Aleks. *In-yer-face Theatre: British Drama Today*. London: Faber and Faber 2001.

Sloterdijk, Peter. *Critique of Cynical Reason*. Trans. Michael Eldred. London: Verso, 1988.

Stallabrass, Julian. *High Art Lite: British Art in the 1990s*. London: Verso, 1999.

Williams, Raymond. *Drama from Ibsen to Eliot*. London: Chatto & Windus, 1952.
_____. "Drama in a Dramatized Society." *Writing in Society*. London: Verso, 1983. 11-21.

Ravenhill's Wilde Game

Jozef DE VOS

Universiteit Gent

Mark Ravenhill's notorious *Shopping and Fucking* (1996) undoubtedly constitutes one of the most representative examples of the recent wave of what has come to be called "In-yer-face theatre" (Sierz). Though this play did not actually spark off the movement, it is remarkable how many similarities it bears with *Look Back in Anger*. Like John Osborne's famous début, its frankness of tone and content caused controversy. Both plays also offer a picture of a disorientated young generation that voices its disgust with existing society, but at the same time seems to be desperately in need of something to hold on to.

Indeed, *Shopping and Fucking* lives up to the promises of its almost programmatic title: it contains some explicit sex scenes and depicts a society ruled by money and consumerism. The characters are hopelessly adrift in a world that has abandoned its "grand narratives." With its rapid, cinematic structure and nervous dialogues, *Shopping and Fucking* perfectly reflects the contemporary urban culture. Beneath the surface of this picture, however, lurks a moral undertone. The slightly sentimental end scene, in which the three youngsters seem to reunite and feed each other, creates a gleam of hope in this ruthless environment. So does the character of Lulu, the only woman in this male gay milieu, who almost pathetically tries to keep "the family" together.

In spite of its shocking language and stage pictures, *Shopping and Fucking* mainly uses a conventional, realistic code and may even be seen as a "slice of life." It therefore comes as a surprise to hear Robbie make explicit reference to J. F. Lyotard's theory of the loss of grand narratives:

> I think ... I think we all need stories, we make up stories so that we can get by. And I think a long time ago there were big stories. Stories so big you could live your whole life in them. The Powerful Hands of the Gods and Fate. The Journey to Enlightenments. The March of Socialism. But they all died or the world grew up or grew senile or forgot them, so now we're all making up our own stories. Little stories. It comes out in different ways. But we've each got one. (64)

The contemporary uprootedness and lack of values are thus directly and expressly put in the context of postmodernism.

That Ravenhill was not altogether unfamiliar with postmodernist discourse very clearly transpired from his next play *Faust* (*Faust is Dead*) (1997), which almost reads like a dramatic comment on some postmodernist issues. Featuring as characters a Foucault-like philosopher, the son of a Bill Gates-like tycoon, and a boy who only appears on the computer screen, the play entirely focuses on the blurring of reality and the virtual world. As Aleks Sierz points out, it also dramatises postmodern ideas about the volatility of character and the indeterminacy of the subject (136).

It should come as no surprise then that Ravenhill's *Handbag* (1998) presents itself as a fully postmodern, highly intertextual play, in which the author consciously refers to and skillfully uses Oscar Wilde's *The Importance of Being Earnest* in order to create his own contemporary comedy of manners. The intertextual framework allows Ravenhill to develop different levels of action and meaning that put each other in perspective. Whereas in *Shopping and Fucking* the awareness of the "postmodern condition" was almost too explicitly voiced by one of the characters and felt as if imposed on the play, *Handbag*, in a seemingly effortless way, creates a structure in which a historical and a contemporary level intertwine, characters appear and re-appear with different names and clothes, and which reinforces the theme of sexual mores.

In the relatively complicated plot structure, two levels—a Victorian, Wildean one and a contemporary one—must be distinguished. In the contemporary strand, a male homosexual and a lesbian couple decide to have a baby by means of artificial insemination. Various infidelities seem to undermine this attempt at alternative parenting. The baby even gets kidnapped and eventually dies of neglect. The Victorian plot offers a "prehistory" to Wilde's play. We see the characters twenty-eight years before the action of *The Importance of Being Earnest*, and we actually witness how Prism, who is far more interested in novel writing than in child care, puts Jack in a handbag and, before fleeing to Worthing, conspires with the philanthropist-paedophile Cardew to let him "mistake" her bag for his own.

The two plots are carefully and adroitly juxtaposed. Critics of *The Importance of Being Earnest* have drawn attention to the play's extreme formality, which is even said to approach the codification of dance. W. H. Auden also commented on the "pure verbal opera" of the dialogue" (Jackson 171). Ravenhill seems to have seized upon and even intensified this quality by creating an equally balanced configuration of characters in his plot: Gwendolen and Cecily have their counterparts in the lesbian couple Mauretta and Suzanne, while Algernon and Jack are paralleled by the homosexual "fathers" of the baby, Tom and Davies. The nanny Lorraine who in Ravenhill's play kidnaps the baby of course embodies the present-day Miss Prism. Besides these parallelisms, the actors' doubling performance of the characters of Mauretta-Augusta, Suzanne-Constance, David-Moncrieff, Tom-Cardew, and Lorraine-Prism also reinforces the connections between the Victorian and the contemporary strand in *Handbag*.

Far from being a gratuitous game, Ravenhill's shrewd juxtaposition and intertwining of the two plots in a few crucial scenes proves to be a procedure which foregrounds several essential aspects of the play. The author's "Wilde game" offers a convenient framework for a contemporary comedy of manners. The wittiness of Oscar Wilde's comedy is so baffling that William Archer's reaction to its first production in February 1895 still remains one that spectators or readers can easily sympathise with:

> What can a poor critic do with a play which raises no principle, whether of art or morals, creates its own canons and conventions, and is nothing but an absolutely willful expression of an irrepressively witty personality? (Wilde xxxiv)

In spite of the almost paralysing effect of the consistently farcical tone, critics have increasingly recognised a serious layer of social comment beneath the flippant surface of the play's plot and characterisation. Wilde repeatedly turns upside down all social conventions in order to reveal the empty formality of the society about which he writes (Knox 98-99). Recently, Sos Eltis's careful study of Wilde's revisions has shown that he systematically sharpened the satirical and subversive thrust of *The Importance of Being Earnest*. Likewise, Ravenhill draws a critical picture of contemporary mores, particularly in the gay community. The formality and politeness of Victorian society is juxtaposed with contemporary frankness and directness, especially in sexual matters, but both sets of attitudes are shown to be just a veneer covering the characters' cynicism and lack of emotions.

Handbag starts off with a scene in which Suzanne, Mauretta, and David are waiting for Tom, who is supposed to masturbate so as to donate his sperm for Mauretta's artificial insemination. This immediately sets the scene for a play concerned with today's sexual mores. The two couples apparently have decided to have a baby. By the time the child is born in Scene Seven, David has been having intercourse with Phil, and Suzanne has been flirting with Lorraine. Clearly the characters appear incapable of engaging in an enduring relationship and of bearing personal responsibility. The more stable ones in the gay foursome are Mauretta and Tom. Already in Scene One, as the latter enters holding a cup with his sperm, Mauretta expresses her intention of doing better as a mother than her own parents:

> When I was a kid my dad walked out. One day he came home and he packed a bag and he stuck his head round the door and he said: "I'm going out." And that was it. He was gone and we never mentioned him again. But people would look at you and they'd say: "It's not right. A mum and a dad's best for a kid. A kid's gotta have a mum and a dad." (3)

Tom also seems to be convinced he will be able to give a far more loving and positive upbringing to his child than most ordinary parents:

> **Tom**. Sorry. I just want everything to be … You see so many kids. At the end of school, the parents come and pick them up. And I watch them from the staffroom window, and they grab hold of the kid's hand and it's: "shut up"—swipe—"keep your fucking mouth shut." I mean, how's a child supposed to grow, develop and grow, when there's so much anger and, and … ugliness? And that's why I want … We can do so much better than that. We can create something calm and positive. We can do that. (5)

Typically, Tom only has words of contempt for the pornography David brings along "to do the trick."

David's frivolous lifestyle is strikingly illustrated by the fact that he misses the birth of the baby, because at the very moment he is having sex with Phil. In an earlier sex scene between David and Phil (Scene Three), the latter's concluding remark after fellating David—"Twenty quid. Come on. Nothing's for nothing. Twenty quid" (15)—clinches the commodification and commercialisation of love and sex. The reader/spectator may wonder whether the frankly mercenary approach to life and marriage of Lady Bracknell differs much from the attitude demonstrated by Phil.

The confrontation of the mores of the Victorian upper classes with those of the generation of the late twentieth century implicitly raises a number of uncomfortable questions. The lesbian couple's hiring and treatment of Lorraine as a nanny invites comparison with the situation of Miss Prism in Wilde's play. As well as their Victorian counterparts, Suzanne and Mauretta entrust the upbringing of their child to a nanny. In the course of a century, the social relation between employer and employee does not appear to have gained in humane quality. Not only is Lorraine exploited, but she is also humiliated by having a camera monitor her.

At the centre of the play are problems concerning responsible parenting and child care. On the Victorian level, parents give responsibility to a nanny, who is only interested in novel writing.

> Really, how am I to deal adequately with fiction when reality keeps making such rude interruptions on my time? Because, really, you are a single infant.

You really won't make one bit of difference to the world. Whereas this is a novel. Think of the emotion and instruction in a three-volume novel and think of the thousands of readers. (78-79)

On the contemporary level, the gay parents either neglect the child or employ a nanny, who kidnaps the baby to set up home with the drug addict Phil, a situation which leads to the final shocking episode in which the child is virtually killed. This hallucinatory scene of horror in fact constitutes one of the intriguing moments when the two strands of the play not only intertwine, but even merge. For an instant, even the two babies—that of the gay couples and the Victorian one—seem to become identical.

The issue of child neglect is foregrounded in the play by the story which Mauretta tells immediately after the birth of her baby. It parallels and, as if by way of anxious premonition, foreshadows what is to happen to her own child:

I had this woman on my show. Some girl took her baby. And the hospital had it all on video. The security camera. "Could it be someone you know?" So they showed her the video, but you couldn't see the face because of course the camera was in the wrong fucking place. "I can't see the face." "Oh, but there's a moment when she looks over her shoulder. Put it on freeze frame and you can catch the face." But it's all blurry and you can never quite make it out. She watched it over and over but ... They found the baby a week later in a dustbin. (31)

The combination of the different strands in the play sheds light on the complexity of the issues discussed, and prevents the spectator from drawing easy conclusions or deriving moral guidelines. Rather than providing solutions, Ravenhill invokes doubt and disturbing questions. In the Victorian plot, Constance and her husband are responsible for neglecting their child. Moncrieff's reaction to his wife's intention to "do [her] duty" [viz. breastfeed the child] exemplifies the cold, inhumane attitude of the upper classes. He does not want his wife to fulfil what he calls "the duty of an animal" (78). Prism, into whose care the baby is entrusted, only hopes "the bogeyman" will come along to take it away, and therefore has no qualms about passing it on to a paedophile. But the project of alternative parenthood of the gay couples, who voice idealistic intentions in the beginning, soon turns into a muddle and ends in horror.

The most disturbing aspect of the play, however, concerns the role of Cardew, who runs a home for foundling boys, but who has to flee to Worthing after a crowd has set fire to his house. To Aleks Sierz, the author of the recently published first survey of "In-Yer-Face Theatre," Ravenhill declared that the play's central meaning is "that it is impossible to have children as a selfless act in a society that is basically selfish, that can create the Lorraines and Phils" (143). Cardew too has his selfish, sexual motives for "fathering" the boys, but in the context of *Handbag*, it may be argued that he is one of those who take the most responsibility for the children and who most represents the quality of "caring." However sinister and ambiguous, he is not depicted as an incarnation of malevolence. Though I cannot agree with Aleks Sierz, who thinks that Ravenhill gives us a "sympathetic portrait" (143) of Cardew, it should be noted that he is never shown as a child abuser. The final scene, then, which juxtaposes Lorraine's cradling of the bin bag containing the dead body of the present-day baby with Cardew's cradling of the baby taken from the handbag, may suggest the rather unsettling conclusion that Cardew's treatment remains the more humane one.

The most intriguing character in *Handbag* is probably Phil, who also features in both plots of the play. Phil comes closest to being a tragic victim. He makes his first appearance in the play with blood running from his nose, probably the result of an abortive attempt at stealing a handbag. Ravenhill portrays Phil as a lost boy who wants to be his own person. More than the others, he has the impulse to be a responsible and caring parent, but he tragically fails, because he cannot cope with the problems related to a lifestyle of drug addiction and instant sex. The opening of Scene Fourteen offers a striking theatrical moment, when Phil, while bathing the baby, invokes a sort of vision in which he, as a father, exorcises the drugdealer/child abuser. This, of course, echoes Scene Ten, in where he recalled a situation in which he gives in to the dealer's pressure to prostitute his infant daughter. When in the final scene Phil desperately attempts to make the baby breathe again by stubbing his cigarette into its eyes, he virtually kills the child. Phil's howling then appropriately concludes the play.

The tragic character of Phil fulfils a pivotal function, because he provides the structural link between the contemporary and the Victorian levels. This allows Ravenhill to develop the relationship between Phil and Cardew. In each of the two key scenes where the two strands come together, Cardew is also involved. In a thrilling theatrical moment in Scene Nine, by making Phil have a fix, the playwright transposes him as well as the audience into Victorian times, as Cardew appears to be looking for his lost boy Eustace, whose role is taken up by Phil. Both Phil and Cardew then act out their fantasy of adopted child and guardian. The second scene in which the two levels of the plot intertwine is the play's gripping finale, to which I have already referred. Seeking help for the baby, Phil ironically turns to Cardew, from whom he has been trying to break away throughout the play.

Shaking off Cardew's influence forms in fact a part of Phil's quest for identity, which features at the heart of the play. The latter is trying to throw off the shackles of control by others and to confirm his own individuality. That Ravenhill wanted this to be a central issue in *Hand-*

bag is shown by the subtitle of the play's first production, "The Importance of Being Someone" (Sierz 141). Again, Wilde's comedy, described by Melissa Knox as a "drama of identity," obviously provided a convenient point of departure. The main characters, Jack and Algy, are as interchangeable as Gwendolen and Cecily. As Knox says, "Wilde seems to want to impress on his audience that they have no identities of their own. They are carbon copies. At the same time, there is an artificial splitting of characters into several different identities: Jack and Algy both adopt the name of Ernest in order to assume another role. Identity is unstable: easily assumed, carelessly discarded" (98). The love of the two girls depends on the triviality of the proper name Ernest. As Lady Bracknell herself puts it, "We live, I regret to say, in an age of surfaces" (62), a statement echoed by Ravenhill's Augusta: "To challenge substance over style is quite a challenge to society is it not" (7). Names, appearances, surfaces are the elements that matter and that constitute identity, which therefore cannot possibly be fixed. As Neil Sammells says, what Wilde gives us is

> a picture of identity as radically decentered and dispersed. The characters in *The Importance of Being Earnest* all speak in the same way, with that extraterritorial perfection which has nothing to do with naturalism and everything to do with Wilde's assertion that language is the parent and not the child of thought. These are more versions of the poststructuralist subject, defined by what they say rather than what they are, and characterised by indeterminacy and instability. (109)

Ravenhill's treatment of characters, then, appears to be a radicalisation of Wilde's. The rapid, nervous style of the play contributes to creating a world in which the characters continually oscillate between various options, assume different roles, and thus lack any stable identity. Phil's attempt "to be his own person" travesties Jack Worthing's search to find out who he is. Typically, his quest turns out to be a failure. Scene Ten, in which Phil, dressed in Victorian clothes, sings a Victorian ballad as Cardew watches and "arranges" (58) him theatrically, allows the audience to visualise the manipulation and control of Phil's personality by Cardew. How loosely identity sits upon character also appears from the varying use of names. In Scene Nine, in which Phil is transposed into the Victorian plot, Cardew welcomes him as his lost boy and calls him Eustace. Phil insists that he be given a different name. Cardew later addresses him by the names of Jack and John. At the beginning of Scene Fourteen, Lorraine and Phil enact a small ritual in which their kidnapped baby is born (again) and rechristened Eustace.

Besides the very concept of the play and its conscious intertextuality, the determining presence of the media equally contributes to its postmodernist outlook. Baudrillard describes the present-day order as one of "simulation" and one that is "controlled by the code" (quoted in Bertens

150). This order is also the order of the media, which form and embody the code (Bertens 150). The new media and means of communication omnipresently pervade the world of *Handbag*. The characters are incapable of establishing a relationship; paradoxically, even their casual and quick moments of (sexual) contact are continuously broken off by mobile phones and pagers. Typically too, they work in television and advertising. Both David and Phil know Lorraine from her appearances on television. In the maternity ward scene, right after the baby is born, Mauretta expresses her anxiety about children getting lost by referring to a story of "this woman on my show." Later on, Mauretta and Suzanne monitor their nanny by means of video cameras and actually watch the video. Another striking instance of the impact of television is the appearance in the play of the Teletubbies. In Scene Eleven, whilst Phil is trying to make love to Lorraine, he does so wearing the mask of Tinky Winky. While masturbating her, he puts the mask on Lorraine. Aleks Sierz reminds us of the fact that, Tinky Winky as a cult figure for clubbers, was denounced as gay by the American preacher Jerry Falwell in 1999 (141). In each of these cases, the characters seem to have lost their grip on reality and are only able to refer to a mediated version of it. If this brings us close to Baudrillard's hyperreal, the systematic relationship of *Handbag* with Wilde's "phenotext" also contributes to creating a hyperreal world. Nearly all the characters and a part of the action itself appear as reproductions of the images of *The Importance of Being Earnest*.

Besides the structural and thematic links between the two plays, Ravenhill also incorporated stylistic and humorous elements that function as echoes of the original comedy. The text teems with details that remind the reader/spectator of Wilde. A few jokes can be singled here to reinforce the Wilde connection. Aleks Sierz (141) says that most reviewers quoted Ravenhill's line of Wildean humour in Scene Five, where Constance is about to give birth:

Constance (off) *cries out*

Cardew Good lord. What a terrible noise.

Moncrief Not at all. It's the sound of labour.

Cardew Labour? Isn't that something that happens in Manchester? (23)

Equally witty and reminiscent of Wilde is Phil's conclusion after hearing Prism's account of the accident with an omnibus which "overturned, depositing [her] on the pavement": "Then you must be a Fallen Woman" (53).

Needless to say the cumulative effect of the "prequel," the parallels in character and style, and the numerous allusions make for a pastiche, which, as Frederic Jameson has argued, is the postmodern genre par excellence. But, as appears from my analysis, the shrewd juxtaposition and intertwining of the Victorian and contemporary world also allows the author to shed critical light on twentieth century mores and to infuse the play with a moral dimension.

Works Cited

Bertens, Hans. *The Idea of the Postmodern. A History.* London and New York: Routledge, 1995.

Eltis, Sos. *Revising Wilde.* Oxford: Clarendon Press, 1996.

Jackson, Russell. "The Importance of Being Earnest." *The Cambridge Companion to Oscar Wilde.* Ed. Peter Raby. Cambridge: Cambridge UP, 1997.

Knox, Melissa. *Oscar Wilde. A Long and Lovely Suicide.* Yale: Yale UP, 1994.

Ravenhill, Mark. *Handbag.* London: Faber and Faber, 1998.

Ravenhill, Mark. *Shopping and Fucking.* London: Faber and Faber, 1996.

Sammells, Neil. *Wilde Style. The Plays and Prose of Oscar Wilde.* Harlow: Pearson Education, 2000.

Sierz, Aleks. *In-Yer-Face Theatre. British Drama Today.* London: Faber and Faber, 2000.

Wilde, Oscar. *The Importance of Being Earnest.* Ed. Patricia Hern and Glenda Leeming. London: Methuen Students Editions, 1981.

Political Currents
in Caryl Churchill's Plays
at the Turn of the Millennium

Amelia HOWE KRITZER

University of St. Thomas

Over the past twenty-five years, Caryl Churchill's plays have offered a theatrical critique of international social and political developments—whether in Britain or abroad—delivered with an activist energy oriented toward progressive change. Turn-of-the-millennium events, however, from the killing of a toddler by ten-year-old boys in England to the mass murder and systematic rape in Bosnia, have posed problems that seemed to invalidate activist solutions. Concurrently, the post-Thatcher political scene in Britain, with the demise of the Left and the vagueness of a political landscape defined by New Labour, tends to negate activist approaches to social conflicts and economic disparities. The deconstruction of social and political categories and goals in the perspectives of postmodern theory further complicates the situation. This difficult environment has silenced many playwrights of the Left, but Churchill, who has never hesitated to take on the most intractable issues, and whose work is known for deconstructing assumptions of both Left and Right, has addressed herself to the current situation. Her latest plays give theatrical power to the shock, dismay, and disillusionment which have been widely shared responses to recent events, and use deconstructive methods to stimulate thinking about patterns of human behavior implicated in these events. Churchill's turn-of-the-millennium plays, though less direct in their use of political ideas than earlier works, express a continuing concern with divisions, violence, and inequalities among people, and struggle toward new ways of thinking about these issues.

The direction of Churchill's turn-of-the-millennium political preoccupations emerged in her 1994 translation of Seneca's *Thyestes*. The *Thyestes* narrative, in which the thirst for power or revenge leads to generations of intra-family violence, including the killing and cannibalization of children, has been transmitted in various forms from the beginning of Western culture, but still has the power to shock. In her preface to the translation, Churchill reflects on the surprising topicality of the original, the malleability and immutability of language, the terrible time in which the Roman playwright Seneca lived (the reign of Nero), and the persistence of the will to vengeance. In the wake of these reflections, Churchill has intensified her longstanding preoccupation with the individual who willfully sacrifices others to increase or exercise personal power. The will of the individual is examined in relation to others in the family, the future, and the larger world. At the same time, Churchill has turned away from realistic or epic styles to embrace an absurdism that decontextualizes the ordinary and strips distancing historicity from the horrific.

The emphasis on personal actions and responsibility returns Churchill to the territory of her earliest plays—for example, her first radio play *The Ants* (1962)—before her association with politically active theater companies such as Joint Stock and Monstrous Regiment enabled her to find a collective voice. The breakdown of the Left in post-Thatcher Britain has deprived those who seek change of an identifiable and coherent position to serve as a starting point for collective voice or action. The recent works *Blue Heart, This is a Chair*, and *Far Away*, indicate this change, as they resonate with a strong sense of loss and emptiness. They present characters and situations with tragic potential, but this is subject-less tragedy, in which individuals are never fully revealed or defined. Indeed, a sense of identity and coherence seems to be what these characters seek in their futile attempts to connect with others. The only redemptive power in these plays, as in the German *Trauerspielen*—baroque plays about the martyrdom of tyrants— analyzed by Walter Benjamin in the 1920s, lies in the element of play (Benjamin 80-82).

The political content of a work of art, in the view of Fredric Jameson, is most fundamentally expressed in the form of that work (Jameson 1981). The recent plays, in which Churchill acknowledges the confusion or erasure of previous oppositions and alliances, uses absurdist form. In particular, these theatrical works employ disruptions of language and narrative to turn experience inside out and expose the unconscious patterns of thought and behavior. The gaps thus created in the fabric of representation subvert the expected form of communication that mandates audience passivity, involve the audience in a common dynamic, and invite participation in the element of play.

This is a Chair, first performed at the Royal Court Theatre in June 1997, consists of eight brief, disconnected scenes with Brechtian-type titles to be announced or displayed. The titles refer to highly visible national or international issues with complex implications: "The War in Bosnia," "The Labour Party's Slide to the Right," "Animal Conservation and Third-World Economies: The Ivory Trade," "Hong Kong," "Genetic Engineering," "Pornography and Censorship," "The Northern Ireland Peace Process," and "The Impact of Capitalism on the Former Soviet Union." The scenes bear no clear relationship to the displayed titles. For example, in the one that takes place under the title "The War in Bosnia," a woman arrives for a date with a man who is waiting for her with a bouquet of flowers, only to announce apologetically that she has "double-booked" herself for that evening and then rush off to keep her other engagement. "The Labour Party's Slide to the Right" has a drug-addicted man jump off a balcony and commit suicide, just as two brothers of his girlfriend arrive at his flat with the intent of beating him up as a punishment for getting their sister involved with drugs. In "Animal Conservation," two young women discuss a painful hospital test one of them has undergone, while in both "Pornography and Censorship" and "The Northern Ireland Peace Process," a mother and father try to persuade their child to eat her dinner. Although guessing at possible implied relationships between the titles and the action of the scenes contributes to the playful quality of this short work, the apparent lack of connection also creates a sense of alienation from meaning that intensifies with each repetition. The pattern seems to be that of juxtaposing the words defining a political crisis with the material of a personal crisis, and the dialectic thus created holds the personal and the political in an uneasy and constantly tilting balance.

The scenes, which focus on the personal, contain the energy of enactment, while the titles, denoting the political, consist only of words. As the scenes progress, however, their form changes: the dialogue is robbed of some of its words. In the scene "Hong Kong," Tom and Leo quarrel intensely and then make up: their emotions, though complete in a nonverbal sense, are given verbal expression only in fragmentary phrases such as "never did anyway" (20) and "what the fuck you" (20). These phrases serve well enough to convey the general tone of the interaction, but do not define it in any specific way. What might otherwise have been an encounter between the two men over very specific issues instead becomes generic and universalized. Their personal specificity is lost, even as the minds of audience members join in the play to bridge gaps and create coherence. The final scene, titled "The Impact of Capitalism on the Former Soviet Union," has no action or dialogue. It is as though the political is warring with the personal, and the political wins, silencing the personal altogether by stealing its words. *This is a Chair*, then, projects the sense of individual consciousness threatened by the events and concerns outside the personal sphere, which demand recognition even though they are confined to the margin of individual experience. Gradually, however, individual consciousness loses the power to articulate its own crisis. The final result is a failure of communication in both spheres—the personal and the political.

The title *This is a Chair*—in addition to being a playful reference to the image of Magritte's painting "This Is Not a Pipe," reproduced on the cover of the published playscript—carries the implication that a very simple fact is being taught, as it reinforces the play's preoccupation with words. The deliberate estrangement of word and meaning emphasizes the fact that there is no inherent relationship between the word *chair* and the object or its use; even if an inherent relationship existed at some previous time, it has been lost. *Chair* is the term English-speaking people agree to apply to a particular class of objects and, by extension, a leadership function. It is only through agreement to make completely arbitrary connections that communication of even the simplest matters can take place. These agreements structure consciousness as a dialectic between the individual and others, but mandate a shared—or social—consciousness if meaning is to be produced. Word and object attain meaning only through their linkage in a shared consciousness; similarly, the individual attains identity only in relationships defined through shared understandings. Disconnection from a specific context, paradoxically, only serves to place the individual into a wider, more universalized context. Individual consciousness cannot be articulated in the absence of shared consciousness; the very desire for individuality implies a collectivity. Thus, the personal cannot be separated from the political—or, in a broader sense, what lies outside the self—even when political events and issues are so complex, protracted, and painful that an individual may feel driven to cut them out of consciousness.

What the strange dissociation between the titles and action shows most clearly, however, is the absence of a defined relationship between ordinary individuals and the external events of the world. The issues posed by the scene titles defy a simple "for" or "against" dichotomy. They necessitate complex thinking and multi-leveled strategies rather than action proceeding from a single alliance or point of view. The individual, while needing to identify with a larger commonality, cannot rely on familiar forms and patterns of identification in the face of turn-of-the-millennium events. While acknowledging the discomfort and sense of loss inherent in displacement from the familiar, the play attempts to signal the potential of this situation. The final scene, empty of action, is open to the imagining of a new scenario, new forms of relating, and new meanings for given words.

Blue Heart, first produced by Out of Joint at the Royal Court Theatre in August 1997, consists of two thematically related one-acts, "Heart's Desire" and "Blue Kettle," linked by a focus on disrupted family relationships. In "Heart's Desire," an aging couple, Brian and Alice, are expecting the arrival of their adult daughter, who lives in Australia and is coming for a visit after years of absence. The eagerness with which they anticipate the daughter's homecoming is poignant, but in the tension of waiting, the two engage in irritable bickering that at times escalates to bitter blaming and recrimination. The oddball appearance and disconnected chatter of Aunt Maisie, who lives with them, provides a counterpoint of mildly lunatic cheerfulness. As Brian and Alice worry over whether they should have gone to the airport, whether they should eat lunch now or wait, and how they should behave toward the daughter when she arrives, Alice blames Brian for the estrangement from their offspring. For his part, Brian confesses that he entertains a bizarre fantasy of eating himself. The mood also changes when Lewis, an alcoholic son, who lives with them but has little contact, comes in drunk and initiates an unpleasant scene. When the doorbell rings, everyone stops expectantly, anticipating the daughter's arrival, only to be confronted with the unexpected. Successively, the door admits a horde of children, two gunmen, the daughter's female lover, a police officer, and a ten-foot-tall bird.

The most remarkable aspect of this play lies in the way in which the action itself is disrupted. Again and again it stops, resuming at a previous point and repeating parts of scenes. Reiterated scenes often speed up or become telegraphic. Each repetition moves toward the moment when the doorbell rings and someone—or something—arrives. Only in the last recurring scene does the long-awaited daughter arrive. In this scene, Brian starts to greet her with the phrase that forms the title of the one-act—"heart's desire"—but fails to complete the statement and only says "You are my heart's," before the action is interrupted and resumes from the beginning point. The play ends with its first image of Brian putting on his cardigan sweater. All the apparent action has brought about no dramatic progression. Again, Churchill uses theatrical means deliberately to create a sense of estrangement, by negating the standard formula for the communication of meaning in drama. Furthermore, she shows the audience unexpected and dramatic possibilities each time the characters, despite their doubts and hesitations, respond to the ring of the bell by opening the door.

In "Heart's Desire," Churchill seems to be returning to the psychological terrain of her earlier short plays, such as *Abortive* (1971), *Schreber's Nervous Illness* (1972), or *Three More Sleepless Nights* (1980). The one-act seems to represent a desire for reunion—rather than the reunion itself—and the action may be located in the mind of Brian, who wants to but never actually speaks the word *desire*. The scenarios of reunion encompass varied elements that alienate the family's members from one another, but at the core of them is Brian's fixation on and submerged loathing of himself, expressed in his fantasy of self-eating. Brian's fantasy of devouring himself, similar to Tantalus' offering of his children as food for a god, represents an extreme of attempting to isolate the self. Both of Brian's children seem to have responded to their father's egocentrism—with its undercurrents of obsessive control—by distancing themselves. The daughter has lived for a considerable time in Australia, and her homecoming may be no more likely to occur than the other outlandish possibilities enacted in the continually repeated arrivals. The son lives within the household, but, by mutual agreement, separated from its other members and accomplishing his escape through alcohol.

While the one-act play can be viewed in merely psychological terms, it is more interesting as a representation of contemporary England. The failures of the generation that currently holds political power are embodied by the self-loathing Brian, the responsibility-denying Alice, and the incompetent Maisie. The response of the next generation has been to separate in ways that deny this dysfunctional family a future. Total disengagement from either past or future, however, shows itself as impossible through the many repetitions of the action. Though the three who are waiting agree that the daughter's return from Australia will constitute a unique moment, it can only be defined as such through linkage with the past and future, as well as with the many alternative scenarios that exist for that particular moment. All the characters seem trapped in time by their repetitive patterns, but opening the door never fails to admit some new possibility. Opening the door, then, together with the curiosity and hope implied by this act, constitutes the one aspect of the repetitive behavior patterns that offers hope for a future.

A focus on family relationships continues in the second one-act, "Blue Kettle." The primary character in this play, a forty-year-old man named Derek, tells an elderly woman that he is the son she gave up for adoption as a newborn. She reacts with warmth and interest in continuing the re-established relationship. In the following scenes Derek recounts the same story to three more elderly women, who in varying degrees admit him into their lives. In scenes with his girlfriend and his actual mother, now hospitalized with dementia, Derek says that he is conning the women in order to get money from them; however, his girlfriend suggests that his "hobby" (47) of initiating these relationships is a "hangup" (61). In one scene, Derek brings two of the women together, and both initially suppose the other to be his adoptive mother. When they discover that neither of them was, and that they both think they are his biological mother, Derek goes on to tell Mrs. Plant, the first of the women he contacted, that he knew her son and that the latter died in Indonesia. The play ends with Mrs. Plant trying to decide whether to believe him and struggling with what all these revelations mean for her.

Like "Heart's Desire," "Blue Kettle" employs a non-realistic technique to disrupt the unfolding of the narrative. Language becomes problematic as the words "blue" or "kettle" randomly substitute themselves for other words in conversation. At first, the substitutions do not obliterate the sense of conversational statements, as the missing words are easily inferred from the context. As the play continues, however, the substitutions occur more frequently, and the substituted words disintegrate into their component syllables and phonemes. The final sentences consist of the following: "T b k k k k l?" and "B.K." (69). This technique serves to highlight the link between language, experience, and identity. As Derek imposes a new identity on the women he cons, some other mysterious force obstructs communication and subverts the control of speakers over their statements. Again, the dialectic between individual and collective consciousness emerges through language. As the language of each individual character disintegrates, the context becomes more and more important in determining meaning. Context depends on the existence of a common awareness. This common consciousness functions as a kind of invisible chorus, providing the necessary framework for expression, but the visible individuals who present their personal experiences and thoughts remain the focus of the action.

The action of "Blue Kettle" serves to question individual experience and identity. Derek embodies contemporary British individualism. He exists with minimal human connections—a girlfriend of less than a year and his mentally disabled mother. He moves outside this isolation by constructing artificial relationships that he defines and can presumably control. In his claim to represent the continuation of a life they had excluded from their own and remember only vaguely, Derek, consciously or not, problematizes the sense of continuity, identity, and memory in the women he approaches. Derek's quest also reveals the artificial nature of group consciousness. All of the women in Derek's circle of "mothers" are defined as mothers through the action of the play. Although the experience of meeting a forty-year-old man who claims biological kinship is similar for all of the women concerned, each nevertheless reacts differently to this new relationship and changed identity, from Mrs. Plant, who is married with several children and has told her husband about the baby given up for adoption, to the single and childless Miss Clarence, who has kept the illegitimate birth a secret. Paradoxically, their individuality manifests itself in their articulation of the identity they share, even though this identity is based on a long-ago event from which they had cut themselves off and which has now been artificially imposed on them by a dishonest and manipulative stranger.

Derek's identity, too, changes in the course of the play. His claim that he is meeting with the women in order to con them weakens as the action shows him getting more involved in these relationships and allowing the women some power over his life. He readily slips, along with the other characters, into the play's unique language indicating a shared context of unconscious desire. In fact, it is a strong desire for connection that impels both characters and audience. That need, as the one-act demonstrates, can bridge gaps and overcome obstacles. The gaps and obstacles themselves, as well as the artificial configuration of multiple mothers, suggest possibilities for new forms of relationship that might avoid the pain and harm evident in the stories elicited by Derek from the women he contacts.

Far Away, which premiered in November 2000 at the Royal Court Theatre, is the most overtly political of Churchill's recent work, functioning as a kind of parable indicting the Left for its failures in the twentieth century. Recorded sounds of birds chirping and a painted front drop romantically depicting a cottage in an English country landscape greet the audience as it enters the theatre. When the play begins, the front drop lifts to reveal a spare and dark interior where a middle-aged woman sits mending. A young girl in a long white nightgown enters, hugging a stuffed animal. At first, the girl, Joan, seems to be merely having trouble getting to sleep in a guest room at her aunt's house; however, this impression changes as the scene continues. With single-minded intensity, the girl asks one question after another, gradually revealing that she has witnessed acts of bloody violence taking place just outside the house and that she is seeking an explanation for them. The aunt, Harper, tries to reassure her—by saying the screaming was "an owl," the blood on the ground from "a dog [...] run over this afternoon" (10)—but for each comforting explanation, Joan has another question. Under the girl's relentless inquiry and calm gaze, her aunt's attempts to explain away what Joan has seen appear as patent lies. Finally, Harper takes a deep breath, gathers the girl into her arms, and gives a more extended answer, saying that the bloodied adults and children being moved from a truck to a shed outside are being helped to escape. Harper presents this explanation as "the truth" and impresses Joan with the importance of keeping it secret. Joan's further revelation that she has seen her uncle hitting a man and a child with a metal rod brings out another of the weak fabrications with which Harper began, but this time Joan accepts her aunt's comforting words and approving conclusion: "You're part of a big movement now to make things better. You can be proud of that" (14).

The second scene brings an abrupt shift of time and setting. Now Joan is a young woman newly employed in making hats, a form of art entered in a competition for prizes in a parade. Over several days, Joan constructs an extravagantly theatrical hat, while she gets to know the young man, Todd, who occupies the workbench next to hers. Todd confides his discontent with deteriorating working conditions and corrupt management, as well as his intent to speak with "a certain person" about these issues. As the hats are finished, martial music blares, and the workroom fades from view. Rows of chained and battered prisoners—adults and children—move forward in rows, then exit. They are wearing colorful hats, including the ones made by Joan and Todd. The workroom setting then returns, with the two hat-makers discussing Joan's surprising win in the competition and Todd's talk with the "certain person." Joan regrets the fact that non-prizewinning hats were burned "with the bodies" after the parade, while Todd insists that the joy of the work lies in its ephemeral nature (25-26). Neither acknowledges the existence or fate of those who wore the hats.

The final scene reverts to the unchanged setting of Harper's home, with Harper seated in the same chair. Todd discusses with her his poisoning of some wasps. Their conversation, which initially seems to be about a routine measure of pest control, quickly spins into incomprehensibility as they talk about what seems to be a global war in which nations, animal species, and even natural elements like the weather, have been conscripted to serve in a multi-sided conflict. While they converse, Joan is sleeping offstage. By the time she appears, Harper has discovered some differences with Todd and questions whether or not she should trust him. Joan tells of a grueling struggle to escape from her role in the war and be with her husband Todd for one day. Now Joan no longer occupies a privileged position; dirty and ragged, she is among the world's fugitives. She says she swam across a river on the way, uncertain as to whether the river's current would aid or harm her, because it was the "only way of getting here" (38). The play ends with Joan's description of the moment she stepped into the river, committing herself to its current, while knowing that "you can't tell what's going to happen" (38).

The three primary scenes of the play refer to three failures of modern European socialism. The first scene, between Harper and young Joan, represents the era of Stalinism, under which those supposedly being helped were often harmed, while its apologists defended the system through constantly shifting lies. The second scene, in which Joan and Todd create hats for a competition, points to the narrow perspective of trade unionism—the aspect of Leftist politics with which many British dramatists have been closely associated. While Joan and Todd focus on the rewards of personal achievement and the problems of their particular workplace, they are ignoring the conditions of a world in which their artistic creations serve as absurd adornments for people in chains being marched to their deaths. The final scene suggests the factionalism that characterizes the contemporary Left, along with the chaotic proliferation of intense but indecipherable conflicts around the globe. The title of the play challenges its audience to question how "far away" any of the situations or issues are from its particular lives and concerns.

Few images in contemporary drama are more devastating than the parade of chained and beaten prisoners in single file wearing preposterous hats. The fact that the hats serve as an obvious metaphor for art, even specifically for theatre—reinforced in the fact that the prisoners exit in rows like theatre audiences—offers a powerful acknowledgment of the collusion of art with political oppression. The play insists on the acuteness of the problems which it presents not only by the power of such images, but also by using actual children on stage—a choice unusual in Churchill's plays. This choice seems to remind us of the need to understand our connection to and responsibility for the future, and to act accordingly.

Churchill gives only a hint of how we in the audience might throw off our chains and move toward a better future. This glimmer of a Brechtian "way out" of the dystopia of a world disintegrating in chaotic conflict occurs in the final monologue of the final scene. Joan, who has braved all the bizarre dangers of her conflict-ridden world to be with Todd, if only for a day, demonstrates her choice to make a meaningful commitment, even in a situation where she cannot determine where this commitment will lead. Joan inhabits a world in which great movements for change have been founded upon lies, violence, and the power of a few. She faces a situation in which it is impossible to make simple alliances or separate the dangerous from the absurd. She herself shows the effects of what she has been taught and exposed to, particularly when she evokes her disregard for the "child under five" whom she killed and the "girls by the side of the road" who were bleeding from their mouths (37). Despite all this, Joan embodies a kind of heroism in the extraordinary trust she places in her relationship with Todd and the extraordinary risk she endures in her need to sustain it. Joan does not take this risk unthinkingly, but instead describes a long hesitation when she gets to the banks of the river that separates them. As she explains, "I knew I'd have to go straight across. But I didn't know whose side the river was on, it might help me swim or it might drown me" (38). Her desire for reunion with her loved one overcomes her fear, and, as she describes it, at last she does "put one foot in the river" (38).

Churchill's turn-of-the-millennium plays, thus, deal with the kind of fundamental desires and behavior patterns acknowledged in the plays of ancient Greece, but refer in various ways to the political conditions of contemporary Britain. These plays explore the limits of individual knowledge and responsibility, as well as the failure of individualist and socialist approaches to longstanding social and political problems. They acknowledge the loss of a common vision, while demonstrating the necessity of relationship and communicating hope for the emergence of new collective energy that will help her audience move beyond the destructive patterns of interaction displayed throughout the previous millennium's history and mythology.

Works Cited

Benjamin, Walter. *The Origin of German Tragic Drama.* Trans. John Osborne. London: Verso Press, 1998.

Churchill, Caryl. *Abortive.* In *Churchill Shorts.* London: Nick Hern Books, 1990. 21-36.

_____. *Schreber's Nervous Illness.* In *Churchill Shorts.* London: Nick Hern Books, 1990. 57-93.

_____. *Three More Sleepless Nights.* In *Churchill Shorts.* London: Nick Hern Books, 1990. 245-273.

_____. *Blue Heart.* London: Theatre Communications Group/Nick Hern Books: 1997.

_____. *This is a Chair.* London: Theatre Communications Group/Nick Hern Books: 1999.

_____. *Far Away.* London: Nick Hern Books, 2000.

Jameson, Fredric. *The Political Unconscious.* Ithaca: Cornell UP, 1981.

"Disturbing the Spirits of the Past"

The Uncertainty Principle in Michael Frayn's *Copenhagen*

Donna SOTO-MORETTINI

Royal Scottish Academy of Music and Drama

In 1941, an historic but undocumented meeting took place in Copenhagen between two giants of twentieth-century physics, Werner Heisenberg and Niels Bohr. The tantalising lack of certainty about why the German went to Denmark at this particularly crucial historical time has puzzled scientists and historians ever since—after all, Heisenberg was working under the Nazi regime, while Bohr's country, Denmark, was under German occupation. Michael Frayn's play offers an extended examination of the possible answers to the questions that have surrounded this mysterious meeting, of which no record remains. As Frayn's postscript to *Copenhagen* makes clear "[Heisenberg] almost certainly went to dinner at the Bohr's house, and the two men almost certainly went for a walk to escape from any possible microphones, although there is some dispute about even these simple matters. The question about what they said to each other has been even more dispute […]" (97).

Structurally, *Copenhagen* is a series of repetitions. The actual moment of Heisenberg approaching the door, the Bohrs answering and welcoming him into their home, the ensuing awkward moments are played out a number of times for the audience. The three characters, Heisenberg, Bohr, and his wife, Margarethe, attempt to test their memories against each other's in each staged recollection—as they all try to puzzle out the answer to the recurring questions of the play: what was the meeting about? What had Heisenberg come to say? Why did he put himself and the Bohrs at risk in this way? What was at stake? Frayn places this central public concern within a deeper, more personal replay of memory: at points the Bohrs recall the tragic death of their son, who is swept away by the sea in sight of his helpless father. The memory reoccurs to all three characters, who speak their thoughts out loud in the silence as Heisenberg first appears:

Margarethe: All the things that come into our heads out of nowhere.

Bohr: Our private consolations. Our private agonies.

Heisenberg: Silence. And of course they're thinking about their children again. [...]

Bohr: She's thinking about Christian and Harald.

Heisenberg: The two lost boys. [...]

Bohr: And once again I see those same few moments that I see every day.

Heisenberg: Those short moments on the boat, when the tiller slams over in the heavy sea and Christian is falling.

Bohr: If I hadn't let him take the helm ...

Heisenberg: Those long moments in the water.

Bohr: Those endless moments in the water. [...]

Margarethe: I'm at Tisvilde. I look up from my work. There's Niels in the doorway, silently watching me. He turns his head away, and I know at once what's happened. (29, 30)

As Frayn notes in his postscript to the play, the mystery surrounding the Copenhagen meeting was one that haunted Heisenberg, who actually attempted to discuss the memories of that night with Bohr years later, but reached no conclusion: "We both came to feel that it would be better to stop disturbing the spirits of the past" (97). If Heisenberg's memoirs are unhelpful in providing any conclusive evidence about the meeting that Frayn reconstructs, there is still something for a playwright to admire about the centrality which Heisenberg gives to dialogue in his recollections—a perhaps unexpected demonstration of interest in human exchange on the part of a theoretical physicist. As Frayn points out, in the actual memoirs written by Heisenberg, "dialogue plays an important part [...] because he [Heisenberg] 'hopes to demonstrate that science is rooted in conversations'" (98). This section from the postscript sums up the sophistication of the argument that Frayn's play seems to be putting forth about the relationship between science, history, and memory.

The implication ventured by *Copenhagen* suggests that—like Heisenberg's particular brand of theoretical physics—the "science" of the historian is one which hinges crucially upon including a kind of "calculated" uncertainty within the act of apprehension. This uncertainty inhabits the spaces between language, text and memory. (That "calculation," of course, can never be represented in mathematical terms beyond being expressed as an "X" factor—but its intrinsic *value* is less significant in this context than the effect of its indeterminate *presence*.)

Frayn's dramatic license triggers yet more uncertainties—questions about the value of histories, and about the ways in which we invest histories with an authority that would cause even those making them to feel uncomfortable; and questions about the status of history-as-knowledge altogether, which oscillates in its narrative structure somewhere between what we represent to ourselves as certain and the manifestly uncertain fragments of the past.

Frayn refashions time itself into a repetitive scientific experiment; he incorporates the imaginative in a plethora of possible reasons, excuses, motivations, and associations that tenuously fix and then radically unhinge historical representation in his replaying of the past; he explores the unconscious through continually revealed mistakes in memory, and in the shifting of the roles of Heisenberg and Bohr: as father and son, as brothers, as Others.

A number of things make Frayn's play distinct from earlier British ones dealing with political histories and science, but perhaps it will be most immediately compared to Bertolt Brecht's *Galileo*—with its similar meditations on the relationship between science and ethics, and its questions about ideas of scientific "heroism." If so, the comparison can only emphasise the great distance between the clean bright weapons of Brecht's historical materialism and the more oblique ones available to those writing after the loss of such grand meta-narratives as Marxist theory. Brecht's episodic journey was meant somehow to fracture time and to jolt us out of our ease in the presence of classical narrative structure. Our "surprise" did not come from finding out that Galileo was no hero, but from discovering that we had been lulled somehow into *expecting* scientists to be heroes.

For Frayn, time is not fractured so much as it is inescapably circular. He structures his play like a controlled-observation experiment: conditions surrounding the eve of Heisenberg's visit are carefully set up and played out a number of times, then behaviours and reactions are carefully recorded. Each time, data is analysed, questioned, and the characters become more detached, and more observant of themselves. But their scientific method is not adequate to the task of answering the fundamental question: why did Heisenberg come? What was it he had to say? And in the wake of the scientific disasters of the Twentieth Century, perhaps our "surprise" as viewers is to realise that from our historical perspective no one expects science and heroism to inhabit the same places.

Frayn's "Idea of History"

Any number of reviews of the play centred on Frayn's ability to conflate the difficulties of accurately observing the physical matter of the universe and the difficulties of accurately observing human behaviour, or intuiting motives—either our own or others'. And where this approach leads straight into the territory of human psychology, it does so only in the sense that Frayn's disposition as a historian is also squarely focused there. In the postscript to the play, Frayn declares that as far as he could, he attempted to follow "the original protagonists' train of thought." "But," he writes, "how far is it possible to know what their train of thought was? This is where I have departed from established historical record—from any possible historical record. The great challenge facing the storyteller and the historian alike is to get inside people's heads, to stand where they stood and see the world as they saw it, to make some informed estimate of their motives and intentions [...]" (98-99).

Here Frayn, for all the postmodern sophistication of his characters' debates in *Copenhagen*, harks back to a historiographical tradition as old as Thucydides—and perhaps best framed in our times by R. G. Collingwood in his seminal "The Idea of History." Collingwood attempted to elucidate a method whereby the historian could comprehend the seemingly incomprehensible: the thought processes of historical agents. And despite the objections that have come his way—from those which emphasise history as a totality of mutually conditioning structural and conscious processes, to those which displace subjectivity or agency altogether—here we find Frayn at the end of the century sounding remarkably like Collingwood himself: "The history of thought, and therefore all history, is the re-enactment of past thought, in the historian's own mind" (Collingwood 215).

Collingwood's point, like Frayn's, turns out to be less simple than it appears, since he is keen to make it clear that the historian's own mind is specifically grounded in a contemporary context. But perhaps the most interesting parallel between Frayn and Collingwood occurs when the latter defends history from those who would conceive its discipline as some kind of science. Collingwood saw a major difference between the two fields in that for the "scientific observer nature is always merely a phenomenon presented to his intelligent observation; whereas the events of history are never mere phenomena, [...] but things which the historian looks, not at, but through, to discern the thought within them." (214). Frayn is more wary of apprehending the natural phenomena observed through quantum mechanics as brute or static, but he sees that the more dialectical approach suggested by Collingwood toward human subjects applies to physics as well. Nor does Frayn follow Collingwood down the road of attempting to objectify the process of understanding itself—for throughout his play, there is little objective ground, even when the issues of historical evidence are brought up.

Still, for both Collingwood and Frayn, the historian's primary interest seems to be ferreting out the secrets of intention manifested in the historical act. As Collingwood's critics have pointed out, even if he fails to take into account the larger picture of socio-structural determinants in history, he does so on humanist grounds, and his fundamental project aims to elucidate his assertion that history constitutes above all a "humanistic" discipline with a specific and progressive function. The sting in the comparison is in the tail of this last sentence: one must work hard to find the evidence of a "progressive function" in Frayn's history, although it remains a deeply humanistic approach in the telling.

History and Physics

The fundamental question of *Copenhagen* is voiced over and over again by its characters: "[...] what exactly had Heisenberg said?" (34). Margarethe suggests that "The person who wanted to know most of all was Heisenberg himself" (35); and Bohr, stymied by the same inability to recall his own words confesses: "Heaven knows what I said" (39). At one level, the play appears to be about the ways in which historical inquiry at many points becomes an almost metaphysical inquiry—one which beavers away at uncovering the tomes of what Louis O. Mink once called the "omniscient chronicler" (see Louis O. Mink). In fact, Mink could be suggesting what Frayn's fictional Niels Bohr character states: "Heaven knows." Heaven: the presumed domicile of the omniscient chronicler—that ideal scribe who knew, who recorded the WAY IT WAS, but never publishes, leaving the lesser mortal historians to endlessly scratch away, trying to fill in the details of a Platonic historical form.

"Did these things really happen to me?" asks Heisenberg. "We wait," he says, "for the point of it all to be revealed to us" (46). In another time, of course, another kind of historian—Collingwood, for one— would have seen this grand act of narrating events from a distance to be charged precisely with this purpose: to reveal the point of it all. In Frayn's play, the physicists come to realise that quantum mechanics—in a sense—returns man to the centre of the universe by insisting that the physicist's perception of the universe will always be inextricably linked to the knowing subject. But once they reach this conclusion, they simultaneously realise that the man at the centre of the universe can see absolutely everything except himself.

> **Bohr:** We put man back at the centre of the universe. Throughout history we keep finding ourselves displaced. We keep exiling ourselves to the periphery of things. First we turn ourselves into a mere adjunct of God's unknowable purposes, tiny figures kneeling in the great cathedral of creation. And no sooner have we recovered ourselves in the Renaissance, no sooner has man become, as Protagoras proclaimed him, the measure of all things, than we're pushed aside again by the products of our own reasoning! [...] Then, here in Copenhagen in [...] [the] [...] mid-twenties we discover that there is no precisely determinable objective universe. That the universe exists only

as a series of approximations. Only within the limits determined by our relationship with it. Only through the understanding lodged inside the human head.

Margarethe: So this man you've put at the centre of the universe—is it you, or is it Heisenberg? [...] If it's Heisenberg at the centre of the universe, then the one bit of the universe that he can't see is Heisenberg. (73-74)

And this dilemma—the historical agent with a panoptical blindness—is for that aforementioned historian the very problem that drives his vocation: the idea that from a distance, discrete events in the historical field ultimately converge into patterns, into shapes that reveal some significance. Which of course is why when Heisenberg and Bohr are debating the ontology of matter (are we talking ultimately about particles, which Bohr calls "things, complete in themselves"? (71) or are we talking about waves, which he describes as "disturbances in something else" (71), they could just as easily be describing the historian's difficulty in apprehending what s/he see in the historical field. Does the historian discern "things, complete in themselves"—perhaps easily identifiable agents of historical change—or does the historian see "waves," disturbances that shape something else such as historical agents? The latter could be said to fairly describe a kind of "structuralist" approach to history that seeks perhaps to write history without a subject. The former could maybe describe pre-structuralist histories—Collingwood's history. The extraordinary thing about *Copenhagen* is that its conclusion argues vigorously for the validity of "complementarity" in physics—which asserts that matter is both wave and particle. And once through the piece, it becomes difficult not to think that what Frayn is putting forth, knowingly or not, is that the validity of any historical understanding may also, crucially, depend on its ability to adopt an approach of "complementarity." In other words, history is both structure and subject; its ontological status oscillates; and it is both and neither.

But Frayn's physicists go on to make another deeply problematic point about complementarity in the field of quantum mechanics—which is that oscillation does not yield a viable point of view. Indeed, as the fictional Niels Bohr exposes, he cannot understand Heisenberg because to do that he must treat him "not just as a particle, but as a wave. I have to use not only your particle mechanics, I have to use the Schroedinger wave function." (71). But as he goes on to explain, the smallest bits of matter are "either one thing or another. They can't be both—we have to choose one way of seeing them or the other. But as soon as we do, we can't know everything about them." In other words, if we try to translate this into an historiographical problem, when we view the historical field, we know that it contains both particles (subject/agents) and waves (structures: linguistic, cultural, political etc.). We can intellectually appreciate that to apprehend historical motion in any kind of totality, we must be continually oscillating our point of view between particle and wave, but if Bohr is correct, ultimately we must choose. Because to align oneself theoretically with one is, perforce, to deny the other. And yet, to position one's method of apprehension from only one point of view entails forever living with partial sight. Here, ultimately, lies the fundamental paradox of postmodern physics, postmodern thought, and postmodern history—uncoupled from certainty the questions begin to oscillate from the one extreme to the other: if there are no answers, then any answer will do.

Quietly Collapsing History

From the point of view of the historical subject on the ground, we know that this final paradox is simply one clever conundrum too far. If any answer will do, we are left with no ground on which to pitch a moral argument—and in the end, Frayn's play remains a deeply moral piece of work. His characters stay centred around the moral dilemma of the physicist working in Hitler's pay. For all the sophistication of their arguments, the final moments of the play are given over to questions of good and bad, right and wrong:

Bohr: So perhaps I should thank you.

Heisenberg: For what?

Bohr: My life. All our lives.

Heisenberg: Nothing to do with me by that time. I regret to say.

Bohr: But after I'd gone you came back to Copenhagen.

Heisenberg: To make sure that our people didn't take over the Institute in your absence.

Bohr: I've never thanked you for that, either.

Heisenberg: You know they offered me your cyclotron?

Bohr: You could have separated a little 235 with it.

Heisenberg: Meanwhile you were going on from Sweden to Los Alamos.

Bohr: To play my small but helpful part in the deaths of a hundred thousand people.

Margarethe: Niels, you did nothing wrong!

Bohr: Didn't I?

Heisenberg: Of course not. You were a good man, from first to last, and no one could ever say otherwise. Whereas I ...

Bohr: Whereas you, my dear Heisenberg, never managed to contribute to the death of one single solitary person in all your life. (93)

A simple—rather disturbingly simple—place in which to leave this highly sophisticated meditation on the ways in which lived experience and survival so often prevents one from the practical exercise of moral and ethical reason and certainty.

On one level, this is where Frayn's drama brings us squarely before what Keith Jenkins calls the linguistic contradictions between "life" and the "writing up of life." The context in which Heisenberg and Bohr made their choices was one in which the deductive or syllogistic logic driving moral decisions could not apply. The very specific context in which the physicists made their choices therefore yielded a terrain on which their conclusions about good or bad were quite startlingly incongruent. As Hayden White has pointed out: "[...] you need another kind of logic to talk about practical affairs, a logic of praxis. The logic of praxis cannot follow the logic of identity and non-contradiction [...]. Society creates situations in which you must act in contradiction [...] you need a theory of the representation of life lived in contradiction. That would allow you to account for the syntax of real lives" (quoted in Jenkins 122). Frayn's play does not provide this "logic of praxis," but it does throw the contradiction of which White speaks into a strange relief. Hayden White's point is also made eloquently by the fictional Heisenberg:

Complementarity, once again. I'm your enemy; I'm also your friend. I'm a danger to mankind; I'm also your guest. I'm a particle; I'm also a wave. We have one set of obligations to the world in general, and we have other sets, never to be reconciled, to our fellow-countrymen, to our neighbours, to our friends, to our family, to our children. [...] All we can do is to look afterwards, and see what happened. (79-80)

Comparatively, where other modern and postmodern dramatists—Brecht, Trevor Griffiths, Caryl Churchill, for example—write plays and characters reminding us that history is in the eye of those living it, and that a single event is recalled in myriad ways, they do so to complicate history, to raise unbridgeable gaps. But they do not, in the end, suggest what Frayn's uncertain characters do: which is to put forth that the contradiction between logic and a "narrated memory" is unresolvable. *Copenhagen* questions the breach between ethical language and socio/practical language and behaviour, but, of course, in its tropological structure (in which Bohr's lost son and his own helplessness in watching that loss become a metaphor for Bohr's relationship with Heisenberg), the play goes much further. It concludes, ironically, by collapsing its own historical specificity and transforming a particular moment into an ongoing universal tragedy of the human condition. In the final moments before Heisenberg departs, the characters once again voice their thoughts aloud, in an exchange much like one earlier in the play:

Margarethe: Silence. The silence we always in the end return to.

Heisenberg: And of course I know what they're thinking about.

Margarethe: All those lost children on the road.

Bohr: Heisenberg wandering the world like a lost child himself.

Margarethe: Our own lost children.

Heisenberg: And over goes the tiller once again.

Bohr: So near, so near! So slight a thing!

Margarethe: He stands in the doorway watching me, then he turns his head away...

Heisenberg: And once again, away he goes into the dark waters. (95-96)

But if Bohr and Heisenberg metaphorically represent Bohr and son, then they are both, in their turn, figurative emblems of a greater "trans-historical" tragedy: the tragedy in which those on the firm ground of a world apprehension based on the syntax of logical deduction/identity/non-contradiction will always be condemned to witness the loss of their certainties in the maelstrom of socio/political praxis, whether that loss is sustained in the context of the Third Reich or the Manhattan Project.

This collapse of history, ultimately, allows Frayn to rescue an older, simpler notion of morality from an arguably "deconstructive" approach to historiography. By the end of the play, we have watched his characters drag a barely breathing moral "body" out of the burning buildings on the postmodern landscape, which leaves us with many questions about the play's ideological implications. Hayden White's idea of a language able to accommodate "lived contradiction" remains no more than a theoretical sketch. And in the place of an ethical theory elegant enough to match the grace and complexity of quantum physics, a play like *Copenhagen* must inevitably, perhaps, make way for the concluding judgements that operate under the yet-to-be-replaced meta-narratives of Marxism or Christianity, whose baseline guidance in questions of right or wrong still hold tenuous sway amidst the particles and the waves.

Works Cited

Collingwood, R. G. *The Idea of History.* Oxford: Clarendon Press, 1946.
Frayn, Michael. *Cophenhagen.* London: Methuen, 1988.
Jenkins, Keith. *Why History.* London: Routledge, 1999.
Mink, Louis O. "Narrative as Cognitive Instrument." *The Writing of History.* Ed. Robert H. Canary and Henry Kozicki. Madison: University of Wisconsin Press, 1978.

Im/Migrations, Border-Crossings and "Willful Internationalism" in Timberlake Wertenbaker's *The Break of Day*

Maya E. ROTH

University of California, Berkeley

Timberlake Wertenbaker's "dances" with history foreground roving geographies. Provocatively, her plays explore intersections of geography, power, and identity, not only in her most famous play *Our Country's Good*, in which all characters are displaced, or in her sharp-edged feminist journeying plays such as *The Grace of Mary Traverse* and *New Anatomies*, but also in her more *explicitly* contemporary plays of the 1990s—*Three Birds Alighting on a Field*, *The Break of Day*, and *After Darwin*—and her first play of the new millennium, *Credible Witness*. By focusing on complicated "roots" and "routes"—to borrow designations from anthropologist James Clifford—Wertenbaker imagines new forms for Anglophone drama.

While dispossessions and im/migrations have infused Wertenbaker's writing from early on, they vividly haunt all of these recent plays, all situated in relation to contemporary England within their playworlds.[1] In *Three Birds Alighting on a Field*, for example, a work ostensibly about the contemporary art world, Wertenbaker sets the entire dramatic action in England, and yet the characters stretch the play's—and Britain's—boundaries in multiple directions. Written in 1993, this play includes the following cast of characters: a white Briton who grew up in Africa; a mixed race British-Indian raised in England; U.S. Americans who live and work in England; a Romanian seeking international economic

---

[1]   In *Three Birds Alighting on a Field* (1993), the entire play roves through present-day England. In *The Break of Day* (1995) the first and last acts are likewise set in contemporary England, as is part of the second act. *After Darwin* (1998) incorporates a contemporary English theatrical frame set in London, where a multicultural theater ensemble creates a history play. *Credible Witness* (2001) locates much of its action in a Refugee Asylum Center in today's London.

sponsorship to bring home; a blueblood British woman married to a wealthy "foreigner" (in her words); her husband—a Greek émigré who seeks acceptance as a British gentleman more than as an immigrant or Greek; and a Turkish organ donor, flown in to Britain by a private hospital, who sells his kidney so he can raise money for his family.

Although there is a strong tradition of exposing class hierarchies in leftist British history plays, and of unmasking gendered hierarchies in feminist plays, Wertenbaker's theater conscientiously interweaves those concerns with border-crossings.[2] To that end, both the content and form of her plays are insistently multiple, intercultural, and hybrid. This dramatist foregrounds complex foreigners and multicultural figures situated in relation to an unusually wide range of settings and themes, which help not only to complicate but also to enrich received constructions of place and politics, history, and home. Persistently, Wertenbaker's plays question Who and What is English.[3] How do shifting socio-cultural boundaries re-shape identities, memories, economies, subjectivities, and social relations? Repeatedly too, her plays probe the issue of how to re-imagine narrative and theatrical space in order to recognize diverse cultures and activate an internationalist civics.

Wertenbaker's investigation of the intersections between geography, power and identity issues exemplifies a recent turn in critical focus as the world moves toward increasingly global markets and political cultures that simultaneously dispossess the poor, spur travel and large-scale im/migrations, and propel nativist movements. In her plays of the 1990s, Wertenbaker situates historic and contemporary England in global relation, particularly to its former colonies (e.g. India, Egypt, the U.S.) and to varied European constellations (the European Union, Western Europe, Eastern Europe, the "New" Europe etc.). By emphasizing historical relationships to and in space—*geographies of history*—in these and other plays, Wertenbaker illuminates historicized migrations based variously on: servitude, colonization, and post-colonialism; warfare, exile and waves of exodus; travel, technological advances and global economies. Places register as constituted and contested by those living both "inside" and "outside" their changing and politically-invested designated borders. Even when Wertenbaker's plays are not about international collisions per se, cultural differences introduced by

---

[2]   Her focus on immigrations extends across widely varied plays. In fact, I would hazard that among extensively produced British playwrights, Wertenbaker most often explores the complexities of immigrations. For related arguments, see Bassnet, "The Politics of Location," and Carlson, "Language and Identity in Timberlake Wertenbaker's Plays." Also see Wilson, "Forgiving History and Making New Worlds: Timberlake Wertenbaker's Recent Drama" (148).

[3]   For example, see Wisehammer's and Liz' exchange in 2.1 of *Our Country's Good*, 1.3 and 1.9 of *Three Birds Alighting on a Field*, and 1.3 of *After Darwin*.

im/migrations lead these dramatic works to direct their focus to the historical relations in which today so many countries find themselves: moments of hybrid identifications and heated contestations over whose voices should be heard in given places, histories, and civic spaces.

By focusing on political geographies undergoing change with regard to history, Wertenbaker demonstrates how civic cultures—and nations —are construed in relation to interconnected, changing geographies— and that this has been the case for centuries. For example, as one character in *The Break of Day*'s Not Romania explains, "This country is not (*gestures width*), but it is (*gestures depth*). Ancients, Greeks, Romans, Khans, Byzantium, Turkish Yoke, Russian Yoke, now West. I show you ancient monuments and new monument by American democracy" (Act Two, 48).[4] Wertenbaker's focus on layered geographic history emphasizes that appeals to ethnic purity or native rights are political stances, and that most nations have a range of intercultural mixing.

Wertenbaker, herself, is a former journalist who, while Canadian-American, grew up in the "Basque country" of southwest France. She studied in the U.S., and then lived and worked briefly in Greece. For more than two decades, she has been active as a playwright in London, where almost all of her plays have premiered—and where recent waves of post-colonial immigrants and war refugees have increasingly diversified the city. In this context, it is perhaps unsurprising that her plays seek to create openings for more complex notions of identity, intersecting transnational histories, and women "on quests in this world," engaged beyond the "smallness of naturalism" (Wertenbaker, *Rage and Reason* 140). It is also not surprising that she centers on questions of citizenship and dispossession, their relationships to multicultural space, and theater as a social arena in which to imagine other possibilities.

Wertenbaker's traveling paradigm—in which her theatrical spaces migrate from one history to another, one theatrical register to another, one character's perspective to another's, and, persistently, from one *topos* to another—creates epic plays with more diasporic and multicultural practices of home, nation, justice, and identity/ies than the source materials which she famously re-works (e.g. classic plays, historical narratives, novels).[5] Further, the plays themselves migrate, developing

---

[4] For best clarity, internal citations begin with the act relevant to all publications of the play, followed by the page number specific to the edition used here. Unlike most Wertenbaker plays, *The Break of Day*, as a more Chekhovian work, features no internal scene divisions within acts.

[5] "Dramatic geographies" and" performance geographies" are two phrases I have developed to articulate a spatialized dramaturgical analysis. I use "dramatic geographies" to refer to the geographic imaginaries (seen and unseen) scripted by plays' stories. I use "performance geographies," instead of "performance texts," in order to

what I call an alternate journeying principle. Often the theatrical space itself shifts—from disjointed and roving dramatic geographies to plays within plays, from performance geographies of character monologic audience address to critical interventions (via songs, scene titles, and metacommentary). In making flux and geography such central aspects of her work, Wertenbaker exemplifies the spatial turn shaping post-modern culture and fuelling post-colonial approaches to social theory, including history.[6]

Nowhere are these heterotopic dislocations more central, or have they been more disorienting for theater critics, than in her 1995 work, *The Break of Day*. In the second act, for example, there are at least twenty-two discernible shifts of theatrical focus (from narrative action in a range of discrete locations, to songs and direct storytelling address to the audience, or to jumps in time). The play's multiplicity of spaces, as well as its lack of closure, underscore a migratory, versus stable, subject ground for its theatrical subjects as well as for its audiences. In part, the play simulates the layered complexities, and sometimes conflicting dislocations of post-modern and im/migrant experience. It also accents the very kinds of displacements which *The Break of Day*'s dialogue suggests saturate late twentieth-century lives, making it difficult to chart paths to self, action, and more just futures. The play leads its audiences to cross borders—of gender and genre, national focus, narrative perspective, cultural identifications, and interpretive locations—not, ultimately, in order to point to meaninglessness, but rather to encourage linkages across difference.

This paper excavates how *The Break of Day* emphatically links multiculturalism with internationalist ethics—leading Wertenbaker to interrogate roots and routes, including in her transformations of theatrical space. Indeed, a dramaturgic focus on this play sheds light on Wertenbaker's ongoing search for new forms of drama that imagine—and practise—different models of civics. While I believe *The Break of Day* is due for a critical re-evaluation more respectful of its situated range and innovations, as suggested below, I offer it for shared examination here because it productively illuminates the distinctive contributions that Wertenbaker's drama has provided for creating a civic theater that navigates crucibles of cultures. This play highlights the stakes that fuel

---

accent the deeply spatialized and embodied sensibilities of theater in and as production.

[6] My dissertation—*Opening Civic, Feminist and Theatrical Spaces: The Plays of Timberlake Wertenbaker*—closely examines this correlation. See my chapter five, "Performing Contemporary Civic Praxis, Re-Imagining History in *After Darwin* and Other Recent Plays."

her plays of the last fifteen years and their increasingly explicit multicultural histories.

***

In *The Break of Day*, Wertenbaker revises Chekhov's domestic cosmopolitanism, locating feminisms, civics, and millennial malaise in transnational registers. Directed and commissioned by Max Stafford-Clark, *The Break of Day* was co-produced by The Royal Court Theatre and the fringe company Out of Joint to be performed in touring repertory with Wertenbaker's adaptation of Anton Chekhov's *The Three Sisters*. The two plays are thematically linked.[7] Wertenbaker sets her play at the turn of the twentieth century just as Chekhov's was contemporaneous with his time, the turn of the nineteenth century into the twentieth. Both plays look to the future with uncertainty, seeking hope amidst underlying social change, even unresolved havoc, in the intimate lives of the primary characters. Like Chekhov's, Wertenbaker's is a deep ensemble play, bringing a range of characters (many of them intellectual, artistic, and professional) into conversation with each other regarding relationships, politics and ethics. With twenty-four characters, Wertenbaker's play features twice as many as Chekhov's. His main characters are three sisters, Wertenbaker's three close friends who were sisters in the feminist movement of the 1970s.

Chekhov's work emphasizes the sisters' sense of displacement in their provincial setting, their desire to circulate in a more cultured, cosmopolitan environment, specifically Moscow, where they grew up. Meanwhile, over the course of the play, they experience literal displacement from their home as the middle-class Natasha, their sister-in-law, supplants them, the landed gentry, and their values. Each act dispossesses the sisters further, with scenes occurring in a proximal yet slightly different location; the play's—and the sisters'—homespace moves from an expansive drawing room, where they host many guests, to a small shared bedroom for Irina and Olga hidden away on another floor, and finally to the garden as they bid farewell to their friends and prepare to move to small quarters in town, their dreams of Moscow silenced.[8] Class and cultural revolution press dramatic changes on their lives, pointing to larger social trends, whether they realize it or not. The play meditates on modernity, the great social transformations ushered in

---

[7] The pair of plays was also produced in association with the Bristol Old Vic and Leicester Haymarket theatres.

[8] See Hanna Scolnicov's chapter 8, "Preferring Insecurity," of *Woman's Theatrical Space* for illuminating spatial readings of Chekhov's *The Seagull and The Cherry Orchard*. Chaudhuri's scattered references to Chekhov's plays in *Staging Place* (e.g. 11-13, 25) are particularly relevant to the distinctions between nostalgic exile and concrete exile which I am proposing.

with industrialization; of course, it also anticipates the specific changes brought by the Russian Revolution.

In *The Break of Day,* Wertenbaker's late twentieth century companion piece, global economies, technological revolution, and im/migrations press on the characters' lives even more than they realize, equally pointing to larger social trends.[9] Disenchanted by the state of affairs they see in England—market influences in hospitals and universities, feminism's unrealized goals, over-stimulation, a culture of immediacy and individualism, fatigue and powerlessness to effect deep change—and by a lack of fulfillment in their personal relationships, the primary characters, female and male alike, seek ways to believe in the future, to bring meaning to their lives. They make it to Moscow, as it were, and yet they still feel alienated, isolated. For two of the middle-aged sisters of feminism—Nina, a singer-songwriter, and Tess, a journalist—parenting calls as an answer. The other, April, continues to seek meaning in her work— teaching at a university, uncurtained from the world, as she explains at play's end, by romance or child.

Wertenbaker's first act takes place in an English country garden, part of Tess and Robert's weekend country home to which they have invited their old friends. The second act, of equal length in playing time, volleys between varied locations in Not Romania (airport, church, hotel room, streets, Ministry of Health, courthouse, and more), where Nina and Hugh spend several weeks seeking an international adoption, and fewer repeated locations in London (Dr. Glad's expensive fertility clinic and a flat), where Tess, with the mitigated support of Robert, seeks a pregnancy through medical technology. *The Break of Day*'s final act, really a brief coda, happens backstage after Robert's performance as Vershinin in *The Three Sisters*, set in a Northern provincial theatre in England; here the extended group of characters from Act I stay together into dawn trying to understand "what's happened," as Tess says (Act Three, 94).

As unexpected as each new act's settings may seem in *The Break of Day,* all were explicitly situated for the play's premiere audiences. Moreover, the primary dislocations of each act differently "place" the play in relation to *The Three Sisters*. The contemporary English country setting establishes a current British parallel for its audiences. The second act initiates exchange with a present-day equivalent of Chekhov's Eastern European setting. Then, the final act moves to include a situated production environment in which *The Three Sisters* has recently been performed—as was the case during the premiere tour. Even more impor-

---

[9]   Wertenbaker makes sure that her audiences recognize these larger social trends through crafting patterns of political-philosophic conversation across social positionings—as in Chekhov—but also through her idiosyncratic departures in theatrical space.

tantly, Wertenbaker anchors her play—one most concerned with mothering, debating feminism, and intimate relationships—in the context of transnational geographies.[10] Almost as disconcerting to reviewers, she locates an ostensibly "British" play, the one most explicitly critical of the state of the nation and social democracy in England, in relation to Not Romania, which occupies the focus for much of the second act.

The poetics of exile, so prominent in modern play-writing—as Una Chaudhuri has described in *Staging Place: The Geography of Modern Drama*—and so central to *The Three Sisters*, becomes re-positioned in Wertenbaker's drama to focus on literal refugees, waves of exile and im/migrations. In the last moments of the first act, for example, amid the country weekend reunion for the main characters of *The Break of Day*, an elderly neighbor, Mr. Hardacre comes by bringing fresh tomatoes, as requested, from his garden. He carries them in a battered suitcase—and tells them he is commencing a walking protest "against the atrocities of history." Wertenbaker places this monologue just before the intermission:

> My wife's father was a Jew from Macedonia, he had a good business in France. When they were rounding up the Jews, this is 1943 now, I was in the RAF, she and her mother escaped. This was her suitcase. I met her in 1949. She taught at the village school here and to this day old pupils come looking for her, I think because she brought an air of history with her. She was such a good teacher, she had a temperament, the children loved it, she used words like art, truth, beauty, not very English, you might say. She always kept her suitcase. She died three years ago just when the war in Eastern Europe started. I watch the television all the time now. And I see them. I think I see her. People with suitcases, walking, walking with their suitcases. I thought we'd never see those images again. Do you remember in Denmark how everybody wore a Star of David as a protest against the Nazis? To say we are all one. This suitcase is my Star of David. I'm going to march with my suitcase every day for the rest of my life. I'm going to protest against history. (42-3)

A walking memory of history, Mr. Hardacre can be seen to clarify the kind of "willful internationalism" Wertenbaker's plays advocate. It is not a rootless, romantic trope of universalism, nor a tourist cosmopolitanism. Instead, it constitutes a conscious political stance, a humanist and historicized response to waves and waves of slaughter, refugees "walking, walking with their suitcases." It is at once a diasporic ethic that says people are interconnected across geographies, an historical

---

[10] I suspect that part of theater critics discomfort with this work resulted not only from its "mommy focus" and its radical dislocations, as noted by Carlson, yet also from its pairings of those elements. In so doing, Wertenbaker places female subjectivity in relation to an explicitly political, internationalist civics.

education for audiences, and a call to political action. For audiences during the premiere, this play crafted specific focus on the contemporaneous ethnic genocide and rising trends of nationalism throughout Europe (specifically the Balkan Wars of 1992-95).

In addition to Mr. Hardacre's wife, the maid in the country home, Natasha, is an émigré and, as Tess and April gather, a war refugee, although her English is too limited for her to tell her story. Natasha's limited linguistic access functions as a reminder of the material and psychic challenges of immigration. Not exactly a cipher, for she tries to communicate her desire to and for April, Natasha's inability to testify reminds audiences of all the untold other histories co-present in the spaces of their lives, all they do not hear or even imagine. It also re-acquaints audiences with the reason why Wertenbaker's theater seeks to fill some of those gaps. "Because we don't know where she's from, and her life has ceased to interest us, although we cry for her on television, because our imagination has been depleted by this terrible century—because words like compassion and humanity have cracked in the last fifteen years and we've let it happen," says April, the professor character (Act one, 24). Robert, an actor working on *Three Sisters* throughout the play, compares this weariness to the "sense of waste" and of "being outside history" in Chekhov's play.[11] By the time *The Break of Day* actually migrates to Not Romania, the multiple reasons for doing so, beyond and related to the plot function, are clear: English citizens should know about *contemporary* Eastern Europe, a place so different from Chekhov's setting of one century ago, yet also so different from contemporary England, with which it is simultaneously inter-related. Doing so will connect them with their sense of history, the past, and the present (in England and Eastern Europe), and perhaps also help them to imagine better futures.

Just as *The Three Sisters* motivates Nina to speak of—and perhaps also to remember—her family's history, her Eastern-European descent, so does *The Break of Day* hail its audiences to place themselves in relation to multivalent histories, across national boundaries. The proximity and *differences* of multiple cultures and political geographies become particularly prominent in Act Two, across countries and within them: "History, my friend, moves and we move with it," says

---

[11]   Meanwhile, Nina, who has earlier said she "never thinks about the past," is compelled by Robert's performance research for *Three Sisters* to reveal to him alone that her grandmother "started life like one of those sisters but then she found herself in St. Petersburg during the famine. She often told me how she went in search of bread to bring back to her son, my father, but ate it all on the way back [...] A lot of those Russians went around missing their estates, but I think she enjoyed it, migrations, husbands, lovers, history. Even when she was old she kept moving house. I have her restlessness and I envy her experience of history" (Act One, 25).

Mr. Statelov to Hugh and Nina, as their adoption plans in Not Romania must circumnavigate the flux of a country in turmoil: "History moves very fast in Eastern Europe: Government will fall any day. Then who knows who rises, Turks, gypsies, worse: Jews" (Act Two, 76). Nina and Hugh, dizzy from the multiple ethnic, cultural, and political layers of Not Romania, discover the complexities of border-crossings as they negotiate a touch-and-go international adoption with the assistance of a range of people, most importantly the elder couple Mihail and Eva. Meanwhile for audiences, the changes of location in Wertenbaker's play accentuate the diversity of perspectives, as well as the fast pace of lives at the end of the millennium—market and technologically-driven in first world nations like England, and driven by socio-economic upheavals, global markets, political and ethnic divisions in Not Romania, for example.[12] By pointing to and from many complex locations, Wertenbaker seeks to engage her audiences in multivalent critical inquiry, shifting identifications and imaginative civic praxis. Yet, too, she crafts a different kind of civic space, bolstered by a model of inter-subjectivity that incorporates dislocation as culturally meaningful and which also performs cross cultural co-habitation as challenging, necessary, and long-standing.

The most radically de-stabilizing of *The Break of Day*'s many departures and dislocations occur in the second act. Particularly in performance, this act seems to interlay two different acts in different countries, for the action migrates rapidly from one nation to another, some moments even prospectively overlapping as the action unfolds, typically, in separate parts of the stage space.[13] Each country's dynamic and its differential resources become visible in *relation,* not only in juxtaposition. Not Romania's infrastructure is crumbling: fax machines and phones do not work; jobs disappear at a moment's notice; the government is up for grabs; nearly everyone must hustle either for resources and/or to avoid persecution; there is no petrol; and the imported free market promise has taken hold with no sense of this country's long history. England, meanwhile, is de-territorialized, its relative privilege exposed. It becomes as if foreign to those who live within it, as if they traveled away or became outsiders; its inhabitants are thus enabled to see it differently situated, in migration and from a distance. In these

---

12 Even in the first act, characters arrive from London and mobile phones ring. Thus the porous proximity of different places in a technological age and the rapid mobility of people with money stand in juxtaposition to the extended stretches of time foregrounded in Chekhov's late nineteenth-century work and its sisters' long distance— given gendered constraints, transportation options, and means of communication— from the city.

13 The compression of two acts into the same compound act may well explain why Wertenbaker's play consists of three acts to Chekhov's four.

various ways, Wertenbaker's willful internationalism navigates and negotiates between interconnected social worlds.[14]

Here, as in other plays, Wertenbaker's units of focus—nations, families, spaces, selves—are rendered as multicultural, helping her to layer complex histories and traditions, refuting singular identifications.[15] This is perhaps best exemplified by The *Break of Day*'s "cross-border children," wards of the state kept in hospitals and orphanages, whom the committed Marxist character Mihail struggles to pair with families abroad, such as the couple formed by Nina, a Briton of Eastern-European descent, and Hugh, a Jewish-American expatriate living in London. In cross-border children, Mihail, who has built a community of friends across ethnicities, sees hope for the future:

> I have known fear but now I see people suffer the greatest fear of all: fear of the future. I loved the future, even if I feared the present, with its sudden disgraces. I refuse to recant. I still believe in history. Now, it will be in the hands of the children, possibly most of all, these cross-border children I have helped to get out. Born in one country, loved and raised in another, I hope they will not descend into narrow ethnic identification, but that they will be willfully international, part of a great European community. I hope they will carry on history with broad minds and warm hearts. They have the complexity from their childhood: change, migration, indifference and uncertainty came to them early. Now, established, secure, educated. Is it unfair of me to place the responsibility of history onto them? We must not go into the next century with no ideal but selfishness. (Act Two, 83)

By staging this monologue as a direct address to the audience, Wertenbaker casts this revelatory query in direct relation to their lives. She positions the cross-border child as an antidote to the rise of ethnic nationalism and, also, the selfishness of capitalism. The baby girl is the future to which the play's title refers—"Little girls are important/at the break of day,"—which Nina sings towards the end, drawing from a traditional English folksong.[16] The child of the future—of England's

---

[14] Susan Carlson aptly observes that both Tess and Nina buy children, operating from their relative privilege (146). I would add to this the distinction that whereas Nina and Hugh's international adoption connects them more consciously to a diverse social world, Tess' fertility treatments and her seemingly endless string of medical interventions isolate her from her politics, her husband, her work, her former life; ultimately unsuccessful, the medical technology displaces her even from her body, exposing technology not only as a marker of privilege, but also as an illusory symbol of ultimate power for an individual—and a nation.

[15] Carlson makes a similar argument (134).

[16] In a play where Western feminist characters had chartered their lives trying to create and claim greater expressive and social equity for themselves and other women, in a world where many countries value baby girls far less (to the point of targeted abor-

future no less than the world's at the dawn of a new millennium (the break of day)—is *multicultural*. In that, she is embraced as a metaphor for, and citizen in, a better future. In this trope of the cross-border figure, Wertenbaker locates hope—for a more ethnically connected internationalist consciousness, for a more multicultural, feminist ethics.

Although it is tempting, I cannot end my discussion here. For however much im/migration operates as a metaphor for moving into a better future, connected to history and claiming multiple identifications, the play nonetheless draws attention to the material conditions—economic, political, cultural—that accompany immigration and the difficulty of navigating border-crossings. The international adoption market, for example, is placed within the context of widely disparate national economies and cultural access. This is not a naïve, simplistic vision. My earlier discussions of transnationalism emphasize a parallel focus in the play, materialism and humanitarianism being developed side by side, posited as necessary companions to internationalist civics and social change.

The Break of Day exhibits a refusal to fix identities, narratives or politics in a set location, instead foregrounding complex variety and relation. Even more than a restlessness, this play promotes an ethic maintaining that various experiences and tensions be held if not at once, at least in the same imaginative (theatrical, psychic, civic) space. The play advocates that no center become fixed, that identities and places be recognized in specified variety, that people strive toward complex cohabitancy and internationalist ethics. Thus Wertenbaker's performance geography navigates multiplicities, experimenting with how to embrace many different voices, places and competing needs, many different cultures and rights—without silencing, sublimating, or fully integrating them. With this goal, it boldly reshapes dramatic contours of expected genre, re-imagines cultural webs of relation, and opens geographic boundaries.[17]

When preparing for his performance in Chekhov's play, his own act of commitment to a meaningful future as opposed to commercial projects which pay the bills, Wertenbaker's actor character Robert says that "In *Three Sisters* characters contemplate the end of their century with that same sense of waste, of being outside history" as England is experiencing in the late twentieth century, "but Vershinin intoxicates himself

---

tions, neglect and/or social subservience, child prostitution, or infanticide), this song has prospective personal, socio-political, and international resonances.

[17] Una Chaudhuri posits that "The challenge of multiculturalism [...] is not only that of including new voices and faces in drama, but also that of effecting an ideological transformation, a transvaluation of the once-impacted relationship between place and personhood" (*Staging Place* xiv).

with a vision of a better future. I don't think Chekhov intends to mock that. He kept building schools: humanity could become better" (Act One, 24). In *The Break of Day*, Wertenbaker seeks to re-connect audiences with a sense of history and to cultivate a politically-conscious internationalism, imagining that "humanity could become better." Wertenbaker's school is the theater. She advances a deeply committed interculturalism and internationalism, which is strengthened by her plays' complex critiques of singular identity tropes, whether based on class, culture, bodies, or nations. With creativity and theatrical immediacy, she foregrounds hybridity and co-habitation as vital remedies to the human casualties of rigid conceptions of identity, country, or place.

Works Cited

Aston, Elaine and Janelle Reinelt, eds. *The Cambridge Companion to Modern British Women Playwrights*. Cambridge: Cambridge UP, 2000.

Bassnet, Susan. "The Politics of Location." *Cambridge Companion to Modern British Women Playwrights*. Eds. Elaine Aston and Janelle Reinelt. 73-81.

Carlson, Susan. "Language and Identity in Timberlake Wertenbaker's Plays." *Cambridge Companion to Modern British Women Playwrights*. Eds. Elaine Aston and Janelle Reinelt. 134-149.

Chaudhuri, Una. *Staging Place: The Geography of Modern Drama*. Ann Arbor: U of Michigan P, 1997.

Chekhov, Anton. *Five Plays: Ivanov, The Seagull, Uncle Vanya, The Three Sisters and The Cherry Orchard*. Trans. Ronald Hingley. Oxford: Oxford UP, 1998.

Clifford, James. *Routes: Travel and Translation in the Late Twentieth Century*. Cambridge, MA: Havard UP, 1997.

Roth, Maya. *Opening Civic, Feminist and Theatrical Spaces: The Plays of Timberlake Wertenbaker*. Doctoral Dissertation. U of California at Berkeley, 2001. Ann Arbor: UMI, 2002.

Scolnicov, Hanna. *Woman's Theatrical Space*. Cambridge: Cambridge UP, 1994.

Stephenson, Heidi and Natasha Langridge. *Rage and Reason: Women Playwrights on Playwriting*. London: Methuen, 1997. 136-145.

Wertenbaker, Timberlake. *After Darwin*. 1st ed. London: Faber and Faber, 1998.

_____. *The Break of Day*. Royal Court Theatre. 1st ed. London: Faber and Faber, 1995.

_____. *Timberlake Wertenbaker: Plays One*. First ed. London: Faber and Faber, 1996.

Wilson, Ann. "Forgiving History and Making New Worlds: Timberlake Wertenbaker's Recent Drama." *British and Irish Drama Since 1960*. Ed. James Acheson. New York: St. Martin's, 1993.

The Flexing of Muscles and Tongues: Thug Rituals and Rhetoric in David Mamet's *American Buffalo*

Alain PIETTE

*Ecole d'Interprètes Internationaux de l'Université
de Mons-Hainaut/Université Catholique de Louvain*

American Buffalo (1975) entirely takes place in Don's junkshop, no doubt a telling metaphor for modern-day America. The owner of that microcosm, Don, has just sold what he ignored was a rare coin, a buffalo-head nickel, for the hefty sum of $90. Convinced, however, that his customer did not give him enough money with regard to the true value of the coin, Don immediately plans a burglary to steal the nickel back from its new owner. Therefore, he entrusts his feeble-minded protégé, Bobby, with the surveillance of the customer's apartment. Soon after, Teach, who also hangs out regularly at the junkshop, imposes himself as the executor-in-chief of the burglary, and both of them subsequently oust Bobby from the deal to plot the robbery. But all they do is talk about it, as they never actually come around to committing it, and this for two reasons: first, because a third accomplice, Fletch, fails to show up as planned by Don (we will learn at the end of the play that he is lying in hospital with a broken jaw after a mugging); second, and perhaps most importantly, because the men's own incompetence and passivity in effect prevent them from putting their plan into action. At the end of the play, Teach lets out his frustration at the stillborn robbery by hitting Bobby violently on the head and then smashing the junkshop to pieces. The play finishes with the image of the devastated junkshop and of Don's picking-up of the bleeding Bobby to drive him to the hospital.

American Buffalo undoubtedly stands out as the cornerstone of David Mamet's work, as the play that marks the true beginning of everything for the playwright and that provides critics with the norm by which to measure the rest of the work. Indeed, *American Buffalo* is at the center of much Mametian secondary literature, which must be credited for establishing the critical vocabulary that was to be used in

the assessment of the other plays, the screenplays, the films, and even
the essays written by David Mamet.

In their respective analyses, Steve Lawson, Timothy J. Wiles, and
Thomas King,[1] to mention only a few critics, examined the quintessential Mametian belief that language equals action and that, in the theater,
talk is action and action is talk. Several other critics, as for instance
David Worster, focused on the concept of speech-act play with regard to
Mamet's work. Finally, Anne Dean devoted a whole monograph to the
subject, *David Mamet: Language as Dramatic Action*. As regards
American Buffalo itself, most of these critics argued that the three
characters of the play engage in sterile logorrhea instead of proceeding
with the planned robbery precisely because, for them, talk is action.
Many commentators have also expatiated on the pettiness of the three
characters, a Mamet trademark, as in many of his plays marginality
becomes mainstream. In his review of *American Buffalo*, Walter Kerr
uses the phrase "small-time hood[s]": after all, is not a man's character
usually said to be defined by his actions, whereas the three men in
American Buffalo apparently do nothing, indulging merely in what Chris
Bigsby calls "excessive verbiage" (269). I myself have written in my
piece on David Mamet's *Oleanna* that, for Mamet, language is action
and that, in Mamet's world, you are how and what you speak (Piette
178-179). In this respect, it seems particularly significant that Fletch, a
would-be accomplice in the burglary, who never actually appears onstage, should fail to materialize to perform the robbery: the fact that he
is now lying in the hospital with a broken jaw literally prevents him
from participating in the (speech-)action. Incidentally, in the film adaptation, the very verbiage of the play turns out to be the film's main
liability, failing to make a successful transition from the stage—the
realm of the verbal—to the screen—the realm of the visual. One reviewer even went as far as to write "Oh! Shut up, Dustin!" thus venting
the general feeling of the audience toward Dustin Hoffmann's unbearable performance in the role of Teach in the film. The stage production
has to my knowledge never suffered from the same problem, which
constitutes further proof that, in the theater, language *is* indeed part of
the action.

The other, somewhat related, perspective under which the play has
been studied is that of the teacher-student relationship that appears
central to so many Mamet plays (*A Life in the Theatre* [1979], *Sexual
Perversity in Chicago* [1977], *Oleanna* [1992], and *American Buffalo*,
among others). Many critics have indeed underlined the "pedagogical"
overtones of Teach's pontificating—even if his pedagogical method

---

[1]   See "Works Cited" for complete bibliographical details of all the critical pieces
referred to in this paragraph.

remains rather summary: "The only way to teach these people is to kill them" (11)—as well as Teach's and Don's patronizing attitude toward the younger Bobby (see Hubert-Leibler). Added to which, of course, the obvious onomastics of Teach's very name—which is in fact a nickname, his real name being Walt—also convey the idea of "pedagogy." This second approach also bears heavily on the first (linguistic) perspective, as language provides the primary raw material of education and teachers are generally regarded not as people who "do" things. I believe it was George Bernard Shaw (1856-1950) who said: "Those who can, do; those who can't, teach" (The anecdote is probably apocryphal).

A third reading of the play by critics tends to highlight the affinities that exist between Mamet's work and that of some of his illustrious predecessors like Chekhov (1860-1904), Pinter (1930), or even Beckett (1906-1989). Mamet actually directed *Uncle Vanya, 42nd Street,* and Pinter directed *Oleanna* in London. Furthermore, many commentators have indeed appositely observed that the long wait of Don in the third act (first for Teach, who shows up late, and then for Fletch, who fails to arrive altogether) has resonances of Didi's and Gogo's unsuccessful waiting for Godot in Beckett's eponymous play. The same can be said about the absence itself of the much-talked-about nickel buyer and that of Grace and Ruthie. I would, moreover, like to suggest here that the connection between *Waiting for Godot* (1953) and *American Buffalo* is more than simply that: just as the highly original plays *Fortinbras* (1991) by the American playwright Lee Blessing (1949) and *Rosencrantz and Guildenstern Are Dead* (1967) by the British Tom Stoppard (1937) respectively expand on *Hamlet* (1600-1601) by having as their central protagonists secondary characters who usually get cut in the performance of the Shakespeare original, it seems to me that Mamet has written a kind of sequel to *Waiting for Godot,* or rather an inflated version of its last line and final stage direction: "[...] let's go. *(They do not move)*" (88). *American Buffalo* can indeed be seen as a two-act variation on the immobility that paralyzes Beckett's characters as the curtain falls on the last act of *Waiting for Godot.*

To cut a long story short, the criticism on *American Buffalo* is abundant, most of it is thoroughly convincing and, by and large, I agree with the views put forward. Yet, two elements in that criticism (including my own) have always left me quite frustrated: the alleged lack of action in the play and the sleight-of-hand treatment that the character of Bobby has consistently received in various analyses of *American Buffalo,* no doubt a consequence of his apparent moronic feeble-mindedness. In view of Mamet's avowed predilection for the con game, for manipulation, for deceiving appearances, and for leaving things unsaid or unexplained, for allowing portentous events to take place offstage (like Beckett, Pinter, and Chekhov) so as to force the spectator-reader to infer

meaning from the interstices or silences in the play, I would like to
suggest in this essay, first, that there is far more physical (as opposed to
"linguistic") action in this play than initially thought by most critics and,
second, that Bobbie's role in it is perhaps more important than meets the
eye. I hold this to be the case despite the fact that, granted, Don and
Teach get the lion's share of the performance, and that Grace, Ruthie,
and Fletch, although they never actually appear onstage, arguably focus
more attention from Don, Teach, and the audience than Don's protégé.

In contrast to what much of the criticism tends to aver, the action in
American Buffalo is not restricted to the mere linguistic level. It takes
the physicality of performance and its visceral impact—as usual with
Mamet—to make one realize that the play's characters are far more
active than is generally assumed by its readers. One need only read the
reviews of the play's 1981 Broadway revival with Al Pacino in the role
of Teach to be convinced. In his review significantly entitled "Al
Pacino's Supercharged *Buffalo*," the *New York Times* critic Walter Kerr
appositely stresses Pacino's barely restrained physicality and the "brutally foolish incompetence of his plans for the evening", thus laying bare
the frenetic, near-hysterical violence that pervades the play. The physical violence contained in *American Buffalo* must indeed be considered
as action in the primary sense of the word, just as its linguistic violence
is generally considered as action in the figurative or metaphorical sense.
This active physicality starts in Act I with the hyper-animation or histri-
onics of Teach who, as Gregory Mosher confirmed in an interview,
consistently exerts "a kind of dramatic pressure on the others in the
play" (Jones and Dykes 22), and it ends in Act II with his vicious attack
on Bobby and subsequent material destruction of the junkshop.

In between these two extremes, we are led to surmise that the junkshop's internal confusion and violence are in fact externally determined
by, or are at least a reflection of, what is going on in the outside world.
Police cars regularly patrol the neighborhood—Teach mentions them
twice—apparently to no avail, since they cannot prevent Fletch's mugging, no doubt itself an external dramatic prefiguration of the internal
aggression to which Bobby falls a victim. Teach's intention to carry a
gun during the burglary merely reflects similar attitudes in the dangerous world out there: the mark might defend himself and hit his burglar
with a cleaver, the police are armed to the teeth. "They have the right
idea," says Teach, "Armed to the hilt. Sticks, Mace, knives ... who
knows what the fuck they got. They have the right idea" (88). As Teach
again puts it, the outside world is peopled with "Ax murderers" (87), it
is a place where "Guys go nuts" (87) and where "Social customs break
down, next thing *everybody*'s lying in the gutter" (88).

This scene occurs only minutes after Teach himself has unwillingly provided us with a cause for the disintegration of the social consensus in one of his appalling pontificating speeches:

TEACH: You know what is free enterprise?

DON: No. What?

TEACH: The freedom ...

DON: ... yeah?

TEACH: Of the *Individual* ...

DON: ... yeah?

TEACH: To Embark on Any Fucking Course that he sees fit.

DON: Uh-huh ...

TEACH: In order to secure his honest chance to make a profit. Am I so out of line on this?

DON: No.

TEACH: The country's *founded* on this, Don. You know this. (74-75)

Despite the fact that the junkshop seems to be an enclosed microcosm, it is far from being hermetic and protective. Bobby and Teach come and go, bringing in with them upon their return some of the infection and contamination at large in the world out there: the patrolling cops, the nickel buyer, Fletch, Grace and Ruthie, the telephone conversations, all external elements, contribute to the perverse atmosphere in which the junkshop is steeped. Furthermore, cheating and robbing are a way of life both inside and outside the junkshop. Inside, the customer cheats Don out of a supposedly valuable coin; Don plans to cheat it back from him; Don and Teach con Bobby out of the deal; Don does not fully trust Teach, who does not fully trust Don. As Teach himself says, "Bad feelings, misunderstandings happen on a job. You can't get away from 'em, you have to deal with 'em" (49). Indeed, when he sees Bobby in the junkshop later that night, Teach immediately assumes that Don and Bobby are intent on double-crossing him out of the deal. Later still, Don briefly attempts to cheat Bobby out of another buffalo-head nickel. Bobby manages to wrestle fifty dollars out of Don and twenty dollars out of Teach in what might possibly be a con trick on his part—more about that later. Outside now, Fletch steals Ruthie's pig iron, which is probably the one that Don is reselling in his junkshop, thus being a receiver of stolen goods. (This unfamiliar object itself is particularly symbolic of the pervasive violence of the play: it is supposed to keep a pig's hind legs apart to facilitate its goring, bleeding and gutting.) Fletch, Ruthie and Grace cheat at cards. Finally, inside and outside come together when Teach and Don get suspicious of a potential collusion between Fletch and Bobby to double-cross them out of the burglary altogether. Cheating is thus omnipresent and general. In Teach's own words, "You stiff this one, you stiff that one ..." (105); "You fuck your friends. You *have* no friends. No *wonder* that you fuck this kid around" (104). There is, then, plenty of action in the junkshop of *American Buffalo*, mostly of a violent nature, just as there is plenty of action outside it. It is this pervasive all-encompassing decay and collapse, as also the emblematic buffalo symbol, that has led June Schlueter and Elizabeth Forsyth to conceive of Don's resale shop as a fitting metaphor for America itself (492).

In view of the omnipresent violence and suspicion that pervade the junkshop, conceiving of it as a refuge or a protective womb out of which the characters would be reluctant to emerge to commit their burglary, as has often been suggested, is not altogether plausible. In her recent monograph on David Mamet, *Weasels and Wisemen*, Leslie Kane appropriately remarks how homes, even metaphorical ones as the junkshop, are consistently self-contained hells for Mamet, places to run away from, as one of his latest plays, *The Cryptogram* (1995), a domestic family drama, clearly evidences (186). The junkshop, Don's, Bobby's and Teach's surrogate or proxy home as it were, is definitely not a comfortable cocoon that lulls the characters of the play out of their drive for action. Quite on the contrary, it partakes of the violent action of the world at large and does not function at all, as Teach would have it, as the "Fort" that they will defend from outward aggression (37). Teach's description of the junkshop as a fort and his alertness to the police cars outside give us the impression that the junkshop is under siege and about to be raided. Teach's allusion to one of the most traditional settings of western movies, the Fort, as also the central metaphor of the play—the buffalo-head nickel—inevitably arouse our anticipation of some brawny bullying action. Before going to battle, the men flex their muscles and engage in a kind of tribal ritual, which is both physical and verbal, evoking the thug rituals of the title of this essay.

Much has been made in the criticism of the fact that the burglary does not actually take place, despite its act-long planning, to stigmatize the characters' passivity. Indeed, the promise of action apparently remains unfulfilled. But if one pauses an instant to consider the true nature of the burglary with regard to its potential loot, one is then forced to conclude that the action inside the junkshop probably provides far more excitement than the aborted robbery itself. Consider this: the target is a buffalo-head nickel, whose actual value remains vague and highly uncertain, as it is comprised between five cents—its face value—and ninety dollars—what the customer paid for it. Any higher estimation by Don and Teach is pure conjecture: even if it amounts to five times that, as Don enthusiastically alludes to (32), it still remains quite petty. It hardly seems worth the trouble, even for three small-time hoods. There is action in *American Buffalo*: it simply unfolds elsewhere than in the anticipated burglary only.

I would argue that it is perhaps also to be found in the character of Bobby, Don's apparently moronic gopher. At the end of the day, he comes across as the only one who has achieved some result: he unexpectedly shows up in the shop with a buffalo-head nickel that he tries to sell to Don and Teach. At first suspicious that he might have committed the robbery alone and for himself, Don and Teach quickly shrug off the idea and brush Bobby off by giving him some money, respectively fifty and twenty dollars, as they are convinced that this is not THE buffalo-head nickel that they are after. Bobby's explanation that he bought it from a coin shop is then taken for granted, both by Don and Teach and by the audience and critics. Only when Bobby comes back to tell them that Fletch is in the hospital, do Don and Teach take the possibility of Bobby's double-crossing them seriously. They interrogate him and, when he gets the name of the hospital where Fletch is supposed to be wrong, they are finally convinced of his betrayal. Accordingly, Teach violently hits Bobby on the head with a heavy object to get a confession out of him, thus paralleling, indeed parodying, the potential defensive gesture of the nickel buyer of whom Teach was so afraid earlier, when he wanted to carry a gun during the burglary. But when the telephone rings and news comes in that Fletch is indeed in the hospital, only not the one Bobby mentioned, they instantly drop the charges—as do we— against Bobby. Instead, they are in a hurry to bring him to the hospital in his turn for he is badly wounded.

It seems to me that Bobby is let off the hook all too easily. Fletch's actual mugging does not exclude Bobby's guilt altogether. Searching for clues in the play for that possibility, one must go back to the very beginning and to the initial characterization—direct and indirect—of Bobby by Don and Teach. In the opening scene of the play, Don and Bobby are together in the junkshop. They reminisce on the card game of the night before and on the nature of Fletch's talent for poker:

DON: I mean, Fletcher, he plays *cards*.

BOB: He's real sharp.

DON: You're goddamn right he is.

BOB: I know it.

DON: Was he born that way?

BOB: Huh?

DON: I'm saying was he born that way or do you think he had to learn it?

BOB: Learn it.

DON: Goddamn right he did, and don't forget it.

Everything Bobby: it's going to happen to you, it's not going to happen to you, the important thing is you can deal with it, and you can *learn* from it.

And this is why I'm telling you to stand up. It's no different with you than with anyone else. Everything that I or Fletcher know we picked up on the street. That's all business is ... common sense, experience, and talent. (5-6)

I would argue that Bobby is perhaps a far better student than one generally credits him for. We now know in retrospect that Fletch cheats at cards: that is what he has picked up on the street in this perverse social milieu. Cheating might also be the lesson Bobby learns here. Don and Teach's assessment of Bobby's feeble-mindedness, which may be due to drugs, becomes ours a little too quickly as it is predicated solely on Bobby's failure to get the breakfast order of the other two men right. He comes back without Don's coffee and with a Pepsi for himself, whereas Don had advised him to buy something good for his health. For the rest, Teach's initial suspicions toward Bobby, albeit for the wrong reasons, after all prove true in the course of the play: Bobby is just not reliable. First, after his outburst against Grace and Ruthie in the junkshop, Teach asks Bobby, who is going for coffee, not to talk to the two women about his insulting bout. Yet, when Bobby returns, he has obviously been talking to them as he reports that they are not mad at Teach. Second, Teach and Don briefly allude to a previous burglary in which Bobby betrayed their trust:

TEACH: We both know what we're saying here. We both know we're talking about some job needs more than the kid's gonna skinpop go in there with a crowbar ...

DON: I don't want you mentioning that.

TEACH: It slipped out.

DON: You know how I feel on that.

TEACH: Yes. And I'm sorry, Don. I admire that. All that I'm saying, don't confuse business with pleasure.

DON: But I don't want that talk, only, Teach. You understand?

TEACH: I more than understand. I apologize.

Pause.

I'm sorry.

DON: That's the only thing.

TEACH: All right. But I tell you. I'm glad I said it.

DON: Why?

TEACH: 'Cause it's best for these things to be out in the open.

DON: But I don't want them in the open.

TEACH: Which is why I apologized.

Pause.

DON: You know the fucking kid's clean. He's trying hard, he's working hard, and you leave him alone.

TEACH: Oh yeah, he's trying *real* hard.

DON: And he's no dummy, Teach.

TEACH: Far from it. (25-26)

We understand that Bobby has already betrayed their trust at least once and gone solo, possibly to buy himself some drugs. In the light of Don's early observation to Bobby that "Things are not always what they seem" (7)—Mamet's artistic creed as it were—and of Teach's own realization that "Bobby's got his own best interests, too" (36), I am tempted to conclude with Don that Bobby is indeed no dummy and that he has learned quickly from the ambient atmosphere of deception and double-crossing. My proposed interpretation and ending would perhaps be in line with similar endings of David Mamet's films like *House of Games* (1987) and *The Spanish Prisoner* (1996), if less evident here. After all, if we except the big bump on the head, Bobby is the sole beneficiary of the evening: he has got seventy dollars and a potentially valuable buffalo-head nickel in his pocket. *A qui profite le crime?*

Works Cited

Beckett, Samuel. *Waiting for Godot. The Complete Dramatic Works*. London: Faber and Faber, 1986. 7-88.

Bigsby, Christopher W. E. *David Mamet*. London and New York: Methuen, 1985.

Dean, Anne. *David Mamet: Language as Dramatic Action*. Rutherford, New Jersey: Fairley Dickinson UP, 1990.

Hubert-Leibler, Pascale. "Dominance and Anguish: The Teacher-Student Relationship in the Plays of David Mamet." *Modern Drama* 31 (1988): 557-70.

Jones, Nesta, and Steven Dykes. *File on Mamet*. London: Methuen, 1991.

Kane, Leslie. *Weasels and Wisemen. Ethics and Ethnicity in the Work of David Mamet*. New York: St. Martin's Press, 1999.

Kerr, Walter. "Al Pacino's Supercharged *Buffalo*." *The New York Times* 14 June 1981, late ed.

King, Thomas. "Talk and Dramatic Action in *American Buffalo*." *Modern Drama* 34 (1991): 538-48.

Lawson, Steve. "Language Equals Action." *Horizon* (November 1977): 40-45.

Mamet, David. *American Buffalo*. London: Methuen, 1984.

Piette, Alain. "The Devil's Advocate: David Mamet's *Oleanna* and Political Correctness." *Staging Difference: Cultural Pluralism in American Theatre and Drama*. Ed. Marc Maufort. New York: Peter Lang, 1995. 173-187.

Schlueter, June and Forsyth, Elizabeth. "America as Junkshop: The Business Ethic in David Mamet's *American Buffalo*." *Modern Drama* 26:4 (December 1983): 492-500.

Wiles, Timothy J. "Talk Drama: Recent Writers in the American Theater." *Amerikastudien/American Studies* 32:1 (1987): 65-79.

Worster, David. "How To Do Things with Salesmen: David Mamet's Speech-Act Play." *Modern Drama* 37 (1994): 375-90.

The Complexities of Intertextuality: Arthur Miller's *Broken Glass* and Maria Irene Fornes' *Fefu and Her Friends*

Barbara OZIEBLO

University of Málaga

The intricacies of intertextuality—that postmodern proposition which playfully points in the direction of constant interlinking and interconnecting in order to assuage the dire fragmentation of the individual in the second half of the twentieth century—may yet offer up some answers (never mind the question). Both Maria Irene Fornes and Arthur Miller are fascinated with the individual in society and attempt to reconstruct the shards of glass with which we hope to protect ourselves when our self-image has been shattered and disconnected from that of others. But the solutions they offer show up the conflicting claims of their subjects, the women and men they place before us. For Maria Irene Fornes, the answer may be found in the bonding of women. For Arthur Miller, the answer would depend on women giving up the gains of feminism and returning to the role of prime nurturer.

This essay will bring together these two seemingly antithetical playwrights and their evidently disparate plays, Maria Irene Fornes' *Fefu and Her Friends* (1977) and Arthur Miller's *Broken Glass* (1994). Fornes has stated quite vehemently that she dislikes Arthur Miller because he romanticizes the suffering of his characters; she claims that in her plays "people are always trying to find a way out, rather than feeling a romantic attachment to their prison" (Savran 55). Miller, of course, can afford to ignore Fornes' dislike: his position in the canon of American Drama is impregnable; Fornes, on the other hand, finds herself equivocally positioned as an ethnic minority feminist on Off-Off-Broadway. Even today, *Fefu and Her Friends* represents a highly innovative piece that juggles the audience and the theatrical space in order to dramatically implicate us in the predicament of its women characters; Miller takes no such risks, as he unrelentingly unmasks his male protagonist's insecurities and failings. The two plays are quite different in their conclusions, their theatrical shape, and in the stories they tell.

Thus we are surprised to see that both authors, writing in 1977 and 1994 respectively, should have turned independently to the same metaphor—a woman afflicted by psychosomatic immobility—in order to examine the paralysis brought on by the horrors unceasingly perpetrated by our civilization in the spirit of patriarchal superiority: the oppression and annihilation of the "other," inevitably seen as inferior and weaker on both the private and the public front. Fornes' Julia lost the use of her legs when she was scared by a shot, which killed a deer; "the hunter aimed ... at the deer. He shot [...] Julia and the deer fell. [...] She had convulsions ... like the deer. He died and she didn't" (17). This surreal, even absurd, account of the accident given by Cindy explains nothing; in contrast, the more literal-minded Christina aptly personalizes a previous incidence of violence when she insists that "One can die of fright, you know" (12). Miller's Sylvia Gellburg is also terrified by violence done to others; in this case, it is the newspaper reports of *Kristallnacht* that bring on the "hysterical" paralysis, which mystifies her family and doctor.

Before I go on to examine how these two cases of physical paralysis brought on by external events have been used by Fornes and Miller, I would like to point out other coincidences in the two plays, the most obvious being that both are placed in the 1930s. In Miller's case, this proves contingent on his choice of historical setting, while Fornes has said that she wrote the play in order to use six 1930s dresses she had bought in a thrift shop (Robinson 253). The names Julia and Sylvia have a similar ring to them and, in *Fefu and Her Friends,* the women listen to Schubert's "Who is Silvia" (the words of this song are Shakespeare's and it was sung in honor of Silvia, who had displaced Julia in Proteus' heart in *Two Gentlemen of Verona,* Act IV, Scene 2). The husband in each play—Fefu's in *Fefu and Her Friends* and Sylvia's in *Broken Glass*—bears the august name of Phillip; both Julia and Sylvia do—for a moment in Part Three of *Fefu and Her Friends* and in Scene Eight of *Broken Glass*—appear to be able to walk; Sylvia's dream, which she tells her doctor, can be related to Julia's hallucination and also to Cindy's dream, dismemberment and violence being key issues in all three cases. The rabbit that Fefu kills also finds its way into *Broken Glass*: Dr. Hyman horrifies Sylvia when he boasts that as a boy he had delighted in the gratuitous killing of rabbits "with sling-shots. [...] To see if we could. It was heaven for kids" (50). Then there is Fefu's "constant pain" which she tries to describe to Emma: "It's not physical and it's not sorrow [...] it's hard to describe" (29), and Sylvia's equally stumbling "I seem to have an ache [...] my whole body seems ... I can't describe it" (16).

For all their disagreements and differences, the two playwrights share the conviction that the individual's place is within society. In *Broken Glass*, Sylvia's paralysis is willfully equated with the horrors of *Kristallnacht*, thus structurally linking the private with the political; in *Fefu and Her Friends*, this link is spelled out by Cecilia in her long speech at the beginning of Part Three: "We cannot survive in a vacuum. We must be part of a community, perhaps 10, 100, 1000. It depends on how strong you are. But even the strongest will need a dozen, three, even one who sees, thinks and feels as he does" (44). Miller and Fornes also share the conviction that the theater can, in Miller's words, at least "shift the consciousness of a certain number of people" (Bigsby, *Cambridge Companion* 9), although we might feel that Fornes is more demanding in this respect; in an interview with Savran, she has declared that: "The play is there as a lesson, because I feel that art ultimately is a teacher"(56). In *Fefu and Her Friends* Fornes has indeed reshaped the play into a lesson; Emma gives us the clue to this transformation when she passionately affirms that "Life is theatre. Theatre is life. If we're showing what life is, can be, we must do theatre" (22). For Penny Farfan, the *mise-en-scène* of Part Two reinforces Cecilia's recognition that we cannot survive as isolated individuals; she argues that "in reconfiguring the conventional performer-spectator relationship, [the play] realizes in theatrical terms an alternative model for interaction with the universe external to the self such as that proposed by the metatheatrical actress/educator-character Emma as a means of transforming Fefu's pain. In this respect, *Fefu and Her Friends* posits postmodern feminist theatre practice as a constructive response to the psychic dilemmas of the play's female characters" (443). Indeed, in Emma's dramatized speech in Part Three, borrowed from the educator Emma Sheridan Fry, the didactic function of theatre is lucidly stated: it will teach us to flee "indifference that is death," while "a sense of life universal surges through our life individual" bringing us "slowly and painfully into recognition of ourselves" (46-47). We can apply the lesson taught by Emma to the characters of *Broken Glass*: Sylvia and Phillip Gellburg are afflicted by an indifference/impotency, which prevents them from recognizing their individuality and thus their common humanity. As Joyce Antler succinctly puts it: "To be blind to oneself makes us blind to the world about us" (19).

What are we to make of such multiple coincidences? The fact that both dramatists uphold the political and didactic possibilities of the stage merely emphasizes a common theatrical heritage. But what of the minor details? Should we search for deeper meanings in the interstices revealed by—possibly—shared literary allusions? Or, should we assume that Miller, in an act of revenge for Fornes' avowal of "dislike" expressed in such personal terms, perhaps plundered her play for a suitable metaphor—hysterical psychosomatic paralysis— to show us yet again, characteristically and unforgettably, how intertwined the political and the personal are? Frankly, I doubt the latter hypothesis. Added to which, Christopher Bigsby put paid to any such unworthy speculation in his program notes for the London National Theatre production in 1994, when he disclosed that the image of a woman who had inexplicably lost the use of her legs had fascinated Miller for fifty years; moreover, the woman's husband, like Phillip Gellburg, always dressed in black. And Miller confirmed this to Amanda Hopkinson, when he insisted that the idea had been "an itch in the back of [his] mind" for 56 years. Given that fanciful speculation is rarely illuminating, I shall disregard the trifling coincidences I have discovered, and engage the two plays in a hypo-thetical conversation with the hope that it might yield some answers as to the potential intertextuality between them.

In spite of Steven Drukman's contention that "[t]he best way to wrap your mind around the plays of Maria Irene Fornes [...] is to abandon all hope of understanding them" (36), there have been many attempts at explicating *Fefu and Her Friends*. These studies generally adopt a more or less radical feminist stance (Kent 123), and explore the relationship between the women, particularly that of Julia and Fefu; if we heed Fornes' warning that symbolical meanings should not be wrung from the play (Marranca, "Interview" 106), both the actions of the women and the ambiguous ending escape interpretation. And yet, unless we accept Toby Zinman's absurdist reading, we feel obliged to search for meanings; although Julia has been seen as a symbol of oppression, a victim, as Fefu's potential savior and even as her double (Keyssar 125; Austin 79), all critics seem to agree that the play exposes "suppressed truths about (women's) social circumstances" (Kent 119). The eight very different women who appear in the play establish connections and relationships with one another as they move from scene to scene, their interrelatedness made clear by their repeated appearances in the differ-ent rooms of Part Two as much as by their conversation. Going through college together created a common bond between them which still holds good in the face of patriarchal oppression, and we see them immersed in a fund-raising project with educational goals, a worthy cause to which they are devoted.

In her first appearance, Fefu perplexes her interlocutors and her au-dience with the bizarre assertion that her husband had married her "to have a constant reminder of how loathsome women are" (7). In spite of its initially absurd repartee, this dialogue, rather than showing that life is senseless, ends with the chilling truth that we have to recognize those hidden, private surfaces that are not exposed to public view: "It is another life that is parallel to the one we manifest. It's there. The way worms are underneath the stone. If you don't recognize it [...] it eats you" (10). Thus, from the very beginning, Fefu establishes the theme of the play as the danger of the suppression of true instincts and desires (see Fuchs); but her warning applies equally well to Phillip and Sylvia Gellburg in *Broken Glass* as to her friends. The arrival of Julia, crippled in a surreal accident, draws our attention to the fate of a woman who did dare to recognize her true identity as a woman, and who is now paying the consequences for going beyond the boundaries of self-knowledge permitted to women. In the scene where the audience stands above her and she lies hallucinating on a mattress in a makeshift bedroom, she discloses the psychological reasons for her metaphorical—albeit real—paralysis. She has been beaten, dismembered, tortured into accepting that "the human being is of the masculine gender" (35), and forced to renounce her personhood—her capacity to walk independently. She is not so much the weak, cringing victim, but rather, in her acceptance of a paralyzed life, in her resignation, she reminds us of our mothers and grandmothers who, before Betty Friedan named the "problem that has no name" (29), lacked the words to do so. Although Julia submits to the loss of independence implicit in the wheelchair, she is extremely brave in her defense of Fefu for whom she fears her own fate; as she pleads with her judges that Fefu is "only a joker" and not at all "smart," we sense her pride in the fact that her friend has so far outwitted the judges and "is still walking" (34).

Julia is fortunate to be surrounded by her friends, women who, although they may not quite understand her hallucinations, appear prepared to take her seriously and also to joke, cavort, and play with her; and finally, after Fefu has taken the male weapon into her own hands and symbolically killed the rabbit, they join her round Julia's wheelchair. This communion of women demonstrates that neither Julia nor Fefu are alone; in their struggles as individuals and as members of a community that they hope to improve by bringing the arts into education, they have only to reach out to one another. This empowerment of women through bonding and mutual support has been signaled by Phyllis Mael (190) and Deborah R. Geis (175), among others. Fefu's threat that once "women recognize each other" (15), they will have the power to blow the world apart, thus becomes the dominating message of the play. Such an interpretation refutes Bonnie Marranca's claim (*American Playwrights* 61) that Fefu kills Julia out of despair that she will ever fight the feminist struggle again, and refuses to acknowledge the fact that Julia is still fighting, still struggling with the judges in her hallucinations, and risking her own "cure" by protecting Fefu; her paralysis and her hallucinations teach us, the audience, as well as the other women in the play, the extent of the power of patriarchy.

Patriarchal authority is shaken when Fefu, who has mastered its tools and strategies—she is an efficient plumber and markswoman—shoots and kills the rabbit. In their very different readings of the play, W. B. Worthen and Toby Zinman both recognize that the conventions of realism, understood as a patriarchal mode of representation, have been deeply undermined; but perhaps we could go even further and read the rabbit as a symbol of lust and of the repetitive reproduction enforced on women by patriarchy. Thus, by killing the rabbit, Fefu "kills" the male construct of woman as submissive mother, as a machine for the continuation of the human race, thereby allowing women to create their own image. Strong women such as Julia expose the patriarchal order whose weaker representatives feel threatened and retaliate by torturing them into submission and paralysis. Fefu's daring act has metaphorically killed the "woman-as-victim" (Keyssar 125; Pevitts 317), saving Julia and allowing the friends who now surround the wheel-chair to hope that she will walk again—after all, Fefu has seen her walking previously and believes that she can do so. But, most importantly, the women do gather around Fefu and Julia, and we recognize the community they create, and the power they will now wield.

In *Broken Glass*, there is no such female understanding, and my initial pleasure at finding a woman protagonist in a male-authored play ended in disappointment when I realized that Miller had cast Sylvia as the mere instrument of the true protagonist's tragedy. I had automatically assigned the principal role to Sylvia; perhaps, as a woman, I was simply looking for a woman to identify with and, in spite of decades of conditioning, contrived to ignore the "natural" protagonist, the male. Conversely, Fornes has commented that men find *Fefu and Her Friends* difficult because there are no men for them to relate to: "I began to notice," she says, "that a lot of the men looked at the play differently from the women. They wanted to know where the men in the play were; they wanted to know whether the women were married. They insisted on relating to the men in this play, which had no male characters" (Fornes, "The'Woman' Playwright Issue" 90). Although in *Broken Glass* Miller seems to focus our attention on Sylvia, the victim of an undiagnosed ailment, critics have ascertained that he "builds his dramatic argument around the diagnosis of her emotionally constricted husband" (Winn). Joyce Antler considers that "the woman's story [...] is less fully developed" (19) and, as we shall see later, believes this has serious repercussions in the play. Once we recognize that Phillip Gellburg is Miller's protagonist, we can read the play as his (conscious or not) reply to Fornes' answer to the problems of women.

Ostensibly, the patient in *Broken Glass* is Sylvia Gellburg, who, for no reason that the medical profession can uncover, is paralyzed from the waist down. The family practitioner, Dr. Hyman, although not trained in psychoanalysis, decides to take on the case, and both he—and the audience—soon realize that Sylvia's obsession with the horrors of

Kristallnacht are not at the root of her problems. Dr. Hyman advises Phillip to give her the love she needs; we suspect from early on that he would be happy to make good Phillip Gellburg's deficiencies, only he does not quite dare. Although Phillip makes out that his sexual life with Sylvia is perfectly normal, we are not at all surprised when she reveals that he has been impotent for twenty years, and the cause barely needs to be explained as we already know that Sylvia is an intelligent woman, who had loved her work as a bookkeeper; she withdrew from her husband when he refused to allow her to go back to work after the birth of their son. Tormented by the "problem that has no name" (Friedan 29) even before it had been identified, by frustration, boredom, and perhaps a desire for revenge, she refused to have more children, and refused to give Phillip the image of himself that he needed in order to function in patriarchal society. As he finally admits, he felt that "didn't want me to be the man here" (60).

Phillip's case is complex: not only does he need to see his own image reflected in the mirror of his wife's eyes, but his immaturity, exacerbated by his self-denial and self-hatred as a Jew, pushes him back toward the maternal womb. Tellingly, Phillip confesses to Dr. Hyman "I never told this to anyone … but years ago when I used to make love to her, I would feel almost like a small baby on top of her, like she was giving me birth. That's some idea? In bed next to me she was like a … a marble god. I worshipped her, Hyman, from the day I laid eyes on her" (70). This little speech, full of conflicting images, encapsulates Phillip's dilemma: he is unable to see his wife as a woman of the flesh with her own desires and ambitions. In short, Phillip has never successfully separated from his mother, has never come to terms with his own identity as a man and as a Jew; he wants and needs to be mothered by Sylvia, yet he casts her as a "marble god"—cold, frigid, superior, and therefore masculine—who, by the very nature he has imposed on her, cannot give him the nurturing he requires. Phillip openly questions Sylvia's maternal instincts (and her Jewish pride) when he reproaches her with lack of interest in their grown son's achievements; he cannot accept that she does not share his delight that their son—"That's your son" he throws out at her (19)—a Jew, has not only entered West Point, but is clearly headed for a highly successful military career. Phillip cannot acknowledge that Sylvia's skills go beyond the confined space of the home; she loved her work as head bookkeeper because she "always enjoyed … you know, people depending on me," as she explains to Dr. Hyman (35).

Contrarily, Sylvia, who thrived in a position of responsibility in the public sphere, cannot accept that her husband depends on her in the home; in Scene Ten, the only moment when the three women who appear in the play are seen together, Sylvia confesses how she has

survived so far: "The trouble, you see—was that Phillip always thought
he was supposed to be the Rock of Gibraltar. Like nothing could ever
bother him. Supposedly. But I knew a couple of months after we got
married that he ... he was making it all up. In fact, I thought I was
stronger than him. But what can you do? You swallow it and make
believe you're weaker. And after a while you can't find a true word to
put in your mouth. And now I end up useless to him ... just when he
needs me!" (64). The other two women, Harriet, her sister, and Margaret, Dr. Hyman's wife, are no "jury of her peers"; they react as good
women, in Miller's books, should: Harriet offers to bring along some
pot roast, while Margaret advises yet more resignation and submission.
This is not the life-saving community of women that Fefu's friends
create; Margaret and Harriet sit with Sylvia and help her out--but they
refuse to understand or bond. They remain distant, incapable of the
imaginative leap needed to overcome indifference on the personal and
the political plane. These two women have fully internalized the text of
the lesson that Julia in *Fefu and Her Friends,* is still struggling with:
"They say that when I believe the prayer I will forget the judges. And
when I forget the judges I will believe the prayer. They say both happen
at once. And all women have done it. Why can't I?" (35).

In spite of Sylvia's refusal to be the nurturing home-bound mother,
Phillip adores and worships her; but he is so indifferent to his own
humanity that he can only see the "marble god" in her and cannot
acknowledge the drives and desires of the intelligent, ambitious woman
he has married. The passive adoration of her body that Phillip offered
could not satisfy Sylvia for long; "idealization is not intimacy," as John
Lahr has rightly indicated (95). Sylvia needed the acknowledgement of
the larger stage, the community which Phillip is incapable of handling
and prefers to ignore, hiding away in his ten/eleven hour workday from
himself as much as from the world. Just as Julia, in *Fefu and Her
Friends,* has to pretend to submit to the judges in order to buy moments
of freedom, Sylvia creates a personal world of pretence, which, for
twenty years, has made it possible for her to play the part of dutiful
wife. The insidious inferiority which she affects and her subsequent
paralysis of mind, as much as the feigned indifference to her situation,
eventually bring on the psychosomatic paralysis that finally alerts others
to the serious danger of such spiritual inertia. And in *Kristallnacht,*
Miller found the perfect reflection of the consequences of private indifference in the public sphere.

The solution to Phillip's personal dilemma comes with his heart attack; this represents a real, masculine illness, one that is comprehensible, easily diagnosed, and treatable. The pain is real—and Sylvia finally
breaks down and transfers responsibility from Phillip to herself: "I'm
not blaming you, Phillip. The years I wasted I know I threw away

myself" (73), she cries out in her attempt at reconciliation, echoing her older sister Elizabeth of *The Crucible*, who also nobly exonerates her husband from blame, taking his adultery upon herself. But it is when Phillip falls back unconscious that Sylvia can, from the male point of view, recover her own true self. She recognizes that he is helpless without her and accepts the role of the nurturing mother; overcoming her paralysis, she gets to her feet and goes to him.

Critics have not attached importance to the different endings of *Broken Glass* (Abbotson 79, Roudané 192), but the reading I have just proposed only works with the supposedly final version of the play, in which Phillip falls unconscious and his fate is unclear. The earlier version, in which Phillip dies, would imply that Sylvia recovers the use of her legs once her husband, her oppressor, is no more, thus turning the play into a man-hating tract, which would turn the spotlight on Sylvia as the protagonist rather than on Phillip. But as Joyce Antler has pointed out, Sylvia's character and motives are "too airily sketched" to be convincing, thus a resolution which placed her in the position of protagonist must have rung false and would "account for the trouble Miller had in ending the play" (19).

The coincidences between the two plays are resolved by reading *Broken Glass* as Miller's reply to the feminist spirit, which Miller presumably fears, of *Fefu and Her Friends*. For Miller, the Phillips of this world are not to blame for the frustration and paralysis of their wives or of society in general—before we can achieve a society which is loving and nurturing women must return to their primary role of carers, must learn to reflect the image their husbands want to see. Fornes' conclusion, for all the dangers of reductionism that today we recognize in the supposed haven of a global women's community, is still more appealing than Miller's desire to see only the nurturing, forgiving mother in his women characters.

Works Cited

Abbotson, Susan C. W. "Issues of Identity in *Broken Glass*: A Humanist Response to a Postmodern World." *Journal of American Drama and Theatre* 11 (Winter 1999): 67-80.

Antler, Joyce. "The Americanization of the Holocaust." *American Theatre* 12.2 (February 1995) 17-20, 69.

_____. "The Madwoman in the Spotlight: Plays of Maria Irene Fornes." *Making a Spectacle: Feminist Essays on Contemporary Women's Theatre*. Ed. Lynda Hart. Ann Arbor, MI: U of Michigan P, 1989. 76-85.

Austin, Gayle. "The Madwoman in the Spotlight: Plays of Maria Irene Fornes."
  Ed. Lynda Hart. *Making a Spectacle: Feminist Essays on Contemporary
  Women's Theatre.* Ann Arbor, MI: U of Michigan P, 1989. 76-85.
Bigsby, Christopher. "Miller's Journey to *Broken Glass.*" London National
  Theatre, Lyttelton Theatre Program for *Broken Glass,* 1994.
_____. *The Cambridge Companion to Arthur Miller.* Cambridge: Cambridge
  UP, 1997.
Drukman, Steven. "Notes on Fornes." *American Theatre* 17.7 (September
  2000): 36-39, 85.
Farfan, Penny. "Feminism, Metatheatricality, and *Mise-en-scène* in Maria Irene
  Fornes's *Fefu and Her Friends.*" *Modern Drama* 40.4 (Winter 1997): 443-
  53.
Fornes, Maria Irene. *Fefu and Her Friends.* New York: PAJ, 1990.
Fornes, Maria Irene. Ed. Gayle Austin. "The 'Woman' Playwright Issue."
  Performing Arts Journal 7:3 (1983): 87- 102.
Friedan, Betty. *The Feminine Mystique.* 1963. Harmondsworth, England:
  Penguin, 1992.
Fuchs, Elinor. "*Fefu and Her Friends*: The View from the Stone." Ed. Marc
  Robinson. *The Theater of Maria Irene Fornes.* Baltimore: Johns Hopkins
  UP, 1999. 85-108.
Geis, Deborah R. "Wordscapes of the Body: Performative Language as *Gestus*
  in Maria Irene Fornes's Plays." Ed. Helene Keyssar. *Feminist Theatre and
  Theory.* London: Macmillan, 1996. 168-88.
Hopkinson, Amanda. "Broken Glass." *New Statesman and Society* (5 August
  1994): 31.
Kent, Assunta Bartolomucci. *Maria Irene Fornes and Her Critics.* Westport,
  Conn.: Greenwood Press, 1996.
Keyssar, Helen. *Feminist Theatre: An Introduction to Plays of Contemporary
  British and American Women.* London: Macmillan, 1985. 121-25.
Lahr, John. "Dead Souls." *New Yorker* (9 May 1994): 94-96.
Mael, Phyllis. "Fornes, Maria Irene." *Dictionary of Literary Biography* 7. Ed.
  John MacNichols. Detroit: Gale Research, 1981. Pt. 1: 188-91.
Marranca, Bonnie. "Interview: Maria Irene Fornes." *Performing Arts Journal.*
  2:3 (Winter 1978): 106-11.
_____ and Gautam Dasgupta. *American Playwrights: A Critical Survey.* New
  York: Drama Book Specialists, 1981. 53-63.
Miller, *Broken Glass.* London: Methuen, 1994.
Pevitts, Beverley Byers. "Fefu and Her Friends." Ed. Helen Krich Chinoy and
  Linda Walsh Jenkins. *Women in American Theatre.* New York: Theatre
  Communications Group, 1987. 314-17.
Robinson, Marc, ed. "Notes on Fefu." *The Theater of Maria Irene Fornes.*
  Baltimore: Johns Hopkins UP, 1999. 221-23.
Roudané, Matthew C. *American Drama Since 1960: A Critical History.* New
  York: Twayne, 1996. 188-92.
Savran, David. "Maria Irene Fornes." *In Their Own Words.* New York: Theatre
  Communications Group. 1988. 51-69.

Winn, Steven. "A Woman's Personal Holocaust: Miller Looks Through *Broken Glass* Darkly in Static Play." *San Francisco Chronicle* (25 April 1994): E3.

Worthen, W.B. "Still Playing Games: Ideology and Performance in the Theater of Maria Irene Fornes." Ed. Enoch Brater. *Feminine Focus: The New Women Playwrights.* New York: Oxford UP, 1989. 167-85.

Zinman, Toby Silverman. "Hen in a Foxhouse: The Absurdist Plays of Maria Irene Fornes." Eds. Enoch Brater and Ruby Cohn. *Around the Absurd: Essays on Modern and Postmodern Drama.* Ann Arbor: U of Michigan P, 1990. 203-20.

The Postmulticultural:
A Tale of Mothers and Sons

Harry J. ELAM, Jr.

Stanford University

"We are in a postmulticultural time," or so the student said assuredly. It was October 2000, and I was visiting a class on issues of diversity and social change in drama at the University of Minnesota, discussing concerns arising from August Wilson's now famous address to the Theatre Communications Group Convention in January 1996, when the student made this remark. It stuck with me. Because of our academic affinity for "posts" (postindustrialism, poststructuralism, postcolonialism, postmodernism, post-postmodernism), "postmulticulturalism" seemed the perfect addition. Why the postmulticultural? Certainly the current politics of race in America demand new classifications and correspondingly compel new representations of race within the theater. Multiculturalism, the concept of embracing racial difference, that "defined the 1990s," no longer seems sufficient to engage the new dynamics of race in America. As an article in the *New York Times* entitled "Beyond Multiculturalism, Freedom?" argues, "In the 2000's the time has come to move on to new ground" (Cotter 1). W. E. B. DuBois famously proclaimed in *The Souls of Black Folk* that the primary problem of the twentieth century was "that of the color line" (54). If this in fact was the question of the twentieth century, what now of the twenty-first? Where shall race and American racial politics figure in the new millennium? How will new understandings of race factor into theatrical representation? How do America's changing racial demographics figure in this equation?

The 2000 Census marked the first occasion in American history in which respondents could check more than one ethnic category, in effect creating new assignations of mixed race identities. And so 7 million Americans filled in multiple boxes declaring themselves or their families to be of mixed race. While 1.9 percent of adults identified as being of mixed race, 4.2 children fit into this new category, suggesting that these numbers will continue to escalate. What these Census statistics do not account for, however, are those who decide, like playwrights August Wilson and Cherríe Moraga—one of the authors featured in this essay— to self-identify as exclusively within one ethnic denomination, although they are of mixed parentage. Born of a white German father and a black American mother, Wilson perceives himself as black, and situates himself as well as his political and artistic roots within African American cultural traditions. Moraga's father was also white, but she, like Wilson, defines herself in terms of her mother's background. Despite her light complexion that enables her to pass as white, she perceives herself as a Chicana and locates herself within intersecting identities of race, gender, and sexuality as a Chicana lesbian. The positions of both Moraga and Wilson underscore the constructedness of race as a political and social category. In fact, the biology and genealogy of Wilson and Moraga would appear to add weight to the supposition that the number of mixed race peoples is more than likely much higher than the Census 2000 figure. Yet, on the other hand, we cannot claim Moraga or Wilson as mixed because *they* do not chose to do so. The ability to check the "mixed race" boxes on the Census only reminds us that race has always been and remains a critical component in the process of self-identification. Critical then to the postmulticultural is the potential meaning of new self-definitions and coalitions, the space to claim a new ethnic positionality.

Within its postmulticultural context, the 2000 Census furthered the importance of race, even as it nuanced this significance in new and different ways. The politics of race, as we well know, has always been critical to the determination of American identity and the dissemination of American social resources. Conscious of impact of racial designations on federal resources, African American, Latino, and Asian American activists feared that the mixed race designation would dilute the total numbers of their respective constituencies and agitated against coloring in more boxes. After all, is not everyone inherently mixed? Mixed race activists, on the other hand, call for the recognition that race is not monolithic or fixed, that increasingly Americans migrate between identity positions and racial identifications. Mixed race designations, they argue, enable the subject not to foreclose aspects of her or his identity through one single racial determination, but to foreground the nexus of affiliations. And yet, what are the risks that those who do unequivocally proclaim mixed race status, might represent a new ethnic homogeneity, a new tradition of identity politics that they purport to oppose? In an essay entitled "Passing and the Problematic of Multiracial Pride (or, Why One Mixed Girl Still Answers to Black)," novelist Danzy Senna, herself of mixed parentage, maintains that

> One of my concerns about the multiracial movement is that it buys into the idea of race as a real, biological category. It seems to see race almost as

chemistry: Mix black and Japanese, you get Blackanese. Mix Caucasian, Black, Indian and Asian and you get Cablinasian. I wonder if it will work toward a deconstruction of race, or a further construction of it. When we look at societies that acknowledge racial mixture—such as Haiti, Brazil, and South Africa—it becomes clear that multiracial pride does not necessarily mean the end of racism. Even when we look at the history of our own country—blue vein societies, brown paper bag tests, and light-skinned privilege—it becomes clear that a Multiracial Identity can live happily with racism and white supremacy intact. (Senna 77)

Senna cautions that mixed race identities can reify racial categories, even as they seek to transcend them. Nonetheless, she does not allow for the potential of mixed raced identifications to affirm a different experience or experiences of race and identity, experiences that fall outside the normative or normalizing circumstances of those more easily or visibly classified by race. Understanding, negotiating, or interrogating the politics and potentialities, the contradictions and the consequences of new mixed race categories is a crucial practice finding new articulations within the postmulticultural.

Yet, the postmulticultural marks not only the contestation of racial categories but, potentially, also the evacuation of the concept of minority as a point of reference and of identity. The 2000 Census testifies that California not longer has an ethnic majority. Significantly, the numbers of Mexican Americans in particular and Latinos in general have dramatically increased in the last decade. Mexican Americans now account for some sixty percent of the 35.3 million Latinos in the United States, followed by Puerto Ricans and Cubans respectively. The growth of Latinos is notable, because it has occurred not only in states such as Texas and California that share a border with Mexico, but in states such as Nebraska, Georgia, and North Carolina. Soon, in fact, the United States as a whole will not have a white majority. The Hispanic designation on the Census also testifies to the increasing significance of hybridity and mestizo or mixed identity positions within the postmulticultural. The Census form designates Hispanic whites as well as Hispanic blacks. Many of those who checked the box for Hispanic also checked multiple designations. At issue, then, is how and whether the Hispanic category constitutes a race or inherently signals racial crossings.

Along with the growth of Hispanic and Latino populations, new strategies of identity politics have emerged that reach across both national and international borders, that identify the significance of language, that allow for difference as well as for the communality of experience. The influx of new immigrants from South Asia has profoundly impacted on the designation Asian American and its inter- and intraracial politics. The racial category "Asian" speaks to the politics of race and, as Lisa Lowe argues, to the heterogeneity, the hybridity and multiplicity of fluid cultural identities, as the term groups together increasingly historically, culturally, geographically, and linguistically diverse groups of people. Hybridity has become an overused word and one that—I would caution—must be used with more critical rigor and consciousness of its historical baggage. Following Lowe, I imagine hybridity as a negotiation of unequal positions of power and domination, and as such hybridity does not indicate assimilation into the dominant culture, nor does it suggest the free oscillation of identity positions. Lowe's notion of hybridity takes into its definition the history of unequal power relationships, as well as the invention of survival strategies and different cultural alternatives to combat them (Lowe 82). Accordingly, "the racial and linguistic mixings in the Philippines and among Filipinos in the United States are the material trace of the history of Spanish colonialism, U.S. colonialism, and U.S neocolonialism" (Lowe 67). Such hybridity recognizes the interactions between the local, the national, and the international, and acknowledges that culture is not fixed but an open and dynamic site. Hybridity then lets us understand that cultural identity, as Stuart Hall argues, concerns not a cultural essence but a "positioning" (6). The collisions between past cultural traditions and the demands of the current historical moment are critical to this process. Cultural identities negotiate with the presence of the past as well as with the forces of progress. They confront the particularities of language and location in a concept that is strategic and positional. The postmulticultural then offers space for new explorations of cultural and ethnic hybridity, for the interrogation of racial meanings, and for a re-thinking of the politics of cultural identity.

A fundamental aspect within the postmulticultural is how cultural identity will be defined, articulated, negotiated, and maintained, and I believe that the theater constitutes an important venue both for the analysis and construction of cultural identity. The unique conventions and inventiveness of the theater allow for provocative explorations of identity not possible in the outside social environment. Theatrical performances not only reflect the changing dynamics of cultural identity within the existent social order, but potentially make their own claims, structure their own circumstances, and raise significant questions about how race operates and how it interacts with issues of gender, sexuality, class, and culture. Within the postmulticultural, new playwrights and new plays have emerged that push cultural identities beyond the historical binaries and constricting definitions of black and white.

As I shall discuss, such issues are paramount in Cherríe Moraga's play *The Hungry Woman: the Mexican Medea* and Suzan-Lori Parks' *In the Blood*. In *The Hungry Woman*, Moraga thematizes mixed race not as a separate status, but as an intraracial issue of Chicano/a identity, as a postmulticultural interrogation of the intra-dynamics, the intersections and tensions of race and sexuality. Perhaps out of a generational affinity for the past, Moraga, like August Wilson, fundamentally maintains that, even in this new day, the politics of earlier cultural nationalism must continue to resonate in the radical insurgencies of artists of color and their current desires to create socially-minded art. As she listened to Wilson's famous 1996 speech to the Theater Communications Group, Moraga "cried out of hunger, out of solidarity, out of longing for that once uncompromising cultural nationalism of the 1960s and 1970s that birthed a new nation of American Indian, Chicano, and Black artists" (Moraga, Unpublished Ms. 2). With *The Hungry Woman: The Mexican Medea*, Moraga attempts to respond to her own cry to renew the spirit and a collective affirmation of identity politics and of earlier strategies of cultural nationalism, while recognizing the contestations and limitations of such potentially essentializing positions.

Suzan-Lori Parks' *In the Blood*, pushes beyond simple racial definitions as it provokes and represents questions of cultural identity. Parks, from a younger generation than Wilson or Moraga, adamantly seeks to move beyond the identity politics of the past black cultural nationalism and has argued for the exploration of new dramatic territory in black writing. "There are many ways of defining Blackness and there are many ways of presenting Blackness onstage [...] BLACK PEOPLE + x = NEW DRAMATIC CONFLICT (NEW TERRITORY)" (19-20). Her play attempts to reach such new territory, as it concerns Hester, a black homeless woman and her wild brood of children, Jabber, Bully, Trouble, Beauty, and Baby, who live underneath a bridge. Hester's children are a multicultural lot, black, Latino and white, played by adult actors who also portray the children's fathers and other significant figures in Hester's life. *In the Blood* features adult actors as children and an interracial progeny that natural selection could never replicate. The multicultural casting stages the fluidity of race and underscores the problematic nature of racial categorizations. The performance of adults as children raises questions about the impact that lessons learned in childhood can have on our developmental processes. Within the theatrical conventions of performances like *In the Blood*, one can seemingly escape the visible markers of the body—an adult can portray a child—even as the action or content of the performance reinforces the power and meanings of the visible body. One can perform, but also subvert conventional cultural roles. Thus, within her portrait of these children and of Hester's world, Parks questions what is "in the blood." Hester's problems simultaneously involve and obscure race. She is a victim, but also tragically complicit in her own oppression. Her tale offers a poignant, contradictory conjunction of suffering and survival, institutional neglect, and individual abuse. Parks constructs complex interactions between race, sexuality, economics, and culture, as the marginalized figure of a black homeless woman takes center stage and perceptions of this ostracized other must undergo reassessment and critique.

While these two plays are not by any means definitive, they both imaginatively engage the question of how to construct a politics of identity within the postmulticultural without succumbing to an essentializing identity politics. These are works that resist and critique national or racial embodiments of what Donald Pease calls a "universal subject":

> The national narrative produced national identities by way of a social symbolic order that systematically separated an abstract, disembodied subject from resistant materiality such as race, class, gender. This universal body authorizes the discrimination of figures who can be integrated within the national symbolic order and matters "of race, gender, class" external to it. Because the coherence of the national narrative depends on the integrity of its universal subject, that figure is transformed into a tacit assumption and descends into the social unconscious. (3)

Significantly, the universal subject within the American national "symbolic order" as articulated by Pease finds reiteration in the exclusionary politics of a Chicano nationalism that restricts gays and lesbians or in a black arts movement that circumscribes creative processes for black authors, as well as in recent multicultural paradigms that reify difference as they practise new forms of exclusion. Each of these examples, as Pease would say, implicitly and explicitly "authorize discrimination" and "systematically separate," as they support their own particularized view of a homogenized cultural subject. Consequently, a critical space for postmulticultural politics involves subverting or inverting such national and nationalistic narratives that impose or suppose a universal subject. My sense is that both *In the Blood* and *The Hungry Woman* partake in such a project.

Both plays focus on the internal dynamics of the family as it operates as the nexus for dramatic conflict around issues of cultural identity. The family has always been an important subject in American drama, from Eugene O'Neill's *Long Days Journey Into Night* onwards through to August Wilson's *Fences.* Yet and still, this concentration on family is all the more significant in our postmulticultural times, when the nature and constitution of the American family and normative national narratives of family are contested by the presence of new gay and lesbian family units, by the increase in interracial marriages and mixed raced families, by the new upsurge in immigration and new immigrant communities, by the rise in single family households across race and class, and by the assertion of cultural dynamics that affirm the importance of the extended family. Ultimately, in each of these plays, mothers kill sons in acts that contain historical, cultural, social, and political resonance. These murders function as gestures of symbolic resistance against the tyranny of a national symbolic order that not only restricts the roles that women or people of color may play, but also preordains the place of progress and how one's offspring can even function within this system.

Moraga's *The Hungry Woman: Mexican Medea* reveals a crisis of cultural identity predicated on essentialized racial as well as sexual identities. She sets her reworking of the Medea myth in "a near-future of a fictional past, one only dreamed in the Chicana/o imagination" (*Hungry Woman* 294). Within this site, she imagines the political paradigms of Chicano cultural nationalism of the 1960s and 1970s carried to an extreme fruition. "An ethnic civil war has 'balkanized' the United States. Medea, her lover, Luna, and child, Chac-Mool, have been exiled to what remains of Phoenix, Arizona. Located in the border between Gringolandia (white Amerika) and Aztlán (Chicano country), Phoenix is now a city-in-ruin, the dumping site of every kind of poison and person unwanted by its neighbors" (Setting, *Hungry Woman* 294). Aztlán, the mythical home of the Aztecs and the symbolic home of the Chicano nation within Moraga's dramatic vision, is a land founded not on cultural pride and acceptance, but on and through the practice of ethnic absolutism and essentialism. Accordingly, anyone who has not got a prescribed percentage of native Indian blood or who is not heterosexual, gets excluded from the homeland. But how do they know who is straight or gay? Who is mixed or pure? Mixed race, like sexual orientation, is not always self-evident, not simply visual. Those on a racial or sexual continuum—those whose racial or sexual identity seems unmarked—challenge the very categories which are self-evidently marked in the play. To have a politics of inclusion, you need to have categories, borders that appear fixed if only to cross them. Inclusion in this case may be a Trojan horse, because it explodes the boundaries that enable that very inclusion. It is this inclusionary/exclusionary dynamic of the Chicano homeland that causes the tension within the play. Medea and her lesbian lover Luna have been exiled because of their sexuality. Jasón, the father of Chac-Mool, now seeks the return of his son to Aztlán, because Jason himself lacks the required heritage of indianismo and thus Chicano authenticity. Jasón needs the presence of his son to assure his belonging.

In the Blood also fundamentally examines issues of alienation, displacement, ethnic legitimacy, sexual deviance, and cultural belonging. Like her namesake Hester Prynne in Nathaniel Hawthorne's *Scarlet Letter*, Park's Hester La Negrita has been ostracized from society because of her sexual transgression. At the opening of the play, the word "slut" is scrawled on the wall under the bridge where Hester and her illegitimate children live. It marks a public branding and abasement, just as from the outset of Hawthorne's novel, Hester Prynne is publicly humiliated and exorcized from the community as she exits from prison.

While Hester Prynne is forced to sew into her clothing the scarlet letter A announcing her adultery and publicly acknowledging her shame, Hester La Negrita during the first scene of *In the Blood* kneels on the ground and awkwardly etches the letter A with chalk on the cement. Her eldest child Jabber teaches her to read and write, as she is illiterate. Yet, the action testifies to another form of literacy, a cultural literacy that she must learn to appreciate through the course of the play. Culturally, La Negrita—Spanish for the little black girl—embodies the symbol of black female deviance. She is the black homeless woman and welfare queen, who produces illegitimate children without concern for their welfare and parasitically lives off the legitimate efforts of the hard-working, morally conscious citizens. Parks riffs on this politics of legitimacy and morality, as her Hester finds herself continually exploited by the Doctor, the Reverend, and the Welfare Lady, representatives of supposedly ethical orders that should protect and help her. Equally significant, Parks' depiction of her five bastard, mulatto children, the bitter fruit of her mother's racial crossings, repeats and revises an implicit tension of legitimacy that lies beneath the politics of multiculturalism and the American legacy of mixed raced identities. Historically, mulattos were marked with scarlet letters as abnormal and aberrant products of "illegitimate" liaisons between slaves and their white masters. The word mulatto originated from the Spanish word for mule, the ungainly, sterile offspring of a donkey and a horse. The original meaning of hybrid is equally pejorative. It designated the progeny of genetically desparate parents. Implicitly and explicitly, then, Parks interrogates matters of racial and cultural literacy and legitimacy as her Hester searches for a place in which she and her family can belong and feel free.

Through the figure of Medea—like Park's Hester, another reworking of a classical female victim of alienation and community vilification—Moraga questions the conventional position of women within the politics of Chicano liberation. Similar to Hester La Negrita, Medea is a repetition with revision of a legend—not simply the legend of Medea, but of women from Aztec mythology. The title of the play, *The Hungry Woman: The Mexican Medea*, signifies this conflation. The Hungry Woman of Aztec legend, the goddess Tonantzin, the mother goddess of earth, of regeneration and rebirth, represents an insatiable figure. She has many mouths and is always hungry. She is fed through the human sacrifice of blood, as well as through natural rainfall whose drops replenish the flowers and the grass for which she is responsible. Other women in Aztec myth often figure as sites of desire and danger. Coyalxauhqui, who led a war band against the mother of the god Huitzilopochtli on his birth, in an attempt to stop him from coming into existence, and Malinalxochitl, a witch who could kill men at a glance.

Moraga's Hungry Woman desires love as sustenance and eventually sacrifices her own son, Chac-Mool. Like the Hungry Woman of Aztec legend, she excels in the use of herbs and employs *curandera* herbs in this sacrificial act. With her reworking of the Ancient Greek and Aztec mythology, Moraga decries the devaluation of women and women's work in the Chicano cultural nationalistic espousals of Aztlán. Her Medea's personal plight links the political, racial, sexual, and cultural. Medea recognizes and desires the security, the authority, and the sense of cultural identity that come from belonging to a homeland. Still, branded as different and deviant, as woman and lesbian, she remains a liminal outsider struggling for re-entry. In an earlier essay, "Queer Aztlán: The Re-formation of the Chicano Tribe," Moraga idealizes an imaginary and inclusive Aztlán that accepts gay and lesbian Chicanos even as it celebrates Chicano cultural identity. "A Chicano homeland that could embrace all its people, including its jotería" (Moraga, "Queer Aztlán"). With *The Hungry Woman: A Mexican Medea*, Moraga calls for such a culturally and sexually specific decolonization through the body of Medea. As Chicana, as a *mestiza*, a woman that is inherently of mixed blood, she fundamentally confounds simple racial categorization. Alicia Arrizón writes that, "Neither Anglo-American nor indigenous, the *mestiza* body troubles the borders of feminist practices, nationalism, and colonial discourses" (31). Medea in this play represents what Arrizón terms the "native woman": "The body of the native woman does not necessarily assert the presence of an authentic self because it challenges cultural 'purity.' The 'native' body's presence in Chicana (and Latina) cultural productions and critical theory becomes a metaphor for the process of the political unconscious" (Arrizon 32). As a native woman wrapped in her racial and sexual ambiguity and ambivalence, Moraga's Medea resists and challenges conventional ideas of Chicano identity and authenticity.

In her portrait of ethnic balkanization, Moraga reveals the inherent dangers within past systems of identity politics and cultural nationalism. Cultural identity and affiliation remain problematic territory that must constantly be interrogated. Border guards literally patrol the "cultural borders" protecting against the entry of those who do not belong. The action of the play moves between the present—with Medea in a cell in a psychiatric hospital after the death of her son—and the past—with flashbacks to the events that transpired prior to his demise. Given our knowledge of the classic Medea story and the re-occurring image of Medea as a prisoner in the hospital ward, the tragic fate of her son Chac-Mool is never in question. Rather, the play explores the personal trajectory and social circumstances that lead Medea to act. The play unfolds as a ritual sacrifice and a requiem not only for Chac-Mool and Medea, but for the lost urgency and direction of the Chicano Movement. The personal collides with the political as the characters perform Medea's memories and inner turmoil.

In Parks' *In the Blood*, borders of difference are not erected around cultural nationalism and ethnic absolutism, but around cultural chauvinism and class prejudice. Hester La Negrita finds herself excluded and denigrated because of her poverty and alleged immorality. The Welfare Lady explains her purposeful patrol of socially delineated borders:

I walk the line

Between us and them

Between our kind and their kind.

The balance of the system depends on a well drawn boundary line

And all parties respecting that boundary. (42)

The social order, the differentiation of self from the other, she argues, requires the maintenance of such strict boundaries. The Doctor, who through his street practice attends to the needs of the underprivileged, further indicates Hester's difference and the necessity to prevent her from being an increasing burden upon society. He intends to sterilize Hester, to "remove her woman parts," as he says, or as the Welfare Lady puts it to "spay" her in order to prevent her from having future children that become the financial responsibility of the state. The Reverend D continues this degradation of Hester by insisting that she come to the back, not the front door of his new church.

Parks contrasts the ethical purity of these characters, their disdain for the impoverished and supposedly parasitic Hester with the hypocrisy of their sexual proclivities, their fetishized desires, and their ultimate exploitation of La Negrita. In a series of staged confessions, the other adult characters admit to their perversions and rationalize their sexual misuse of Hester. The Welfare Lady avers that she arranged for Hester to partake in a *ménage-à-trois* with her husband and her, after her husband grew bored with the routines of their lovemaking. The Doctor concedes that he had unprotected sex with Hester on the street. The Reverend, sexually aroused, attracted by her supplication before him and her destitute circumstances, asks her for a blowjob. He offers no child support for their baby, only avoidance. Then, in his confession he admits that

Suffering is an enormous turn on ...

She had that look in her eye that invites liaisons

Eyes that say red spandex. (45)

Sadomasochistically, the Reverend yokes his desire to Hester's pain. Her suffering and poverty, rather than encouraging his religious compassion, stimulates his prurient sexual urges. The Reverend dodges her solicitations for financial support and "backing" for their child, by claiming that he himself must wait for his own backers. "Do you know what a 'Backer' is? ... It's a person who backs you ... My backers are building me a church" (44). In a scene similar to the encounter between the Baron Doctor and the Venus Hottentot in Parks' *Venus*, where the Baron Doctor turns his back to the Venus on the bed and masturbates, the Reverend turns his back to her and pleasures himself sitting on a rock while Hester reveals her vision of an eclipse that engulfed her like hands of fate. His arousal, like that of the Baron Doctor's, is both a removal from and degradation of Hester's fetishized difference, but also an admission that suffering and difference excite his desire. "That's how we like our poor. At arms length" (44). She embodies for him "poverty erotica." The Reverend and the others, the Doctor and the Welfare Caseworker, use Hester for masturbatory, self-gratification, and self-indulgent fulfillment of their missionary desires. They justify their exploitation of Hester through the narcissistic celebration of their own charity towards her, the erotics of benevolence. Consequently, sexual desire enables boundaries of class and of propriety to be crossed, and therefore complicates constructions of identities and hierarchies of difference. Still, while sex complicates these relations, the existent power dynamics and boundaries of identity remain intact. These border crossings, like the sex act itself, are temporary, ephemeral, and only result in the further ostracization of Hester La Negrita. She finds no sense of self, no freedom in these acts. Sex does not liberate her from but only imprisons her more in the system.

Hester as black woman is objectified, sexualized, and silenced. The sexual exploitation of Hester reaffirms the historic role of black women as sexual objects of desire, subject to the abuse of the white master in slavery. Yet, not unlike Parks' title character in her exploration of the sad history of the Venus Hottentot in *Venus*, Hester is not simply a sexual victim. Her figure is not solely defined by her sexual subjugation. Hester, like Venus, does not merely embody a desired object, but also a desiring subject with a degree of agency even within her oppressive circumstances. Hester chooses not to tell on or turn in to the Welfare authorities any of the fathers of her children. At her most desperate and depressed times, when the care for or her decision to give birth to her five children seem most problematic, she affirms her love for and her desire to have children. As with Parks' Venus, Hester's situation allows for few options other than to use her body in an attempt to change her socio-economic circumstances. Moreover, Parks reveals that the problems Hester encounters are not simply the result of her racial marking, not simply a matter of black and white. The welfare caseworker who patronizes and exploits Hester economically and sexually is black. The self-serving, duplicitous Reverend who fathers her most recent child and avoids paying child support even as he requests sexual favors, is also black. Through these divergent representations Parks problematizes questions of community and collectivity or shared understandings of blackness. The interactions of race with issues of class, gender, and sexuality contest simple definitions of blackness.

Through Medea, Moraga too ponders the relation of sexuality and gender to her cultural and racial identity. Medea like Hester attempts to use sex to her advantage, but to no avail. She sleeps again with Jasón in a vain attempt to keep Chac-Mool and to facilitate her return to Aztlán.

Jasón: Medea, why the sudden change of heart?

Medea: I want what's best for my son. He'll be forgotten here in this ghetto.

Jasón: I'm ... sorry

Medea: Are you?

Jasón: You don't have to stay here either, you know.

Medea: I don't know that.

Jasón: You're not a lesbian, Medea for chrissake. This is a masquerade.

Medea: A seven-year old one?

Jasón: I'm not saying that you have no feelings for the relationship, but you're not a Luna.

Medea: (*Sadly*) No, I'm not. (327-28)

Medea, is sexually and culturally uncertain. She recognizes her own inability to commit fully to lesbian identity as does Luna, because this sexuality identity conflicts with her desire to return to and live in her cultural homeland, Aztlán. She sees how in this world her employment of sexuality can change her own social circumstances and those of her son. Sexuality is inextricably linked to racial and cultural identity. Yet, Moraga's fictive Aztlán excludes gays and lesbians, not because they procreate and produce racially impure progeny but because their sexual difference undermines the heterosexist imperative that maintains the stability of this racialized state. The lesbianism of Luna, Medea, and others is a form of pollution. Samuel R. Delaney writes in "Some Queer Notions about Sex" that "Homosexuality pollutes the family, the race, the nation *precisely because* it appears to reduce the threat or menace of pollution to others—the mutual menace that holds the boundaries of a given family, race in tense stability" (273). Still, Medea complicates notions of pollution and exposes the fluidity of the borders between gay/straight and Chicano/other, because she did procreate and produce the Indio son Chac-Mool that Jasón desires.

Scarred by Medea's sexual ambivalence, Luna, the spurned lover, takes on another lover, a black woman, Savannah. Jonathan Dollimore argues that "desire for, identification with the cultural and racial other brings with it a complicated, ambivalent history" (25). Yet, with this interracial relationship, Moraga does not focus on the complex interactions of racial and sexual difference. Rather, Luna and Savannah come together over sameness. They share a politicized cultural identity as lesbians. *In the Blood*, Parks takes a different tact on interracial lesbian desire. Amiga Gringa, Spanish for "white friend," confesses to having lesbian sex with Hester as a means of making money. She charges the neighborhood men to voyeuristically watch their libidinous interactions. "The guys in the neighborhood got their pleasure/and we was our own boss so we didn't have/ to pay no joker off the top" (43). With Amiga Gringa and her confession, then, the act of lesbian sex is not a place to affirm sexual identity, difference, and autonomy, but rather a site to exploit for economic advantage and self-determination. With Amiga and Hester as well as Luna and Savannah, the racialization of sex and the sexualization of race through their interracial desire complicate these categories and understandings of both race and sex.

Trapped within a word of ruptures and liminalities, Medea's son Chac-Mool is fatally impacted by intersections of sexuality, gender, and race, as he seeks to determine his own identity as a young man and a Chicano. He is thirteen years old, within the throes of puberty, and moving from childhood into manhood. He lives in the alien space of Phoenix caught between the wills of his father and his mother. While he desires to return to Aztlán and experience the ancient cultural traditions of initiation, Chac-Mool also wants to stay with his mother and Luna. His two names, "Chac-Mool" and "Adolfo," given to him by his mother and father respectively, reflect the paradoxes of his cultural identity. The nickname Chac-Mool—the name he has tattooed into his arm, etched into his being—is the name of the ancient Mayan messenger to the gods and thus a symbol of Chicano cultural heritage and pride. On the other hand, he dislikes Adolfo, the name given to him by his father, because he associates it with Adolph Hitler and Nazism. Chac-Mool's liminality raises the following question: is it possible to reaffirm cultural identity without also reinforcing exclusivity, separatism and ethnic absolutism? Through Chac-Mool, Moraga also asks if it is possible to raise a new culturally sensitive Chicano man who does not perpetuate the sins of the father. "The man I wish my son to be does not exist, must be invented" (339-40).

Significantly, the boy-child Chac-Mool is the only male actor in the piece. In *The Hungry Woman: A Mexican Medea*, Moraga asks that women play all the male roles, including the husband Jason, but not the boy, Chac-Mool. She demands that an actual young man portray him. Conventional Western drama, in concert with the hegemony of the male gaze, identifies with the male figure and inevitably makes the man the protagonist. In such an economy, Chac-Mool becomes the hero and focus of the piece. Moraga exposes this malecentric prejudice in a scenic moment that breaks the fourth wall and in Brechtian fashion compels the audience to think about the meanings of Chac-Mool and gender within the production. Standing at the border between Aztlán and Phoenix, a Border Guard chastises Chac-Mool by pointing out his difference, "It's your play ... You're the source of the conflict. You're also the youngest, which means you're the future, it's gotta be about you. *And*, you're the only real male in the cast" (344). Through this explicit rupture of the theatrical convention, Moraga exposes the unmarked and interrogates the power of patriarchal authority. Consequently, the true focus of *The Hungry Woman: A Mexican Medea* is not on the son, but on the mother, Medea.

When Jason betrays her again and the loss of her son is imminent, Medea performs the act of infanticide, poisoning Chac-Mool with *curandera* herbs. This act immediately connects her to other cultural traditions and to other mothers in history who became either vilified or celebrated for the murder of their children. This heritage includes Margaret Garner, the escaped black slave, who when re-captured, killed her children rather than see them sold back into slavery. Medea's act saves Chac-Mool from returning to a politically segregated and ideologically bankrupt Aztlán. She prevents him from carrying on traditions of patriarchal oppression. Most specifically, her act joins her with La Llorona, the weeping woman of Mexican legend, who when wronged by her young husband, threw her children into the river. Within more recent feminist appropriations, La Llorona symbolizes the loneliness and agony of the disparaging mother, a woman without agency in a patriarchal society. In the stage directions, Moraga asks that her Medea's relation to La Llorona, the "Mexican Medea," be made tangible after the death of Chac-Mool:

> *their lament [the chorus'] is accompanied by the soft cry of the wind in the background that swells into a deep moaning. It is the cry of La Llorona, The moon moves behind the mountains. The lights fade to black.* (357)

Significantly, La Llorona needs the light of the moon to appear and Medea too needs her Luna.

In *In the Blood,* Parks too repeats and revises the trope of Margaret Garner and of La Llorona of Sethe in Toni Morrison's *Beloved*, women of color who killed their children rather than risk to see them entering into lives of oppression. When her last chance at the dream of an ideal marriage in a white dress fades, Hester lashes out. Chili, Jabber's father—a Latino man with whom Hester got involved when they were both very young and who abandoned Hester subsequently—returns now wealthier and wiser, offering not back child support but marriage. He dresses her in a wedding gown which he produces from a picnic basket and places a ring on her finger; she provides the shoes. However, Chili balks at marriage and moves on, taking his possessions with him, when he discovers that Hester is not merely the mother of one fatherless child but five. "I carried around this picture of you. Sad and lonely with our child on yr hip ... My Dear Hester or so I thought. But I don't think so" (48).

Unable to confront the father, Hester hammers his son. Like Medea, she kills the son in a gesture that implicates the father as well as the oppressive class system that surrounds her. Rather than vent her frustrations and rage at the men who have betrayed and abandoned her or the social system that exploits her, Hester kills her son Jabber in an act of indirection and transference. She murders the one thing that she loves most, one of her children, the ones she has gone without for and determined to protect. At the end of the play, she is forced to leave them as she stands accused and damned by the very system that has used and abused her. A chorus that includes the Doctor who wanted to sterilize her after they had sex, the Welfare lady who used her for threesome with her husband, and the Reverend who asked her for a quick blow job, stands over her as she sits alone in her prison cell. They chant: "She is the Animal, No skills, 'cept one, cant read, cant write ... That's why things are bad like they are 'cause of girls like that"(50). Their hypocrisy is glaringly evident. The final scene then works to refocus the power of perception and invert the virulence of their indictment by illuminating the damage done *to* Hester, but not *by* her.

Both Parks' Hester and Moraga's Medea end up in jail punished for their crimes. Yet, these acts resound in ways that are far more than personal. The killing of their sons marks both an ending and a beginning, it signals the indictment of corrupt social orders and the tragic corruption of the protagonist's mind. The murder of their sons disrupts the patrilineal legacy, the tradition of carrying on the father's name and heritage through the son. The killing of the son is then perhaps a futile way of fighting back against patriarchal hegemony. But sacrificing the child in your midst forecloses not simply the possibility of patrilineal ascension, but also the potential for a mixed race future. These violent acts then portend an ambivalence and ambiguity for the children of mixed blood, as within their hybridity they possess the potentiality for affecting social, cultural, and racial change, even as they embody or carry with them complex and often problematic histories, legacies, inequities, interstices, circumstances that must be confronted.

The deaths of Jabber and Chac-Mool dramatize the ultimate despair of the family through these interdynamics of family functioning as a metaphor for the intraracial struggles present in the postmulticultural. Accordingly, the debate around mixed race and the checking of multiple boxes in the 2000 Census is not simply an argument for and against normative whiteness, but a familial debate, an intraracial as well as interracial argument. How within race do we place questions of multiethnic identification? What kinds of racial insurgencies are possible within the postmulticultural? These plays raise but leave these questions unresolved, even as the sons' deaths act as pleas for change in restrictive cultural and social covenants that demarcate and prescribe identities. These works reflect on the tensions operating within the postmulticultural, as we struggle to find a politics that enables difference and diversity, but still encourages a sense of collectivity and communal affirmations of identity.

Works Cited

Arrizón, Alicia. "Mythical Performativity: Relocating Aztlán in Chicana Feminist Cultural Productions." *Theatre Journal* 52 (March 2000): 23-49.

Cotter, Holland. "Beyond Multiculturalism, Freedom?" *The New York Times* 29 July 2001, sec. 2: 1.

Delaney, Samuel R. "Some Queer Notions about Sex." *Dangerous Liaisons*. Ed. Eric Brandt. New York: The New Press, 1999. 259-289.

Dollimore, Jonathan. "Desire and Difference: Homosexuality, Race, Masculinity." *Race and the Subject of Masculinities*. Eds. Harry Stecopoulos and Michel Uebel. Durham, NC: Duke UP, 1997. 17-44.

DuBois, W. E. B. *The Souls of Black Folk*. New York: Penguin Books, (1903) 1969.

Hall, Stuart. "Introduction: Who Needs Identity?" *Questions of Cultural Identity*. Eds. Stuart Hall and Paul Du Gray. London: SAGE Publications, 1996. 1-17.

Lowe, Lisa. *Immigrant Acts*. Durham, NC: Duke UP, 1997.

Parks, Suzan-Lori. "An Equation for Black People Onstage." *The America Play and Other Plays*. New York: Theatre Communications Group, 1995.

_____. "In the Blood." *American Theatre* (March 2000): 31-50.

Moraga, Cherrie. "Queer Aztlán: The Reformation of the Chicano Tribe." *The Last Generation*. Boston: South End Press, 1993. 145-174.

_____. *The Hungry Woman: A Mexican Medea. Out of the Fringe: Contemporary Latina/Latino Theatre and Performance*. Eds. Caridad Svich and María Teresa Marrero. New York: TCG Press, 2000. 289-364.

_____. Unpublished manuscript, April 1997.

Pease, Donald. *National Identity and Post-Americanist Narratives*. Durham, NC: Duke UP, 1994.

Senna, Danzy. "Passing and the Problematic of Multiracial Pride (or, Why One Mixed Girl Still Answers to Black)." *Black Renaissance/Renaissance Noire*, 2.1 (Fall/Winter 1998): 76-79.

An Untold History: The Challenges of Self-Representation in Asian American Women's Theater[1]

Eriko HARA

Tokyo Kasei University

In multicultural contemporary theater in the United States, American women artists of Asian descent—Wakako Yamauchi, Genny Lim, Velina Hasu Houston, Gennie Barroga, and Elizabeth Wong—all attempt to find a way to deconstruct American identity, which has been constructed primarily from a Western white male perspective. For these Asian American women playwrights, this enterprise constitutes the performative dimension of an untold history and the expression of a fundamental cultural need for self-representation. Asian American culture in particular, including theatrical culture, is "about recapturing various histories differentiated by the specificities of each group, histories of survival and endurance, stories of love and heroism which would otherwise be lost" (Ling 4). In the face of this historical erasure and silencing, how can Asian American women artists in particular—who are doubly marginalized by gender and race in so-called mainstream of U.S. culture—possibly recapture their heretofore untold histories?

In *A Different Mirror*, Japanese American historian Ronald Takaki, a proponent of American multiculturalism, concludes that "as Americans, we originally came from many different shores, and our diversity has been at the center of the making of America. While our stories contain the memories of different communities, together they inscribe a larger narrative" (428). Asian American women artists such as Yamauchi, Lim, Houston, Barroga, and Wong look to Takaki's "different mirror" in examining U.S. national history on the stage from the perspective of diversity, viewing theater as an apparatus for both visually and aurally

---

[1] I wish to thank the English Literary Society of Japan for the support given me under the travel grant scheme. This made it possible for me to present a shorter version of this essay at the drama conference "Crucible of Cultures: Anglophone Drama at the Dawn of a New Millennium" in Brussels (May, 2001).

narrating the historical truth of their authentic human experiences. For these dramatists, theater is a site for re-remembering the past and sharing communal memory.

Despite their varied ethnic backgrounds, these Asian American women artists each reclaim untold histories from their personal and communal pasts that have been silenced or erased within a national history mapped in visible "differences" across boundaries of nationality, culture, gender, race, and ethnicity. This paper explores how these artists resurrect memory to (de)construct (gendered and racialized) American identity in resisting stereotypical images of the historical Other and representing their authentic self.

In writing history by means of autobiography, these Asian American women playwrights interrogate, criticize, and intervene in the seemingly monolithic, hegemonic American White male identity. In the practices of these artists, theater offers a powerful voice to women of color, making them visible. As Vietnamese American artist Trinh T. Minh-ha provocatively argues:

> Autobiographical strategies offer another example of ways of breaking with the chain of invisibility. Diaries, memoirs, and recollections are widely used by marginalized people to gain a voice and to enter the arena of visibility. [...] Memories within come out of the material that precedes and defines a person. When she creates, they are the subsoil of her work. Thus, autobiography both as singularity and collectivity is a way of making history and of rewriting culture. Its diverse strategies can favor the emergence of new forms of subjectivity[...]." (*When the Moon Waxes Red* 191-92)

As Trinh observes, and artists such as Yamauchi, Lim, Houston, Barroga, and Wong demonstrate, memory affords the possibility of narrating the untold histories of the marginalized, thereby recovering their historical subjectivity.

Turning first to a trailblazer in the dramaturgy of memory and history, second generation Japanese American Wakako Yamauchi has established important directions in Asian American women's theater. In plays such as *And the Soul Shall Dance* (1974) and *The Music Lessons* (1977), Yamauchi dramatizes the harsh experiences of Japanese immigrants to the Imperial Valley of California, who were forbidden to own land under the Alien Land Act of 1913. *And the Soul* focuses particularly on the sense of connectedness shared by immigrant women, and their endurance in "keep[ing] the dream alive" (152) despite isolation combined with racial and socio-economic oppression. As an immigrant woman points out in *And the Soul*, "White people among white people ... that's different from Japanese among white people" (153); for Yamauchi, the central project of reconstructing and mapping the ethnic memories of Japanese women immigrants must recognize their particular historical location within the dominant culture.

In her introduction to *And the Soul*, Yamauchi asserts that "the play is based on memory, but I embellished it" (quoted in Berson 130). Projecting from the playwright's own recollections through the perspective of American-born teenager Masako, *And the Soul* foregrounds the unspoken collective memories of immigrant women struggling to conform to the gendered roles of patriarchal Japan, even as they confront their lives in America.

Yamauchi focuses on the secret past of one woman immigrant Emiko, relentlessly unveiling both her reasons for leaving her "real home" in Japan to come to America as a second wife, and her reasons for "planning to go back" (145). In America, Emiko "has nothing to live on but memories" (148), and spends her days drinking *sake* to escape domestic abuse and violence at the hands of her husband. Ultimately, Emiko's dream of returning to Japan to recapture a lost romance is completely destroyed when her husband Oka spends her entire savings on his own dream of Americanizing his newly arrived daughter Kiyoko.

In Yamauchi's representation, even Asian American history fails fully to do justice to the immigration of Asian women, denying them any roles as active and central players in U.S. national history; against this backdrop, Yamauchi's final scene provides an opportunity for an Emiko who is "in exile now" (152) to let her soul dance along with her favorite Japanese song, "And the Soul Shall Dance," in her beautiful kimono against a desert background.

Significantly, it is through Japanese songs and dance that the play conveys Emiko's sense of transience and displacement; as Simon Firth observes, "Music seems to be a key to identity because it offers, so intensely, a sense of both self and others, of the subjective in the collective" (110). At the same time, the desert landscape within which Emiko locates herself as an exile reflects her interior landscape, a space doubly displaced, remote from both the Japanese American community and the larger U.S. society. *And the Soul* thus suggests both through musicality and the spaces of memory that "identity is *mobile*" (Firth 109); that is, that identity is not fixed.

Nonetheless, Emiko's desert symbolizes "the land of the perpetual beginning; of the place-no-place whose name and identity is not yet" (Bauman 21). In the final scene of the play, after Masako witnesses the "fantasy" of Emiko dancing to "And the Soul Shall Dance" while carrying a branch of sage, the American-born teenager then "picks up the branch Emiko has left" (174). By suggesting that Emiko's memory will haunt a second generation Masako, the dramatic finale offers a significant exploration of ethnic transgenerational memory, transformed as a particular historical location, to be reconstructed and re-articulated in a geo-political space not unlike the American desert.

Yamauchi's *The Music Lessons* also explores the conflict between an immigrant mother and her Japanese American daughter, a conflict rooted in differences of gender, ethnicity, and sexuality. Contrasting the memories and dreams of widowed Chizuko and her teen-age daughter Aki, *The Music Lessons* depicts this conflict through the competing attractions that they both feel for the Japanese male, itinerant Kaoru. Yet, as he hopes to become a violinist in the U.S., he can instruct Aki to play the violin. Through Aki's acceptance of music lessons from him as her means of self-representation, she comes to acknowledge her immigrant mother's memories and dreams; for Aki, they are "dead!" and her mother has "nothing to look forward to" (94). *The Music Lessons* thus reveals that it is not by separating from a mother's memory but rather through the "re-membrance" of her untold history that a daughter maps her particular historical location both within the Japanese American community and the larger American society.

Pursuing similar concerns, Chinese American Genny Lim narrates the histories of poor, oppressed, and exploited Chinese in such plays as *Paper Angels* (1978) and *Bitter Cane* (1989). *Paper Angels* concerns the Chinese experiences of "paper sons," who had to use false documents in emigrating to the U.S. because of the 1882 Chinese Exclusion Act—the first American immigration legislation to bar a particular race and class from entering the country. An old timer, Chin Gung, is a man "who's been in the United States long enough to cultivate American habits, but who's never lost his traditional Chinese values and outlook on life" (18). After a trip to China to bring back his wife, who has waited to join him for forty years, Chin Gung finds that upon re-entering America he is mistaken for one of the "paper sons." Ultimately, he commits suicide.

Speaking of America, Chin Gung insists, "[...] I know this land, I ache for her sometimes, like she was my woman [...]. If you treat her with respect, she responds, just like a woman. A lot of whites don't know this [...]" (40). What Gung refers to by this is "the propensity" of whites "to imagine an essentialized Asian American identity that 'generalizes Asian American identity as male'" (Lee, "'Speaking a Language That We Both Understand'" 149). His comment is itself a reflection of white cultural nationalism, a construct in which the land is cast as female and its ownership as well as American identity as male (Mason 232).

Like *Paper Angels*, *Bitter Cane* deals with the history of Chinese immigrants; the play exposes the system of oppression and exploitation prevailing at Hawaiian sugarcane plantations in the 1880s, within which people of color were relegated to hard labor, and women, in particular, to prostitution. Tracing the untold family history of its protagonist, the play reveals how this system was intricately related to the white, male desire to conquer and dominate both land and women.

In both *Paper Angels* and *Bitter Cane*, Lim challenges assumptions based on a gendered construction of American identity. By simultaneously narrating how lower-class Chinese women survive, resist, and cope with exploitation/victimization both in discriminatory U.S. immigration practices and patriarchal Chinese society, these plays suggest how important "an evocative memory that fills" one's "inner thoughts" (Lim, *Performing Asian America* 153) is in an untold history.

For instance, in Scene One of *Bitter Cane*, an old mother's voice emphatically articulates the importance of "the seeds of memory" in order to "break the cycle of pain" or "pursue another grievous lifetime" (165). These messages are closely intertwined with Lim's personal memory; Lim is herself a descendant of the detainees of the Angel Island in San Francisco. According to Velina Hasu Houston, "Lim calls history 'the repository of the memory, the memory of where we've been as people'" (*The Politics of Life* 159); Lim's plays similarly suggest that the mapping of ethnic memories comprises a means of deconstructing the imposed gendered and racialized identities accruing to location on, and the ownership of, American land.

This project of mapping memory within the contours of, in Lim's words, "dominant Western imperialistic society" (*The Politics of Life* 154) is "a process of reverse history" (Uno 12) that works to subvert the monolithic dominant conception of national identity, as well as the binary oppositions of gender and racial identity.

The most representative example of conquering the land and domination over it can be shown through memories related to histories of U.S. wars in Asia. They are well depicted in plays such as Wakako Yamauchi's *12-1-A* (1981), Japanese Amerasian Velina Hasu Houston's trilogy, *Asa Ga Kimashita (Morning Has Broken)* (1980), *American Dreams* (1983), and *Tea* (1983), and Filipino American Jeannie Barroga's *Walls* (1989). These plays provide concrete proof that Asia is viewed as feminized Other and Asians/Asian Americans are represented as Other in so-called mainstream culture.

This representational practice has complex roots in reminiscences of gendered wars conducted beyond U.S. borders, particularly World War II and the Vietnam War. Out of the effects of gender and race oppression/discrimination/exclusion related to war, there emerged a new conspiracy to suppress Asian American women as historically active agents within a structured system of hostilities. For instance, Yamauchi's *12-1-A* depicts the effects of this conspiracy in the imprisonment by race and gender for Japanese American women during World War II internment. Houston's trilogy also reflects a similar concern in the stories of her Japanese mother's long-concealed "war brides." Both Yamauchi and Houston attempt the deconstruction of the traditional gendered roles that are frequently depicted in the white male representation of war. More importantly, both artists also pursue the recasting of the U.S. national narrative into one that represents both the ethnic self and the historical subjectivity of Asian American women. They do so, moreover, through similar theatrical strategies of constructing a site for narrating untold history as gendered war.[2] What their untold histories reveal is that the discourses of gender and race are inextricably imbricated with the representation of national identity.

This imbrication is also evidenced in Jeannie Barroga's documentary play *Walls*, which examines the gendered history of the Vietnam War as, in Barroga's words, an "essentially racist war" from the perspective of women of color. Barroga deals with the process that led to the construction of the controversial Vietnam Veterans' Memorial in Washington D.C., a process deeply informed by memories of the war. It is noteworthy that in *Walls* Barroga includes a subplot centering on Maya Lin, the designer of the monument. This subplot serves the strategic purpose of resisting the stereotypical representation of Asian American women characteristic of dominant historical discourse, that is, the discourse of U.S. imperialism, which is conducted primarily from the white male perspective.

As far as the subplot is concerned, the actual Maya Lin—upon whom the character is based—is a Chinese American woman who, as a twenty-one-year-old undergraduate at Yale University, won the anonymous competition by which a design for the Vietnam War Memorial was selected. However, Vietnam War veterans opposed Lin's design for a black, abstract modernist, V-shaped monument, because they felt that it did not represent them. The heated national controversy that ensued was waged on both sides from their respective perspective of the war, a perspective that determined how the two black granite walls inscribed with the names of the American dead were to be interpreted. The veterans' objection to Lin's design was rooted in this Asian American woman's otherness of gender and race.

In *Walls*, Barroga examines the art war conducted between Maya Lin and the veterans, the differences that divided them (though both Lin and the veterans are marginalized), and finally, the role of the media in posing to the American audience the question of whether it was even

---

2   See Eriko Hara, "The Politics of Re-narrating History as Gendered War: Asian American Women's Theater," *The Journal of American and Canadian Studies* 18 (Tokyo: Institute of American and Canadian Studies/Sophia University, 2000): 37-49.

possible for a national monument designed by an Asian American woman to represent the American nation. At the core of the polemic is Lin's identity "as a citizen" who "continues to be located outside the cultural and racial boundaries of the nation" (Lowe 6). In regard to this issue, Marita Sturken observes, "In the debate, Lin's status as an American disappeared, and she became simply 'Asian'" (55). Resisting this erasure of Lin's status as an American, a voice in Act One, Scene One of *Walls* answers the questioning of Lin's ability to represent America definitively: "This [memorial] represents an entire war a nation meant to forget" (209). Barroga thus argues that as art, the Wall (as the memorial is often called) *does* represent memory and difference within the concept of nation, transcending the limitations of an Asian American woman's otherness.

By drawing attention to both the art war and discrimination/prejudice against women and people of color, Barroga's portrayal of memories of the Vietnam War reflects her intention of creating a stage whereupon the attempt can be made to break down "all the walls people build around themselves and between each other" (Stiehm 29). It is for this reason, beyond her subject matter of the Wall, that Barroga titles her work *Walls*. I contend that for Barroga, the symbolic walls of her title represent the complex mechanisms that define cultural and racial boundaries by which the Other is excluded from a seemingly monolithic American identity. As Lisa Lowe notes, "A national memory haunts the conception of the Asian American [...]" (6); as regards the memories that comprise American identity, at issue is the question not of "aesthetics but about to whom the memories belong" (Sturken 56).

In deconstructing an American identity that has been affected by the nation's politics of memory, *Walls* persuasively argues that the value of Lin's art was what made it worthwhile for her to speak out; as Sturken writes, "Lin emphasized her position as a[n] outsider by consistently referring to 'the integrity of my design'" (55). Barroga, therefore, reproduces Lin's comments on the Memorial faithfully:

> MAYA: [...] I just want to say this memorial is meant to be reflected on. People should be mesmerized. They should face it, approach it, and perceive the names before they read them. Touch them and realize in the black reflection they've touched something in themselves. They shouldn't just see a bunch of names or even a political statement. Even the process of killing the grass in order to build this is important. I meant to show what it's like to die. (221)

Barroga also consistently characterizes the Vietnam Veterans' Memorial of Lin's design as a de-gendered American cultural representation. In analyzing Lin's role in the power politics of the memory of the Vietnam

War, Barroga undoubtedly referred to her own experience as an outsider graphic artist in the white male-dominated art world.

By making the reporter an Asian American woman, as well as by her attempt at multiracial/multi-ethnic casting, the author of *Walls* furthermore suggests that her audience should acknowledge differences of gender and race. Even though characters such as "a ghost in fatigues" and "various offstage voices," including SOLDIERS 1 and 2, MAN, WOMEN, WWII VET, and HIPPIE (208), are invisible and thus marginalized onstage, *Walls* gives these characters voices, empowering them to speak up and be heard about their respective Vietnam War experiences. In the final scene, all of the characters in the play stand together in front of the self–reflective mirror of the Wall sharing space, time, memory, and a sense of the proximity of life and death; the audience is thus presented with a harmonious and totalizing reflection of a "multiethnic, multigendered, multi-abled America" (Lee, *Performing Asian America* 215).

Turning from documentary to autobiographical theater, second generation Chinese American Elizabeth Wong's *Letters to a Revolutionary Student* (1989) traces a ten-year correspondence between Bibi, a Chinese American reporter based loosely on Wong and Karen, a native Chinese woman. This correspondence starts in 1979 with their meeting in Tiananmen Square, and ends suggestively with the 1989 Tiananmen Massacre. In taking up the example of the Tiananmen Massacre, Rew Chow interrogates the legacies of European imperialism and colonialism, viewing media coverage of the Massacre as "another instance of Western imperialism dominating a 'third world' culture—this time by way of a claim to objective news-making" (165). Expanding upon this perspective, *Letters* is the first Western play to examine this tragic event in the context of Western imperialism.

In articulating varied issues of Western hegemony, *Letters* demonstrates clearly that the Massacre was closely related to both U.S. imperialism and internalized colonialism. This relationship is reflected specifically in the untold history of Karen, who becomes involved in the Tiananmen Square due to her belief that "a new China" will have "a system that will respect the individual" (304) in the manner of the American system. Karen's internalized American colonialism originates in the fixed American identity that was constructed in the political process of the American transition to independence, that is, from its status as European-colonized Other to that of sovereign nation-state founded on an ideology of democracy, freedom, and equality. Out of this process emerged a nation's history premised on the understanding that the heterosexual, patriarchal, Eurocentric perspective alone can represent national history perfectly; American history has thus been constructed exclusively in terms of Western white male subjectivity.

This process of constructing American identity entailed the ingenious mimicry and repetition of European patriarchy, and the colonization of those "who form the constitutive outside to the domain of the subject" (Butler, *Bodies that Matter* 3). In other words, *Letters* implies that internalized American colonialism has always been identified with European patriarchy. Such a fixed essentialist notion of American identity is gendered, and can be understood in terms of Judith Butler's notion of "performativity":

> The parodic repetition of gender exposes as well the illusion of gender identity as an intractable depth and inner substance. As the effects of a subtle and politically enforced performativity, gender is an "act," as it were, that is open to splittings, self-parody, self-criticism, and those hyperbolic exhibitions of "the natural" that, in their very exaggeration, reveal its fundamentally phantasmatic status. (*Gender Trouble* 146-47)

From this understanding of performativity, it follows that American identity is not predetermined and substantive. On the contrary, it is rather a result of performativity, appearing as it does "through a signifying practice" (*Gender Trouble* 145) that intensifies its political meaning. Butler assures us that this "signification is not a founding act, but rather a regulated process of repetition that both conceals itself and enforces its rules precisely through the production of substantializing effects" (*Gender Trouble* 145).

Letters pursues a strategy of first exposing the structure of the system by which White American identity is constructed, and of then resisting the representation of women of color as an embodiment of the Other. Over the course of the play, Bibi comes to recognize how she has identified with White American cultural identity through the influence of the American Dream and U.S. capitalism, and specifically through her travel to China, her relationship with Karen, and their decade-long correspondence. On the other hand, as her name reveals, "Karen" is a product of White American culture; Karen "chose" this "new name in secret" (277), she "—adopted an unofficial American name—" because of her belief in democracy and "Freedom of speech. Freedom to choose" (298). Yet, Karen is fully aware of neither multicultural America nor of America's character as "a nation of shoppers" (299), let alone of a monolithic American identity as such.

Reflecting the contrast between Bibi and Karen, the stage of *Letters* is set with "two separate areas representing China and the United States respectively," as well as a "center space" that "is a neutral territory wherein the rules of time and geography are broken" (268). Bibi and Karen place themselves in this borderland that is neither China nor the United States, but they also come and go constantly between the two separate areas. As a whole, this setting can also be understood to represent the binary oppositions of inside/outside, self/other, and subject/ object, as well as the borders dividing these concepts.

Thus, as Trinh maintains, the "to and fro movement" of Bibi and Karen, like their correspondence, connotes the possibility of a new form of subjectivity lying beyond the limitations of categorization and identity politics, "while unsettling every definition of otherness" (*When the Moon Waxes Red* 74). Karen says to Bibi, "[...] I look at you and it is as if I look at myself in a glass" (278); by using a self-reflective mirror to reveal that "You are me" (278), that is, that the self/other binary comprises an identity, Wong suggests that the American identity with which Karen hopes to identify is a gendered fantasy. In addition to Wong's use of chorus members who play multiple characters, the borderland setting of *Letters* represents a space to create an identity that is mobile and plural while encountering self and other. In Trinh's words, *Letters* provides a "mutual voyage into self and other," as well as a rethinking of "the fixed boundaries and the crossing-borders as a disturbing yet potentially empowering practice of difference" ("Other than myself/my other self" 21).

In 1990, several months after the Tiananmen Massacre, Bibi reads aloud her letter to Karen. At the end, she says, "I want you to know that I haven't forgotten you. [...] Love, Your Good Friend, Bibi" (308). Although this letter is meant to be torn up and not to be received by Karen, the play appeals to its audience to recognize the significance of narrating memory of the other in order to reorient the self. *Letters* thus becomes a portrait of memory for Karen, who says, "I want to be a part of history" (279), as well as an act of Chinese American self-representation for Bibi.

Consequently, the dramatic works of the Asian American women artists discussed here offer insight into a completely different paradigm, one (de)constructing American identity. The theater of these Asian American women posits what might be termed a "mutual" American identity forged in an ongoing dialogue between claiming America as home and imagining America as a nation, as well as through continual negotiation with Asian American identity and White American identity.[3] Locating this negotiation on a theatrical site enables the emergence of a new form of subjectivity, the subjectivity of de-colonized and de-essentialized self/other.

Similarly, Yamauchi, Lim, Houston, Barroga, and Wong conduct striking "mutual" dialogues between memory and history, inhabiting the

---

[3]   For further discussion on this point, see Dorinne Kondo, *About Face: Performing Race in Fashion and Theater* (New York: Routledge, 1997), 189-209; David Leiwei Li, *Imagining the Nation: Asian American Literature and Cultural Consent* (Stanford: Stanford UP, 1998), 185-203.

theatrical site with stories spun for untold numbers of individuals in "a large narrative" of U.S. history. These playwrights thus demonstrate the significance not only of reconsidering the differentiation of the national/transnational, cultural, ethnic, and racial, but also of transgressing gender borders and the boundaries of Eurocentric art. I argue that these Asian American women dramatists have attempted to perform a "vision" through self-representations that both deconstruct the hierarchy of the dominant culture and change its potential for artistic representation. Through their emphasis on fundamental conceptual questions of difference, these artists direct their audiences toward a greater awareness of the politics of representation and borders.

Regarding this awareness, Asian American activist-chronicler Helen Zia maintains that the Asian American heritage is a part of the American history which "every American should know" (313) and understand as a vision "that has sustained Americans from every shore" (317) in their dreams. In Zia's view, this represents "the memories of where we've come from, the lessons of what we've been through, and the visions of roads we have yet to walk in this land called America" (319). In this sense, the theater of the Asian American women considered here poses the question of American identity and multiculturalism: how can the American people map memory in the twenty-first century in order to cross the borders of "difference" by living their American dreams?

Works Cited

Barroga, Jeannie. *Walls. Unbroken Thread: An Anthology of Plays by American Women.* Ed. Roberta Uno. Amherst: U of Massachusetts P, 1993. 201-260.

Bauman, Zygmunt. "From Pilgrim to Tourist—or a Short History of Identity." *Questions of Cultural Identity.* Eds. Stuart Hall and Paul du Gay. London: SAGE Publications, 1996. 18-36.

Butler, Judith. *Gender Trouble: Feminism and the Subversion of Identity.* New York: Routledge, 1990.

_____. *Bodies That Matter: On the Discursive Limits of "Sex."* New York: Routledge, 1993.

Chow, Rew. *Writing Diaspora: Tactics of Intervention in Contemporary Cultural Studies.* Bloomington: Indianapolis UP, 1993.

Firth, Simon. "Music and Identity." *Questions of Cultural Identity.* Eds. Stuart Hall and Paul du Gay. London: SAGE Publications, 1996. 108-127.

Houston, Velina Hasu, ed. *The Politics of Life: Four Plays by Asian American Women.* Philadelphia: Temple UP, 1993.

_____. *Asa Ga Kimashita (Morning Has Broken). The Politics of Life.* 220-274.

Houston, Velina Hasu. *American Dreams.* Unpublished manuscript, 1983. 1-72.

_____. *Tea. Walls. Unbroken Thread: An Anthology of Plays by American Women.* Ed. Roberta Uno. Amherst: U of Massachusetts P, 1993. 155-200.

Kondo, Dorinee. *About Face: Performing Race in Fashion and Theater.* New York: Routledge, 1997.

Lee, Josephine. *Performing Asian America: Race and Ethnicity on the Contemporary Stage.* Philadelphia: Temple UP, 1997.

_____. "'Speaking a Language That We Both Understand': Reconciling Feminism and Cultural Nationalism in Asian American Theater." *Performing America: Cultural Nationalism in American Theater.* Eds. Jeffrey D. Mason and J. Ellen Gainor. Ann Arbor: U of Michigan P, 1999. 139-59.

Li, David Leiwei. *Imagining the Nation: Asian American Literature and Cultural Consent.* Stanford: Stanford UP, 1998.

Lim, Genny. *Bitter Cane. The Politics of Life: Four Plays by Asian American Women.* Ed. Velina Hasu Houston. Philadelphia: Temple UP, 1993. 151-204.

_____. *Paper Angels. Unbroken Thread: An Anthology of Plays by American Women.* Ed. Roberta Uno. Amherst: U of Massachusetts P, 1993. 18-52.

Ling, Amy, ed. *Yellow Light: The Flowering of Asian American Arts.* Philadelphia: Temple UP, 1999.

Lowe, Lisa. *Immigrant Acts: On Asian American Cultural Politics.* Durham: Duke UP, 1997.

Stiehm, Jamie. "Breaking down the Walls." *Palo Alto Weekly* (24 May 1994): 29.

Sturken, Marita. *Tangled Memories: The Vietnam War, the AIDS Epidemic, and the Politics of Remembering.* Berkeley: U of California P, 1997.

Trinh, Min-ha T. *When the Moon Waxes Red: Representation, Gender and Cultural Politics.* New York: Routledge, 1991.

_____. "Other than myself/my other self." *Traveller's Tales: Narratives of Home and Displacement.* Ed. George Robertson. New York: Routledge, 1994.

Takaki, Ronald. *A Different Mirror: A History of Multicultural America.* Boston: Little, Brown and Co., 1993.

Wong, Elizabeth. *Letters to a Student Revolutionary. Unbroken Thread: An Anthology of Plays by American Women.* Ed. Roberta Uno. Amherst: U of Massachusetts P, 1993. 261-308.

Yamauchi, Wakako. *And the Soul Shall Dance. Between Worlds: Contemporary Asian American Plays.* Ed. Misha Berson. New York: Theatre Communications Group, 1990. 128-74.

_____. *The Music Lessons. Unbroken Thread: An Anthology of Plays by American Women.* Ed. Roberta Uno. Amherst: U of Massachusetts P, 1993. 53-104.

_____. *12-1-A. The Politics of Life: Four Plays by Asian American Women.* Ed. Velina Hasu Houston. Philadelphia: Temple UP, 1993. 46-100.

Zia, Helen. *Asian American Dreams: The Emergence of an American People.* New York: Farrar, Straus and Giroux, 2000.

"Imagine All the People"

Hip Hop, Post-multiculturalism, and Solo Performance in the United States

Robert H. VORLICKY

Tisch School of the Arts, New York University

When in 1992 Anna Deavere Smith exploded onto the United States theatrical landscape with *Fires in the Mirror*, the press, commercial and regional theatres, and academic communities hailed her artistic undertaking—her solo docudrama about the tragedy in Crown Heights, Brooklyn—as a new genre, a new American-inflected theatre. The title of this essay pays tribute to Smith's achievement, as well as to those of John Lennon, David Henry Hwang, Danny Hoch, and Sarah Jones— other middle- to late-twentieth-century artists who explore the range of representations and possible presentations when one's body and voice are alone on stage.

In her search for American character through the *On the Road* series (over twenty different performances which began in 1982 and include *House Arrest* [2000]), Anna Deavere Smith has given voice on the United States stage to many of the previously unheard, the once predictably under-represented. In her docudramas, she has transcribed interviews with actual people, shaped the conversations into reality-based fiction (or plays), and presented as well as performed *her* drama constituted from reformulated "characters." In the live performance of these, Smith does not try to embody or become another person. Rather, her primary goal as a performer is to capture the *voice* of her subject: his/her tone, rhythm pattern, pitch variations—from the striking characteristics to the nuances that individualize the sound of one's speaking voice. She does not imitate her subjects in an Aristotelian fashion, nor does she approach her work from a Stanislavskian, psychological perspective. Rather, she desires to convey an "essence" of her characters through her imitation of speech patterns. "I can learn to know who somebody is, not from what they tell me," concludes Smith, "but from *how* they tell me. [...] My goal would be to [...] become possessed, *so to speak*, of the person" ("Word" 51; emphasis added).

Language, for Smith, constitutes her "major fascination in the world" ("Word" 55). It is through language that one can act, can "become the other. [Yet] to acknowledge the other, you have to acknowledge yourself" ("Word" 51). Voice, in turn, conveys character. To create characters, Smith assumes that her body—specifically the voice within her body—will respond to the speech patterns of her subjects: the artist repeats the words until she "begins to feel [the subject's] *song*" and that helps her to "remember more about [the subject's] body" ("Word" 57).

No voice seems to be beyond the range of Smith's skillful method of repeating sound and language. In *Fires in the Mirror*, she transforms vocally from a Lubavitcher woman to a teenage Haitian girl, an Australian Jewish man, a Black "bad boy," and from a Russian Jewish mother to such recognizable public figures as Angela Davis and Reverend Al Sharpton. Unshackled from the burden of conventional mimetic representation—one that presumes that she will "inhabit" the body of her Other from sex and racial markings to ethnicity and age—Smith "presents" in docudramatic context a fictionalized schema of her highly edited, diversified subjects. Her bold form of theatre—whereby a sexualized, racialized body presents a panoply of voices that constitute fictionalized characters of the actor's "others" on stage—has connected with a growing audience in the United States.

Smith's public—which started to take identifiable shape in the post-Reagan years as her work moved from New York's Public Theatre to Broadway, and from the pages of scholarly journals to *Time* magazine—has spilled over into the artistry of other soloists who specialize in the creation of multiple characters. Quite specifically and importantly, there are characters whose sex, race, age, ethnicity—to name only a few features—do not reflect those of the performer. To define the audience drawn to these performances may seem, at first, insignificant. And yet, it is the composition of these spectators and their reception of this "new genre" that have slipped by many critics. It is an eclectic, heterogeneous group—one whose ages range from youth in secondary schools to senior citizens, many of whom have been exposed to feminism, interrogations of race and class, democratic socialism (whether theoretically or through lived experience), capitalism, exploitation, technology, pop culture, music, travel, hip hop and its "poetry," the fluidity of daily living, classroom and street knowledge, violence, hype, and a constant barrage of words and images that saturate day-to-day living in United States culture. Anna Deavare Smith's spectatorship represents what many of us have come to experience with steady consistency as the twenty-first-century U.S. urban audience.

Arguably, the most influential feature of Anna Deavere Smith's work that has had tremendous impact on a new generation of solo performers is an extension of artistic license whereby the individual body claims the stage and presents, as a soloist, a range of (fictive) lives other than her own—characters who cross any identifiable or presumed boundaries of the performer's own embodied sex, race, ethnicity, and age. In turn, the performer is able "to pass language back and forth across borders," which is a primary goal of Smith's artistry ("Word" 59).

Two of the United States' most dynamic soloists to advance Smith's original breakthrough in performance practice are Danny Hoch (who, like Smith, is now also a stage, television, and movie talent) and Sarah Jones (a stage and film performer, and National Poetry Slam winner). At the brink of 2002, their audiences are not unlike those of Anna Deavere Smith's, yet they have also noticeably expanded upon Smith's base to include a sizable portion of people who are part of, on the one hand, what performance artist Guillermo Gómez-Peña identifies as the "Fourth World" (7) and, on the other hand, what has been coined in the mid-1990s as "hip-hop theatre."

In order to contextualize Danny Hoch's and Sarah Jones's solo performances and thereby differentiate their work from Anna Deavere Smith's, I shall first turn to Gómez-Peña to identify and to locate the eclectic spectatorship that now exists in United States theatre—perhaps its most diversified since the 1960s—and I shall examine the emergence of hip-hop "culture" that liberates solo bodies in theatrical performance.

In his essay, "The Free Trade Agreement," Gómez-Peña argues that "[i]n reaction to the transculture imposed from above, a new essentialist culture is emerging, one that advocates national, ethnic, and gender separatism in the quest for cultural autonomy" (11). His activist reaction to this drive for a homogenized global culture reads as follows: "a grassroots cultural response that understands the contextual and strategic value of nationalism, as well as the importance of crossing borders and establishing cross-cultural alliances" (11). While suggesting a political strategy to combat essentialism through "cross-cultural alliances," Gómez-Peña also intimates a kind of performance practice that I see happening in Danny Hoch's and Sarah Jones's solo work. Gómez-Peña anticipates this association when he suggests the rise of a "hybrid culture"—or a Fourth World—in the United States: "the hybrid"—who is cross-racial, polylinguistic, and multicontextual—"expropriates elements from all sides to create more open and fluid systems. Hybrid culture," within which I would identify *hybrid performance practice*, "is community-based yet experimental, radical but not static or dogmatic [...] [and it] fuses [...] the problematic notions of self and other" (11-12).

Gómez-Peña's postulate is worth quoting at length in order to more fully appreciate its interconnectedness to performance practice. He argues:

> An ability to understand the hybrid nature of culture develops from an experience of dealing with a dominant culture from the outside. The artist who understands and practices hybridity in this way can be at the same time an insider and an outsider, an expert in border crossings, a temporary member of multiple communities, a citizen of two or more nations. S/he performs multiple roles in multiple contexts. [...] S/he speaks from more than one perspective, to more than one community, about more than one reality. His/her job is to trespass, bridge, interconnect, reinterpret, remap, and redefine; to find the outer limits of his/her culture and cross them. (12)

In November 2000, playwright David Henry Hwang, speaking to my students at New York University, identified his version of Gómez-Peña's "hybridic artist" as one who is a "post-multiculturalist"—one who is aware of *and/or* actually embodies the (complexities of the) *construction* of racial, ethnic, and/or gendered categories. This acknowledgement, however, does not presume that the articulation and the aliveness of hybridity erase the subjectivity of those who are traditionally considered marginalized. In critically revealing ways, it is not dissimilar from locating cultural identity within the (psychic) spaces suggested by intersubjectivity (Benjamin 19-24, 221-224). Clearly, both Hwang and Gómez-Peña see a major shift in identity politics and its impact on staged representation and presentation in the United States. They raise a central issue about the "place" of subjectivity in contemporary performance in a post-multicultural theatre practice. This theorization materializes in the 1990s through the work of several major solo performers—including Danny Hoch and Sarah Jones—who engage in hybrid performance practice, a style marked by its post-multicultural, hip-hop theatrical influences.[1]

"Hybrid culture" might just as easily have been Danny Hoch's phrase when describing his neighborhood in the "Introduction" to his Obie award-winning 1994 solo, *Some People*: "I'm a third-generation New Yorker, lucky enough to grow up during the birth of Hip-Hop culture in a towering brick-and-asphalt outer-borough neighborhood, where there was no racial majority or minority" (xi). Citing both solo theatre's roots in pre-Roman and Greek culture and its relationship most

---

[1]   Arguably, the genealogy of solo hip-hop theatre originates in the United States with the writings of playwright Adrienne Kennedy. Current hybrid performance practice is indeed greatly indebted to the pioneering theatrical experimentation by Adrienne Kennedy. Beginning with *Funnyhouse of a Negro* (1964), Kennedy utilized postmodern techniques (such as pastiche, multivocality, fragmentation, transformation, as well as sex and race changes) and theatricals that—nearly forty years later—would become a foundation for hip-hop theatre in the 1990s.

dynamically to the African griot, Hoch is wholly committed to "theatre [that] is *about* language. Oral, physical, and spiritual language," which invigorates him to create, "oral theatre, the ancient way, but with modern themes and today's language" (xi-xii).

Surveying the landscape of United States culture in the 1990s and commenting on its theatrical history, Hoch surmises that Americans are

not terribly familiar with solo theatre. We are, however, accustomed to stand-up comedians, talk-show hosts, mimes, magicians, politicians, rabbis and priests. Those are the solo performers we are accustomed to. Well, I wanted to be an urban griot for the communities of urban North America. I don't tape-record or interview people to then play them on stage. A few people think I am some anthropological/theatrical case-study guy. *This is my world!* These are my inner monologues, layered composites of stories and voices from me, my family, my neighborhood, my people. I think all the hoopla about my work comes from people not being accustomed to seeing traditionally *peripheral* characters in a center-stage setting. Well, these characters are center-stage in *my* world." (xiv, italics added)

Hoch deliberately separates himself from the performance practices of Anna Deavere Smith. Unlike Smith—who mixes and matches characters from the various centers and margins of United States culture— Hoch is committed to presenting on stage "some people," those who remain traditionally marked as peripheral characters. Among them, in *Some People*, are a live-wired Carribean DJ; a good-natured Polish handyman; an egomaniacal guy from New Jersey; a young, sexy Latina; a grieving, elderly Puerto Rican father; and an outspoken Jewish mother. His subsequent work, including *Jails, Hospitals, & Hip-Hop* (1998), continues to focus on those who are marginalized within the dominant social power structure.

What is critical to note, however, is Hoch's previous reference to the "hoopla about [his] work" (xiv). His remark relates to the subsequent interest that "Hollywood people" had in him (after *Some People*) as a writer and actor in television and film (xv), offers that he continues, in general, to bypass.[2] But the "hoopla" also refers to the undercurrent of criticism that surfaced about Hoch's work in public post-performance discussions or panels and (some) academic scholarship: who, after all, is this straight white man to be "playing" African American men, Latinas, or Jamaicans? Is his work simply minstrelsy legitimized through a kind of assimilated hip-hop theatrical aesthetics? Is it misogynist and racist in its portraits of women—a drag performance void of political, social consciousness?

---

[2]   He filmed *Some People* for an HBO-TV premiere in 1998, however, and he released an independently produced film version of *Jails, Hospitals & Hip Hop* in October 2001.

While participating in a panel discussion on "Cultural Appropriations" that I attended at New York's Joseph Papp Public Theatre on
October 24, 1994, Danny Hoch was asked by an African American
woman in the audience about his "right to represent blacks" on stage.
The question, certainly a legitimate one in its impulse to challenge the
borders of representation, reminds me today of the now infamous
August Wilson-Robert Brustein public exchange in 1996 that focused,
in print, on the colonizing impulse versus the worthy merits of multicultural casting (Wilson; Brustein). Essentially, the young woman at the
Public Theatre went to the heart of one facet of the issue of cross-racial,
cross-gender, cross-ethnic, cross-sexual casting—a facet that is embedded in the performance of any solo artist who does not do autoperfor-
mance. In this case, how can the white man's body "represent" its
"other"? Hoch's answer, measured and direct, demonstrated not only
that he had been asked this question before, but that it was, in fact, a
crucial realization that he had had to come to prior to this moment—in
order to understand why he does what he does on stage: "I never represent someone else," he replied, "I can only *present* characters whose
voices I hear and then, as an actor, bring them to stage-life through my
voice and body."

Like Anna Deavere Smith, the voices of his people are a source of
inspiration. But unlike Smith, whose sources are recorded *in* life, Hoch
is inspired *by* life, by the sounds and languages of his "hybrid[ic] cultural" background, recalling Gómez-Peña's assertion about the already
thriving Fourth World, or David Henry Hwang's "post-multicultural"
society. Like his contemporary, Sarah Jones, Hoch lives in the bodies—
as well as in the voices—of his characters while on stage. The highly
selective detail in physical work evidenced in his performance style is
pivotal to the individualization of each character he creates: gestures,
facial expressions, and activities accompany the attention paid to the
rhythm, tempo, pitch, volume, and variance in his vocal delivery.

Michael Peterson identifies three key aspects of the politics of
Hoch's show, the first one being

> a function of the greater diversity of characterization, coupled with an atten-
> tion to linguistics where some performers might concentrate on accent. [...]
> [Hoch creates] the performance of cultural fluency. (165-66)

The second aspect discerned by Peterson is the" structure of the individual character" (166).

> In standing center stage with these characters, Hoch perhaps decenters the
> straight white male authorial and spectatorial presence. (169)

To which he adds as a third element "[t]he place of the performer's self
in the work" (169). Peterson's observations are astute and extremely

helpful in linking Hoch's work back to its roots in hip hop: Hoch's diversity of characters; his attention to linguistics, to the poetry of languages, his experience with and presentation of cultural fluency; his ability to "decenter" the straight white male's authority without denying his body's whiteness; and the inspiration of his own "cultural hybridity," which gives him passage through any number of performances of race, sex, class, ethnicity, and age. Unlike Anna Deavere Smith whose tape recordings inspire her collage of stage portraits, Hoch's neighborhood moves right onto the stage and remains until, like Prospero's action, the spell woven by the artist's imagination is broken by the audience's applause. It is the sound of urban life that drives Hoch's monologues, the lyrics of his hip-hop aesthetics, and the politics of his version of hip-hop theatre.

Hip-hop theatre, Holly Bass reminds us, like "hip-hop music and culture,"

is not a genre that sprang up overnight. The music itself has been around for over twenty years and has always contained a strong theatrical element. The Broadway hit *Bring in'Da Noise, Bring in 'Da Funk*, with its rhyme-heavy libretto penned by "hip-hop poet" Reg E. Gaines, introduced the hip-hop aesthetic to a vast mainstream audience in the early 1990s. (18)

But what exactly *is* hip-hop theatre? "Like the music," Bass notes,

it means different things to different people. [Playwright Robert] Alexander defines it as theatre informed by the sensibilities of rap music, just as August Wilson's plays are informed by the blues, or Ntozake Shange's works by jazz. "For something to be truly a hip-hop theatre piece it has to contain certain elements of schizophrenia and rebellion, creativity and destruction," Alexander elaborates. "There has to be a marriage between heaven and hell, light and dark, revolution and complacency and all of our various contradictions, whether it's a performance piece or a traditional play with dialogue." (18)

Central to Bass's analysis is the identification of the stage "conventions," so to speak, in hip-hop theatre that involves more than one "character." Bass contends that the "four cornerstones of the culture," and therefore of hip-hop theatre, are: (1) emcee-ing (i.e., rapping, rhyming), (2) deejay-ing [one's use of two turntables and a microphone], (3) graffiti art, and (4) breakdancing (18-19). These four elements, I suggest, are not required features of solo hip-hop performance, which I identify within the context of this essay as a *solo hybrid performance (practice)*.

For Hoch—and for his contemporary Sarah Jones—hip-hop theatre speaks to the people of Gómez-Peña's Fourth World—which is also a conceptual space, one that can be and is inhabited by *some people* from the First and Third Worlds. "Hip-Hop Theatre is the most relevant and timely theatre that exists in America today," Hoch wrote in his welcome to the First New York City Hip-Hop Theatre Festival (*First* 1), which he curated during the summer of 2000 at the East Village's renowned PS 122. Hoch produced the festival, which showcased for ten weeks, among other hip-hop performers, twenty-six-year-old poet/actor/playwright Sarah Jones in her solo, *Surface Transit*, a play composed of eight different characters. Jones's drama includes an array of men characters, from a homophobic Italian American cop to a bitter white supremacist and a frustrated black rapper; among the women are an African American homeless woman from the southern states, a white Russian immigrant speaking to her biracial daughter, a young Black English woman, a Jewish mother, and a ghetto girl.

For Jones, this gig was a publicity coup—it followed right upon the heels of her highly publicized, standing-room-only solo play, *Women Can't Wait*, performed at the United Nations during the International Conference on Women in June 2000. This gripping piece focuses on eight different women from around the world, who are subject to laws that violate their human rights. Using only one prop, "a diaphanous shawl" to cover her head, to tie around her neck or waist, or to toss over her shoulder, Jones becomes an "international population": from a "timid woman from India working up the courage to talk about beatings by her husband" to a "vivacious Frenchwoman defying laws against women working at night," Jones also brings to stage life women from Japan, Jordan, Uruguay, Israel, Kenya, and the United States (Crossette 1).

Jones's latest piece, *Waking the American Dream*, commissioned by the National Immigration Forum (a grantee of the Ford Foundation), is to premiere in February 2002. Subsequently, it will be videotaped and broadcast on public television. This will be the first piece of Jones's to be publicly available, since her solos are currently neither published nor on film. *Waking the Dream* was initially to open in December 2001, but it was delayed in response to the World Trade Center disaster on September 11, 2001 in New York City. The writer-actor expects the finished piece to include immigrants' reflections upon this national tragedy.

Addressing why hip-hop and specifically a talent in hip-hop theatre like Sarah Jones burst forth onto the United States cultural landscape, Danny Hoch concludes unequivocally: "precisely BECAUSE we were ignored." He continues:

> Our neighborhoods were ignored, our language, our accents, our struggles. Our teachers dragged us to see productions of Shakespeare and *Cat on a Hot Tin Roof*, and *Our Town*, as if that was the only culture that was important, the only perspective that mattered. But us kids had an entirely different per-

spective that was being shaped by Reaganomics, Eighties greed, Corporate and Police assault on our communities, accelerating technology and yes ... Disco. We as a generation need theatre that is by, about, and FOR us. We also need to be INVITED, and we need to be able to afford theatre. (*First* 1)

I must qualify Hoch's assertion about his audience, and ostensibly that of Sarah Jones's and other gifted hip-hop theatre practitioners. While the generation about which Hoch speaks may well need a "theatre that is by, about, and for [them]," his audience—and Jones's audience upon the three occasions I saw *Surface Transit*—constitutes one of the most diversified gatherings of people I have been with during my many years of theatergoing. Absolutely no single profile characterizes their audiences—spectators were of a noticeable array of ages, races, and ethnicities. The presence of so many different patrons in one theatre space to see plays proved exhilarating and with limited precedence. My observation is not unlike that of Psalmayene 24, a hip-hop writer/performer, who said during the 1999 National Black Theatre Festival in Winston-Salem, North Carolina, "It's really an organic movement for hip-hop to go into the theatre and theatre to go into hip-hop. [...] Theatre is a reflection of the culture. If it's jazz time, you're gonna have jazz plays. We're bridging the gap between youth and our elders, and the momentum is going to continue to build" (Bass 19).

Rather than position the hip-hop theatre of Danny Hoch and Sarah Jones as speaking to or for particular groups, they speak *with* an audience about lives that appear either familiar to them or lives that they can readily imagine. The diversified audiences before these performers gather the silent listeners who are already contextualized within the various speakers' narratives. Regardless of their age, sex, sexuality, or race, they know the difference between Reaganomics and a federal government's commitment to all the people, they know racial profiling exists when police indiscriminately arrest citizens, they know the greed of the 1980s, and yes, they even know that the lyrics of disco are frivolous. Performing before just such an audience, Hoch and Jones know and trust, intrinsically, that their own marked bodies can *present* the vast range of their "others" by paying attention to the details of their characters' language usage, verbal expression, physical movement, and "soul"—the fictional site of a character's sense of truth, of spirit, of its imagined "humanness."

Hip-hop solo theatre captures the destabilizing identity of its singular subjects through performance strategies that destabilize the performing body. It is a powerful theatrical choice, one that does not underestimate the destabilized identities of its diverse spectators who—when in the presence of a text and a performance that takes them seriously—eagerly embrace the opportunity to imagine, to listen to fictive lives other than theirs. In this way, spectators, as well as performers, search for opportunities to live both inside and outside their own bodies. The circular nature of theatre production—a world of endless reciprocity—encourages this dynamic possibility between performer and spectator, between art and the streets.

White straight man—Danny Hoch—presents a straight, sexually active Latina, who speaks about her black, gay roommate living with AIDS. Black straight woman—Sarah Jones—presents a homophobic, misogynist Italian-American policeman, who speaks about his physical abuse of a Black English woman at customs in a New York airport. These particular "characterizations" feature no hip-hop theatrical conventions: no rappings, deejaying, graffiti art, or breakdancing (Bass 18). Present, however, are sexually, racially marked "solo" actors' bodies that cross borders of sex and race—through voice and movement— in the process of theatre making. These artists are at the edge of radical theatre performance. In turn, they bring spectators to the edge of their imaginations and then they ask us to take the leap: a leap that solo hip-hop theatre advances, a leap that post-multicultural presentations contextualize, and a leap that cannot be presumed to threaten the postmodern spectator's already "decentered" logic or position. Very simply, solo hip-hop theatre makes sense of the hybrid culture we know as the United States—a culture that has become increasingly more fluid, borderless, and in flux, as have the identities of its inhabitants. It is a theatre of liberation that "imagines *all* the people" on the body of one.

Works Cited

Bass, Holly. "Blowin' Up the Set." *American Theatre* (November 1999): 18-20.

Benjamin, Jessica. *The Bounds of Love: Psychoanalysis, Feminism, and the Problem of Domination.* New York: Pantheon, 1988.

Brustein, Robert. "Subsidized Separatism." *American Theatre* (October 1996): 26+.

Crossette, Barbara. "All Her Stage Is a World; Its Women Call for Justice." *New York Times* 7 June 2000, late ed.: D1+.

First NYC Hip-Hop Theatre Festival. New York: Caseroc Productions, 2000.

Gómez-Peña, Guillermo. *The New World Border: Prophecies, Poems, and Loqueras for the End of the Century.* San Francisco: City Lights, 1996.

Hoch, Danny. *Some People.* New York: Caseroc Productions, 1998.

Jones, Sarah. *Surface Transit.* Unpublished manuscript, 2000.

Peterson, Michael. *Straight White Male: Performance Art Monologues.* UP of Mississippi, 1997.

Smith, Anna Deavere. *Fires in the Mirror.* New York: Doubleday, 1993.

_____. "The Word Becomes You." Interview with Carol Martin. *The Drama Review* 37.4 (1993): 45-62.

Wilson, August. "Common Ground." *American Theatre* (September 1996): 14+.

Irish Disconnections with the Former British Empire: Thomas Kilroy's Adaptation of *The Seagull*

Thierry DUBOST

Université de Caen

In the course of the twentieth century, the relationship between Ireland and England was significantly altered, with climatic crises such as the Easter Rising of 1916, the war of Independence, and also the repetitive tragic events that have characterised life in Northern Ireland since the late 1960s.[1] In Ulster, the place where tensions are still acute, many Catholics regard themselves as the victims of a persistent and lurking form of colonialism, while some Protestants pride themselves on their attachment to the former Empire. Repeated, intense political crises have left their mark on people, but also on art and artists, among whom there is Tom Kilroy, whose plays and adaptations of dramatic works such as Chekhov's *The Seagull* echo past and present conflicts resulting from Ireland's colonial history.

Born in 1934 in Callan, County Kilkenny, Thomas Kilroy is the author of eight plays, a novel, and three adaptations. His theatre breaks away from realism by exposing its artificial nature in numerous ways, a general approach that helps him deconstruct reality. His distancing techniques reinforce comedy or, on the contrary, provide depth to usually one-sided visions, which he displays as mere perspectives on one issue, thus forcing the audience to (re)consider more critically the ambiguous events staged. As an intellectual—he was a professor at University College Dublin and then at the University of Galway—he

---

[1] Whether they live in the Free State (cf. "Do you know, I believe we simply reached a crossroads somewhere in Ulster. Someone mentioned the Free State. The name beckoned. So here we are!" [Kilroy *The Madame MacAdam Travelling Theatre* 2]) or in Ulster, Irish people's outlook on their connection with the former colonial power plays an essential part in the way they define themselves. Living in the South or in the North also has consequences in the way individuals claim or reject their Irish identity. While some define themselves as citizens of a free state—a former colony of the British Empire—others, in Ulster, often have conflicting visions of who they are.

knows the importance of Ireland's colonial past and is acutely aware of
the tragic consequences of the cultural divide between opposite religious
groups. As a playwright, he committed himself to the promotion of a
better understanding between the two communities when he joined Field
Day, the theatre group that Brian Friel and Stephen Rea had created in
Derry with a definite political intent. Each year, a new play would tour
from the North of Ireland to the South, a significant political gesture
aimed at bridging gaps between communities in conflict.[2] Two of
Kilroy's plays were selected and produced by Field Day: *Double Cross*
in 1985, and *The Madame MacAdam Travelling Theatre* in 1991. Both
were performed throughout Ireland, providing spectators with elements
of reflection regarding their identity, play-acting, and the lethal consequences of self-delusion.

While not restricting the scope of his dramatic quest to the issue of
Irish identity, Thomas Kilroy devoted considerable attention to the
relationship between Ireland and England, starting with his first play,
The O'Neill. Staging the story of Hugh O'Neill, Count of Tyrone who
was beaten by the English at the battle of Kinsale in 1601, he questions
the fake, simplistic coherence of history. Through Hugh O'Neill's
undoing, he exposes the various layers of delusion and connects them,
almost accusingly, to Ireland's colonial history, to the waste of human
lives resulting from people's absolute beliefs.[3] Another play, *Double
Cross,* stages two Irishmen, William Joyce and Brendan Bracken, who
joined opposite sides during the Second World War in order to fight
with or against the English. Here again, Thomas Kilroy challenges the
very coherence of the motives that led the characters to such extreme
choices. In his other plays, the Anglo-Irish connection sometimes
provides a background to the action, or is merely alluded to.

Some of his personal writings supply valuable information regarding
his vision of relationships between England and Ireland; however,
because his adaptation of *The Seagull* initially constitutes a rewriting of
colonial history, a study of Kilroy's standpoint as an adapter of Chekhov
may prove even more rewarding than a reflection on his original works.
To understand some of his perspectives on Ireland's colonial and post-
colonial history, the reasons which pushed Kilroy to make the literary

---

[2] Field Day's political stance clearly transpires from the following statement: "All the
directors are northerners; they believed that Field Day could and should contribute to
the solution of the present crisis by producing analyses of the established opinions,
myths and stereotypes which had become both a symptom and a cause of the current
situation." (Field Day Theatre Company *Ireland's Field Day* (London: Hutchinson,
1985) vii).

[3] On that matter, see Thierry Dubost, *"The O'Neill*: premiers regards sur l'identité
irlandaise," *Le théâtre de Thomas Kilroy* (Caen: Presses Universitaires de Caen,
2001) 13-28.

choice of adapting *The Seagull* will be analysed. Indeed, the fact that Kilroy referred himself to a famous play instead of writing a new one provides a number of clues, not only on his own status as a playwright who adapts plays, but also with regard to the new trends informing the relationship between Irish and world drama. The next question that comes to mind is how Kilroy's adaptation of *The Seagull* to an Irish colonial context sheds light on his uncommon perception of past connections with the former British Empire. Finally, beyond the playwright's personal or literary motives, the political significance of his work on *The Seagull* needs to be examined in a context of connections with or disconnection from the former British Empire.

In 1981, Max Stafford Clark, an English artistic director at the Royal Court Theatre in London asked Kilroy to write an adaptation of *The Seagull*. This initial request—which some might be tempted to view as an extended form of colonialism—cannot be considered a remainder of such a process, since it went exactly in the opposite direction, as will be shown further on. The reasons why an author translates the literary production of a foreign writer differ from artist to artist. Still, they can be roughly explained by a wish to give one's fellow citizens access to the specific works of an author, whom the translator deems important on a number of grounds. As far as the decision to adapt a foreign masterpiece is concerned, the motives for such a commitment can less easily be explained, since the works of the foreign author in question are already available to the public. No single answer may prevail, but undoubtedly, through his particular dialogue with Chekhov, Kilroy found the means of redefining past and present Anglo-Irish relationships.

To start with, one should note that a dramatist's willingness to adapt plays constitutes one of his distinguishing traits. Indeed, it forms an integral part of the process of self-definition as a writer in general and as an *Irish* writer in particular. Through his renewed approach to this foreign play, Thomas Kilroy found himself in the position to play a role close to the almost creative one of translators, since his adaptation—as opposed to previous translations—gave an Irish touch to otherwise English-sounding texts. In the Irish playwright's own words:

> Max felt, and I agreed with him, that some English language productions of Chekhov tended towards a very English gentility where the socially specific Chekhov tended to be lost in polite vagueness. He believed that an Anglo-Irish setting would provide specificity, at once removed from, and at the same time comprehensible to an English audience. He also felt that an Irish setting would more easily allow the rawness of passion of the original to emerge, the kind of semi-farcical hysteria, which Chekhov uses in the

scenes between Arkadina, Treplyov and Trigorin in Act Three [...]. ("Adaptation" 80)[4]

Furthermore, what Kilroy wrote in his preface to the play about Max Stafford Clark's offer indirectly relates to Ireland's colonial history:

> [...] I was well aware that the history of drama is a history of adaptations. The good adaptation is always a substantial tribute to its original and it should send us back to that original with an enhanced view of it, as I hope this version will do. ("Introduction" 12)

The perspective put forward—being part of a general culture, a stage in the history of drama—sheds some light on the nature of Kilroy's complex undertaking. This quotation becomes even more significant if one thinks of *Tea and Sex and Shakespeare*—a comedy in which he had humorously depicted a young playwright's unsuccessful attempt at eradicating compulsory English cultural references, when he tried to assert himself as a writer by lessening Shakespeare's influence on his works. Kilroy's serious approach to Chekhov partakes of the same idea as that described in *Tea and Sex and Shakespeare*. Indeed, at a social level, adapting plays that do not belong to a specific English heritage opens new doors to an extended literary fund that, so far, had only been available to Irish people through the frame of English culture. On that matter, it is worth noticing that other major Irish playwrights such as Brian Friel and Frank MacGuinness have taken the same path and adapted famous works by foreign writers.[5] Thereby, each playwright connects himself with his illustrious predecessors, but socially, individual accomplishments take a wider significance. They also indicate that new cultural perspectives are emerging in Ireland in relation to world drama, through a literary disconnection from the former British Empire.

Regarding Kilroy's involvement, one should remember that adapting plays can be a risky venture in terms of ensuing publications. This is unfortunately proven by the fact that his two other adaptations—one of Ibsen's *Ghosts*, and another one of Pirandello's *Six Characters in Search of an Author*—have not been published. His work on *The Seagull*, though, was published, even if, at the time, about ten translations

---

[4]   Other critics have commented on Kilroy's adaptation of Chekhov: see, for instance, Frank McGuinness "A Voice from the Trees: Thomas Kilroy's Version of Chekhov's *The Seagull*," *Irish University Review: A Journal of Irish Studies* 21.1 (Spring-Summer 1992): 3-14; and also, Joseph Long "An Irish Seagull: Chekhov and the New Irish Theatre," *Revue de Littérature Comparée* 4 (Oct./Dec. 1995): 419-26.

[5]   See, for instance, Brian Friel's adaptations of *Three Sisters* and *Uncle Vanya* (After Chekhov). Also see Frank McGuinness' adaptations of Ibsen's *Rosmersholm, Peer Gynt, Hedda Gabler, A Doll's House*; Chekhov's *Three Sisters, Uncle Vanya*; Lorca's *Yerma*; Brecht's *The Caucasian Chalk Circle*; Sophocles' *Electra*; and Ostrovsky's *The Storm*.

were available to the public. Regarding his choice of authors and plays, one notes that family relationships and crises, together with people's connection with society at large, bring indirect echoes of a paradoxically close Irish world. At a wider cultural level, the professor's presence is felt behind that of the playwright. Indeed, plays such as *Six Characters in Search of an Author* added to the culture of theatregoers, who may have been unfamiliar with daring works that challenged conventional opinions of what theatre should be.[6] Consciously or not, Kilroy's creation of cultural landmarks that are initially alien to British culture reinforces his disconnection with the former British Empire.

Besides experimenting with the theatrical genre and offering a reflection on art, Chekhov's *Seagull* and Kilroy's adaptation also present parallels at the social and political levels. The painful economic situation of the Anglo-Irish in the West of Ireland in the late 1870s strongly echoes that of Chekhov's gentry. For instance, the Big House[7] becomes a focal point where people from all walks of life meet, in an atmosphere that forebodes feared changes and characterises a dying world. The signs of impotence reflecting common impoverishment are also reinforced by some characters' awareness of the distance that separates them from the capital and a power they are supposed to represent. In Kilroy's adaptation, the Anglo-Irish stand for *foreign* power, which introduces the dimension of colonialism, one that is absent from Chechov's work. Moreover, various short addenda made to the Russian original also generate specifically Irish political themes and gradually build up a colonial background in the play, as illustrated in the following extract:

> Sorin. And after dinner I accidentally fell asleep again and now every joint in my body aches. I feel as if I'm going through a nightmare, when all's said and done. Peter. And there I was, after dinner, snoozing again in the chair. It's no wonder half the neighbourhood lives in England. This country is asleep. (Chekhov 6; Kilroy, *The Seagull* 18)[8]

Kilroy revisits a specific period of Ireland's colonial history. Like its Russian equivalent in Chekhhov, the Anglo-Irish land-owning gentry has now disappeared. On this basis, Kilroy transforms Russia into

---

[6] Kilroy's adaptation of *Six Characters in Search of an Author* was first staged at the Abbey Theatre, Dublin in May 1996. His adaptation of *Ghosts* was first produced at the Abbey Theatre in October 1989.

[7] The Big house itself possibly symbolises Ireland.

[8] Other similarly discreet elements are mentioned as a part of everyday life, and thus contribute to the creation of this colonial atmosphere. Compare, for instance,
> Medvedenko. We must have tea and sugar, don't you think? (Chekhov 6).
with
> James. [...] *duty* on the tea. I'm telling you, ya don't know the half of it. (Kilroy *The Seagull* 17 [Italics, mine]).

Ireland. The first significant alteration concerns space, when geographi-
cal references turn a Russian landscape into an Irish one. For example,
"The whole district" (Chekhov 12) becomes "this side of the river
Shannon" (Kilroy, *The Seagull* 25); in a similar vein, "the other side of
the lake" (Chekhov 15) evolves into "beyond the lake near to Kilmore"
(Kilroy, *The Seagull* 30). These transformations illustrate the passage
from a Russian to an Irish background, but after Brian Friel's play,
Translations, it would be difficult to view the adaptation of names as a
purely innocent phenomenon. These changes help Kilroy ground his
play into Irish soil, so that the situation of the Anglo-Irish will bring to
his audience echoes of not quite forgotten days. Verbal scenery creates a
fake reality to which Irish—or even English—theatregoers are likely to
relate, since their cultural background will make them fully realise that
through his depiction of helpless characters faced with a predicament
which they cannot possibly master, Kilroy, an Irish playwright, provides
a personal outlook on Ireland's colonial history.[9] If one compares Chekhov's text with Kilroy's, one can easily measure how the two plays
differ when characters talk about the political and financial situation, as
shown by the contrast below:

> Polina Andreevna. He sent the carriage horses for work in the fields, you
> know. And misunderstandings like this go on every day. If you only knew
> how it worries and upsets me! It's making me ill. See, I'm trembling... I
> can't stand his rudeness, I can't. (Chekhov 22)

versus

> Pauline. It's not as if he runs the estate properly. He doesn't. It's bankrupt
> like every other estate in the West of Ireland. You know they've stopped
> paying rents again this past month. The land leaguers will have nothing to
> take of what's left. (Kilroy, *The Seagull* 44)

In both cases, the depicted economic situation derives from the owner's
vain attempt at running the farm in a profitable way. However, in pre-
Revolutionary Russia, the characters' impotence is individualised as the
direct result of personal behaviour or habits, while the Irish perspective
differs. The desperate financial state of the farm does not represent an
isolated case highlighting a specific situation. On the contrary, it reflects
on a wider scale a common poverty shared by landowners, who—in the
West of Ireland—find themselves in financial straits.

Although Kilroy mentions the tension between various social classes,
colonial oppression does, however, not stand out as the major cause of

---

[9]   And this corresponds to Field Day's objectives as stated in *Ireland's Field Day*. In
brief, all the directors felt that the political crisis in the North and its reverberation in
the Republic had made the necessity of a re-appraisal of Ireland's political and cultural situation explicit and urgent.

it. First, similar social tension has occurred at various stages in the rural history of European communities. Moreover, the lurking conflict spurs an almost metaphysical questioning that goes beyond ready-made answers about the harmful rule of England as a colonial power. Landowners undoubtedly thwart communal well being, but their human incapacity to turn Nature into a satisfactory provider seems to prevail over their origins when it comes to the source of the conflict.[10] It follows that the Land Leaguers merely add to the list of factors that prevent landowners from hoping to make some profit out of their farming activities. Kilroy refrains from taking sides, an approach that corresponds to that found in his other works on similar issues, since, apparently, both parties endure a fate that precludes any attempt at improving the general situation.

By depicting the mental background of a dying world—a recurring stage in any communal history—Kilroy connects the specific past of Ireland to a world history of rural desolation. In this respect, his adaptation can be perceived as a way of building new links, of asserting a common ground between the Irish and the rest of the world. To return to the earlier alluded-to links that exist between Kilroy's adaptation and its original, Russian people, in different circumstances, have also endured the harsh consequences of incompetent landowners, symbolising a general human disconnection with Nature. Consequently, Kilroy's adaptation becomes a way of underlining this connection between two peoples, because it underplays the foreign element inserted in the Irish version of *The Seagull*. This strategy adds to the distancing effect from colonial issues, and reinforces the impression of a gradual intellectual disconnection from the British Empire.

While, at first sight, this literary tactic does not seem to give prominence to colonial issues, Kilroy—who thrives on ambiguity and paradoxes—also uses this unorthodox approach to Ireland's past to reconnect Irish people to their history. Subjectively, he re-acquaints them with episodes of their past, and invites them to reconsider their relationship —if not with the former British Empire—at least with the present legacy of their colonial experience. Kilroy challenges expected divisions in several ways. First, he acknowledges—but does not overemphasise—national antagonisms:

---

[10]   The excerpt below further corroborates this:
   Peter. The tenants are in revolt. This man Parnell. Indeed, it has just occurred to me, quite clearly, that we may have to sell—(Kilroy, *The Seagull* 59).
   This extract, which does not correspond to any political allusion in Chekhov's *Seagull*, underlines the idea of a conflict with Parnell, but one feels that Kilroy is wary of creating clear-cut oppositions.

Aston. And you people. I know nothing about you. Indeed, I rather find the
whole experience in this household strange, if you will forgive me, yes, foreign. I have great difficulty in understanding what, precisely, is being said
by you Irish at any particular time. And yet we appear to share the language.
(Kilroy, *The Seagull* 49)

Aston's insistence on the impossibility of understanding the Irish was
added by Kilroy in his adaptation, in order to stress the disconnection
that existed between a representative of England and an ordinary Irish
woman. The word "foreign" sums up the extent of their estrangement,
but while this colonial opposition is marked, one should note that this
state of alienation does not merely concern English citizens. Peter, a
former civil servant in Dublin Castle—where British Imperial power
resided—is now forced to live in the country, in the West of Ireland, but
feels he does not belong there. For the younger generation, the issue of
belonging is even more complex. The Anglo-Irish, as their name indicates, are torn between their loyalty to England and their attachment to
the country where they were born and raised. As the son of a Galway
pedlar and a famous London actress, Constantine suffers from this
feeling of alienation (Kilroy, *The Seagull* 63). Identity confusion obviously affects the Anglo-Irish, but Catholics like James and Dr Hickey
are not spared either. Blind to the needs of his future wife, James fails to
understand the challenges that his marriage with Mary—a Protestant—
entails in terms of self-definition.[11] His complete approval of the values
of a dying world, together with his acceptance of a ready-made social
identity for himself can only lead to a fake harmony. In fact, beyond the
religious divide, the major threat to the contemplated union seems to lie
in personal interrelationships. Mary, a Bovary-like character, will
eventually accept to marry Peter, but their defective marriage will serve
to underline their intimate disconnection. Here, as in many of Kilroy's
plays, the capacity of individuals to relate to someone else is questioned
and exposed as a major existential challenge, a view that diminishes the
importance of the colonial legacy, whose importance as an obstacle

---

[11] By contrast, Mary has no illusions about the perception that James' family has of
their future marriage:

Mary. My James isn't the brightest of creatures and he hasn't a shilling to his
name and he's a Roman Catholic and he has all that awful family of his down in
that awful cottage but I believe he truly loves me. His family look on me as a
kind of loot rifled from the Big House. (Kilroy, *The Seagull* 56)

This situation reminds one of *The O'Neill,* in which Hugh and Mabel, who belonged
to opposite clans, could not agree on a *modus vivendi.*

appears reduced compared to the feeble human capacity for mutual understanding.[12]

Adapting Chekhov proved a challenge for Kilroy, who attempts to keep a critical distance from the political problems which he raises. He rejects realistic theatre[13] but tries to remain authentic, avoiding the trap of folklore-like Irish identity, which George Bernard Shaw had derided as ludicrous in *John Bull's Other Island*. Like geography, language plays an important part in the transformation of Russia into Ireland,[14] but other devices underscore familiar situations to which the audience is likely to relate:

Mary. Oh, I'm stiff with the cramp – (*She goes*)

Dr Hickey. She will go in there and have several stiff drinks before her lunch.

Peter. She's desperately unhappy, poor thing.

Dr Hickey. She will convince herself for a few, brief hours that she is—ecstatic.

Peter. Who can blame her? Dreadful situation. What difference does it make, if the poor thing finds it easier—

Dr Hickey. You will forgive me sir, but you are talking dangerous nonsense—(Kilroy, *The Seagull* 40)[15]

---

[12] One should note that in his three adaptations (*The Seagull, Ghosts*, or *Six Characters in Search of an Author*), the question of identity—posed in terms of insiders and outsiders—is raised.

[13] For instance, compare
> Dorn. That's true, there are very few actors gifted with brilliance nowadays, but the average actor is much, much better than he used to be.
> Shamraev. I just can't agree with you. (Chekhov 12)
versus
> Dr Hickey. We may not have the acting, perhaps, on the old scale but there is more reality on the stage nowadays...
> Isobel. Reality. Fiddlesticks! What on earth has theatre got to do with reality? (Kilroy, *The Seagull* 26)

[14] For instance, "a poor man" becomes "the tinkers out on the road," as exemplified below:
> Medvedenko. Even a poor man can be happy. (Chekhov 6)
versus
> Mary. Even the tinkers out on the road can be happy. (Kilroy, *The Seagull* 17)
Sentences like "Your father won't give me the lend of a horse" (Kilroy, *The Seagull* 70) further contribute to the staging of an Irish identity built on common expressions.

[15] Compare this quote with the one below:
> Masha. My leg's gone to sleep... (*Goes out*)
> Dorn. She'll go and soak up a couple of glasses before lunch.

The characters' remarks about Mary's drinking habit echo the familiar speeches of capitulation found in Chekhov, speeches which reveal a fatalistic acceptance of an unfortunate destiny. Kilroy is, however, wary of overemphasis. He knows the danger of turning his adaptation of Chekhov into a pseudo-realistic portrait of yesterday's Ireland, and adds very few elements that give an Irish touch to the play. Though restricted in number, typically Irish details—some of them unpleasant like alcoholism and the type of delirious ranting that results from it—are nonetheless sufficiently present to enable the audience to connect past and contemporary political situations.

While economic circumstances have evolved, the perception of Dr Hickey and James as Catholic outsiders—together with their Anglo-Irish schizophrenia—contains strong echoes of the present state of affairs. In this respect, the geographical transposition and literary assessment of a specific era that Kilroy makes in his adaptation of Chekhov prove politically significant: indeed, they represent the first steps in an attempt to question and redefine a non-colonial Irish identity. For this purpose, Kilroy resorts to the play within the play, proceeding from the principle that if theatre is a place of artifice, it can also bring some truth when it exposes itself as a mere show. Constantine's play, rejected by his mother as "One of those Celtic things" (Kilroy, *The Seagull* 13), proves interesting in that an outsider—an Anglo-Irish playwright—deals with the issue of Irish identity. He seeks a cultural foundation beyond present divides, and traces the way to discover new roots through an approach that disregards colonialism:

> Lily. Once in every thousand years I speak out and my voice is a voice in the emptiness. And I shall speak again until the spirit of Darkness is defeated and the spirit of Light shines over the land of Banbha. (Kilroy, *The Seagull* 28)[16]

From what is staged in the play, one understands that the spirit of Darkness rules. In his search for renewal—one not limited to the theatrical arena—Constantine aspires to a spiritual rebirth. The fact that an Anglo-Irish character initiates the quest for identity should be noted, because the distant reference in time—"once in every thousand years"—invalidates Catholic claims of a unique and authentic Irish identity. In his first steps towards a redefinition of Irish identity, Constantine partly seeks answers in legends which deny the relevance of present religious divisions. Once pre-Christian times become the accepted framework of

---

Sorin. She has no personal happiness, poor thing.
Dorn. Nonsense, your Excellency. (Chekhov 21)

[16] This passage parallels the following one in the Russian original:
Nina. I open my lips to speak once in a hundred years, and my voice resounds despondently in this barren, desolate place, and no one hears [...]. (Chekhov 13)

reference, British colonialism is reduced to an episode, a period of darkness during which people wait for the spirit of Light to reveal to them who they really are as Irish individuals, and not as the bearers of predefined and stifling social masks.

Chekhov's play *The Seagull* parallels the tragic fate of a bird with that of a fallen woman. One may wonder to what extent, in Kilroy's adaptation, the destiny of the seagull or of Lily does not also become that of Ireland in relation to England and the British Empire. As a country chosen then left alone in its struggle for survival, the consequences for Ireland are close to those experienced by Lily. Proximity means destruction because of the loved one's lack of response. Therefore, links need to be severed so that life may start again, different, plain, perhaps offering few perspectives of success, but at least providing Lily—and maybe Ireland—with the opportunity to be themselves. This point concurs with Kilroy's work as an adapter and the new bonds that it establishes with world literature. Being unable to shed the burden of a colonial past equates the fate of Constantine, who finds himself in a deadlock. He cannot summon up the strength to start a new life, a desperate echo, possibly, of the quandary that afflicts contemporary Northern Ireland. On the other hand, Lily shows him the way by accepting an unflattering self-definition, which nevertheless has the merit of affording her partial disconnection from her past and from the historical past that casts its shadow on Ireland. Obviously, Kilroy is too subtle and cautious to turn *The Seagull* into a political tract. However, one feels that he might favour self-assertion for Ireland and the Irish, and that his adaptation of Chekhov's *Seagull* represents a personal example of such a belief. Consequently, Lily's advice regarding her mental acceptance of what she is may also be understood in terms of a hoped-for, beneficial, and final disconnection of Ireland from the former British Empire. She thus sums it up: "what matters is being able to go on with some small dignity within oneself. That's all, really I feel that, now. I'm not afraid of being alive anymore" (Kilroy, *The Seagull* 85).

Works Cited

Chekhov, Anton. *The Seagull*. Trans. E. K. Bristow. New York: Norton, 1981.
Dubost, Thierry. "*The O'Neill*: premiers regards sur l'identité irlandaise." *Le théâtre de Thomas Kilroy*. Caen: Presses Universitaires de Caen, 2001. 13-28.
Field Day Theatre Company. *Ireland's Field Day*. London: Hutchinson, 1985.
Friel, Brian. *Translations*. London: Faber and Faber, 1981.
Kilroy, Thomas. *Double Cross*. Loughcrew: Gallery Press, 1986.
_____, adapt. *Ghosts (after Ibsen)*. Unpublished manuscript. 1989.

_____. Introduction to *The Seagull (after Chekhov)*. Loughcrew: Gallery Press, 1993. 11-14.

_____, adapt. *Six Characters in Search of an Author (after Pirandello)*. Unpublished manuscript. 1996.

_____. *Tea and Sex and Shakespeare*. Loughcrew: Gallery Press, 1998.

_____. *The Madame MacAdam Travelling Theatre*. London: Methuen, 1991.

_____. *The O'Neill*. Loughcrew: Gallery Press, 1995.

_____, adapt. *The Seagull (after Chekhov)*. Loughcrew: Gallery Press, 1993.

_____. "*The Seagull*, an Adaptation." *The Cambridge Companion to Chekhov*. Eds. V. Gottlieb and P. Allain. Cambridge: Cambridge UP, 2000.

Long, Joseph. "An Irish Seagull: Chekhov and the New Irish Theatre." *Revue de Littérature Comparée* 4 (Oct./Dec. 1995): 419-26.

McGuinness, Frank. "A Voice from the Trees: Thomas Kilroy's Version of Chekhov's *The Seagull*." *Irish University Review: A Journal of Irish Studies* 21.1 (Spring-Summer 1992): 3-14.

Where Is Here Now?
Living the Border
in the New Canadian Drama

Jerry WASSERMAN

University of British Columbia

"Here we are." These first words spoken by a character named Verdecchia open Guillermo Verdecchia's 1993 play *Fronteras Americanas*. "Here we are," he repeats to the audience a line later, the message reinforced by a slide projected behind him: "Here We Are" (19). Apparently self-evident, the meaning of the phrase is challenged by the repetition which isolates the words and holds them up for examination. Verdecchia, a Canadian who emigrated as a child from Argentina, feels himself neither authentically Canadian nor Argentine. For most of his life, he says, "I felt like a liar, a fraud, an impostor. [...] I didn't know what I was nor where I lived." The play "was an attempt to understand, and if possible, resolve this dilemma" ("Spanglish" 10). Constructed as a series of journeys and investigations, it ends in a revelation: "Je suis Argentin-Canadien! I am a post-Porteno neo-Latino Canadian! I am the Pan-American highway!" (*Fronteras* 74). So "here we are" is revealed to be densely problematic as an expression. Where exactly is "here"? Who are "we"? Who is the individual "I" within that collective "we," and what does it mean to *be* him and us, here and now?

Given the Canadian context of Verdecchia's "here we are," some of us who constitute its audience cannot help hearing an echo of Northrop Frye: "It seems to me that Canadian sensibility [...] is less perplexed by the question 'Who am I?' than by some such riddle as 'Where is here?'" (220), he pronounced famously in 1965. Canadian sensibility, demographics, and cultural identity have changed substantially since then; consequently, this truism—one of the most oft-repeated in the catalogue of Canada's obsessive attempts at national self-definition—has become ripe for re-examination. The Fall 2000 issue of the journal *Essays on Canadian Writing*, for example, devoted itself entirely to the question, "Where is here now?" My interest focuses on the ways recent Anglophone drama emerging out of Canada's various multicultures relocates Canadian nationhood and redefines Frye's conundrum. As the pluralism of what Verdecchia calls "this Noah's ark of a nation" (*Fronteras* 73) has come to be increasingly reflected on Canada's stages, the borders between here and there, home and exile, margin and mainstream have blurred. Thirty years ago, the paradigmatic Anglo-Canadian play, David French's *Leaving Home*, dealt with a relatively straightforward binary: Newfoundlanders torn between their originary culture and their adopted central Canadian home. Today, Canadian plays peopled by African-, Latino-, Native- and Indo-Canadian characters, among many hyphenated others, examine personal and cultural boundaries complicated by postcolonial hybridization, media manipulation, and fractious diasporic politics. The construction of new "imagined communities"—distinguished, Benedict Anderson argues, "by the style in which they are imagined" (6)—has become the locus of some of the most exciting work in the Canadian theatre. These are also "discursive communities" in Linda Hutcheon's phrase, "micropolitical groupings" defined by race, ethnicity, and national origin, but also by gender, class, political and sexual choice, age, profession, religion, and so on, such that "we all belong to many overlapping (and sometimes even conflicting) communities or collectives"—the condition, according to Hutcheon, that makes irony possible (92).

This new theatrical profile, along with the styles and ironies inherent in it, has been drawn in particularly vivid ways in the work of four Canadian playwrights writing at the turn of the millennium. Verdecchia in *Fronteras Americanas* and Djanet Sears in her plays *Afrika Solo* and *Harlem Duet* reposition national and geographic borders to frame their evolving definitions of the trans-national, trans-racial, trans-cultural self. Drew Hayden Taylor in *The Baby Blues* and *alterNatives*, and Rahul Varma in *Counter Offence* stage versions of the new culture wars in which battle lines are drawn across, behind, and only sometimes along the traditional borders of race and ethnicity. These writers, and others like Daniel David Moses, refuse familiar definitions of ethnicity, instead challenging the very concept by playfully foregrounding its constructed nature, insisting on ethnicity as performance. Object-lessons in what Verdecchia calls "learning to live the border" (*Fronteras* 77), their plays are redefining and reconstructing the Canadian imaginary.

Three of these writers are immigrants from other countries, Verdecchia coming to Canada from Argentina when he was two, Sears from England when she was fifteen, and Varma from India at twenty-four. Taylor inhabits another kind of border, having grown up on an Ojibway reserve in Ontario, the light-skinned, blue-eyed son of a white father and Native mother. When as a young man he left the reserve for the city, he quickly learned that he confounded people's preconceived notions of how an "Indian" was expected to look and behave: "I became more aware of the role people expected me to play, and the fact that physically I didn't fit in" (*Funny* 9).

The failure to conform to preordained physical, racial, or national categories is a common denominator in these playwrights' lives and work. Taylor, both White and Red, neither White nor Red, declares himself "a Pink Man" (9). His character Angel in the 1999 comedy *alterNatives*, also a writer with a similar racial make-up, is torn between his personal and cultural allegiances to his Native activist friends and his white girlfriend, in neither of whose worlds he comfortably fits. Verdecchia straddles a linguistic border. He says his "first language was Spanglish" ("Spanglish" 10), and in *Fronteras Americanas* he plays himself as both an educated, assimilated Anglophone Canadian, and as his alter ego Facundo Morales Segundo, nicknamed Wideload, who embraces every offensive North American stereotype of "de authentic Méjico" (23). In their own lives neither Taylor nor Verdecchia fits the stereotype of Native or Latino, as evidenced by their failure to get parts in Hollywood-Canadian films and television shows because their ethnicity is deemed insufficiently "authentic." Taylor wryly describes his inability to get himself cast as a Native character in movies: "Politics tells me it's because of the way I look, reality tells me it's probably because I can't act. I'm not sure which is better" (*Funny* 10-11). Verdecchia accepts the verdict of a string of disastrous auditions, admitting that he makes "a lousy television Latino [...]. Perhaps I didn't look Latino enough (too white, too short, too Canadian, too Mediterranean, too nervous)" ("Culture" 15).

Janet Sears, a black girl growing up in England and Canada surrounded by white kids and media images of white physical normativity, has the opposite problem. In the autobiographical *Afrika Solo*, first performed in 1987, she feels herself defined by her all too visible otherness: her "bum [...] way too big," "lips [...] way too thick," "hair [...] so wooly" (28). This despite her strong identification with the pop norms of North American tele-culture, from *Tarzan* (with its obvious ironies for a black girl) to *Star Trek* (an addiction she shares with *alterNative*'s Angel, whose girlfriend deplores his desire to write science fiction rather than "authentic" Native fiction à la Thomas King). Like the crew of the *Starship Enterprise*, Janet feels herself a citizen of everywhere and nowhere. One of her parents is from Jamaica, the other from Guyana, and she herself holds four passports. "I'm gonna find my home," she declares, setting off on a primal pilgrimage to "mother Africa" (41). But despite a series of important self-discoveries there, she ultimately feels unable to define herself as wholly African either. Like Verdecchia's, her journey concludes with her embrace of a diasporic hybrid, a border identity: "African Canadian." As other black Canadian writers have pointed out, however, that identifier is itself neither stable nor uncontested. For George Elliot Clarke "the phrase 'African Canadian' denotes a fragile coalition of identities" (xviii), and Cecil Foster wonders if "such a thing as a black—or, as some call it, an African—community in Canada" really exists at all (20).

Varma's *Counter Offence*, a murder mystery set in Montreal, elaborates a highly complex confusion of communities and identities. An Indo-Canadian activist, Mr. Moolchand, defends an Iranian student, Shapoor Farhadi, who has been arrested and threatened with deportation for beating his Indo-Canadian wife, Shazia. Moolchand's strategy is to accuse the arresting officer of racism. Shazia is represented by an African-Canadian social worker who runs a women's shelter. When the social worker, Clarinda, expresses support for the white cop's effective work against domestic violence, Moolchand reminds her that Montreal's white police have a nasty history of shooting unarmed black men, and he berates her: "there is something wrong with a person who doesn't stand by her own community." Clarinda replies, "Shazia's my community" (54). Whereas Moolchand defines "us"—"the East Indians, the Africans, the Chinese ... you know—people like you and me" (51)—by ethnicity and skin colour, Clarinda delineates her discursive community by gender: "Isn't *she* also one of us?" (52).

In each of these plays the characters live what Homi Bhabha calls "border lives," occupying the "'in between' spaces" where categories overlap and "provide the terrain for elaborating strategies of selfhood—singular or communal—that initiate new signs of identity, and innovative sites of collaboration" (1-2). One strategy elaborated by all these playwrights is the performance of ethnicity, a complex set of manoeuvres which may involve varying degrees of mimicry or minstrelsy. Similar to the way in which, according to Judith Butler's argument, gender is constructed as "an identity instituted through a *stylized repetition of acts*" (270), ethnicity in all these plays is understood as being at least in part a performance—in Taylor's words, the role people expect you to play.[1] Postcolonial mimicry, with its ambivalence and indetermi-

---

[1]   Performing ethnicity as a theatrical strategy for self-consciously interrogating notions of race and issues of power is not, of course, a recent invention of Canadian playwrights. In Jean Genet's *Les Nègres* (1959), for instance, black actors in whiteface masks perform for a white audience a travesty of racist clichés in order to facilitate the black revolutionary actions being organized "offstage." See also George C. Wolfe's *The Colored Museum* (1984). In a different context Sneja Gunew has described as "performing ethnicity" a kind of fraudulent disguise or ventriloquism undertaken by an Australian novelist attempting to claim for herself a certain ethnic authenticity. I use the phrase to describe work more similar to Genet's scenario than to Gunew's, though the ironies attendant on Genet's own racial ventriloquism (as a white writer) and on issues of "ethnic authenticity" in the Canadian plays I discuss make both these texts useful points of reference for my argument.

nacy ("*almost the same but not white*" [Bhaba 89]), carves out a space for exploring new ways of defining the self and reversing the cultural gaze. Similarly, minstrelsy at the turn of the millennium, ironizing on its historic associations with racist oppression, becomes a performative strategy that allows the possibility of "reclaim[ing] from white control the power of racial definition" (Lhamon 283). The characters in these Canadian plays perform their ethnicity self-consciously, sometimes as a way of clarifying it for themselves, sometimes as a way of mocking the assumptions and expectations of the audience or other characters. And sometimes they watch it backfire.

Both as actor and writer, Sears literally performs her ethnicity in *Afrika Solo*, its Sundiata Form a combination of narrative, music and dance traditional to West African theatre (*Afrika* 96). Joanne Tompkins has described *Afrika Solo* as less a performance than an infinite rehearsal of identity which never becomes fixed (36). But the play climaxes with Djanet (having Africanized her name) arriving at a specific semantic determination of her ethnicity precisely by performing it. After running the gamut from reggae, calypso, R&B, and rap to TV theme songs and traditional African music, she sings for her BaMbuti hosts around a campfire in Zaire a "soulful gospel ballad" version of "O Canada" which triggers her revelation of identity: "That's it! See, that's me! The African heartbeat in a Canadian song. African Canadian. Not coloured, or negro .... Maybe not even black. African Canadian" (87-88). An icon of border life, she goes, in her own words, "home—to Canada" (91), bearing her African heritage in her hair, her lips, her hips, wearing an African Boubou wrapped around her head, and the Maple Leaf (figuratively) tattooed on her heart.

In Taylor's 1995 comedy *The Baby Blues*, three generations of Native men perform their ethnicity for the benefit of a young white woman named Summer, an anthropology student and broadly caricatured wannabe who follows the pow wow circuit in order to "breathe in the essence of being Native" (13). The young fancy-dancer Skunk invites her to join him in his "morning purification … cleansing swim, in the lake … Mother Earth's lake … the tears of Mother Earth"—naked, of course, to get the full ritual experience (15). Amos, an elder, impresses her with his aboriginal wisdom ("Eat, drink, and be merry, for tomorrow they may put you on a Reserve" [64]), while at the same time mocking the commodification of aboriginality: "Check the authentic Native totem pole for a 'Made in Korea' label" is one of his wise-elder epithets (64). When Noble, a middle-aged dancer, regales her with fictional tales of his heroic resistance at Wounded Knee and Oka, Summer coos, "I would love to hear your opinion on the socio-political implications of both events in retrospect of today's Indigena political agenda." But Jenny, a Native woman, interrupts: "Somehow I think if it doesn't have beer or boobs, he doesn't have an opinion" (41). Bitter at Noble's having gotten her pregnant and then deserted her eighteen years earlier, Jenny calls attention to his ethnic performance as an abrogation of what should have been his parental performance, an irony that comes home to roost for Noble at the end, when he discovers that Amos is in fact his own long-lost father.

More directly in *alterNatives*, Taylor shows how putting on the ethnic mask can have surprisingly unpalatable consequences. Angel spends much of the play, set amid a dinner party, trying to negotiate his way between conflicting sets of assumptions about cultural and ethnic authenticity. On one side are the expectations of his white girlfriend, a Native Studies professor: that he know how to cook moose, and restrict his reading to books about what he calls "another adventure in an oppressed, depressed and suppressed Native village" (37). On the other is the desire of his "alterNative Warrior" friends to shape him in their politically outspoken image, urging him to join them in subverting non-Native attempts to access First Nations culture. Unable to satisfy either side, Angel makes a confession. He reveals that, years back when he lived on the reserve, he and some other young men made up stories for visiting anthropologists (including his current girlfriend!), concocting them as "the legends of our people" (128). And those 'legends' became a textbook, and that textbook, now in its seventh printing, is on university reading lists, perpetuating lies about Native life to Native students. Here the imagined community becomes a destructive one, the performance of ethnicity revealed as a form of Native minstrelsy that traps the performer in a double-bind similar to the position in which African-Americans found themselves at the historical moment when they began joining blackface minstrel shows: "To adopt minstrelsy is to collude in one's own fetishization; but to relinquish efforts to adapt it is to lose completely a cultural past appropriated by whites" (Gubar 96).[2]

Minstrelsy and the re-appropriation of the cultural past come together in a variety of interesting ways in Sears' *Harlem Duet*, first produced in 1997. The play rewrites *Othello* from the point of view of a black woman named Billie, Othello's first wife, whom he leaves for Desdemona. Set primarily in contemporary Harlem, it re-casts Othello as a university professor who opposes affirmative action and prefers

---

[2]   The cultural pressure on Taylor's Native characters to perform their ethnicity reflects a fact of life in contemporary Canada, according to a recent report about the lucrative German tourist trade in the Yukon. The report notes the extent to which the expectations of many of the tourists continue to be shaped by the enduring Wild West mythology of Karl May's novels. According to the executive director of the Yukon First Nations Tourism Association, "About 95 per cent of the German market is looking for an aboriginal cultural experience. [...] They are expecting to be greeted by someone in a head dress and on horseback" (Matas A10).

white women to black. Defending his decision to marry Mona, he insists to Billie that he is "beyond this race bullshit": "My culture is Wordsworth, Shaw, *Leave It to Beaver*, *Dirty Harry* [...] I am not my skin. My skin is not me" (73-74).

The contemporary action weaves in and out of scenes in which the same two performers who play Billie and Othello also appear as slaves in the antebellum South and as actors in the dressing room of a Harlem theatre circa 1928. The black actor who dreams of performing Shakespeare in 1928 has to cover his face in the black greasepaint of the minstrel, a racially enforced travesty of self. This performance of ethnicity as self-mockery seems to be an expression of Billie's bitterness regarding Othello's newly imagined cross-racial community. It suggests the historical frame within which blacks, in order to enter white discourse, have had to mask themselves. In Othello's case, the mask is whiteface: "A Black man afflicted with negrophobia," Billie calls him; and her friend Magi scornfully adds, "Booker T. Uppermiddleclass III" (66). But Sears provides Othello with ample stage time and sincere, impassioned rhetoric with which to argue his position. The fact that Billie's apartment sits at the Harlem crossroads of Martin Luther King and Malcolm X Boulevards reflects the long-standing and still unresolved ideological battle between integration and black separatism within the larger African-American community. None of the borders in this play is simply or unequivocally drawn. And the late-developing sub-plot in which Billie makes peace with her estranged Nova Scotian father, a man named Canada, further emphasizes the complexity of border life as it is lived along the divides of both gender and racial politics, and at the intersection of African-American-Canadian experience.

The minstrel show model for performing ethnicity as a strategy of cultural re-appropriation and recuperation is used most explicitly by Native playwright Daniel David Moses in his 1991 play *Almighty Voice and His Wife*. Act One intertwines the historical drama of Almighty Voice, a young Cree killed by Mounties on the Saskatchewan prairie in the 1890s after resisting arrest for stealing a cow, with his courtship and marriage of the Cree woman White Girl. Act Two is styled and structured as a minstrel show, complete with the genre's ritual comedy routines, songs and dances, the plantation playlet (here a mock-melodrama about "Sweet Sioux"), the stump speech, and repeated references to the popular endmen, Tambo and Bones. Almighty Voice and White Girl reappear after intermission in white gloves and whiteface make-up, White Girl playing the Interlocutor (the minstrel show's master of ceremonies) and Almighty Voice his own ghost. Their snappy, anachronistic exchanges go on in this vein:

INTERLOCUTOR: Did you know, Mister Ghost, that marriage is an institution?

GHOST: Yes sir, I had heard that said.

INTERLOCUTOR: Well, sir, so is an insane asylum. […] Do you know, sir, how many Indians it takes to screw in a light bulb?

GHOST: What's a light bulb? (93-94)

Moses utilizes minstrelsy as an ironic device to distance the play from the tragic form in which he felt so many similar Canadian Native stories had been petrified, and to challenge stereotypical conceptions of Native identity (see Appleford).

INTERLOCUTOR: Surely, Mr. Ghost—

GHOST: Call me the late Almighty Voice. Call me an early redman. Call me, yes, even call me a ghost—but don't call me Shirley! (69-70)

At the end both characters discard their gloves, remove their make-up, and revert to dancing, drumming and speaking Cree in what appears to be a return to their authentic ethnic selves. But the overt theatricality of the ending suggests that "authenticity" constitutes no less a performance than the minstrel show travesty of racist stereotyping. The impression the play leaves is of an inevitable hybridity, underlined by the name White Girl and by the cross-cultural marriage of Native agency and minstrel show form.[3]

In *Fronteras Americanas* Verdecchia performs ethnicity to brilliant effect, donning the Latino minstrel mask rather than citing any of the specific forms of blackface minstrelsy. The character of Wideload is a deconstructive travesty of the Latino as media creation and nightmarish popular stereotype: "Hey mang, we could be neighbours—would you like dat? Sure, I'm moving in next door to … you … and I'm going to wash my Mustang every day and overhaul de engine and get some grease on de sidewalk and some friends like about twelve are gonna come and stay with me for a few … years" (26). But Wideload also turns the racial gaze around, assuring us that we members of "de Saxonian community" (40) seem just as exotic to him, what with our sexy rituals like the Morris Dance. Ultimately though, Verdecchia recognizes that the minstrel mask of Wideload is a projection of his own ethnic ambivalence, even self-hatred: "I remember my fear, I taste and smell my fear, my fear of young men who speak Spanish in the darkness of the park, and I know that somewhere in my traitorous heart I can't stand

---

[3]   For the best brief history of the minstrel show in Canada, documenting touring troupes from the United States as well as domestic companies, see Gardner (128-35). Attesting to the enduring popularity of the genre was the longevity of Toronto's Calvary Minstrels, who were still performing in blackface as late as 1969 (135).

people I claim are my brothers" (72). His resolve at the end to learn to live the border involves a radical rethinking of the "we" in his initial "here we are," made concrete in a thoroughly theatrical moment in which Wideload and Verdecchia, played by the same actor, somehow speak together (77).

Finally, Varma's *Counter Offence* highlights the performance of ethnicity with one of the trickiest and most unsettling gambits attempted by any of these plays. A richly ironic work, *Counter Offence* continually upsets audience expectations by showing how the discursive communities constructed through racial, gender and family politics, ethnic allegiances, and personal relationships conflict and overlap, and how the agendas attached to each community of interest cause individuals to manipulate each other sometimes ruthlessly. At the centre of the action is the activist Moolchand, who speaks with a thick East Indian accent. He walks a fine line between cynical self-interest and the genuine concerns of his client and the ethnic communities he purports to represent. Midway through the play the Iranian husband Shapoor, just released from jail, is slapped with a restraining order to keep him away from his wife. "Why are they doing this to me?" he implores Moolchand, who responds: "Because you are a Muslim. And they think you are all terrorists, out to get Salman Rushdie, blow up Bay Street, your people breed like crazy … might take over Canada. Don't you get it?" (49-50). What makes the speech remarkable is that, for the only time in the play, as the stage directions make clear, "*MOOLCHAND speaks with a Canadian accent instead of his usual East Indian.*" Even Shapoor wonders, "Mr. Moolchand, what happened to your accent?" (50). Are *all* his other appearances, then, inflected by this conscious performance of ethnicity, the assumption of what he calls his "Bombaywallah accent" (102) being perhaps meant to give him greater credibility in the ethnic community? Does this Brechtian gestic moment reveal a cynical Machiavel or only a pragmatic political realist who understands the shifting borders of a Canada both anxious to appear responsive to its multicultural constituency, and at the same time, as he says with his "Canadian accent," fearful of being overrun by those Others with their dark skin, high birth rates, and internecine violence?

The production history of *Counter Offence* further reflects the complexities of where "here" is and who "we" are in contemporary Canada, as refracted through the unique prism of Quebec's cultural and linguistic politics. In 1999, following two productions in English, the play received its French-language premiere in Montreal. Titled *L'Affaire Farhadi*, it recast the social worker Clarinda—played with a Jamaican accent in the original—as Haitian. And while Shazia spoke perfect French, being a child of Bill 101, the Quebec language law that mandates compulsory French education for the children of immigrants, her immigrant husband and parents spoke to her only in English. (The success of that production caused at least one reviewer in the Québécois press to reclaim Varma himself—referred to as "indien" in most articles and reviews—as "Indo-Québécois" [Labrecque].) After its English-language premiere in 1996, *Counter Offence* was remounted as a co-production between Varma's primarily South Asian Teesri Duniya Theatre (the name means Third World in Hindustani) and Montreal's Black Theatre Workshop. That kind of cultural cross-pollination is evident, too, in the blues tropes that Drew Hayden Taylor and other Native playwrights, including Tomson Highway, share with Djanet Sears and other African Canadian playwrights, the African-American musical tradition adapted to conjure imagined communities of its own (see Wasserman).

"Counter-narratives of the nation that continually evoke and erase its totalizing boundaries—both actual and conceptual—disturb those ideological manoeuvres through which 'imagined communities' are given essentialist identities," Homi Bhabha writes (149). The strategies shared by these playwrights work to undermine the unwritten restrictive covenants that threaten to delimit Canadian theatre and the Canadian identity, not to mention the major Toronto company that first produced *Harlem Duet*, a company calling itself Canadian Stage. In Djanet Sears' words, "Before *Harlem Duet* Canadian Stage had never produced a work by an author of [Black] African descent. And the problem with Canadian Stage is that it's called Canadian Stage, so it represents Canada, and I'm thinking, 'I'm Canadian, so it must represent me'" ("Nike" 30). Representing us, here, now, in all our complexity, is the ongoing project of the new Canadian drama. *And there we are.*

Works Cited

Anderson, Benedict. *Imagined Communities: Reflections on the Origin and Spread of Nationalism*. Rev. ed. London: Verso, 1992.

Appleford, Rob. "The Desire to Crunch Bone: Daniel David Moses and the 'True Real Indian.'" *Canadian Theatre Review* 77 (Winter 1993): 21-26.

Bhabha, Homi K. *The Location of Culture*. London: Routledge, 1994.

Butler, Judith. "Performative Acts and Gender Constitution: An Essay in Phenomenology and Feminist Theory." *Performing Feminisms: Feminist Critical Theory and Theatre*. Ed. Sue-Ellen Case. Baltimore: Johns Hopkins UP, 1990. 270-82.

Clarke, George Elliott. Introduction to *Eyeing the North Star: Directions in African-Canadian Literature*. Ed. George Elliott Clarke. Toronto: McClelland & Stewart, 1997. xi-xxviii.

Foster, Cecil. *A Place Called Heaven: The Meaning of Being Black in Canada*. Toronto: HarperCollins, 1996.

Frye, Northrop. *The Bush Garden: Essays on the Canadian Imagination.* Toronto: Anansi, 1971.

Gardner, David. "Variety." *Later Stages: Essays in Ontario Theatre from the First World War to the 1970s.* Ed. Ann Saddlemyer and Richard Plant. Toronto: U of Toronto P, 1997. 121-223.

Genet, Jean. *The Blacks: A Clown Show.* Trans. Bernard Frechtman. New York: Grove, 1960.

Gubar, Susan. *Racechanges: White Skin, Black Face in American Culture.* New York: Oxford UP, 1997.

Gunew, Sneja. "Performing Ethnicity: The Demidenko Show and its Gratifying Pathologies." *Canadian Ethnic Studies* 28.3 (1996): 72-84.

Hutcheon, Linda. *Irony's Edge: The Theory and Politics of Irony.* London: Routledge, 1994.

Labrecque, Marie. "La couleur du temps." *Voir* 25 February-3 March 1999.

Lhamon, W. T., Jr. "Ebery Time I Wheel About I Jump Jim Crow: Cycles of Minstrel Transgression from Cool White to Vanilla Ice." *Inside the Minstrel Mask: Readings in Nineteenth-Century Blackface Minstrelsy.* Ed. Annemarie Bean et al. Hanover, N.H.: Wesleyan UP, 1996. 275-84.

Matas, Robert. "Teutonic Tourists Flock to Yukon's Open Spaces." *Globe and Mail* (Toronto) 5 May 2001: A1, A10.

Moses, Daniel David. *Almighty Voice and His Wife.* Stratford, Ont.: Williams-Wallace, 1992.

Sears, Djanet. *Afrika Solo.* Toronto: Sister Vision, 1990.

_____. *Harlem Duet.* [Winnipeg]: Scirocco, 1998.

_____ and Alison Sealy Smith. "The Nike Method." *Canadian Theatre Review* 97 (Winter 1998): 24-30.

Taylor, Drew Hayden. *alterNatives.* Vancouver: Talon, 2000.

_____. *The Baby Blues.* Vancouver: Talon, 1999.

_____. *Funny, You Don't Look Like One: Observations from a Blue-Eyed Ojibway.* Penticton, B.C.: Theytus, 1996.

Tompkins, Joanne. "Infinitely Rehearsing Performance and Identity: *Afrika Solo* and *The Book of Jessica.*" *Canadian Theatre Review* 74 (Spring 1993): 35-39.

Varma, Rahul. *Counter Offence.* Toronto: Playwrights Canada, 1995.

Verdecchia, Guillermo. *Fronteras Americanas.* Toronto: Coach House, 1993.

_____. "Spanglish." *In 2 Print* (Summer 2000): 10.

_____, et al. "Culture Inc." *This Magazine* 32 (September-October 1998): 14-17.

Wasserman, Jerry. "Where the Soul Still Dances: The Blues and Canadian Drama." *Essays on Canadian Writing* 65 (Fall 1998): 56-75.

"Where Is Here Now?" Special Issue of *Essays on Canadian Writing* 71 (Fall 2000).

Wolfe, George C. *The Colored Museum.* New York: Grove, 1988.

Humanist Heresies
in Modern Canadian Drama

Anne NOTHOF

Athabasca University

Humanism, which affirms the universal value of human beings, and privileges individual responsibility and self-determination, is an unfashionable term in current critical discourse. Postmodern theory typically prioritizes difference and denies individual agency, asserting instead the formative power of social and discursive structures. As Richard Levin points out in "Bashing the bourgeois subject":

> Anyone who has tried to keep up with the current state of critical discourse does not need to be told that the Bourgeois or Humanist Subject [...] is in very serious trouble. Something like a major industry has developed, primarily among the cultural materialists, new historicists, and feminist critics associated with them, which is devoted to BHS bashing. (76)

According to Levin, liberal humanism has been reinvented and demonized by "leftist" critics, and its long and complex history conveniently ignored. It has been subjected to crude distortions by anti-humanists, and to a myriad of contradictory interpretations. It has become an ideological weapon in debates between evolutionists and creationists, between science and fundamentalism, and reduced to a rationalistic, naturalistic, and secular philosophy. In the theory wars, it has been dismissed as "essentialist," an imperialist mindset responsible for injustice, oppression, and consumerism. Michel Foucault, for example, regarded the "chimeras of the new humanisms" as "warped and twisted forms of reflection," wishing to take "man as their starting point in their attempts to reach the truth" (from Foucault's *The Order of Things*, quoted in Abrams 14). In discrediting humanism, Foucault, Roland Barthes, and Jacques Derrida dismantled the concept of "humanity," arguing that that "the subject is no more than an effect of language" (from Barthes' *Roland Barthes par Roland Barthes*, quoted in Abrams 14). Foucault also denied the possibility of human agency and choice: "in no historical period is cognitive activity 'free,' rather it always occurs within certain determined channels or forms of knowledge that

are given beforehand, and which are simultaneously anonymous, unconscious, and inescapable" (from *The Order of Things*, quoted in Puledda
124). Historical materialists such as Louis Althusser have similarly
argued that cultural productions are determined by the economic structures of their societies.

From its historical beginnings in Greece during the fifth century
B.C., however, humanism has been traditionally viewed as a positive,
liberating, and enabling attitude, emphasising the possibilities for individual capacities, human dignity, and education, beginning with self-
knowledge, as Socrates advised, and acting to shape society. But humanism was not defined as a coherent system of values until the nineteenth-century, when it was applied to the perceived values of the
European Renaissance. It presented a more positive and hopeful image
of "Man" than that of medieval ascetic Christianity, which assumed that
since the "fall" from God's grace, humanity was circumscribed by sin.
"Delight" in mankind and in the human struggle was "an idea launched
in the twelfth century by the forces of humanism as they woke society
from its Dark Ages," according to Canadian humanist philosopher, John
Ralston Saul:

> It was an attitude the humanists embraced in what they saw as a struggle
> between delight and self-loathing—delight in your fellow man and woman,
> sympathy for them; in other words, a sense of society [...] This was then as
> it is now a profoundly anti-ideological idea which takes the human for what
> the human is and believes it is worth trying to do better. (36-37)

Nineteenth century humanists saw in "man" the possibility for the
development of moral, intellectual, spiritual, and physical possibilities,
unconstrained by religious ideology and independent of religious super-
naturalism. With the erosion of a belief in the possibilities of "rationalism" which followed the First World War, humanism was deflected into
an engagement with social and personal values—examining the relationship between the individual and society, and investigating the nature
of the moral values that permeate positive social interaction. In 1933, it
was extensively defined in *a Humanist Manifesto* (published in *The New
Humanist* VI:3—http://www.infidels.org—in the United States) by
associations in Britain and the United States to include social, ethical,
cultural, political and environmental concerns. In the 1970s, "New
Humanism" was even more broadly conceived as a "universal" philosophy, drawing on and bringing into confluence diverse cultures, according its advocates (Puledda 2), and it has been advanced as a global
strategy by such diverse figures as Mikhail Gorbachev and Mario
Rodriguez Cobos (Silo). *The Humanist Manifesto II* (1973) repudiates
the "dogmas" and "myths" of traditional religions and asserts that moral
values derive their sources from human experience, that reason and

intelligence are the most effective instruments of humankind. It affirms the dignity of the individual, and the possibilities of freedom of choice. It advocates civil liberties and a democratic society, the separation of ideology and state, and the development of a world community which exercises environmental and economic responsibility (Lamont, "Appendix" 293).

Humanistic literary criticism also purports to be holistic and inclusive. According to M. H. Abrams, it "deals with a work of literature as composed by a human being, for human beings, and about human beings and matters of human concern" (37). It assumes agency and authorship. Abrams locates himself in the "frame of reference" of Aristotle, Horace, Edmund Wilson, and Northrop Frye. Similarly, the humanist scholars of the "Cambridge School" in the 1930s, such as F. R. Leavis, believed that literature functioned as a resource for the exploration of human values. Leavis assumed the possibility of self-determination and volition—that individuals have choices, both for themselves, and for their societies. They are not wholly determined by religious or secular ideologies: "there is a certain measure of spiritual autonomy in human affairs, and [...] human intelligence, choice and will really and effectively operate, expressing an inherent human nature" (*The Common Pursuit* 184). According to Leavis,

> there *is*, then, a point of view above classes; there *can* be intellectual, aesthetic and moral activity that is not merely an expression of class origin and economic circumstances; there *is* a "human culture" to be aimed at that must be achieved by cultivating a certain autonomy of the human spirit. (*For Continuity* 9)

Self-knowledge, individualism, humanism, a civil society—these are the best aspects of the humanist experiment, according to John Ralston Saul. "Practical humanism is the voyage towards equilibrium without the expectation of actually arriving there"—"the acceptance of time versus the fear of it" (154). In late twentieth-century Canadian drama, these humanist values are assumed, validated, or interrogated. In some respects, as Terry Eagleton has pointed out in his critique of liberal humanism, they are portrayed as having "dwindled to the impotent conscience of bourgeois society, gentle, sensitive and ineffectual," but humanism remains "the best ideology of the 'human' that present bourgeois society can muster" (200). Eagleton sees humanism as "a suburban moral ideology, limited in practise to largely interpersonal matters" (207). In the plays under discussion in this essay, humanism is indeed placed in a suburban context, but the interpersonal matters assume wider implications: domestic space takes on metaphysical dimensions, and the interaction of family members, friends and acquaintances works to validate and/or to question social, moral, and spiritual values.

* * *

Joan MacLeod's *2000* is a domestic play set on the interstices of society and wilderness. It demonstrates the limitations of liberal humanism in a world characterized by the unpredictable and the unknowable, but it also enacts those values that keep intact, even strengthen the human interactions and commonalities that constitute the lineaments of a "civilized" society. The setting quite specifically locates the action in a precarious space between the knowable and the unknown, evoking a technologized consumer culture that cannot entirely displace the elemental forces of nature—"a suburb of Vancouver built up against the mountains" (MacLeod 11). This domestic space is inhabited by a middle-aged husband and wife, Sean and Wyn, and by Wyn's grandmother, "Nanny," whose centenary coincides with the end of the millennium. The title and the characterization clearly suggest that the gyre is finally unwound, and a "Second Coming" is at hand. In the monologue that opens the play, Wyn recounts how a cougar infiltrated the heart of Vancouver society—the Pacific Coliseum. As in Judith Thompson's *Lion in the Streets*, a "rough beast" prowls through urban streets, and through the hearts and minds of individuals. Anarchy and disorder are also embodied in the threatening presence of the "Mountain Man" who lurks outside the windows, and who is invited into the household by Nanny, who recognizes that "a mountain man's property [knows] no bounds" (20). For Sean and Wyn, the Mountain Man is an embodiment of the failures of their society—the homeless, the destitute, the deranged—whom they cannot help despite their liberal philosophies and "good works." He confounds their philosophies and brings chaos into their own spaces. Sean is acutely aware of the limitations of his efforts as a "city planner":

> I go to my job, I work hard. I really try to come up with solutions to improve our lot in the future, that will help correct a multitude of mistakes. I try my best to live in a way that doesn't harm others. [...] When did I become the enemy? (113-14)

Sean's helpless humanitarianism, the philosophy of a White, middle-class, middle-aged male in Western society, has become demonized, not because it is wrong, but because it is inadequate.

However, the faint hope of humanism is evident in Wyn's dreams. She believes that all "signs" are amenable to a rational discussion, that there is a spiritual dimension in life, and that love should function as a cohesive interpersonal and social reality. She attempts to articulate her hope for the new millennium as "world peace, a cleaner planet, an end to hunger et cetera and so forth, and for me, personally, this—the death of yearning" (14). However, she is also disinclined to believe that any of her dreams will be realized: "Well that's the way with dreams, isn't it?

Everything rich and real then BANG! Whack! All gone ..." (15). When she extends sympathetic, humanitarian overtures to the Mountain Man, she is sexually attacked.

There is at least a partial redemption for Sean and Wyn at the beginning of the new millennium. Sean has acquired a "Global Positioning System" that "tells us exactly where we are on the face of the earth" (114). Although he does acknowledge that no philosophical system exists to determine the point—"on land, nothing is level and everything is in the way—dead reckoning is impossible" (115)—he does know that individuals can only survive in terms of community or family: "we're just getting so isolated from one another. Everyone, not just you and me. So we fight that Wyn, we fight against that as hard as we can" (117). Wyn remains pragmatic in her response: she knows exactly where they are—in their own backyard, and it is here that they must realize their values. At the end of the play, they stand together in the dark, gazing at the stars.

* * *

George Walker also establishes a dialectic between nihilism and humanism in his plays. A recurrent theme, from *The Prince of Naples* (1973) to *Heaven* (2000), is the attempted indoctrination of a recalcitrant humanist into an anarchic, anti-humanist position. According to Craig Stewart Walker, the playwright "maintains a troubled bewilderment at the loss of humanist values even as he appears to accept many of the philosophical premises that make the maintenance of humanist values an absurdity" (272). In his "East End" trilogy, Walker explores the possibility of operative humanist values, usually through the person of a woman who defies social anarchy and irrationality. According to Jerry Wasserman, in these earlier plays,

> Walker's women [...] act from a sense of personal imperative based on a vested familial or communal interest in the social world in which they intervene [...] they adopt attainable goals and pragmatic strategies. (41)

In *Better Living*, Nora is a "possibility character" who practises the doctrine of "betterism," a term coined by Walker to explain the possibilities of a humanistic optimism in his *East End Plays*:

> For me it was a matter of letting more light into my plays; just naturally, I felt I had to do that, see what sort of hope—that's not a good word; "possibility" might be better—I could find [...] I'm getting more possibility, more future, into the work. (Wallace 22)

Nora's domestic environment is complicated and fraught, like the larger society which it reflects in microcosm. Each of her three daughters is struggling through the process of self-realization: the youngest, Gail, has abnegated any sense of social or personal responsibility in favour of a liberal sexuality; her middle daughter, Mary Ann, is returning home, having left her baby with her husband; her eldest daughter is a lawyer who appears rational and controlled, but who in fact has been traumatized by her relationship with her father. This long-absent, violent father and husband, Tom, whom Nora and her brother Jack had believed successfully dispatched, returns on a mission to save the family from a Third World invasion. Nora's response is to tunnel out another room under the backyard for her daughters and their present and future daughters. She finds a willing and able assistant in her "late" husband, Tom, whom she contends is someone else. She invents her own reality in order to create a safe space, and resists the nihilism of her brother Jack, a lapsed priest, who believes only that "Life. Is. Dumb" (166):

> No Jack, it's not a hole. It's a room. And it could be more. It could be anything. I could be a new way to live. An underground world. A place to keep vegetables. A safe place to hide. A bomb shelter. (168)

She teaches herself how to overcome each difficulty and to "live better" by "finding the right book" (142), but she recognizes the importance of accessing the knowledge and experience of others. However, Tom's survival strategies—order, control, precision—are essentially fascist and destructive of humanist values. He embodies "the soldier of the total shit future" (205), and his violent tactics can and have been turned against the family. Like the mother in Sharon Pollock's play about social upheaval and the consequences of war, *Fair Liberty's Call*, Nora believes that the future is something you make—and it can be a happy one. Walker sees this journey from nihilism to social commitment as a recurrent pattern in many of his plays: "You begin with anger and energy; but then you face things—the details of life—and you meet the emptiness that you're afraid of" ("Looking for the Light" 27). But he is not pursuing an ideological position: he distrusts ideology "as a limited road to a limited truth" (29).

In the six plays which comprise *Suburban Motel*, Walker's vision is darker, and he rejects the possibility of personal solutions to social and interpersonal disintegration: "I wanted to be healthy, for a long time, in and around *Love and Anger*, I wanted to contribute, to be the good citizen. Now I suppose it's okay to say, I don't give a fuck. I'm that way. So I'm in this thing where I'm not responsible for saving the world, or making it better or anything else." (*Brick* 64). In each play, the end of "civilization" is enacted in a motel on the edge of society, in a room in which the lives of the inhabitants have been reduced to psychic survival. In the play entitled *The End of Civilization*, a husband and wife have relocated to a shabby motel room which symbolizes in microcosm the misery in the "civilized" present. The two have been forced to downsize from their model home and leave their children with the wife's sister when the husband, Henry, loses his job. Lily accompanies him on his ostensible job search to lend support, although she asserts the need for some hope, some purpose in their relocation:

> And if you don't we're all screwed. Because there's just no way I can help. Oh I can be supportive. I can "pull" along with you. Or behind you. But basically it's your rope we're pulling on. And if there's nothing on the end of the rope worth anything then well that's it [...]. We might as well gather up the kids, go home, lock the doors, make up some Kool-Aid with a bit of cyanide in it, and have our own little Jonestown. (258)

It becomes increasingly obvious that Henry is moving beyond rational constraints. He sees his loss as indicative of a corporatist world order, against which he feels powerless—an exemplification of John Ralston Saul's "unconscious society," but his response is wholly destructive. Henry has enacted his rage by murdering other job applicants, and he is being investigated by two detectives: Max, who attempts to effect reason and order in his work and his life, but who enforces a "big brother" attitude to the public good through an exercise of authority primarily used to intimidate and bully; and Donny, his more sympathetic partner, who is acutely aware of the ways in which innocence is lost and souls are destroyed in a system which overrides interpersonal relationships, but who perseveres in his caring for Lily, even though he further complicates and confuses things. In the final confrontation between the humanist, Donny, and the nihilistic Henry, it is Henry who gets shot, ironically while demanding that Donny acknowledge that he was never a victim and a loser.

* * *

The plays of Morris Panych take an even more ambivalent view of humanist values in interpersonal and social interactions, but inherent in their ambiguities is an assumption of common human needs and values that test the deviant behaviours of the characters. They also share with the Theatre of the Absurd a black humour that balances despair and hope, determinism and choice. Panych's dramatic works reflect an existentialist humanism as defined by Jean Paul Sartre, who posited in 1968 "that human beings are never wholly identifiable with their conditioning, that alienation is possible precisely because the individual is free, because the human being is not a thing" (from Sartre's *L'Existentialisme est un humanisme*, quoted in Puledda 84).

Lawrence and Holloman (1998) explores the relationship of two antithetical personalities—one an optimist, the other a pessimist and nihilist. Holloman's name alludes to the title of T. S. Eliot's poem, "The Hollow Men," which delineates the modern world as being without values, without conviction, ending "*Not with a bang but with a whimper*" (*Selected Poems* 80). In Panych's play, however, Holloman's life does end with a "bang": he is accidentally shot by Lawrence after failing at an attempt at suicide. His nihilistic interpretation of life as a joke appears in one sense validated, but Lawrence's final words—that there is some meaning, "a brilliant and complex kind of logic" (127)—is also ironically demonstrated, in that all of Holloman's efforts to destroy Lawrence have resulted in his own destruction. Holloman's testing of Lawrence with a series of disasters also recalls the trials of Job; in this light, then, the disasters can be read as tests of the human spirit. As in MacLeod's *2000*, Panych's play offers no articulate or coherent statement of philosophy: both Janine and Lawrence cannot find the words, but at least their incomplete sentences may be read as an attempt at understanding: "We may not understand the logic of it at times but that doesn't mean it doesn't—doesn't something—doesn't—what's the— what's the—word I'm looking for?" (127). There is no response from Holloman, however. He is dead.

In fact, Lawrence has consistently misunderstood Holloman since their first meeting in a bar—assuming that he is a shoe salesman with no prospects for advancement, a "liberal" who empathizes with losers (15). Actually, Holloman is a calculating nihilist, who determines to destroy Lawrence's simplistic optimistic outlook, one driven by a capitalistic Darwinian philosophy, egocentricity, and ignorance. But Holloman also guesses that Lawrence feels sustained by his optimism, whereas Holloman's superior intelligence and acumen have resulted only in his self-defeating and destructive pessimism, a vision of life as a brief interval between birth and death, signifying nothing.

* * *

The possibility of lived humanist values is also explored in Vern Thiessen's *Blowfish* (1996)—an extended philosophical monologue, spoken by a caterer named Lumiere. He recounts his life in Alberta— from his youth as his father's mortuary assistant, to the trauma of his twin brother's car accident, to the deaths of his parents in the Edmonton tornado of 1988, to his political education, and finally to his own death as a ritualistic celebration. As in *Lawrence and Holloman*, Lumiere's life unfolds as a series of disasters that test his beliefs, but finally which also comprise them. He formulates a philosophy of dying, which is integral to his philosophy of living, and he takes his cue from the first humanist—Socrates—whose dying afforded the opportunity for another dialogue with his followers. The implication is, then, that a humanistic philosophy that values rationality and self-determination is defined through interrogation and debate, not through fixed systems or ideologies. As John Murrell recognizes in his introduction to the published text of *Blowfish*, this inquiry constitutes one of the most important responsibilities of drama, and the creation of theatre is essentially a humanist enterprise:

> I think Shakespeare was trying to do what all creative people have been try-
> ing to do ever since there were creative people [...]. He was trying to flash
> an intense and individual reflection of human existence in our eyes, so that
> its beauty can illuminate us before its anguish causes us to look away. (n.p.)

In *Blowfish*, Lumiere's vision of Socrates is similar to John Ralston
Saul's: Socrates was primarily motivated by the idea of a disinterested
public good. To this end, he applied a mode of inquiry that activated and
energized doubt and irony. Thiessen's play employs a similar process,
pitting the chaotic, irrational forces of a tornado against the positive
constructive elements of the family as a microcosm of human society.
His protagonist is also engaged in a debate that includes political and
social values when he is seduced into the fold of the Conservative Party
through his infatuation with Mila Mulroney, the Prime Minister's wife.
Her advice to him is that he "serve others and others will serve
[him]" (11). From an unemployed philosophy graduate, Lumiere transforms into "a Young Conservative: independent, ambitious, responsible,
debt-free, entrepreneurial, driven" (11). He "progresses" through a
number of jobs from security guard to a writer for an organization called
Canadians for a Better Canada, "whose more radical members were
accused of beating a man into unconsciousness" (11). When the radicals
are convicted, he is out of a job, and relocates to the U.S., where he
meets up with an even more extremist group. His experience with an
American anarchist involved in the destruction of civilized public
society south of the border convinces him that the appropriate response
to irrational human violence is to eradicate it. While preparing for his
final curtain, Lumiere illustrates the "four things that link us as human
beings":

> Number one: Food. We all have to eat.
> Number two: Death. We all have to die.
> Number three: The Weather ...
> [...]
> And number four: Politics.
> [...]
> Politics is people. People like you and me. People converging in groups:
> families, churches, governments, unions, and political parties. The farmer,
> the weatherman, the undertaker. (7-8)

Lumiere contends that what we all need is "Someone to watch, to
witness, to honour, to ... to remember" (42) and he stages his own death
as a ritual celebration shared by the audience in an enactment of
Socrates' death by hemlock. The theatre, then, provides the framework
for such rituals—a communal experience of sharing and understanding.
Modern Canadian theatre shares with ancient Greek theatre this basic
humanist impulse.

* * *

These plays all engage in a humanist perspective, giving "the verdict of lived experience and social character of the culture—the social forms and identities and the way of life the culture generates" (Adams 280). This essay also engages in a humanist perspective, and is necessarily conditioned by sets of organizing ideas coupled with epistemological and metaphysical assumptions which respond only to what they recognize in cultural artifacts. What you see is what you get.

Works Cited

Abrams, M. H. "What is Humanistic Criticism?" *The Emperor Redressed: Critiquing Critical Theory*. Ed. Dwight Eddins. Tuscaloosa: U of Alabama P, 1995. 13-44.

Adams, E. M. *The Metaphysics of Self and World: Towards a Humanistic Philosophy*. Philadelphia: Temple UP, 1991.

Eagleton, Terry. *Literary Theory: An Introduction*. Minneapolis: U of Minnesota P, 1983.

Eliot, T. S. *Selected Poems*. London: Faber and Faber, 1961.

Lamont, Corliss. *The Philosophy of Humanism*. 6th ed. New York: Frederick Ungar, 1982.

Leavis, F. R. *The Common Pursuit*. New York: New York UP, 1964.

_____. *For Continuity*. Cambridge: The Minority Press, 1933.

Levin, Richard. "Bashing the bourgeois subject." *Textual Practice* 3: 1 (Spring 1989): 76-86.

Lill, Wendy. *Corker*. Vancouver: Talonbooks, 1998.

MacIvor, Daniel. *Marion Bridge*. Vancouver; Talonbooks, 1999.

MacLeod, Joan. *2000*. Vancouver: Talonbooks, 1997.

Puledda, Salvatore. *On Being Human: Interpretations of Humanism from the Renaissance to the Present*. Trans. Andrew Hurley. New Humanism Series. San Diego: Latitude Press, 1997.

Panych, Morris. *Lawrence & Holloman*. Vancouver: Talonbooks, 1998.

Saul, John Ralston. *The Unconscious Civilization*. Toronto: House of Anansi, 1995.

Sherman, Jason. *Reading Hebron*. Toronto: Playwrights Canada, 1998.

Taylor, Drew Hayden. *alterNatives*. Vancouver: Talonbooks, 2000.

Thiessen, Vern. *Blowfish*. Toronto: Playwrights Canada, 1998.

Walker, Craig Stewart. *The Buried Astroblabe: Canadian Dramatic Imagination and Western Tradition*. Montreal: McGill-Queen's UP, 2001.

Walker, George F. *Better Living. The East End Plays*. Toronto: Playwrights Canada, 1988.

_____. *The End of Civilization, Suburban Motel*. Rev. ed. Vancouver: Talonbooks, 1999.

_____. "Looking for the Light: A Conversation with George F. Walker." Interview by Robert Wallace. *Canadian Drama* 14: 1 (1988): 22-33.

_____. "A Conversation with George Walker." Interview by Carole Corbeil. *Brick: A Literary Journal* 58 (1998): 64.

Wasserman, Jerry. "'It's the Do-Gooders Burn My Ass': Modern Canadian Drama and the Crisis of Liberalism." *Modern Drama* XLIII: 1 (Spring 2000): 32-47.

Wilson, Edwin. *The Genesis of a Humanist Manifesto.* Http://www. infidels.org/library/modern/Edwin_Wilson/manifesto.

"Look. Look again."

Daniel David Moses' Decolonizing Optics[1]

Ric KNOWLES

University of Guelph

Almighty Voice and His Wife (1991), by Delaware playwright Daniel David Moses from the Six Nations reserve near Brantford, Ontario, is a play obsessed with watching. In its first act, "White Girl," the ironically named Cree wife of the play's title, is herself obsessed with white men's use of telescopes ("clear beads they look though" [15]) to maintain surveillance while remaining themselves invisible. She imagines a white man's glass-eyed god who is "everywhere [and] can see everything" (9), and whom she associates with the power of naming and knowing, with the silver dollars that are posted as rewards for the capture of her husband, and with the all-seeing glare of the daylight sun (15-17, 19-21). But to a greater or lesser degree—though usually much less explicitly—all of Moses' plays are concerned with optics, and with the deconstruction of the panoptic technologies—"they even turn the prairie into a jail" (12)—of the colonizing gaze. In *Almighty Voice and His Wife*, the telescope, the glass god, and the masculinist glare of the sun are set explicitly in contrast to an equally pervasive but transformational and female moon,[2] together with the dreams and "Visions" of White Girl and Almighty Voice that frame and punctuate the play's first act and provide alternative ways of seeing (3, 15, 25, 26, 29). But in the second act, a savagely parodic minstrel show featuring "Almighty Ghost" in place of the absent Messrs. Bones, Tambo, and Drum, the white man's gaze—already openly associated with the objectifications of Western history writing, journalism, capitalism, and the entertainment industry—

---

[1] This essay has benefited from the always astute comments of Christine Bold, to whom I am indebted.

[2] "[T]he dark of the moon" (26) is a constant presence in the stage directions to all of Moses' plays.

explicitly turns into that of the theatre audience itself, as the technologies of theatrical seeing themselves come under scrutiny:

> What's going on! The show. The Red and White Victoria Regina Spirit Revival show! These fine, kind folks want to know the truth, the amazing details and circumstance behind your savagely beautiful appearance. They also want to be entertained and enlightened and maybe a tiny bit thrilled, just a goose of frightened. They want to laugh and cry. They want to know the facts. And it's up to you and me to try and lie that convincingly. (32)

In this act, Moses astutely reverses the gaze, confronts his non-Native audiences with the historical and continuing voyeurism of a European theatrical technology of viewing that parallels that of the telescope and positions the audience safely in a darkened, invisible space where it can observe the objectified, "to-be-looked-at" exotica on the stage as if through a glass, darkly. Moreover, as in all of his work for the stage, he also explicitly associates this gaze with both naming and knowing, and he repeatedly "ghosts" it with spectral presences of various kinds (mists, teepees, and the human dead) that problematize its objectifying relationship with "the real." The reversal of this gaze, which happens startlingly over the intermission in *Almighty Voice and His Wife*, confronts the non-Native audience with its own curiosity and the objectifying cultural work this curiosity, however well intentioned, performs. It also confronts the non-Native scholar and critic, if somewhat less directly, with the role that objectifying and commodifying Western epistemologies have played in the subjection of First Nations Peoples as to-be-looked-at, to-be-understood, labeled, and therefore to-be-consumed others, thereby turning Natives into raw materials for the industrialized Western production of knowledge. "One [*sic*] must always strive for accuracy," argues the "Interlocutor" in parodic white face speaking *as* the internalized racism of White Girl,[3] "Do you have documentation?" (36).

Moses' interest in the technologies of seeing would seem to have emerged at once from his own personal history of bad eyesight and from his learned sense of the optics of cultural location. He attributes some of his interest in "visualizing," imaging, and words, to the accident of having had a "quack" optometrist as a child (Lutz 157), and he describes the experience of being a student in a first-year humanities course at York University in Toronto, questioning the assumption that profit was an essential motive in human nature: "Not where I come from," he argued, disrupting the universalist, ethnocentric gaze of his fellow classmates in a way that he has continued to do, under protest, as he has played the reluctant role of revisionist educator in his subsequent career

---

[3]   "[T]his is what they've done to you?," Almighty Voice cries as he *"looks into her eyes"* [39] in the second act of *Almighty Voice and His Wife*.

as a playwright and poet (Moses, "Adam"). But Moses has always been too aware of the power relationships implicit in the labeling, categorizing, and taxonomic gaze of the Western scientific microscope to rest comfortably on either side of the glass—either under its gaze or employing its (theatrical or generic) technologies: "controlling the naming of things," he argues "is so important" ("Adam")—too important to be taken for granted.

The July/August and September/October 2001 issues of *CanPlay*, the periodical newsletter of the Playwrights Union of Canada, include articles by Moses on early plays by his First Nations contemporaries Tomson Highway and Ben Cardinal. In these essays, Moses challenges the universality of conflict and character, respectively, as being "of the essence," defining features of all drama. Both articles question the taken-for-granted optics of Western generic and theatrical structures and conventions. Moses determined that, "where I was coming from" ("Of the Essence" 6), conflict was less important than contrast, and that the expansive possibilities of space, landscape, and memory mattered more than the determinations of individual character development over linear expanses of historical time. The landscape of Cardinal's *Generic Warriors and No Name Indians*, he writes,

> is a stage where [...] every time seems to exist in familiar proximity. It is the cosmos where an eclipse of the male sun by the female moon is an expression of the possibility of harmony. It is a dream constructed in a way that functions like personal memory or nightmare—pratfalls hard on the images of bloodletting. ("A Bridge," 7)

Moses' recognition of the way Highway's and Cardinal's plays "structured reality and the landscape that reality grew from" might be seen as having framed his own search for non-European optics, and for dramatic structures in which conflict is no longer of the essence, individual character and psychological development are no longer the measures of universal truth, and "time is no longer the straight and narrow line demanded by the progress of history or the history of progress" ("A Bridge" 7).

Almighty Voice and His Wife has been published three times, and will very soon appear once again in an anthology of First Nations Drama in English forthcoming from Playwrights Canada. It is also frequently taught in courses on Canadian and/or Native drama, and it is the only one of Moses' plays–many of which remain as yet unavailable in trade publications–to have received significant critical attention.[4] As a play that directly addresses a non-Native audience, this attention is

---

[4] For further discussion of *Almighty Voice and His Wife*, see Appleford (the best discussion of Moses' work to date) and Knowles.

perhaps not surprising; and, as a non-Native scholar, I want here to seize the opportunity it offers and use the gap between the play's acts as a gateway for non-Natives toward understanding the rest of Moses' *oeuvre*. His overall dramatic output may be read—at least from my own cultural positioning—as a search for and interrogation of dramatic forms, as a moving away from the naturalism of *Almighty Voice*'s first act and its potentially reifying optics towards the kind of *super*naturalist, *performative orality* that, because it requires audience "response-ability" (Lenze 51), is both ethical and transformational, having to do with "metamorphosis" and "possibility" (Lutz 156) rather than realism's reifications. Each of Moses' plays implicitly or explicitly critiques the objectifying optics of naturalism, received dramatic (versus story-telling) forms, and European theatrical technologies of seeing and shaping; each searches for an alternative formal optics; and all are replete with ghosts as the *not-seen*, who model a culturally repressed *what-really-is*, the repressed truth that must be revealed beneath an oppressive realism in order to release the *what-could-be*.

Moses' sequence of four "city plays," in which the same Native family is represented not only at different times but through different generic lenses, can perhaps best be understood as an experiment in optics. The first and most generically familiar of these plays to a non-Native audience is *Coyote City* (1988), the action of which is precipitated, *Hamlet*-like, by a ghost. And indeed, Moses has discussed this play as his first and last experiment with the tragic form (Appleford 22). It tells the simple story of Lena, a young Native woman on a reserve, who receives a phone call from Johnny, her ghostly lover-beyond-the-grave, inviting her to meet him at Toronto's Silver Dollar Tavern (much frequented by that city's "urban Indians"). It traces her (and her family's) fruitless journey in response to that enigmatic call. Even within the frame of contemporary, more-or-less naturalistic (domestic) tragedy, however, the play complicates European formal conventions through its focus less on an individual heroic male figure than on a community of women. It validates the women's seeing of ghosts (and angels) in a community where Natives tend to be invisible at the best of times ("they don't want to see Indians" [44]), and it resists the comforts of conventional closure and cathartic release. The play is peppered with (Native) characters both alive and dead, who complain about their (ghostly) invisibility and plead with other characters "blind to the light" (49) to "open your eyes" (49), or "look at me" (95)—this last line recurs most frequently in the Moses canon. Finally, Moses here introduces a tension between the (objectifying) optics of drama and the (interactive) mode of story-telling. This tension surfaces later in his work to problematize the technologies of the theatrical gaze, as the surface of the dramatic representation is troubled by a parallel oral narrative, "Coyote and the

Shadow People" (Lutz 165). In this parallel story, the trickster Coyote searches for his dead wife, but loses the ability to "see them, the dead people" (43) and "never [...] see[s] that woman of his again in his life" (103).

The three subsequent city plays vary widely (and wildly) in genre, while chronologically following the ongoing story of the characters introduced in *Coyote City*. *Big Buck City* (1991) takes the form of a wildly scatological Christmas farce, city comedy to *Coyote City*'s urban domestic tragedy, in which Lena and Johnny's child, "Babe Fisher," is born; *Kyotopolis* (1993) is a mediatized sci-fi satire about Babe's death/ascension to heaven/space in a space program "tragedy"; and *City of Shadows* (1995) functions as a shadow "play of voices" (v) after the fashion of Dylan Thomas's *Under Milk Wood*, in which all of the characters, now dead, reflect on the action of the tetralogy. *Big Buck City* is perhaps the least successful of the city plays in problematizing the objectifying gaze, though it maintains echoes of *Coyote City*'s focus on looking (35), on seeing or not seeing ghosts (36), on the invisibility of Natives on the streets of the city (where "they treat you like a ghost" [95]), and on the ironies inherent in a world with "all the white faces" and in which "nobody believes in ghosts" (95). It also explicitly critiques the critical, non-Native gaze, in the person of "Mrs. Jones peeking out her drapes" (65), and of the neighbors whose "eyes glaze over every day" (70) as they watch for police cars in front of the home of the play's "Indian business warrior" (9). But the play is primarily a farcically parodic Nativity story, set at Christmas and circulating around the illegitimate birth of the "Babe," the daughter of the earthbound Lena and the heavenly Johnny as ghost/god, in the home of Lena's uncle, a perverse foster-father Joseph figure, the acquisitive and appropriately named "Jack Buck." And it all happens through the complicated agency of a gay Native street kid/trickster/"holy ghost" figure named Ricky Raccoon ("I'm the ghost of Christmas. I can pass through walls" [72]), who knows that "you can't own babies" (100).

All of the same characters (and many more) figure prominently in *Kyotopolis*, the third play in the series. If *Big Buck City* observes, for the most part, dramatic (if farcical) conventions, and touches only lightly on the extra-dramatic need to "tell [...] the story [...] A new story" (95), *Kyotopolis* breaks entirely and outrageously new ground. With fifteen characters, two puppets, a "Tele Presence Operator," "the voice of a Tele Presence system," and a Virtual Reality TV show—not to mention various other lenses, cameras, monitors, and mechanisms for the production and projection of petroglyphs, constellations, space-scapes, and other mediated realities— "this stupid equipment, okay?" (4)—the play is virtually unproducible within the market economies of the professional theatre—which may be part of its point. *Kyotopolis*—in which the

"Babe" (Fisher) appears as an astronaut involved in a Challenger-style tragic explosion that serves both as her (apparent) death and assumption into heaven—not only juxtaposes different technologies of seeing, foregrounding its own radical shifts in perspective; it also goes so far as literally to trap its characters inside television monitors and glass display cases, as it journalistically (and voyeuristically) pursues "the story" of Babe, lost in space, last seen with her face *hauntingly* pressed against the glass window of the space capsule "with that look" (33, my emphasis). "She always looked that way sort of. Pressed up against the glass, trying to get in" (29). The "look" is returned to repeatedly in this media-obsessed play, which frames virtually all of its action within interrogations of what it means to look, to watch, and to be seen, and within a society obsessed with "covering the story" rather than *telling* (and sharing) it: "That's the story?," Ricky Raccoon asks at one point, "[t]hat's the truth?," while the play's journalist, Mary, frames her account of Babe's death as a parodic crucifixion and assumption—"to die for our sins" (51)—even as her birth had been framed in *Big Buck City* as a parodic Nativity. "Do you think Babe has risen from the dead too," Mary later asks Babe's Uncle and agent, Jack Buck (63)? *Kyotopolis* contains what is perhaps Moses' most explicit denunciation of Western epistemologies—"*a team of worried scientists talking to reporters*," as one stage direction has it (77). "Look," Mary argues, "people need to know," which Babe's appropriately named aunt Boo[5] glosses as "People need to feel superior" (64), explicitly articulating the power relationships involved in the interested Western fiction of "objective" knowledge. "Babe didn't belong in their story anyhow," she argues, but "you or somebody else right now is writing it all up, explaining it all away" (64). What kind of knowledge, the play asks, only explains things *away*? "Look," it argues, in the line from which I have taken my title for this essay. "Look again!" (16).

The final, short play in the city tetralogy, *City of Shadows*, set "[o]n that reserve between waking and dreams" (2), presents all of its characters, all familiar from the earlier plays in the cycle, after death, "down and out in the lost and found" (12), and reminiscing about their lives (and the plots of the earlier plays). In *City of Shadows*, "every place we go the dead are talking" (56). The optic shift represented by the play is made clear in one of the most unequivocal of Moses' always evocative epigraphs, this time from "Chief Seattle, Squamish, 1853":

> All night when the streets of your cities and villages are silent and you think them deserted, they will throng with the returning hosts that once filled them and still love this beautiful land.

---

5   This play maintains Moses' interest and faith in ghosts (28, 59).

The White Man will never be alone.

Let him be just and deal kindly with my people for the Dead are not power-less. Dead, did I say? There is no death, only a change of worlds. (1)

The play is rife with explicit, revisionist, and ghostly echoes of all of its predecessors in the tetralogy, revisiting the central, parodic story of Babe Fisher, this time as the Annunciation—"an angel appeared and said I could count on the coming of the Lord"(20). But the tone, now, is elegiac. "What good's having eyes in your head," laments the ghost of Jack Buck, "when the only stars that get in them are the fuckers in the constellation Pizza Pie?" (53-54). Like others of Moses' plays, this short, evocative tone poem abounds with references to eyes, sight, vision, and looking ("Look look look,"[47]), including now familiar variations in Moses' work on "seeing through a glass [...] through my own fogged up breath" (36). Cumulatively, the play shapes a relativist vision of "the truth ... according to me" (16)—"as much and as little [...] as can be accorded to me [...] What I've come down to finally" (17): "You must listen to me," pleads the plays' preacher and "street Indian" (2). "You must listen to the truth" (32). Ultimately, all truth claims in this play are like the stars that also haunt it, but then "blind as a bat, stars are, blinded by their own star shine" (50).

The city plays map and problematize relationships among seeing, vision, perspective, looking ("the gaze"), knowing, controlling, and the objectifying technologies of theatre (versus story-telling), then, as they experiment with genre in ways that insist that there is more in heaven, earth, and the Silver Dollar Tavern than are dreamt of in (Western) epistemologies. Moses' other plays zoom in on specific aspects of these issues and optics, particularly those of story and history. *The Dreaming Beauty* (1988) and *The Witch of Niagara* (1998) might be read together as Moses' "story plays," works that seem to emerge less from the conventions of traditional European dramaturgy than from a combination of First Nations "orature" and Western "story-time" children's theatre—except that Moses rightly objects to "the separation of children from adults in mainstream culture" (Lutz 159) and the condescending catego-rizations that relegate certain works to "children's literature" (Lutz 160). Indeed, he objects to taxonomic and generic categorizations of all kinds, seeing them as a product of "book culture," in which writing "becomes art for art's sake rather than for the story's sake, or for communication's sake" (Lutz 163), preferring to think of his writing as story-telling and as "performance, where you come to realize that every performance is unique" (Lutz 164):

It's a strange technology we're dealing with, this writing our words down on paper and alienating the best parts of ourselves into books. I mean, we

started out using that technology as a storage medium, and instead we've
become oppressed by it. (Moses and Goldie xviii)

The Dreaming Beauty and *The Witch of Niagara*, then, can be read as
attempts to move drama from the realms of book culture and art for art's
sake toward those of story-telling and performance. In an article about
the northern, "rez" tour of Ojibway playwright Ian Ross's Governor
General's Award-winning play *fareWEL*, which deals with Native self-
government, Christine Lenze, an Ojibway critic from the Long Plain
First Nation in Southern Manitoba, has written about the perceptual
differences in reception and response between "drama" and "story" in
ways that illuminate Moses' practice. Lenze usefully distinguishes
between performance-as-story and "drama" as an objectifying Western
genre, aligned, perhaps, with both "book culture" and objectifying
European optics. Quoting Simon Ortiz, she argues that

> The interactive nature of ... performance, and concern over what is *required*
> of an audience, suggest a sense of response-ability to the performance in
> which the "story is not only told but it is also listened to, it becomes whole
> in its expression and perception." (Lenze 51, quoting Ortiz 57)

In a sense, these plays replace the monologism of theatrical optics with
the dialogism of story as socially situated utterance that requires the
listeners' attentiveness and confers "response-ability" upon them.

Both *The Dreaming Play* and *The Witch of Niagara* are story/dream
plays focusing on young girls in lands infected by sickness. The later
play, a retelling of the story of the maid of the mist at Niagara Falls,
begins with "The Girl" "[i]n the story—. The story? In the dream!" It
actually enacts an abrupt shift from the dramatic to the narrative mode at
the beginning of its eighth, penultimate scene, as "the moon grows full"
and The Girl's cousin addresses the audience directly, shifting the action
to story and the story from tragedy to comedy, while at the same time
precipitating a final litany of communal thanksgiving as "the sun and
moon both rise over Niagara Falls" (29). The earlier play, *The Dreaming
Beauty*, is set on the shores of Lake Ontario—"Great Shining Water." It
functions as a simple, lyrical fable about the five-hundred-year sleep
(implicitly the period since contact and colonization) of "Beauty of our
People," the granddaughter of Old Woman Moon, and her decision,
finally, to "walk into the world" again (25). The play begins, after a
brief prologue, with "Look"; it is, moreover, punctuated by "Look.
Look. What do you see?," spoken by the girl's dog, Shiner (21), and it
turns, once again, on ghosts, names, and memory. Here the ghosts—
even Grandmother Moon is herself a ghost—represent the repressed
cultural memories, symbols, and values of a people, and the play's
action is about listening to "Echoes! Echoes. The ghosts of voices" (20).
The key scenes in the play, however, on which both the loss and recov-

ery of the culture turn, are scenes about resistance to European taxonomic seeing and naming. In the face of smallpox—the "sleeping
sickness" that "came with the blankets" when Europeans introduced the
disease by importing infected blankets for trade from the hospitals of
Europe ("they want us to die"[16])–the girl's dying Father makes her
promise not to "let them know your name." "Keep your name a secret,"
her mother tells her. "They'll give you a name they've already killed.
Only pretend to make it yours [...]. Forget your name":

> It is a child's name and it will only get you into trouble. They will use it to
> taunt you. They will use it as if it had no spirit in it. They will say it and
> know nothing of the morning you were born. They want to forget about
> things like mist on the river, the sky blushing with happiness, the dripping
> of dew off corn. (17)

"The Girl," as she is called, nameless throughout the body of the play,
gives her name back to her dying father ("I give him back his Beautiful
Daughter of the Dawn" [18]), and indeed forgets it, pretending to die,
and needing to recover it before she can wake up and see her people
again in order that "Morning will come to [her] and everyone" (25).

If Moses' story plays resist the panoptic "show, don't tell" wisdoms
of traditional European dramaturgy, his history plays–*Brébeuf's Ghost*
(1996) and *Almighty Voice and His Wife*–are reclamations and re-
appropriations of stories involving First Nations peoples that have been
in frequent circulation in the dominant culture in Canada. The latter play
combines the lyrical, moon-drenched poetic naturalism of its first act
with the hysterical historical metatheatre of the second—history *as* a
Victoria-Regina-Spirit-Revival-Show—as Almighty Ghost, the return of
the culturally repressed, performs revenant postcolonial resistance and
effects a kind of purgative cultural healing. The former play, *Brébeuf's
Ghost*, takes the form of a sprawling, apocalyptic historical epic, framed
by an epigraph from Tony Kushner: "The end of the world is at hand.
Hello, paleface" (1). Unlike any earlier retelling of what is usually
framed as the story of "the Canadian martyrs"—Jesuit missionaries,
including the "heroic" Jean de Brébeuf of mainstream Canadian and
Roman Catholic mythology, killed by the Iroquois near what is now
Midland, Ontario, in 1649—this play focuses on this historical episode
from the point of view of the community of Lake Nipissing Ojibway,
surrounded by their Iroquois enemies and literally cannibalized from
within by the ministrations of the Black Robes (the Jesuits). The ghost
of Brébeuf precipitates and haunts the disastrous action, and while
unlike Moses' earlier plays, this one associates the ghostly with the
colonizer, like them it uses the revenants to represent the return of what
dramatic realism represses. Like its predecessors, too, this play has an
interest in looking and seeing beyond objectification ("can't you see?"

[6]; "look at me" [22]; "when I looked into his eyes [...] I saw who he was" [45]). Like them, it associates naming with power ("you leave my name alone" [7]; "You don't know who I am. I could use your name to hurt you" [12]). And like them, it finds more truth in dream (9) and story (115) than in history. Although like *The Witch of Niagara*, the play deals with the exorcism of evils that cannibalize the community, *Brébeuf's Ghost* ends more ambiguously, with less obvious optimism, and it associates the assertion that "Broken Moon" will soon "step into [her] flesh" with the exile of the community and the uncertain disappearance of a cannibal/ghost that might return again.

The most lyrical and evocative of Moses's plays, and the most difficult either to classify or explicate, *The Indian Medicine Shows*, consists in fact of two linked one-act plays, *The Moon and Dead Indians* and *Angel of the Medicine Show*, performed together in that order at Theatre Passe Muraille in 1996 and published together in 1998. Here Moses' search for a contextualizing optic virtually escapes genre altogether, though both plays have historical settings (in late 19th-century New Mexico); moreover, the medecine-show rehearsal of the second play's closing sequences resembles the performative form of the second act of *Almighty Voice and His Wife*, albeit without that play's direct address of the audience. While in *Brébeuf's Ghost* the Black Robe as colonizer is the ghost that cannibalizes the indigenous culture, in *The Indian Medicine Shows* the Indian is the ghost that haunts the landscape and the repressed, collective unconscious of an already decadent capitalist "civilization." *The Moon and Dead Indians*, set in 1878, is most notable for the absence of Indians. Although they exist in the mind of Ma Jones as a constant offstage threat, the Indians, as Ma's son Jonny knows, are all dead, and she is just "hearing ghosts" (18). In the play's most harrowing sequence, which culminates in Ma's suicide, Jonny and his visiting "friend" Billy recall and relive their brutal murder of one of the last of them, a "skinny little Indian who acted all pretty like a girl" (63): "He looked at me Billy [...]. His dark eyes looked at me [...]. The blood looks so black in this light [...]. So black. He looked right at me" (66). This play's obsession with watching, looking, "ghosting," and being looked at is established from the outset, where Ma is discovered, as "*the last fragment of the moon is setting [...] pale in her bedclothes as a ghost, a Winchester rifle in her hands [...] keeping watch*" (13). Guns are associated with looking throughout the play, as Billy tries to confront Jonny with their earlier homoerotic relationship. "Is this what it takes to get you to look me in the eye?," Billy asks, a gun to Jonny's heart. "I just want a good look" (39-40). Jonny pleads with his mother to "look at me," throughout the play and just before her death (49, 68), but it is only after her death, when Billy immediately pleads, "Jonny?

Jonny, look at me," that Jonny makes the essential connection: "See, Billy? See how black the blood looks?" (68).

The action of *Angel of the Medicine Show* takes place in 1890, twelve years after that of *The Moon and Dead Indians*, and it does include an Indian, David, as the key performer—the ghost in the Medicine shows that Jonny is now disastrously running with his lover Angela. But David is the object of everyone's gaze, is hauled off by an angry mob for lynching before the play opens, and is "the one true reason" for audiences to watch the show and be attentive to the spiel about "Dr. Osage Oswald's Omnipotent Elixir," "from a formula handed down from generation to generation by my forefathers, who were chiefs of the Osage Indians [...]. The Indian gave you America and now he gives you the magic secret of health and happiness with long life, the greatest blessing of all" [130-31]). David represents the show's one (allegorical?) claim to authenticity—*as* ghost—since the only "real" Indian is a dead Indian, and "the yokels love to see a wild Indian dance for his keep" (96). He is the object of Jonny's gaze, who calls him "bright eyes" (112 and *passim*) *and* "moon face" (131). "Why can't you look at me the way you look at him?" (123), Angela asks (and he repeats the question to her about the absent and now dead Billy Antrim [124]). "Davy, look at me. Look at me like you used to," Jonny pleads, to which David replies, "Bright eyes died, died and went to heaven" (120). "Look at me, Davy. Don't cry. Look at me!" (121). Jonny's need to be looked at is ultimately revealed as the need to be forgiven—"I need him to forgive me. For what we did to the Indians" (123). "I got to see. I got to see what we're doing," he cries (127). Forced in the rehearsed medicine show to play the ghost (131-34), David ultimately burns the stage and disappears—leaving "*burnt feathers*" (134), and performing, perhaps as an allegory of the proverbial (and wished-for) "vanishing Indian," "[t]hat goddam vanishing act you been dreaming about" (136). "It's better this way," Angela argues. "Look at me. So he's gone now. Look at me, Your Indian's finally done that goddam vanishing act too" (136). A play obsessed with characters opening their eyes ends with Jonny, and not surprisingly, "*his eyes are open*" (138).

As an innovative tour through performance forms and styles, the dramatic *oeuvre* of Daniel David Moses can be seen as a search for a decolonizing optics, a resistance to categorization and naming, a rediscovery of (invisible) ghosts, a return from drama to story, and a refusal to settle into a single way of looking. But as Moses says of most Native writers, he thinks of "formal innovation as not an end in itself, but as part of the story" (Moses and Goldie xiv). And as Christine Lenze argues of the still larger variety of Native theatrical forms in Canada, Moses' resistance to categorization constitutes an "indeterminacy" that is "perhaps a good thing."

It allows First nations writers to work through various forms of performance and narrative *and* allows audiences to respond through various forms of "watching." Native theatre cannot be defined from one place or position. It interacts, changes and forms itself *one stage at a time.* (51)

Works Cited

Appleford, Rob. "The Desire to Crunch Bone: Daniel David Moses and the 'True Real Indian.'" *Canadian Theatre Review* 77 (Winter 1993): 21-26.

Knowles, Ric. "Playing Indian." *The Theatre of Form and the Production of Meaning: Contemporary Canadian Dramaturgies.* Toronto: ECW Press, 1999. 138-50.

Lenze, Christine. "'The Whole Thing You're Doing is White Man's Ways': *fareWEL*'s Northern Tour." *Canadian Theatre Review* 108 (Fall 2001): 48-51.

Lutz, Harmut. "Daniel David Moses." Lutz, *Contemporary Challenges: Conversations with Canadian Native Authors.* Saskatoon: Fifth House, 1991. 155-68.

Moses, Daniel David. "Adam Means 'Red Man': A talk for 'Challenging Racism in the Arts,' a forum at Metro Hall [Toronto] 22 September 1998." 15 September 2001. Http://citd.scar.utoronto.ca/APS/art1.html.

_____. *Almighty Voice and His Wife.* Toronto: Playwrights Canada, 2001.

_____. *Big Buck City.* Toronto: Exile, 1998.

_____. *Brébeuf's Ghost: A Tale of Horror in Three Acts.* Toronto: Playwrights Union of Canada Copyscript, 1996.

_____. "A Bridge Across Time." *CanPlay* 18.5 (September/October 2001): 6-7.

_____. *Coyote City.* Stratford, Ont.: Williams-Wallace, 1990.

_____. *The Dreaming Beauty.* Toronto: Playwrights Union of Canada Copyscript, 1988.

_____. The Indian Medicine Shows: Two One-Act Plays. Toronto: Exile, 1995.

_____. *Kyotopolis.* Toronto: Playwrights Union of Canada Copyscript, 1993.

_____. "Of the Essence." *CanPlay* 18.4 (July/August 2001): 6-7.

_____. *The Witch of Niagara.* Toronto: Playwrights Union of Canada Copyscript, 1998.

—— and Terry Goldie. "Preface: Two Voices." *An Anthology of Canadian Native Literature in English.* Eds. Daniel David Moses and Terry Goldie. Toronto: Oxford UP, 1992. xii-xxii.

Ortiz, Simon. *Song, Poetry, Language: Expression and Perception.* Tsaile, AZ: Navajo Community College P, 1977.

Thomas, Dylan. *Under Milk Wood, a Play for Voices.* New York: New Directions, 1954.

"That Almost Present Dream of Tomorrow"

Daniel David Moses' *Kyotopolis* as Native Canadian Science Fiction/History Play

Robert APPLEFORD

University of Alberta

History has always been fertile ground for storytellers, who venture into the past like explorers into a barely remembered lost city and return with endlessly ample plots and fascinating characters as their booty. But this simile remains of course fraught with irony. The past, in appearance a distant ruin inviting pillage, may in many ways be viewed as a mirage, or perhaps a city where we already live. Those who tell History, whether consciously or not, articulate how we understand our quotidian existence as dwellers in the present, and how we conceptualize present identity in relation to pasts which we either own or desire to own.

For Native artists, the desire to (re)possess one's past is especially problematic, in that so many non-Natives have attempted to stake a claim. Because of this, many Native artists have avoided tackling "historical" subjects in their writing. For example, when considering the apparent lack of interest on the part of Native authors in challenging the historical narratives favored by the mainstream culture, Thomas King suggests that the historical past represents for most Native writers both a creative and ideological dead end:

> Rather than try to unravel the complex relationship between the nineteenth-century Indian and the white mind, [...] most of us [Native writers] have consciously set our literature in the present, a period that is reasonably free of literary monoliths and which allows for greater latitude in the creation of characters and situations, and, more important, allows us the opportunity to create for ourselves and our respective cultures both a present and a future. (King, *Relations* xii)

In relation to plays by Native playwrights, King's observation would seem to be borne out in one respect. While there are hundreds of non-Native dramatic works which attempt (with varying degrees of sensitivity) to explore the world of the nineteenth-century Native, very few theatrical enterprises by Native artists could be termed "history" plays in the generic sense. This being said, I would disagree with King's categorical elimination of the past as a fertile subject for Native writers. Instead, I would argue that most Native plays are informed by a sophisticated understanding of how the past operates within cultures. Historical material is most often used in this context for reasons that have little to do with the aims of traditional historical investigation, such as the delineation of the past as a discrete period or making the past "live" in an uncomplicated fashion for a contemporary generation. For many Native playwrights, the past seems powerful not only as a resource of cultural information but as a potent catalyst for change. Often what is sought is a reordering of the present, what Gayatri Spivak calls "not only the retrieval of the colonial history of the past but the putting together of a history of the present" (139). And the tension between the past as discrete entity and the past as crucible for present action, far from being resolved or ignored, is represented as both inescapable in and necessary for the articulation of a Native subject position.

A science fiction opus set in "a variety of intersections in the global village, that almost present dream of tomorrow" (Moses 12), Daniel David Moses' play *Kyotopolis* explores in an original fashion the ways in which the past is pursued and redemption made possible by a proper relationship with it. One of the play's main themes is the desire on the part of Natives and non-Natives to reconstruct the past to fulfil very personal objectives. At the centre of the play, one finds the elusive figure of Babe Fisher, "shamaness *extraordinaire*," a Native child-star turned New Age guru, who becomes the first Native on a space shuttle mission. Under mysterious circumstances, the shuttle, christened "Crazy Horse," is crippled in orbit and all contact with its crew is lost. Babe Fisher's story is zealously pursued by Mary Oh, the rogue reporter and host of a virtual reality music program. In the tradition of science fiction, *Kyotopolis* presents a critique of technology in contemporary society, with virtual reality powwows and artificial intelligence videophone answering programs portraying a world devoted to what Jean Baudrillard has called the simulacrum, the co-option of the real by its sign. The reporter Mary Oh claims that she has met the ill-fated Babe Fisher, but it is only the repeated viewing of her virtual image from the children's program "Tommy Hawk and the Little People" that causes Oh to affect a personal connection with the mega-star. Oh's quest to discover the "real" Babe Fisher is shown to be impossible in a context where reality has no bearing upon the manufacture and marketing of virtual signs.

The play unfolds in the narrative pattern typified by Welles' *Citizen Kane* with Oh interviewing important Native people in Babe's life, all with a highly subjective and often mutually exclusive history of the central figure. What these histories have in common is the persistent need to cast Babe as a redemptive agent. For instance, Great-Uncle Jack, a slimy Svengali huckster who acted as his grandniece's manager, attempts to reconcile his own ruthless use of Babe for financial gain with his early memories of her as a sweet-natured child. His own narrative of Babe's past is further complicated by the stage convention Moses adopts: the reporter Mary Oh, with whom Jack has a sexual relationship, plays the part of Babe in her family's reminiscences, which introduces a subtext of incest into Jack's relationship with Babe. In terms of public identity, Jack has created Babe Fisher, teaching her camera-ready poses that look "especially Indian" (26), yet he also cannot relinquish his own personal conviction that Babe has a spiritual power beyond market-driven artifice. Similarly, Babe's Grandmother Martha, a born-again Christian, believes Babe to be the second incarnation of Christ, "The Babe," who will redeem the fallen world through her sacrificial death. For her, her granddaughter represents the link between pagan Native spirituality and Western Christianity, a virtual Redeemer in a postmodern age.

Interwoven throughout these competing histories is the mythic narrative of Babe's rescue by Raccoon from her late mother's house and his delivery of the child to the protection of Bear and the Little People, a Native version of fairies. This story is transformed into a street narrative by Ricky Raccoon, a trickster-clown-children's show host, in which Babe's magical protectors become hookers and queers, "Darling, Dear, Bitch and Mary, fairy godmothers all" (83). Babe's past operates as the site of contestatory desires and fictions, and this, in itself, lends *Kyotopolis* the quality of an anti-history play which dramatizes the inaccessibility of the past to present reconstruction.

However, Moses does not simply reaffirm the opaque nature of the historical sign. The necessary path to a redemption of the present, for the playwright, is twofold, involving an imaginative engagement with both the past and the future. While indeterminate and subject to desire, the past in *Kyotopolis* is experienced by the characters through often painful personal visions. Jack describes a trip to Europe which he and his shaman business partner Curly Bear once took to celebrate their creation of Big Buck Enterprises, the parent company soon to orchestrate the meteoric career of Babe Fisher. On the Belgian-German border, they drunkenly explore a castle after visiting hours. Separated from Curly Bear, Jack searches for him:

> I mean it was a long way, more than a couple of storiesdown, once I found them stairs, feeling along the stone walls. And shit, going across that yard, I kept tripping over stuff in the grass. I could hear them laughing in whatever language it was through that window. That's where Curly had gone to. I

looked in and there he was. Tied to a fucking chair. With this circle of guys
in white coats around him, poking him, pinching his skin, looking at his
teeth and just laughing away. And he was laughing along with them. Till
one of them started slipping this blade round the edge of his hair. Taking his
scalp. Shit he mewled like a cat under a boot. And I just knew his hair
would go on display there. And mine too if I let them know for sure where I
was from. I wanted out. But I fell. My hand got a hold of something slimy I
lifted up into the light from the window. A bone. A human fucking bone
from this part of an arm! That fucking yard was full of them. Bones, and
teeth and hair. And there I was, me and that bugger Curly Bear, looking up
at them laughing, looking up out of a glass display case. (32-33)

This episode is a nightmarish corollary to the political struggle of aboriginal peoples worldwide to reclaim their ancestral remains from
institutions. Rather than reflecting upon the pilfered bones from the
pasts of both North America and Europe,[1] Moses forces the audience to
feel the desecration through Jack's imaginative empathy. In this way,
the past is not mourned from a comfortable contemporary position, nor
contextualized within the ordering trope of history, but is performed
viscerally in the present.

This process in a vital way reinscribes the trope of history-telling
with a mythic sensibility. Andrew Wiget, in his study of traditional
Native American narratives, distinguishes between two types of temporal awareness understood by tribal peoples, the historical and the
mythic. The former encompasses the present and the recent past, involving "known personages in identifiable settings," while in the latter
"legendary personages engage in fantastic actions against an ethnologi-
cally familiar background" (Wiget 85). What bears on the discussion at
hand is the nature of the past which the mythic narrative constructs.
Wiget further delineates the mythic category as containing origin myths
and transformation myths, the first relating the creation of the world,
and the second the alteration of this new world resulting in its present
social and physical organization. In *Kyotopolis*, Moses has refigured
what begins as a purely historical search for origins as a mythic narrative of transformation. Despite her shadowy beginnings, Babe comes to
represent (as both Jack and Martha intuit) the potential for rebirth and a
renewal of the relationship between humanity and the cosmos. The play
is framed at its beginning and end by a visual and aural montage which
affirms the synchronic character of Babe's life-journey:

---

[1]   Earlier, Jack relates how the witnessing of a displayed skeleton of an ancient priest in
a church prompted Curly Bear to remark, "How would you like it if somebody pulled
your covers off? How they supposed to rest in peace?" (31)

Darkness.

Then a drum begins an extremely slow double-beat, like a heart from far off in a dream. And with each heart beat there's a pulse of light projecting from a place. First it's a cracked rock face covered with petroglyphs—highly abstracted images of men, women, boats, bears, turtles, Nanabush. Then it's a city seen at night from the air with a freeway a glowing blur. Then it's the Milky Way—and the nearby constellations are very clear. And then it's a path through a clearing. And then the cycle of these four places begins again. And it becomes clear that the crack in the rock, the freeway and the Milky Way are all somehow the path through the clearing, because along it, along them, comes BABE, a little Indian girl, dawdling in the pulsing lights, trailing a red balloon on a string, paying attention to Nanabush, or stars, or cars, or yellow butterflies. (3)

Her journey along "the path through the clearing" unites four sites of signification: the petroglyphs, emblematic of a distant past only dimly understood; the city, filled with ever-present simulacra and desire for the real, the Milky Way; the outward-directed quest for knowledge in futurity; and the "pulse of light projecting from a place," the quintessential metaphysical illumination that underlies all three. These sites are shown to be contiguous rather than discrete, part of a cosmological whole. This cognitive and mythic confluence of time and space is in an important sense in keeping with the traditional ritual performances of many tribal peoples. M. Jane Young describes a Zuni clown performance which took place at the time of the first U.S. moon landings and which enacts a similar cosmological principle:

[…] the clowns in the plaza gave a good rendition of the particular walk that the astronauts in their cumbersome space suits exhibited. Then the clowns climbed to the rooftops and walked on top of one of the sacred kivas. The purpose of these actions, my Zuni consultant said, was to object to the behavior of the astronauts who heedlessly walked on the body of the Moon Mother and pierced her with metal instruments in order to bring back samples for study. This performance was not only a critique of the moon shots, however, but an enactment of Zuni cosmological principles—that the clowns equated the moon with sacred space in this instance was not arbitrary. This coupling suggests a merging of space and time in a ritual context such that the kiva, a ceremonial chamber, sometimes located underground and symbolically associated with the emergence from the underworld, becomes equivalent to the moon, one of the Zuni deities who travels across the sky. Outer and inner space thus occupy the same place at the same time. (Young 275)

Like the Zuni clown ritual, *Kyotopolis* suggests that the mythic conflation of inner and outer space, of past, present and future, promotes a respectful orientation of the self in the cosmos through imaginative engagement.

This synchronic view of history is also symbolized by the Bear figure in the play. He appears in the traditional role of spirit-guide to Babe,
and in a syncretic Christian context afforded by the belief system of
Martha, who asks her granddaughter "does the Bear sleep in Heaven?"
(52). Boo, Babe's aunt, relates a story told to her by her niece and in
which she was visited by a U.F.O. in the woods:

> And I saw there was this bear there, Auntie. Ya, a bear at the controls! [...]
> Well, Auntie, I heard that bear laugh! And the next thing I know we was ris-
> ing up, and flying over the village, and then up through the clouds and,
> Auntie, we got almost to the moon afore we turned around and started head-
> ing back. And do you know how far that is? You look back here at a round
> blue ball and it's the earth and—you don't know how much it looks like
> home. That's where it comes from, Auntie, that's where all this comes from.
> That's where I got my song. That's why I'm going to go there again some-
> day, Auntie. Hey that's what this is all for. (67)

Moses' clever conflation of the tribal myth of origin/transformation with
the narratives of Christian millennialism and extraterrestrial contact,
both retold feverishly in contemporary popular culture, highlights the
similarity between them. The alien contact story, like the prophetic story
of Christ's second coming, is a narrative whose attraction lies in its
promise of a revolutionary alteration in how we perceive our place in the
universe. The bear figure carved in petroglyph, sleeping in Heaven, and
piloting an alien spacecraft, represents a deep-seated desire for human
redemption. Rather than simply lamenting the virtual technological
world and the needs which it leaves unfulfilled in opposition to traditional tribal values, Moses attempts to show the mythic resonance
between them.

As is typical of Moses' work, this narrative of mythic redemption is
not unleavened with irony. Moses' choice of the name Crazy Horse for
the space shuttle feels apt. The story of the Oglala-Brulé tribal leader
(1842-77)—the heroic warrior who routed Custer, galvanized his people, and was murdered at the hands of his enemies—is one of unifica-
tion, tactical prowess (he remains famous for his decoy and feinting
attacks), and ultimate martyrdom. Like Crazy Horse, *Kyotopolis* utilizes
misdirection in the service of a unifying vision. Part of Babe's official
mission on board the shuttle is to use her shamanic powers to gain
insight into the problem of making an uninhabitable space station live-
able. The erratically spinning orbit of the damaged shuttle begins to alter
the gravitational field of the station. In the final scene of the play, the
space station is transformed into "a spectacle of rings and squares,
spheres and cubes—a gigantic high technology astrolabe, a turning
tesseract, a future spirit catcher" (91). In a last confluence of past and
future, Ricky Raccoon notes that the revitalized space station resembles
"that toy the fairy godmothers hung up on the Babe's cradleboard" (90).

Just as the ancient tribal myths of origin and transformation teach the proper manner of living in the present, the play advocates a re-examination of the relationship between temporal and ontological categories to guide humanity as it moves along its own "path through the clearing".

In conclusion, I will return to Thomas King's comments regarding the absence of historical narratives in Native writing. Despite his seemingly categorical rejection of history as a fitting subject for Native literature, King himself frequently incorporates historical narratives into his fiction, but with a predictably ironic twist. Such a twist occurs in his story "Joe the Painter and the Deer Island Massacre," and it is with this tale that I will leave the discussion of history. Joe, the non-Native main character of the story, represents a social outcast whose only real crime is his faith in absolute honesty at all costs. Joe decides to write and produce a historical pageant that he hopes will be performed during his town's centennial celebrations. He chooses as his subject a particularly ignoble event: the massacre of unfriendly Native inhabitants by encroaching settlers, the very massacre that permitted the town's founding. Joe proceeds with the pageant undaunted by its potential unpopularity, confident in his belief that "it's all history. You can't muck around with history. It ain't always the way we'd like it to be, but there it is. Can't change it" ("Joe the Painter and the Deer Island Massacre"105). What proves exciting (and indeed typical) in this story is how King interrogates this assertion of history's inviolability.

In his efforts to add realism to his pageant, Joe enlists the aid of his Native friend Chief (the narrator of the story), whose task it is to round up as many Natives as needed to act as performers. Chief manages to convince his relatives and friends to participate, many of whom view Joe and the project with a bemused eye. They all set up camp on Deer Island, the site of the historical massacre, and make use of the occasion to visit and socialize. Chief relates the charmed atmosphere of the gathering:

> That first night on Deer Island was soft and quiet. Some of us got propped up against the tight clusters of marsh grass and listened to my father and my uncles tell stories. All the kids were sprawled on top of one another like puppies. After the men got things going, Aunt Amy took over. She was the best storyteller. Bernie and James got out a drum and started singing a few social songs, and some of the families danced for a while. Mostly, we watched the fires and watched the fog slip in off the mud flats and curl around the tents. You could hear the frogs in the distance, and the water pushing at the edges of the island. As I went to sleep, I imagined that, in the morning, when the fog lifted, the town and the pulp factory and the marina and Lawson's mansion would be gone, and all you'd be able to see would be the flats stretched out to the trees. (106-107)

The performance, complete with ketchup pouches splattering to simulate blood, predictably disturbs and offends to the town's elite, and another more mundane pageant is picked to celebrate the town's inauguration.

Like many history plays, this story offers a critique of conventional historiography. Joe's conflation of truth and history is shown to be both naively comic and unrepresentative of the general popular desire for historical narratives that flatter rather than challenge. Thus, his pageant does little to shake the town's blithe ignorance of its sordid past. King emphasizes the artificiality of historical representation by stressing the incongruous and makeshift materials of the performance, its ketchup blood and drama department wigs.

If this were the story's only message, King's statements concerning the aridity of historical narrative would appear to be borne out. However, like Moses, he also suggests the potential of the past to transform the present. The actors in Joe's pageant are shown constructing a conceptual bridge between the past and the present, and as a result, none of the participants can view the contemporary environment in a historically isolated way. Instead of simply re-presenting the horror of the massacre, the actors return to the scene of the crime and enact a new narrative, one with a hopeful outcome. The importance of the pageant lies neither in its self-conscious challenge to settler authority nor in its verisimilar depiction of unalterable pain, but in its role as catalyst for the affirmation of communal solidarity. In the words of Russian writer Marina Tsvetaeva, "to continue is, after all, to put to the test" (115). By putting to the test the past's potential as an informing resource for both continuity and cultural change, Native writers like Moses and King avoid the transparent self-authentication of narrative form and the opaque figural gesture that can often result in histories impervious to the possibilities of creative adaptation in the present. The past, far from being a lost city to be mapped and plundered, is both a mirage produced by an ever-present desire and the place where we all must live.

Works Cited

King, Thomas. Introduction to *All My Relations: An Anthology of Contemporary Canadian Native Fiction*. Toronto: McClelland & Stewart, 1990. ix-xvi.

_____. "Joe the Painter and the Deer Island Massacre." *Canadian Fiction Magazine* 60 (1987): 99-112.

Moses, Daniel David. *Kyotopolis*. Unpublished manuscript, 1992.

Spivak, Gayatri. "Feminism in Decolonization." *Differences* 3:3 (1991): 139-170.

Marina Tsvetaeva. *A Captive Spirit: Selected Prose*. London: Virago P, 1982.

Wiget, Andrew. "His Life In His Tail: The Native American Trickster and the Literature of Possibility." *Redefining American Literary History.* Eds. A. LaVonne Brown Ruoff and J. Ward. New York: MLA, 1990: 83-96.

Young, Jane. "'Pity the Indians of Outer Space': Native American Views of the Space Program." *Western Folklore* 46.4 (1987): 269-279.

Drew Hayden Taylor's *alterNatives*: Dishing the Dirt

Robert NUNN

Brock University

> While writing this play, I was fully expecting to become the
> Salman Rushdie of the Native community, for I'm sure there is
> something in this play to annoy everybody. Part of my goal
> was to create unsympathetic characters right across the board.
> And to do this, as the saying goes, I had to break some eggs. A
> close friend, a Native woman, came up to me quite angry and
> said, "So this is what you really think of Native people!" Then
> some time later, one reviewer referred to it as "witless white
> bashing." Evidently I have become a racist! Further proof that
> you never know how your day is gonna end (Taylor, "Fore-
> word" 6).

Drew Hayden Taylor's plays have always gotten at serious themes
through gently subversive humour. One recent play, *alterNatives*,
however, is not nearly as gentle. The tricksterish characteristics of
Taylor's dramaturgy, about which I wrote a couple of years ago,[1] remain
present, but the emphasis lies not so much on playful inversion as on
turning the world upside down in order to do it real damage.[2] By the
play's end, the dinner party which the audience watches from start to
finish, has very possibly left a friendship, a relationship, and a marriage
in ruins. The foremost but not the only agent of this mayhem is the
appropriately named Bobby Rabbit, self-styled "Uber-Indian" and

---

[1] Robert Nunn, "Hybridity and Mimicry in the Plays of DrewHayden Taylor," *Essays
in Canadian Writing* 65 (Fall 1998): 95-119.

[2] *alterNatives* (1999) does not signify a shift in Taylor's dramaturgy so much as a
broadening of scope. More recent plays indeed cover a wide range. *The Buz'Gem
Blues* (2001) returns to several of the characters of *The Baby Blues* (1995) in the
same vein of gentle satire, while *Toronto@Dreamer'sRock.com* (1999) offers a very
dark sequel to the optimistic *Toronto at Dreamer's Rock* of 1989. *Sucker Falls*
(2001) is an adaptation of Brecht and Weill's *The Rise and Fall of the City of
Mahagonny*. The dates given are those of the first performance.

"alterNative Warrior." In this essay, I would like to explore the play through the lens of Lewis Hyde's *Trickster Makes This World: Mischief, Myth, and Art*, in particular through the notion that Trickster throws dirt around—the dirt that a social order rejects in order to protect its purified idea of itself. Neither Whites nor Natives are spared the pain of having their dirt thrown in their faces.

In brief, Lewis Hyde's argument runs as follows:

> [W]e begin to wonder if there is any way to make a general rule about what is dirt and what is not. The anthropologist Mary Douglas [...] suggests we go back to an old saying: "Dirt is matter out of place." [...] To this first definition of dirt, Douglas adds a second: dirt is the anomalous, not just what is out of place but what has no place at all when we are done making sense of our world. [...] In either of Douglas's cases—out of place or anomalous—the point to underline here is that dirt is always a by-product of creating order. Where there is dirt, there is always a system of some kind, and rules about dirt are meant to preserve it [...] whenever humans or gods move [...] to protect order completely from the dirt that is its by-product, trickster will upset their plans. (175-79)

The other aspect of "dirt-work" that Hyde addresses is "shameless speech." Matter out of place is kept *in* its place by codes of silence hedged about by shame. Trickster breaks these taboos by speaking—without shame—about the dirt that nobody is supposed to talk about, let alone notice. Hyde writes:

> You and I know when to speak and when to hold the tongue, but Old Man Coyote doesn't. He has no tact. They're all the same, these tricksters; they have no shame and so they have no silence. (153)

In *alterNatives*, Bobby Rabbit embodies that shameless speaker *par excellence*. Here follows a typical example of Bobby at work. He recounts his conversation with a priest and two nuns on a bus:

> So we started talking religious stuff, you know, all nicey nicey. And then I calmly asked them about their personal perspective on the difference between original sin and ab-original sin. Ab-original sin meaning that being born Native was a horrible affront to God and the Church, paganism and all that. And it had to be corrected as harshly as possible. I went into the whole Jesuit invasion, the Residential school system. You know, the usual. ... Surprisingly, they weren't as receptive as I had hoped. (61-62)

Bobby *will not shut up* about anything where he senses the presence of a conspiracy of silence to avoid all mention of "matter out of place." This is what he calls being an "Uber-Indian," or "alterNative Warrior," a concept he has cobbled together out of Nietzsche, Native tradition, and "a natural flair for turning people and institutions on their ear" (Taylor 54). The dinner party at the centre of *alterNatives* requires a lot of tact in order not to fly apart, as a brief description of the *dramatis personae* will indicate. Colleen, a professor of Native Literature, has been living with Angel, an aspiring Native writer, for some months. She is Jewish, Angel is Ojibway. In the play, they are throwing their first dinner party. Colleen has invited her old friend Michelle and her husband Dale, both non-Native. Michelle tends to get really drunk really fast when there is tension in the air. Dale is a well-meaning blunderer. Colleen has also invited surprise guests, two friends of Angel's, whom she has never met: Yvonne and Bobby, both Native. Neither of them has seen Angel since he abruptly left them shortly before he met Colleen. Yvonne and Angel are former lovers. Bobby once considered Angel a fellow Warrior. Angel's disappearance still rankles with both of them. It would take a miracle to make this party go smoothly. Bobby's presence guarantees that the evening will be disastrous.

The relentless "dirt-work" that dooms this party has many targets, but Bobby leads the attack on one in particular, namely the notion of "Authentic Aboriginality." As Alan Filewod points out, the term "Aboriginality" only exists in the context of colonialism. No people are called—or call themselves—Aboriginal, unless colonized: "the very notion of aboriginality [...] is itself a category of understanding introduced by colonialism" (Filewod 365). Whether the term is applied by the colonists, or adopted by the colonized themselves, it remains fraught with complexities and contradictions, which are routinely swept under the rug. The most basic simplification consists in lumping many nations which differ profoundly from each other under a single heading—such as "Indian." In *alterNatives*, White assumptions of a single homogeneous Native identity come under attack, and from a variety of directions. Taylor's targets range from straightforwardly stupid questions to less obvious assumptions, such as Native opinions on non-Native appropriations of Native voice. In the following excerpt, Dale, speaking to Angel, offers a good example of the stupid question:

> We used to know a Native person, didn't we Michelle? ... Benita. It was Benita. That's it. Benita ... something. I don't suppose you know a Benita? (27)

A more covert form of simplification is exposed in the following passage:

YVONNE
Dare I mention W. P. Kinsella?[3]

---

[3] W. P. Kinsella is a Canadian author, best known for his novel *Shoeless Joe* (1982). He has published several collections of humourous stories set in the fictional Ermineskin First Nations reserve in Hobbema, Alberta, including *Dance Me Outside* (1977) and *The Fencepost Chronicles* (1986).

COLLEEN

We won't even get into that. I'm a hundred percent on your side about him.

YVONNE

My side? How do you even know what side I'm on?

COLLEEN

Well ... uh ... I assumed because of the controversy surrounding his work ... And you're First Nations ... (51)

And, running through the play, is the question of how to cook moose. Colleen, who has bought a moose roast for the dinner, assumes that Angel, as a "Native Aboriginal Indigenous First Nations person" (17), will know how to cook it. But she turns out to be badly wrong: Angel's contribution to the dinner is to bake the Jewish delicacy *rugelach*, whilst the expert on moose happens to be Dale.

Everywhere in the play, there are moments when the gross oversimplification implicit in the concept of "aboriginality" gets dismantled, allowing suppressed differences to come out of hiding. Although she does not appear as abrasive as Bobby, Yvonne is a "dirt-worker" too, but whereas Bobby's targets are White, Yvonne's are Native. She describes her M.A. thesis topic to Colleen: "The working title is 'Selective Traditionalism and the Emergence of the Narrow-Focused Cultural Revival.'" She goes on to explain:

In the last thirty years or so, there has been an amazing cultural revival happening. Languages, practices and traditions, once banned, are not [sic][now] being embraced with almost a fanatical enthusiasm. This in itself is good. Great in fact. We support that [...]. [But] Look a little closer at that picture. In their hurry to recapture the old days of our Grandfathers and grandmothers, these people are being very selective about which traditions they choose to follow, often excluding many ancient practices that would not be considered politically correct in today's society. [...] Centuries ago there were arranged marriages, frequently inter-tribal warfare, slavery, and in some cases, rumours of cannibalism. These are not even mentioned at Pow wows or Elder's conferences. It's as if they didn't exist. It's become a form of cultural hypocrisy. [...] [B]ecause I explore these areas, some people think I'm sabotaging the traditions, or being disrespectful. I am as proud of who I am and where I come from as the next Nish. But I can't believe it's so wrong to ask these simple questions. (75-78)

Yvonne points out that the Peterborough Petroglyphs, which were "carved somewhere between five hundred and a thousand years ago," are under the custodial care of the Curve Lake First Nations, in other words of Ojibways who migrated to Central Ontario in the 1820s and who have no connection whatever with the people who created the carvings. The subtext of this arrangement, from Yvonne's perspective, does not seem so far removed from "We used to know a Native person, her name was Benita, do you know her?"

The other term subjected to scrutiny in this play is "authenticity," equally an effect of colonialism. It too is forced to disgorge a lot of dirt. Criteria of authenticity have been regularly imposed by the settler culture on Natives: in a kind of sleight of hand which hides the reality of colonial aggression, "authentic" Native culture is taken to amount to only that which remains uncontaminated by contact with the settler culture. As Terry Goldie explains, it is Whites, not Indigenes, who test indigenous culture for authenticity: "A corollary of the temporal split between this golden age [pre-contact indigenous culture] and the present degradation is to see indigenous culture as true, pure, and static. Whatever fails this test is not really a part of that culture" (17). On the other side of the fence, an "authentically" Native cultural identity can be constructed by First Nations people as an act of "strategic essentialism"—Gayatri Spivak's term—countering the identity imposed by colonialist discourse with a discursive construct of one's own (Ashcroft et al. 79). The intractable problem for both cultures is the actual hybrid nature of contemporary Native cultures. White criteria of authenticity discount signs of hybridity as "degradation" or "corruption": as Alan Filewod argues, "mediation (most commonly by urbanization and post-colonial deracination)" is often seen by White critics of contemporary Native art as "the condition that diminishes the authenticity of a culture. In this essentialist and humanist view (which owes much to Rousseau), the more authentic the culture, the less mediated it is" (Filewod 364-65). Meanwhile, Native construction of strategic essentialism can equally fall into the same trap of dismissing hybridity. For as Gareth Griffiths points out, "markers of cultural difference may well be perceived as authentic cultural signifiers, but that claim to authenticity can imply that these cultures are not subject to change" (Ashcroft et al. 21). Angel, for instance, is attacked from both sides for wanting to write science fiction. He has abandoned Bobby and Yvonne partly because Bobby kept "urging me ... no, practically ordering me to quit wasting my time on my silly stories and write something that would help the cause" (103-104). He has left them to live with Colleen, who insists "You have such potential, you could create the great Canadian aboriginal novel, but instead you want to squander it away on this silly genre" (102). Somehow there is no room within "authentic" aboriginal identity for such a hybrid as a Native science fiction writer. The problem with Angel's desire to write science fiction throws the problem with essentialism, strategic or otherwise, into high relief.

But the worst beating "authenticity" takes in this play is not revealed until the end. Angel's mysterious unwillingness to tell Colleen what reserve he is from becomes finally cleared up when Angel takes a book from Colleen's shelf and tells how it came to be written. It is a collection of Ojibway legends, harvested at the Curve Lake reserve when he was a boy. In fact, he belonged to a group of several boys on the reserve who were approached by White researchers and asked to recount ancient legends, since the elders of the community refused to tell them any. For fifty cents a legend, they complied:

> ANGEL
>
> We told some great legends, huh? Fantastic stories that only an eleven-year-old could come up with. And that's what we did. We made them up. We would take the fifty cents they gave us, go to the store and buy pop, chips, popsicles, all sorts of garbage, sit around on the church steps, and make up the story we'd tell them the next day. (129)

The first time Angel picked up the book, he was shocked to find at least four of the stories which they made up published, and to discover that the book is in its seventh printing, that it actually features on the reading list of a half dozen university Native Literature courses, and that Native teachers are teaching the book to Native students. Colleen teaches it too. Bobby was the ringleader, whilst Colleen, then a young graduate student, belonged to the research team. Angel remembers her buying him an ice cream cone. She has not, until this moment, recognized him. So the search by White researchers for authentic—that is, uncontaminated—Native culture has harvested a pack of lies told by eleven-year-old boys out of sheer mischief. Colleen is devastated. Angel feels guilty. He reproaches Bobby for instigating this, accusing him of spending his whole life playing "stupid little games [...] to make fun of people" (130). So much for the "alterNative Warrior."

Just a minute though. Is this not just the sort of thing that Trickster is constantly doing? The fallout from this trick calls into question all the unspoken assumptions—and exclusions—underlying the very concept "authentic," just the kind of "dirt-work" Trickster loves to perform. And it would not be the first time that Trickster has passed off wildly inventive lies as the real article, as a reading of Paul Radin's study of the Winnebago trickster cycle makes abundantly clear. Maybe this mischief is as "authentic" an expression of Ojibway culture as the old legends, with this difference: the legends belong to the past—otherwise they do not count—while the boys' inventions are of the living and changing—and hybrid—culture of the present.

Angel may reject Bobby and all his destructive games, but I would argue that the play does not. Bobby is the character who keeps everything on edge, challenges every given, turns simplistic categories inside out, and creates a really impressive chaos out of a nice dinner party. In his study of the trickster in Shakespeare, Richard Hillman suggests that while Trickster's mayhem may lead to a revitalized order, no such

higher purpose should be attributed to Trickster himself. His destruc-
tiveness only has the potential to renew life, but is not engaged in with
that aim:

> [T]he trickster's creativity is indeed part of his significance, but he is essen-
> tially "undifferentiated," and in many of his particular adventures he is
> merely destructive. This is where the subversive principle, as I conceive it,
> conflicts with the reassuring teleological orientation of more traditional
> "festive" criticism, such as C. L. Barber's, according to which "ritual" dis-
> order already contains its own undoing. My view presupposes that whether
> the potential is realized [...] is contingent precisely on his spontaneous and
> unconditional embracing of what appears to be merely destructive. In order
> for there to be power, there must be danger, not merely some form of cir-
> cumscribed and more-or-less tolerated misrule. (Hillman 14)

Bobby has certainly left a trail of destruction behind him. Whether
the relationship between Angel and Colleen will weather this storm is
doubtful. Colleen's sense that Angel incarnates "The Authentic Indian"
(with a little help from her) has been seriously shaken. Angel has coun-
tered her assumptions with a demonstration that Colleen, in spite of
being Jewish, knows far more about Native culture and language than
about her own cultural roots. The questions: "Are you with me because
I'm Native?" and "Are you with me because I'm white?" (135) receive
no answer, and how could they, when this evening has forced each of
them to recognize what a hybrid the other really is. It seems equally
uncertain whether Michelle and Dale's marriage will survive the revelation that Dale has had enough of being Michelle's prize convert to the
cause of vegetarianism. It is even less certain that Angel will renew his
membership in the "alterNative Warriors." But, interestingly enough,
the play ends on an almost upbeat note. Angel, the only member of the
dinner party left in the apartment, is joined by Dale, and the two of
them—the Native carnivorous science fiction writer and the non-Native
vegetarian science fiction fan—sit down to a plate of perfectly cooked
moose. There is a mood of peace and sensual enjoyment, in which
Angel tells a story that sounds like an unashamed hybrid of Native
concerns and science fiction conventions. Two men who may have just
lost a great deal are content to savour the moment calmly, and face
perhaps a very different future. "alterNative" humour may have been
destructive, but not merely so. This play constitutes a sort of rite of
passage. Characters who lived a life overly free of dirt have had it
thrown in their faces: as the saying goes, their certainties have been
destroyed, but truth, which embraces anomalies, contradictions, and
"matter out of place," proves greater than certainty, and much more
alive. And I sustain the thesis that the "matter out of place" in this play
is colonialism's byproduct.

I would like to conclude with some speculation about the relation between "alterNative" humour and post-colonial resistance. Drew Hayden Taylor's comedies are not isolated instances of Native humour, while everybody else is writing ultra-serious books with titles like *Bury My Heart at Wounded Knee, The Dispossessed* or *How a People Die* (Angel by the way has hidden the latter book in the freezer). Taylor forms a part of a wave of new visibility of Native humour (I mean of course new to non-Natives): Tomson Highway's plays and novel, and Tom King's fiction and his just-finished five-year run of the radio program *The Dead Dog Café Comedy Hour*, represent two other major examples. Taylor recently produced a film on Native humour for the National Film Board of Canada, titled *Redskins, Tricksters and Puppy Stew*. Allan J. Ryan borrows the term "the trickster shift" from Carl Beam to title his study of humour and irony in contemporary Native art. These works and many others celebrate Trickster humour as a revived element of Native culture: "Weesageechak begins to dance," as the Toronto theatre company Native Earth Performing Arts titles its annual festival of new work. Indeed, Tomson Highway claims that "Without the continued presence of this extraordinary figure [the Trickster], the core of Indian culture would be gone forever" (Highway 12-13). I would argue that the Trickster seems particularly apt at negotiating the perilous relation between Aboriginal cultures and their post-colonial situation. He does so by subverting the colonizer's essentializing gaze, by preventing the strategic essentialism of the colonized from hardening into a rigid ahistorical identity, and by revelling in the impurity and hybridity that the colonizer habitually dismisses as "degradation." By its very nature, colonialism is an order that has had to pretend that mountains of dirt do not exist, through such means as the Freudian dream-mechanism of "distortion," about which Homi K. Bhabha writes in his celebrated essay "Signs Taken for Wonders." As "dirt-worker" *extraordinaire* and "alter-Native warrior," the post-colonial Trickster has his work cut out for him: to put the non-Native spectator (such as myself obviously) on the couch, so to speak, and oblige him or her to work backward through distortion to the latent content of colonialism; and at the same time, to affirm a living, changing Native culture. Trickster humour cuts both ways.

Works Cited

Ashcroft, Bill, Gareth Griffiths and Helen Tiffin. *Key Concepts in Post-Colonial Studies*. London: Routledge, 1998.

Bhabha, Homi K. "Signs Taken for Wonders: Questions of Ambivalence and Authority under a Tree outside Delhi, May 1817." *Europe and its Others. Proc. of the Essex Conference on the Sociology of Literature, July 1984*. Ed. Francis Barker et al. Colchester: U of Essex, 1985. 89-106.

Filewod, Alan. "Receiving Aboriginality: Tomson Highway and the Crisis of Cultural Authority." *Theatre Journal* 46 (1994): 363-73.

Goldie, Terry. *Fear and Temptation: The Image of the Indigene in Canadian, Australian, and New Zealand Literatures.* Kingston: McGill-Queen's UP, 1989.

Highway, Tomson. *Dry Lips Oughta Move to Kapuskasing.* Saskatoon: Fifth House, 1989.

Hillman, Richard. *Shakespearean Subversions: The Trickster and the Play-Text.* London: Routledge, 1992.

Hyde, Lewis. *Trickster Makes This World: Mischief, Myth, and Art.* New York: Farrar, Straus and Giroux, 1998.

Nunn, Robert. "Hybridity and Mimicry in the Plays of Drew Hayden Taylor." *Essays in Canadian Writing* 65 (Fall 1998): 95-119.

Radin, Paul. *The Trickster: A Study in American Indian Mythology.* London: Routledge, 1956.

Ryan, Allan J. *The Trickster Shift: Humour and Irony in Contemporary Native Art.* Vancouver: U British Columbia P, 1999.

Spivak, Gayatri. "Criticism, Feminism and the Institution." Interview with Elizabeth Gross. *Thesis Eleven* 10/11 (November-March 1984-85): 175-87. Cited in *Key Concepts in Post-Colonial Studies* by Bill Ashcroft, Gareth Griffiths, and Helen Tiffin. London: Routledge, 1998. 79.

Taylor, Drew Hayden. *alterNatives.* Vancouver: Talonbooks, 2000.

Theatrical Capitalism, Imagined Theatres and the Reclaimed Authenticities of the Spectacular

Alan FILEWOD

University of Guelph

> Public opinion is the highest and sole court
> of jurisdiction in literary and artistic matters.
> And what is success? [...] it is the fiat of the
> people [...] (Dion Boucicault, quoted in
> Witham 292)

The focus of this probe into a question of theatrical capitalism, post-colonial nationhood, and the historical fantasy of national theatre is a case study drawn from contemporary Canadian theatre, but it raises issues that apply with equal pressure to contemporary theatre culture throughout the world. This inquiry is triggered by the problematic critical response to the Disney Theatricals production of *The Lion King* in its several replications. The paralyzed critical reception to Julie Taymor's celebrated *mise-en-scène* suggests that contemporary theatrical capitalism has enacted a fundamental shift in the cultural location of the spectacular, by exposing the historical contingency of the discursive contradiction between national theatre movements—and their corollary of the popular—and the transnational circulation of elite aesthetics historically evident in the alliance of high culture and the avant-garde. My argument, briefly put, is that *The Lion King* restages the vocabularies of avant-garde and of community-based popular theatre aesthetics as a performance of the transnational culture promised by global economic movements towards free trade, opened borders, and the subordination of nations as markets.

This point can be developed productively by situating the Toronto performance of *The Lion King* in the context of the dislocated Broadway that grounds the cultural text of its reception. Only then is it possible to address the challenge posed by Susan Bennett in her review of the play in *Canadian Theatre Review*, when she writes that "It is too easy to critique this show as endemic of the pitfalls of an international market-place, and we need to better understand how such theatre works into the specificity of location" (68).

The problem to which Bennet alludes is the fact that the phenomenal popular success of shows like *The Lion King* upsets the premise in which theatre culture has developed in Canada. Postcolonial nationhood is founded on fantasies of absent authenticity (commonly described as a crisis of national "identity"), and nationhood itself is enacted in a theatre culture that reclaims this imagined cultural authenticity: imagined because it never exists, but the gaps of its absences are the emotional structures of nationalism. The idea of national theatre—of an institutionalized theatrical industry that announces and enacts the historical presence of the nation through a canon of performed texts—is in this sense an historical artifact originating in nineteenth century visions of popular mass nationhood, and it presents a particular problem in the postcolonial settler nations of the anglophone world. In my reconsideration of the conjunction of these two unstable terms (theatre and nation) as a metahistorical fantasy that enacts historicized constructions of nation, I paraphrase Benedict Anderson's celebrated argument to suggest that the theatre as it is *imagined*—formally (through policy, canonization, spectacle, and critical discourse) and informally (through polemics, noncanonical textualities, pageants, literary closet dramas, and failed aspirations)—constitutes the legitimizing performance of the imagined community that is the nation. National theatre, in the postcolonial context, refers to performances of desire and surrogation, of "lost" authenticities reclaimed through the elation of spectacle. In this space of the imagined theatre, the problem of transnational spectacle exposes a crisis in the contemporary relationship of theatrical representation and nationhood.

The Toronto production of *The Lion King* is one of seven currently playing in the world (the others are in New York, Los Angeles, London, Hamburg, Tokyo, and Fukuoka). Each carries the *imprimatur* of Taymor and Disney Theatricals, and each serves its market as the "authentic" production—and in fact may mark spheres of authenticity. The Toronto production has sold 850,000 tickets in the year since it opened, more than recouping its 20 million Canadian Dollars investment, and it plays to a market that covers the entire Great Lakes heartland of North America. It operates, needless to say, as a major anchor of cultural tourism in Toronto.

In her study of discourses of nation and the use of "culture" in the rhetoric of national policies, Donna Palmateer Pennee has identified "global capitalism's takeover of, but necessary articulation with, the nation-state" (194) in terms of a shift from "the ideological enemy of the Cold War to the ideology of capital in the onset of the Market Wars"

(191). In this era of the Market Wars, the international franchises of commodity spectacle enact a nation understood as a structure of industrial production in which spectacle is both the visible display of power and the commodity by which the market is controlled. And because theatrical capital functions to acquire value in reproduction, the discourse of the theatrical and the material terms of production adapt to the imperative to reproduce. In consequence, theatre as it has been understood through the twentieth century gives way to the larger notion of the "entertainment industry," in which the theatre merely represents one of several platforms for spectacular pleasure. Spectacle capital sees no difference between a stage musical, a rock concert, a theme restaurant, or a sports team.

Although megamusicals like *The Lion King* have restructured theatre culture in national metropolises for the past two decades, the terms of business in North America shifted in the early 1990s, when Garth Drabinsky's Live Entertainment Corporation of Canada (Livent), producer of *The Phantom of the Opera* in Toronto and of a subsequent series of popular and critical hits (including *Showboat* and *Ragtime*), crossed cultural and financial borders opened by the North American Free Trade Agreement. Livent typified the economic warfare of the late twentieth century, and like industries in other sectors, it used an arsenal of stock issues, leverages, off-shore production, tax-dollar partnerships, and saturation marketing to compete for market share. Livent was also the immediate structural and productive model for Disney Theatricals, which adapted its system of "vertical integration" of show development, marketing, and real estate acquisition.

As founder and CEO of Livent, Garth Drabinsky's main achievement was not simply the (re-)invention of "vertical integration," but rather the wider integration of theatrical business in the diversified productive economics of transnational capital, by bringing to the theatre the systems of corporate partnerships and sponsorships that had developed in the film industry. His production of *The Phantom of the Opera* was marketed with sponsorships from American Express, Labatt, and Pepsi, and, as Malcolm Burrows notes, the sales campaign included "14 different merchandizing items (including a line of *Phantom* clothing being pushed by the leather goods chain Roots" (7). The saturation advertising campaign for *Phantom* (with its unavoidable mask logo and incessant iambic radio tag, "Buy *Phantom* by phone") revolutionized theatrical marketing; according to one commentator, "it changed the very nature of modern entertainment advertising" (Potter). Adapting the logic of film marketing, Drabinsky had created a system in which a production could generate profit through advance sales and tie-ins even before it opened, and could thereby lever the financing for subsequent productions.

In his remodeling of theatrical production, Drabinsky had, as he claimed, adapted the Hollywood system to the Broadway musical (63). In the larger context of Canadian theatrical nationhood, the significance of Livent's achievement was not just that he erased national borders, importing American talent to work with Canadian investments, tax dollars, and labor to build products for export. That has always been the market logic of commercial theatre in Canada and the United States: production follows the dollar, but the reward of distinction and re-capitalization has always been New York. The real significance is that the methods and structures which Drabinsky commanded revived models that had dominated theatrical production a century before, which had provided the template for the Hollywood system, and which had similarly erased the national borders in North America.

Cultural folklore conventionally assumes that the rise of film distribution had spelled the end of the live theatre business in the 1920s, and turned theatre into a minority niche market. To a limited extent, this is true; as Jack Poggi has noted in his economic history of American theatre, the number of touring companies playing in the U.S. declined from 239 in 1900 to 41 in 1918 (30). The decline of the theatre business was due to many factors: in addition to film, Poggi suggests over-expansion of theatrical touring companies (leading to deterioration of quality), increased labour costs, and increased social mobility as a result of the automobile. Working class audiences moved towards film for reasons of cost, novelty, and availability, and theatre owners converted vaudeville palaces to cinemas because, as Poggi points out, "from an economic point of view, the development of the motion-picture industry was [...] a more convenient and less expensive means of distributing the product" (261). Poggi makes the point that

> What happened to the American theater after 1870 was not very different from what happened to many other industries. First, a centralized production system replaced many local, isolated units. Second, there was a division of labor, as theater managing became separate from play producing. Third, there was a standardization of product, as each play was represented by only one company or by a number of duplicate companies. Fourth, there was a growth of control by big business. (21)

But the Hollywood model that Drabinsky adapted to theatrical production had originally developed in New York in 1896 with the establishment of the Theatrical Syndicate. The Syndicate was an inevitable application of the expansionist economics of the age of monopoly capital to theatrical production, because revolutions in transportation and electrical communication enabled new forms of centralized distribution, just as it did in manufacturing industries.

The Theatrical Syndicate constituted an alliance of booking agents, who controlled large regional theatre circuits that had developed when rail transportation enabled "combination companies" to take to the road. The Syndicate contract stipulated a commercial merger in which the partners agreed to book shows only in Syndicate-controlled theatres. They would pool net profits, cease all competition amongst themselves, and forbid contracted shows and companies to play in non-Syndicate houses. For fifteen years, until the monopoly was broken in the "theatre wars" by the upstart rival Shubert chain, the Theatrical Syndicate effectively controlled all theatrical booking in North America through contract and coercion. Beginning with a pool of seventy playhouses across the United States, by 1904 David Belasco estimated that they owned or controlled five hundred theatres in the United States and Canada. Two decades later, a study of the theatre business commissioned by Actors Equity revised this figure to "seven hundred theatres—perhaps even more" (Bernheim 52).

As Daniel Frohman, the dominant partner in the Syndicate, wrote in *Harper's Weekly*, "It is the business system which obtains with the large business and banking institutions, and it is intended for the best interests of actors, playwrights and employees" (Witham 190). Just as in the 1990s many Canadian theatre workers welcomed Drabinsky's shows, so did many of the artists contracted by the Syndicate, for similar reasons of employment and security. The British actor Charles Hawtrey, who starred in Frohman's 1904 production of the long-forgotten *Saucy Sally*, defended the system to the readers of the *Fortnightly Review*:

> Playing, as I am doing, under the direction of Mr. Charles Frohman, and in the Syndicate theatres, I cannot but admire the perfection of the system, the ease and absence of friction with which attraction follows attraction, the novel and striking form in which the newspaper and other advertising is done, and the method of "advance work," in the newspapers, programmes etc. (1014)

Many others, of course, remained less convinced, including the few remaining independent managers and producers in New York, and the visiting stars who allied with them. The most spectacular display of the Syndicate's power was the sight of the world's first theatrical superstar, Sarah Bernhardt, touring in a tent because she had previously played a non-Syndicate house in New York. The major concern about such centralized power sprang from the effect it inevitably had on theatrical creativity, and through that, on national culture. The Syndicate consolidated a system in which the box office was the only marker of value— "the fiat of the people," as Dion Boucicault announced. Detractors feared that the Syndicate degraded the larger stream of culture by forcing artists and producers to create works that would feed the system and, as a result, legitimize an aesthetic structure of value based on mass taste.

This seemed a particularly critical issue in the 1890s, when theatrical modernism was one of the sites that produced the idea of a transnational avant-garde, with its rupturing contempt for the popular and the pedagogical, and its ambivalence towards the national.

Conventional histories of Canadian theatre have examined the impact of this development on national theatre culture in unproblematized terms of cultural colonialism. The monopoly wars of the American theatre established the material conditions in which Canadian theatre came to be articulated as a deferred aspiration. In the first imaginings of a national theatre in Canada, Frohman's virtual monopoly on British plays in North America proved particularly problematic. The liberal nationalist critics who identified American control of Canadian playhouses as a form of cultural colonialism that retarded the anticipated maturation of national culture, recognized that the Syndicate control was an economic problem that could be solved through tariffs and trade regulations. But Frohman represented a more profound problem, because he controlled Canadian access to the new British work that modeled alternatives to the populist dramaturgy of American mass theatre. In a series of famous talks, Bernard Sandwell spoke at length about "our adjunct theatre" and the "annexed stage," pointing out that the erasure of the border on the theatrical map of North America meant that "Canada is the only nation in the world whose stage is entirely controlled by aliens" ("Annexation" 23).

Canadian critics envisioned a theatrical nationhood founded on the principle of the repertory theatre movement, of which Granville Barker was the most tireless exponent. In Canada, the idea of a theatre company dedicated to the best dramatic literature and released from the tyranny of mass taste and the box office also corresponded to a vision of a restored theatrical border. Consequently, Canadian critics perceived a binary opposition between American commercialism and the modernism of the European "free theatre" movement. American, "alien" control meant that the American monopolies were "excluding from the Canadian theatres, nearly all of the best work of the English and European stage" (Sandwell, "Adjunct" 101). It is in this gap between the binaries that the theatre culture in Canada developed in the twentieth century to equate productive industrial structure and postcolonial nationhood.

Critics in Canada, as elsewhere but perhaps more complicitly, identified American touring shows as proof that cultural and economic colonialism were reciprocal, and this experience conditioned the reception of the later twentieth-century theatrical franchises, beginning with *Cats* in the mid-1980s. These productions—up to and including *The Lion King*—occupied an ambivalent space as products of sophisticated local theatrical industries and as imported valorizing texts; these shows were perceived as neither foreign nor local, they seemed dislocated and deracinated enterprises, "belonging" to no place, but never of *this* place. The transnational spectacles profit from this cultural unspecificity. Their location is an imagined Broadway that circulates in popular culture. Even when the shows originate in Europe, Broadway functions as a critical referent of value. A useful example is Drabinsky's *Show-boat*, directed by Harold Prince in Toronto in 1991, which exposed the crisis of location and specificity so clearly played out in *The Lion King*. An offshore venture capital production using American products and mostly American labour, funded by Canadian incentive schemes and tax breaks (this itself clearly a model of the Canadian economy), marketed and received as a "Broadway-bound," *Showboat* was not a Broadway production. But neither was it ever not a Broadway production: Broadway becomes the sign of a dislocated, transnational economic structure which transforms systems of reception and critical value. "Broadway" no longer corresponds to an identifiable district, or a contained realm of production, but rather to a domain of reception and reward. The real Broadway is wherever you have to go to win a Tony award. Just as a film only needs a screening in Los Angeles to win an Oscar, a Broadway show needs only one performance in New York to win a Tony. Like "Hollywood," "Broadway" has become synonymous with a moment of reception. In contemporary theatre capitalism, Broadway—the arrival in New York and subsequent recognition or failure—functions as the structure of value which enables the replication of the show as consumer commodity, particularly in touring markets.

And yet, if Broadway does not represent a place and constitutes neither a productive site nor an originary from which an aesthetic emerges, what is the cultural place of shows like *The Lion King*? The question is not just how they work "into the specificity of location," as Bennett asks, but how they produce the underlying concept of location itself. It is in the context of this question that I am drawn to what I have already identified as the paralyzed critical reception of *The Lion King*.

This paralysis was occasioned by the disruptive presence of Taymor's *mise-en-scène*: disruptive because it ruptures the categories of reception that, on the one hand, valorized avant-garde staging as a sign of cultural sophistication, and on the other, dismissed mass market musicals as vulgar and sentimental populism. The fusion of Taymor's theatricality and Disney's sentimental cartoon produced an incoherent critical response that repeatedly evoked the idea of magic. In her introduction to her book on Taymor's (pre-*Lion King*) work, Eileen Blumenthal identifies the "[...] theatrical tastes and skills that would color Taymor's work for years: formal elegance, filmic manipulation of scale and viewing angle, and a braiding together of global stage forms" (14). Taymor's stage effects were not in themselves particularly new; many of them can be seen in her previous work, and many of the theatrical forms she deploys have circulated widely in community theatre work, particularly by Welfare State in the United Kingdom, Neil Cameron in Australia, Shadowland in Canada, and numerous other processional, popular, and environmental troupes. Like Robert Lepage, Taymor personalizes the commonplace vocabularies of theatrical illusion in sequences of lyrical visual poetry.

By hiring Taymor, and thereby acquiring the cultural legitimation attached to her work history, Disney set out to expand the market of spectacle beyond the prestructured market created by the source animated film. In its first stage musical, *Beauty and the Beast*, Disney had replicated the film on stage as closely as possible, thereby targeting an audience already formed by the film, but at the same time contained by it. With *The Lion King*, the Disney team saw an opportunity not just to enter the theatrical market, but to dominate it by capturing the structures of critical distinction.

The strategy worked famously. Reviews of the premiere production in New York focused on Taymor's staging techniques and their genealogy in her work rather than on the narrative of the Disney story (which had already sold some 30 million videocassettes of the animated film). Analysis dissolved to expressions of wonder. Taymor herself enabled this response by claiming the production as "my *The Lion King*" and locating it in her canon. A reading of the critical reviews produces a series of terms that express astonishment:[1] "a whole new vocabulary of images to the Broadway blockbuster" (*New York Times*); a "dizzying, often mystifying array of theatrical techniques" (Jack Kroll, *Newsweek*); a "cornucopia of dazzlements" (John Simon, *New York Magazine*); a "theatre of miracles" (Clive Barnes, *The New York Post*), in which "Julie Taymor is our theatre's supreme wizard of spectacle" (Donald Lyons, *The Wall Street Journal*). The key term that recurs is "magic," which, as Brecht suggested, represents a term that denies the labor that makes it, and in critical discourse signifies paralyzed awe and the elation produced by exposed illusion. One should bear in mind that Taymor's staging is ornate but mechanically simple, and that the most wondrous scenes use stagecraft right out of Sabbatini. In fact, the effect produced by her staging is markedly similar to the effect that Giorgio Vasari identified in Renaissance Italy, when he observed that in the court spectacles "It seemed that everyone remained dumbfounded by some new and charming marvel" (Pallen 106) so that " it quickly seemed that its make-believe show would surpass truthful action" (113).

---

[1]   Quotations from the New York reviews have been taken from the citations included in *The Lion King* website (http://www.thelionking.cjb.net/ [21 April 2001]).

Taymor's choice to situate *The Lion King* in a theatre of miracles was strategic; as she told Richard Schechner, "When I worked on the story of *The Lion King* I ultimately knew that this is a classic story. It doesn't have to be so absolutely amazing. What needs to be amazing is the telling of the story" (51). On Disney's fable of manhood and natural law inscribed in a mysticized circle of life (as seen from the top of the food chain), Taymor developed a spectacle of interculturalism grounded in a dehistoricized, dislocated myth of primal Africa. Although she wanted "something real cross-cultural" (54), the interculturalism of the show builds on a fantasy of an invented Africa, legitimized by South African musical forms and the black bodies of the performers. Even in the Japanese productions, which resituates the play away from the racialized binary of black/white that supports its intercultural fantasy in North America and Europe, the mainly Japanese casts are legitimized by the inclusion of African performers. (Takeyashi). The choice of a fanta-sized as opposed to a pedagogical interculturalism seems to have been a deliberate strategy to gesture to the shifting politics of race without engaging in local specifics. Prior to the opening of the Los Angeles production, Taymor made this point when she told *Variety* that "it's not about race, but that doesn't mean it doesn't support and celebrate race" (Isherwood). She reiterated the difference between cultural specificity and fantasy when she told Schechner that, "*The Lion King* isn't about racism the way, say, *Ragtime* or so many other plays with black per-formers are. In this regard, *The Lion King* is totally refreshing—a kind of glimpse of the future" (54).

The fantasy of an invented Africa, sustained by intertextual signs of South African cultural experience (including a program note that explic-itly compares Musafa, the Lion King, to Nelson Mandela), allows the show to adapt to the cultural particularities of its various sites (Princess of Wales Theatre 77). The polysomatic performing bodies of *The Lion King* play back a mutiplicity of readings, as cross-cultural puppeteers, as signifiers of blackness, as celebrants of contemporary diversity. The Toronto production takes place in The Princess of Wales Theatre, a new theatre decked in comfortable citations of theatrical traditionalism with its plaster scroll work on boxes and gently curved galleries. The audi-ences sit in these signs of theatrical tradition, watching signs of cultural tradition: an imagined theatre watches an imagined Africa. But the spectators and the performance are real, realizing each other in a mo-ment of reclaimed authenticity that time and again moves audiences to tears. Taymor's comments on this in an interview with Richard Schechner suggest that she recognizes this emotionalism as a response manufactured by the theatrework of the show:

And everybody always talks about this crying. The most common statement is, "The giraffes came on and I burst into tears." From adults. You know,

children don't say that. And you ask, "Why is that?" [...] The fact that as a
spectator you're very aware of the human being with the things strapped on,
and you see the straps linking the actor to the stilts, that there's no attempt to
mask the stilts and make them animal-like shapes—that's why people cry.
(51-52)

This reclamation, this authenticity expressed in sentiment and the elation of spectacle, is an effect produced by illusion, but it is experienced
as the restoration of a sense of community; and the more Taymor's
mise-en-scène exposes the machinations and labors of spectacle, the
firmer the illusion that these support.

That *The Lion King* enacts a vision of an imagined intercultural
world sustained by a deep myth of patriarchy and natural justice will be
quite apparent to anyone familiar with Disney's animated film. In this
performance of real and invented interculturalism, the question is
whether *The Lion King* also models the ideology of transnational economics, legitimized by critical reception that focuses entirely on the
elation of the spectacle produced by Taymor's staging of global culture
as the location of pleasure and wonder. But the idea of "global" culture
and "global" markets are themselves generated by rhetoric. The market-
place that is so often cited as the natural regulator of commerce does, of
course, not exist; it coincides in fact with a flow of information and
power. The metaphor is necessary because it defines an imagined cultural location of commercial interaction. As James Laxer has pointed
out, "'Money' has become an industry in itself. The financial sector now
enjoys a global freedom of action that has sharply reduced the authority
of the state [...]" (64). Because of its demand that nations eliminate all
financial, labor, and environmental regulations that might restrict this
imagined equality and hinder the flow of capital, the new economic
globalism has often been critiqued as an attack on the very premise of
the nation-state. In his analysis of the Business Council on National
Issues and its pivotal role in the sharp right turn undertaken by the
Mulroney government in Canada in 1984, Tony Clarke argues that "the
ultimate aim" of the BCNI's agenda of deficit reduction, deregulation,
and free trade "has been to redesign the state itself" (37).

Transnational capital cannot be reduced to a single vision of an intercultural world, nor does it project a common vision of the nation-state. It
is rather reflexively constructed by the discourses of nation, state, and
regulatory economy that it must always seek to adapt. It would be
reductive to conclude, for instance, that the business community (an
imagined community if there ever was) desires to eliminate the nation-
state. In the global economy of borderless capital and the unregulated
flow of profit, the imagined nation is a qualitative domain that enfran-
chises corporate power by sustaining the principles of citizenry and
policy, principles which enable corporations to claim the legal rights of

individuals, and to demand recourse when government policies restrict those rights.

Theatrical nationhood, in all of its phases, has enacted totalizing discourses of the nation, as empire, federation, or public sphere. Corporate nationhood, in contrast, enacts the fragmentation of nation as a set of practices. In this decentered nationhood, the corporate theatre models the structures of a transnational economy, with its flags of convenience and nominal allegiances to national origin. Theatrical capitalism remodels theatrical structures of financing and production to literally promulgate the neoconservative vision of the nation as an economy, a site and mechanism of entrepreneurial competition for resources and market share. The utilization of public subsidies through tax relief, land development deals, and indeed, through the labor training and talent development provided by the not-for-profit cultural sector, all serve to reinforce this legitimization of the transnational economy.

In the postcolonial imaginary, transnational spectacles like *The Lion King* not only occupy the economic and material place of national theatre; they function as a structural and emotional simulation of national theatre by filling all of its defining absences. Imperial spectacle pleasures its audiences by confirming place in a universalizing order. In this respect, *The Lion King* is no less—and no more—an "authentic" enactment of nationhood than Shakespeare has been in the construction of postcolonial theatre cultures. And just as the various Shakespearean Festivals planted around the post-imperial world promulgated a myth of canonical high humanism for the twentieth century, theatrical capitalism today enacts its no less hegemonic visions of a deregulated intercultural market in the theatrical language of cultural democracy.

Works Cited

Anderson, Benedict. *Imagined Communities: Reflections on the Origin and Spread of Nationalism*. London: Verso, 1983.
Bennett, Susan. "Disney North: The Lion King." *Canadian Theatre Review* 105 (Winter 2001): 67-68.
Bernheim, Alfred. *The Business of the Theatre: An Economic History of the American Theatre, 1750-1932*. New York: Benjamin Blom, 1964.
Blumenthal, Eileen and Julie Taymor. *Julie Taymor: Playing with Fire*. New York: Harry N. Abrams, 1995.
Burrows, Malcolm. "Marketing the Megahits." *Canadian Theatre Review* 61 (Winter 1989): 5-12.
Clarke, Tony and Maude Barlow. *MAI: The Multilateral Agreement on Investment and the Threat to Canadian Sovereignty*. Toronto: Stoddart, 1997.
Disney Theatricals. *The Lion King* website. 21 April 2001. Http://www.thelionking.cjb.net/

Drabinsky Garth, with Marq de Villiers. *Closer to the Sun: An Autobiography.* Toronto: McClelland and Stewart, 1995.

Grover, Ron. *The Disney Touch: Disney, ABC & the Quest for the World's Greatest Media Empire.* Chicago: Irwin, 1997.

Hawtrey, Charles. "Theatrical Business in America." *The Fortnightly Review* 73.438, n.s. (1 June 1903): 1010-16.

Isherwood, Charles. "'King' preps for L.A. coronation." *Variety* (September 18-24, 2000).

Laxer, James. *In Search of a New Left: Canadian Politics after the Neoconservative Assault.* Toronto: Penguin, 1997.

Pallen, Thomas A. *Vasari on Theatre.* Carbondale: Southern Illinois UP, 1999.

Pennee, Donna Palmateer. "Culture as Security: Canadian Foreign Policy and International Relations from the Cold War to the Market Wars." *International Journal of Canadian Studies/Revue internationale d'études canadiennes* 20 (Fall 1999): 191-213.

Poggi, Jack. *Theater in America: The Impact of Economic Forces, 1870-1967.* Ithaca: Cornell UP, 1968.

Potter, Mitch. "Fantasies and Follies: Fall of Garth Drabinsky." *Toronto Star* 5 December 1998.

Princess of Wales Theatre. *The Lion King* program. *Performance* (March/May 2001).

Sandwell, Bernard K. "The Annexation of Our Stage." *Canadian Magazine* 38 (Nov. 1911): 22-26.

_____. "Our Adjunct Theatre." Addresses Delivered before the Canadian Club of Montreal. Season 1913-1914. Montreal. *Canadian Club* (1914): 95-105.

Schechner, Richard. "Julie Taymor: From Jacques Lecoq to *The Lion King.*" *The Drama Review* 43.3 (1999): 36-55.

Takahashi, Hidemine. "Harmony among People through Music: B. B. Mo-Franck." 29May 2001. Http://jin.jcic.or.jp/nipponia/nipponia14/live.html.

Walmsley, Ann. "Canada Inc." *Report on Business Magazine* (June, 1993): 45-56.

Witham, Barry, ed., Martha Mahard, David Rinear, and Don B. Wilmeth. *Theatre in the United States: A Documentary History, Volume 1. 1750-1915: Theatre in the Colonies and United States.* Cambridge: Cambridge UP, 1996.

Derek Walcott's *The Odyssey*: A Post-Colonial "Odd Assay"[1] of the Epic Genre as a Regenerative Source of "Latent Cross-Culturalities"

Valérie BADA

Université de Liège

Derek Walcott's *The Odyssey. A Stage Version* was commissioned by the Royal Shakespeare Company in 1992. That a Caribbean poet and playwright should be asked by the most venerable theatre institution in England to dramatise Homer's epic raises a few questions. Symbolically and interestingly enough, Walcott won the Nobel Prize for Literature within the week the play premiered at the RSC. So, Stratford called a post-colonial bard from a "far archipelago" to rewrite the "master narrative" of European civilisation, Homer's *The Odyssey*. Does the post-colonial writer, in all creative freedom and integrity, "write back to the centre," or does he seek some classical validation or legitimisation through the appropriation of a Western literary monument? Does the "centre" attempt to recuperate the talent blooming in its margins to regenerate its own imagination? Is this theatrical project the visible and official sign of an ancient but subterranean reconfiguration of the creative imagination, one whose virtue it is precisely to have neither boundary nor centre? Walcott's *The Odyssey* encapsulates all these problematic questions and takes us to what lies at the heart of post-modern literary analysis: a questioning of the concept of unity and homogeneity as well as an unmasking of the mechanisms that we know as "binary oppositions": the centre versus the margins, classical culture versus popular cultures, "master narrative" versus "smaller narratives." According to Lyotard, the two principal conditions of postmodernism are break-up and reconstruction on the one hand, and the loss of a belief in

---

[1] Assay\n: **1 b**: a chemical test to determine the presence or absence or more often the quantity of one or more components of a material; **c**: tested purity, value or character; **d**: a substance to be tested or being tested; **2 a**: archaic: assault, attack. *Webster's Third New International Dictionary.*

an overarching "metanarrative" on the other. Walcott's rewriting of Homer's epic does offer such a deconstructive literary revision: it evinces a geographic recontextualisation of the Mediterranean epic, a destabilisation of the genre, a decentering of the subject through the metaphor of exile, as well as self-referential metatheatrical features akin to another "epic" theatre, Brecht's conception of dramaturgy. But it probes much deeper beneath the surface of a post-modern textual disarticulation and offers partial glimpses of subterranean poetic and mythic recurrences. It especially does so through a creolisation rooted in the Caribbean landscape, folklore and poetic imagery, as well as in Yoruba cosmology. It reveals a comparative scrutinising of archetypal patterns in order to disclose "latent cross-culturalities" (Harris, "Quetzalcoatl" 40, quoted in Maes-Jelinek 37), i.e. a subterranean cross-cultural polyphonic structure.

In this essay, I want to focus on the problematic relation between postmodernism as a theoretical force spurting from a "crisis of representation and values" in Western societies and the post-colonial rhetorical strategies of intertextuality, irony, and questioning of history as displayed in Walcott's *The Odyssey*. Walcott's adaptation shows a subtle shift from a self-reflexive, fragmented, discontinuous, palimpsestic, thus experimental post-modern play to an intuitive, reconnecting, revisionary, Protean, thus cross-cultural text. To a post-modern refusal of closure, the play opposes a cross-cultural intimating of unresolvable partiality of vision epitomised in the trinity of blind poets, Homeric *alter egos* echoing and transforming the epic poem across space and time.

To channel the discussion on postmodernism and on crossculturalism as a possible alternative to its "depthlessness" (Jameson 6),[2] I wish to concentrate on a double dimension of Walcott's rewriting, i.e. his questioning of the epic genre as a founding narrative and the subsequent decontructive reading of its rhetoric on the one hand, and his poetics/politics of relocation of the epic on the other. Walcott's cartographic reconfiguration of the epic unites the Mediterranean (Europe and Africa/Egypt) and the Atlantic world (Africa/Nigeria and the Caribbean) through the fluid continuity of the poetic imagination, thereby transforming Homer's epic into a true overarching "metanarrative" released from its cultural fixity. Cross-culturalism, as it has been coined and defined by the Guyanese writer Wilson Harris, implies the existence of "an unbroken thread that runs throughout humanity" (Harris, *Radical Imagination* 26). This fundamentally essentialist conception of human

---

2   This comparison between postmodernism and cross-culturalism as theoretical forces engendered by the contemporary "sense of an ending" (Kermode, quoted in Maes-Jelinek 145) and void is eloquently discussed by Hena Maes-Jelinek in her seminal article "Teaching Past the Posts."

creativity, closer to philosophy than theory, seems to lie at the heart of Walcott's *The Odyssey* and allows a glimpse of latent bridges between cultures through the intuitive discovery of metaphorical and mythical similarities.

As an isthmian text, Walcott's *The Odyssey* thus connects three traditions, cultures, and sensibilities, a balance foregrounded straight from the beginning with a "Prologue" sung by Blind Billy Blue, a blues/calypso singer, a Protean Homeric *alter ego*, whose verse "stitches" (54, 122) stories across the seas. Throughout the play, he assumes the part of the two Homeric blind court poets, Demodocus and Phemius, the first a poet in Scheria at Alcinous' palace, the second in Ithaca. Significantly, Walcott displaces these two Homeric projections (Hamner, *"The Odyssey"* 103): Demodocus becomes Ithaca's poet and Phemius the bard at the Court of King Alcinous. This fusion of three characters—the Homeric story-teller whose voice introduces *The Odyssey* and the two displaced court poets—suggests a fluid continuity of the poetic voice echoing through space and time:

Since that first blind singer, others will sing down the ages

Of the heart in its harbour, then long years after Troy, after Troy. (160)

They represent crucial articulations of a larger discursive setting in which the Aegean text is constantly stretched by the Atlantic world. Just as Odysseus passes "through this world's pillars, the gate of human knowledge" (i.e. through Hercules' columns separating the Mediterranean sea from the Atlantic ocean; 27) and reaches for the "Other('s)" side beyond his own geographic and cultural sphere, Phemius' poem "will ride time to unknown archipelagoes" (59), and Demodocus, coming from "a far archipelago," connects both worlds with a common source of imagination, "the sea [that] speaks the same language around the world's shores" (122).

The "sound of surf" opening the Prologue sets from the very beginning the metaphor of the sea as a poetic continuity of imaginative visions and revisions through a cross-cultural dialogue:

Andra moi ennepe mousa polutropon hos mala polla ...

The shuttle of the sea moves back and forth on this line,

All night, like the surf, she shuttles and doesn't fall

Asleep, then her rosy fingers at dawn unstitch the design. (1)

The first verse[3] of Homer's *Odyssey* preserved in its original Greek form signals the cross-cultural dialogic pattern of Walcott's version. The

---

[3] "The hero of the tale, which I beg the muse to help tell, is that resourceful man" (Homer 1).

Greek text recedes in three dots, both eroded and regenerated by the
eternal flux of creativity, "the shuttle of the sea." The tidal motion is
associated with Penelope's endless weaving and unweaving of the
tapestry, "just as the sea's shuttle weaves and unweaves her foam"
(135). The metaphor of the sea as a poetic site is emphasised in Penelope's transformation of her twenty years of waiting into a fecund
creativity: although "that hot blue sea stays empty [...] its line is my
bow-string, and its waves my lyre" (21). Just as the horizon is an ever-
receding line blurred by the movement of the waves, poetic revisions
represent creative rhythms that ceaselessly produce mutating meanings,
a dynamic whose very *meaning* actually lies in its own motion: "the
gates of imagination never close [if] harp songs ripple the water" (35,
25). Revisionary waves and weaves produce "knot[s] of pain" (129)
echoing in the "sibilance [of the] surf" (37). The unstitched knots of
Penelope's tapestry, whose completion is constantly deferred, are juxtaposed to the useless nautical knots of Odysseus' lost vessel, whose
return home is constantly deferred. Both slow, repeating motions are
conflated into a single metaphor of the revisionary poetic process,
"verse stitch[ing] stories across the seas" (54, 122). The perpetual
deferral of closure embodied in the tapestry corresponds to Odysseus'
perpetual wandering across the seas which seems to end but resonates
with ambiguous Tennysonian accents. Indeed, Penelope's association of
the sea with the lyre echoes another recurrent metaphor which blends
poetic creativity and the fecund possibility of exile, i.e. the metaphorical
association of Odysseus with the turtle whose shell Hermes transformed
into a lyre. Odysseus inherits Achilles' shield after arguing with Ajax
who, bitterly looking at the shield "covering" Odysseus, curses him:
"Bear it, you turtle! Take ten years to reach your coast" (4). Just as the
turtle carries its "home" on its back, Odysseus accumulates in his twenty
years of wandering memories that form the very "shell" of his personality, his mythified as well as dark sides:

ODYSSEUS

My house has dark rooms that I dare not examine.

PENELOPE

Where's your house?

ODYSSEUS

Here. (He touches his temple)

The crab moves with its property.

PENELOPE

And turtles. (131)

Walcott thus brings into sharp focus the ambivalent nature of homecoming and injects his own Caribbean sensibility into the core of the Greek text: the figure of Odysseus appears as a personification of the "Caribbean poetic subjectivity [...] a migrant condition perennially poised between journeying and a desire for home" (Thieme). When Odysseus is shipwrecked on Sheria, Nausicaa notices: "the map of the world's on your back. The skin's peeling" (50). Odysseus' back, like a turtle's, represents the somatic expression of his psychic heritage: the world has become his home, his exile a "pleasure" (Lamming *The Pleasures of Exile*). This Donne-like metaphysical conceit reflects in cartographic terms the restlessly questing Caribbean spirit longing for a "home," but at the same time resisting psychic and cultural enclosure.

The metaphor of cartography also provides the model for a postmodern artistic expression which recharts the space of the contemporary "alienated city" and enables the "practical reconquest of a sense of place and the construction or reconstruction of an articulated ensemble" (Jameson 51). Jameson called this organising principle "cognitive mapping," a concept that applies to social, aesthetic, theoretical as well as ideological formations. But "the very global space of the postmodernist or multinational moment" (Jameson 53) remains strictly confined to the post-industrial city, the "urban [...] unrepresentable totality" (51), where the individual is no longer able to "map and remap [...] alternative trajectories to reconnect with the "ensemble of society's structures as a whole" (51). The post-modern cartography, "cognitive mapping," thus excludes socio-cultural spaces outside its own sphere of emergence and development. In other words, the margins of the post-modern "cognitive" map still represent "blanks," discarded territories "beyond the gate of [post-modern] imagination " (*Odyssey* 35) and interest.

Contrasting with the suffocating space of the post-modern "alienated city," the sea metaphor is a key concept in the work of Walcott, who by adapting Homer's *Odyssey* creatively opens the geographically enclosed Mediterranean world and expands it to the New World. Odysseus' exile across the seas reflects an existential condition which allows the "mapping and remapping" of overarching "alternative trajectories." The "sea's bitterness" (10) is equated with the "bitter ecstasy" (120) of homecoming, the "homeless parasite" (124) he is perceived to be on his return to Ithaca conjures up "the homeless waves" (109) whose rhythm still makes "the earth sway under [his] feet" (112).

His return home has Tennysonian accents which are echoed by Anticlea, Odysseus' mother:

Wasn't this the promise I made you, Odysseus,

That in an oak's crooked shade you would take your ease

> Quiet as a statue, with a stone bench for your plinth,
>
> That here in this orchard is where you would end your days,
>
> With memories as sweet as the honeycomb's labyrinth?
>
> Now your heart heaves, not from the Cyclops' boulders
>
> But that your mother's prophecy should come to pass? (158-59)

"Quiet as a statue" expresses Odysseus' fear of stasis, and the "stone bench" suggests the petrified world he would have to bear if his mother's vision were to materialise. Against the perspective of home-coming as sterile fixity come Athena's final words: "the harbour of home is what your wanderings mean" (159), echoing Menelaus' conception of home as "God's trial. We earn home like everything else" (29). "God's trial" before "earning home" is here "desupernaturalised" and interpreted as the existential ordeal of confronting the "soundless shadows"(151) of his mother and of his dead friends. The invocation of the dead through the blood of a sacrificed ram as it is depicted in Homer's "The Book of the Dead" is culturally transposed into an Afro-Caribbean Vodun ceremony in which Zeus and Athena are invoked alongside Ogun, Erzulie, and Shango. "Odysseus' eyes are wrapped in a black cloth" (88) and he is given a wooden sword which symbolises the duality of human nature as well as of the cosmic order: "the world/the underworld", "body/soul" (88), life/death, known/unknown. As an "archetypal protagonist of the chthonic realm" (Soyinka, "Morality" 3), "the shadow of imagination" (85), he undertakes an inner voyage whereby these antinomies will make "each other whole" (88) and which, as a result, will enable him to reach Ithaca with a deeper knowledge of himself.

He must symbolically "wound the ground" (88) and descend to the innermost reaches of his wrestling mind through "this crack of the heart-broken earth" (88). He removes "the bandage" from his eyes and, with his eyes peeled and his own wound exposed, he goes through the "womb" of the earth to reach his dead mother, Anticlea. Odysseus' utter vulnerability represents a gate within himself which opens the doors of "home." The metaphorical association of the wound with the womb comes up again in the next scene, when Odysseus reaches Ithaca after painfully passing through the "drifting rocks" Scylla and Charybdis, "curled up" on his raft and "cower[ing and] whining" (106) like a child. Simultaneously, his nurse Euryclea "is rocking a cradle" (106) and singing a lullaby:

> Sleep, my lickle pickney, don't 'fraid no monsters,
>
> As me launch your lickle cradle into dreaming seas
>
> [...]

So, cradled in him comfort, a child see what grows

From his shadow to shapes on a nursery wall. (106)

Odysseus is reborn through the wounds of experience symbolised by his descent into Hades, and then through the womb of his own unconscious, the terrifying drifting walls, "these monsters [from] a child's imagination" (106). Wilson Harris uses a similar conflation of metaphors in his latest novel, *The Dark Jester*: it is the "experience [of] a Wound that takes us back to Childhood, a mysterious Childhood we have largely forgotten, even as it brings us close to a recognition of transfiguration, yes, transfigured possibilities, yes, and deadly dangers in ourselves, partial dangers we may reinforce into absolutes" (Harris 6). Significantly, the scar of an old wound on Odysseus' leg allows him to be recognised by his nurse under the dirty rags of a homeless beggar and welcomed "home."

The body as the metaphor of concentrated experiences is also used in the dramaturgy of the play. In the tradition of Amiri Baraka/Leroy Jones's *Dutchman*, Hades is relocated in the underground, "earth's stomach" (89), where Odysseus is confronted with his mother's reflection in a mirror. The dramatic use of a mirror presents Odysseus confronted with himself as a "being inhabited by presences" (Walcott, "Muse of History" 2), which belong to his past and with which he webs a dialogical relationship to reach another level of self-consciousness. The disclosure of a latent heteroglossia within the individual reflects on a metaphorical level the underpinning "multi-voicedness" of Walcott's *Odyssey*, now revealed as a "chambre d'échos" (*Barthes* 78), a chamber in which the echoes of other literary works ranging from the classics to popular calypso are endlessly reflected. The hellish underground is depicted as "a station, echoing arches" (89) where "every mirror echoes [the] mannerisms" (90) of the "eclipsed" presences within the self. The metaphor of the entranced voodoo devotee Odysseus holding up the mirror not to nature, as Hamlet puts it, but to his fragmented self points to a kaleidoscopic referentiality which reflects the structure of the text itself. In other words, thematic introspection corresponds to textual and dramaturgical introversion, i.e. a self-conscious turning towards the form and mechanism of the performance. This textual as well as dramaturgical ritual of deconstruction shows its ultimate disarticulation when the epic becomes split into an "alphabet of the souls, Ajax to Zeus" (92) within the space of the letter "L" drawn on the earth—a liminal space of ritual revelation which symbolises the entrance to Hell. The stark nakedness of the signs stripped of the sophistication of epic poetry and reduced to their minimal contextual meaning reveals the complete dissolution of the heroic substance of the epic when names are the only mnemonic traces left. It reflects Odysseus' angst of being "turned into a name" (130) and thereby stripped of contradictions and ambiguities, the very stuff as man is made on. In reaction against his epic dehumanisation, he depicts himself as a "devious [...] divisive [...] liar" (53-54), echoing Phemius' intuitive assertion that

what lasts is what's crooked. The devious man survives [...] That's the way

with tears. Crooked streams join their rivers. (54)

This double entendre reflected in the word "crooked" (dishonest and curved, twisted) translates Odysseus' ambivalent personality: Menelaus describes him as a "smart [...] acquisitive [...] sacker of cities," materialistically-inclined and interested in taking "his share" (32). The Odyssean virtues defined by the recurring epithets *"polutropos"* (1), *"polumechanos, polutlas, polumetis* [italics mine]"[4] (110) are counter-balanced by their excess or perversion. These adjectives defining a positive intelligence are turned into antithetic flaws. His exceptional cleverness becomes "natural cunning" (60), the man of invention (he conceived the conspiracy of the Trojan horse) becomes the "man of evasions, man skilled at lying" (110).

Odysseus appears as an extension of the Afro-Caribbean trickster figure, Anancy.[5] This cross-cultural association is further emphasised by his "Egyptian" slave and nurse Eurycleia, who cradled Odysseus as "Egypt [...] cradle Greece till Greece mature [*sic*]" (9). She says:

Nancy stories me tell you and Hodysseus [...] People don't credit them now.

Them too civilize. (8)

These flaws reveal a complexity that the Homeric Odysseus possesses but only fleetingly discloses. The final scene showing on stage the massacre of Penelope's suitors connects Odysseus' murderous revenge to the tragic hubris of the Yoruba god of iron, Ogun. As the stage darkens, Odysseus warns the suitors by uttering "say your prayers [...] it fans the forge whose anvil hammers lightning" (142). "A loud rambling noise, echoing" (145) is heard, and that "reverberation" comes from the "great door groaning from dividing iron" (145). The Nigerian playwright Wole Soyinka sees Ogun as the embodiment of Yoruba tragedy, i.e. the merging of the dichotomy creation/destruction into complementary forces. In his adaptation of *The Bacchae of Euripides,* Soyinka fuses Dyonisos with Ogun and describes him as "the god of seven

---

[4]   *Polutropos* and *polumechanos* mean "resourceful," "shrewd," but also "shifty" and "full of tricks"; *polutlas* means "much-enduring"; and *polumetis* refers to Odysseus' archetypal quality, his exceptional cleverness.

[5]   Anancy is a cultural retention of the Yoruba Voodoo god Esu Elegbara and the Fon (Benin) god Esu Legba, the crippled messenger of the gods and the guardian of the crossroads.

paths" (Soyinka 295), who "makes an anvil of the mountain-peaks/Hammers forth a thunderous will" (251). Just like Odysseus, Ogun battles the forces of the chthonic realm, "the transitional yet inchoate matrix of death and becoming" (Soyinka, "Fourth Stage" 142). He forged an iron axe as Odysseus used his sword to "hack a passage through primordial chaos for the gods' reunion with man" (Soyinka, "Morality" 27). Odysseus' mass murder of the hundred suitors is described by Penelope as "a second Troy" (154). She scornfully accuses him of "hack[ing] [his] way through mankind [and] dismember[ing] its branches" (154). Her description is strongly reminiscent of Ogun's "tragic error," i.e. his slaughtering of his own people at a battlefield in a fit of drunken madness. The cross-cultural identification of Odysseus with Ogun articulates some latent similitudes between the Greek and the Yoruba myths and thereby points to "a kind of ontological cross-culturalism which subverts and dismantles Western assumptions of a superior cultural heritage" (Maes-Jelinek, "Latent Cross-Culturalities" 1). The Greek and the Yoruba epics are thus interwoven in an intricate pattern of mythical correspondences which question and creatively contaminate the cultural purity of the genre.

At the end of the play, in a fit of vertiginous consciousness described as "madness" (151), Odysseus nearly kills the poet Blind Billy Blue/Demodocus for preserving the epic tradition and for translating the former's rejection of the war, "Troy's rain [...] Wounds. Festering diseases" (151), into the celebratory "Troy's glory" (151). The poet's epic lines are compared to a "succession of arrows [...] huge oars [...] thudding like lances on to the heart of this earth" (54). Odysseus' fury reflects the thorny intricacy of *history* and *narrative*, of factual historical *reality* and its transmission through *literature*. Odysseus wants to kill the poet "for telling boys that lie!" (151), i.e., for turning a reality of destruction and suffering into a glorious epic. Unlike Jameson's understanding of the post-modern as "bereft of all historicity [where] the past as 'referent' finds itself gradually bracketed, and then effaced altogether, leaving us with nothing but texts" (Jameson 322), Walcott suggests that the dilution of the *real* in the epic narrative represents an unbearable "lie" that must be exposed before reformulating the latent links bridging *realities*, in this case a reality of war and destruction, and the subjective imagination. As a post-colonial writer questioning the validity of the coloniser's hegemonising historiography, he sees the "significance of history [...] in both the event and its narration, however fictionalised and subjective," while postmodernism focuses on its "own awareness of this fictionalization" (Maes-Jelinek, "Teaching" 141) and the impossibility of retrieving any meaning from its referential illusions, let alone recovering a sense of purposefulness and potentiality from the debris of historical catastrophes.

So, Walcott's adaptation of *The Odyssey* is grounded in a revisionary process of the epic genre whose acclaimed heroism and metaphorising compulsion lead to the disappearance of the historical subject into poetic abstraction. Walcott infiltrates into the interstices of the traditional Homeric epic a critique of the genre and is, at the metafictional level, engaged in the same conflict as Odysseus with the poet identified as the voice of "metaphor" (121). Walcott says

> one reason I do not like talking about an epic is that I think it is wrong to try to ennoble people [...] And first to write history is wrong. History makes similes of people, but these people are their own nouns. (Walcott, quoted in Bruckner 397)

Instead of a glorifying, dehumanising and artificial epic language, Walcott offers an elemental epic poetics in which language and nature are engaged in a creative dialectics of sounds and meanings, in a fashioning of an elemental totality through language. The "islands" echo the name Odysseus as "sea, sea, sea" (36), "father" as "farther, farther" (37). Nature repeats the essential connection between the utterance and its wider symbolic significance, and creates a link between language and its infinite mutating reverberations across time and space. Odysseus fuses with the "sibilance" (37) of the "hissing surf" and the "hissing wheels" (139): "Odysseus. His name sounded like hissing surf" (122). The name swirls across the seas to the "green leaf and clear vowel" (109) of home, echoing Penelope's unbroken marriage vow, to the poplars and spring of Mount Neriton which talk the tongue that he recognises "from the crackle of their consonants ... Ithacan" (109). Unlike the post-modern sense of alienation, man, language, and the undetermined vastness of the *real* seem to be here organically united.

So, it seems that despite the sense of being lost in a terrifying void, despite dislocation and utter alienation, the existential "centre" still holds, the accumulated remains of fragmenting/ed historical experiences can be articulated. The connection between man in all his frailty and contradictions and the indeterminacy of the *real* still exist. In other words, the depth of experience beneath the surface of referential illusions or "partial appearances" (Harris, *Unfinished Genesis* 214) can be probed through the intuitive resources of "Adamic" (Walcott) language.

Walcott's *The Odyssey* creatively fluctuates between transformation and continuity, thus showing a post-colonial ambivalence which contradicts and at the same time expands the Homeric literary myth beyond the boundaries of cultural constrictions. In his *odd assay* of the epic genre, a "crucible of cultures" indeed, Walcott *tests* the antique text to determine the presence of essential components, recuperates these thematic *essentia*, and extracts from them a contemporary *substance* by discerning post-colonial concerns in the interspaces of the Western narrative. Through the exploration of the transformative and therefore fertile potentialities of the Homeric text, Walcott "assays" and assaults the static character of tradition and enters a syncretic dimension of creativity capable of engendering a new cultural ethos.

Works Cited

Baraka, Amiri. *Dutchman*. 1964. *Black Theatre USA. Plays by African Americans. The Recent Period 1935-Today*. Ed. James V. Hatch and Ted Shine. New York: The Free Press, 1974. 381-91.

Bruckner, D. J. R. "A Poem in Homage to an Unwanted Man." *Critical Perspectives on Derek Walcott*. Ed. Robert D. Hamner. Washington D. C.: Three Continents Press, 1992. 396-99.

Hamner, Robert. "*The Odyssey:* Derek Walcott's Dramatization of Homer's *Odyssey.*" *ARIEL: A Review of International English Literature* 24:4 (October 1993): 101-108.

Harris, Wilson. "Quetzalcoatl and the Smoking Mirror. Reflections on Originality and Tradition." *Wasafiri* 20 (Autumn 1994): 38-43.

_____. *The Radical Imagination. Lectures and Talks by Wilson Harris*. Ed. Alan Riach and Mark Williams. Liège: L3, 1992.

_____. *The Unfinished Genesis of the Imagination. Selected Essays*. Ed. A. J. M. Bundy. London, New York: Routledge, 1999.

_____. *The Dark Jester*. London: Faber and Faber, 2001.

Homer. *The Odyssey*. Trans. E. V. Rieu. Harmondsworth: Penguin, 1946.

Jameson, Fredric. *Postmodernism, or the Cultural Logic of Late Capitalism*. Durham: Duke UP, 1991.

Kermode, Frank. *The Sense of an Ending. Studies in the Theory of Fiction*. Oxford: Oxford UP, 1966.

Lamming, George. *The Pleasures of Exile*. London: Allison and Busby, 1984.

Lyotard, Jean-François. *La condition postmoderne: rapport sur le savoir*. Paris: Minuit, 1979.

Maes-Jelinek, Hena. "Teaching Past the Posts." In *Liminal Postmodernisms. The Postmodern, the (Post)Colonial, and the (Post-)Feminist*. Ed. Theo D'Haen and Hans Bertens. Amsterdam, Atlanta: Rodopi, 1994. 139-60.

_____. "Latent Cross-Culturalities: Wilson Harris's and Wole Soyinka's Creative Alternative to Theory." *European Journal of English Studies* 1/2.1 (1998): 37-48.

Roland Barthes par Roland Barthes. Paris: Seuil, 1975.

Soyinka, Wole. *The Bacchae of Euripides. Collected Plays*. Oxford: Oxford UP, 1973. 233-307.

_____. "Morality and Aesthetics in the Ritual Archetype." *Myth, Literature and the African World*. Cambridge: Cambridge UP, 1976. 1-36.

_____. "The Fourth Stage." *Myth, Literature and the African World*. 140-60.

Thieme, John. "Derek Walcott's Odysseys." Paper delivered at the conference "Moving Words, Moving Worlds." University of Leeds. September 1994.

Lord Tennyson. "Ulysses." *A Book of English Poetry. Chaucer to Rossetti.* Ed.
    G. B. Harrison. Penguin, 1950. 361-62.
Walcott, Derek. *The Odyssey. A Stage Version.* New York, Boston: Faber and
    Faber, 1990.
_____. "The Muse of History." *Is Massa Day Dead? Black Moods in the
    Caribbean.* Ed. Orole Coombs. New York: Doubleday, 1971. 1-27.

Portrayals of Masculinity/ies in
Wole Soyinka's *The Lion and the Jewel*

Erol ACAR & Martina STANGE

University of Paderborn

Wole Soyinka, the Nobel prize-winning Nigerian playwright, poet, and novelist, is considered by many to be Africa's finest writer. Though apparently influenced in his dramas by the Irish playwright J. M. Synge, Soyinka links up with traditional popular African theatre and its combination of dance, music, and action. In fact, his writing is based on the mythology of his Yoruba people. In a paper delivered at a Swedish conference in 1967, Soyinka underlined that "the artist has always functioned in African society as the record of the mores and experience of his society and as the voice of vision in his own time" (Hughes). This essay will focus on the process of gendering, on the metaphors of gendered power, and on the relation between "hegemonic" and "subordinate" masculinities as exemplified in Soyinka's highly popular comedy *The Lion and the Jewel* (first performed in 1959 and published in 1963). Soyinka's imagery does not only imply a particular perception of the relation between the sexes, it also makes statements on the social value of phenomena within a network of abstract relationships between masculinity and power. Assumptions of supremacy and hierarchy have, for many years, been a key area of postcolonial perception and imagining, turning around notions like "progress," "improvement," "tradition," "heritage," or "dislocation." Already as a young playwright, at a point when Nigeria had not yet reached independence, Soyinka was very much preoccupied with the questions of cultural difference, encounter/conflict, and the potential hybridization of social habits (as well as languages) resulting from contact with other cultures. In his play, the village of Ilujinle serves as the site of a meeting point of African and European traditions, and yet it differs radically from a black-and-white portrayal.[1] Although the white man remains absent, the Yoruba commu-

---

[1] Soyinka has, in many interviews, defended his conception of what the African heritage is against "Neo-Tarzanist" critics. See, for example, the "Introduction" to *Six Plays*: xiv-xvi.

nity of Ilujinle is not static or traditional. Neither of the two opposing protagonists of the play can be called representatives of Western or Yoruba civilisation. Soyinka rather recommends a "syncretistic approach" (Gibbs 53) to the understanding of the supposed embodiments of British and Yoruba cultures.

In his very entertaining play, Soyinka explores traditional Yoruba principles of life and death as opposed to European innovations and the imitation of Western attitudes. Of major interest for our investigation are the two main male characters of the play, Lakunle and Baroka, the lion of the title, and their interaction with Sidi, the village belle, and Sadiku, the chief's head wife. The teacher Lakunle, an unpopular "know -all," attempts to imitate what he thinks is a modern male role model in the Western tradition, a model which, however, he has only come in contact with through British books. His counterpart, Baroka, is interested in the same woman as the teacher, the aforementioned Sidi, and tries to achieve his aim in the Yoruba way. They both suffer a rebuff, because Sidi proves to be a rather emancipated Yoruba woman, though far from being a "women's libber." In this area of conflict, the audience witnesses a competition of male self-realizations and masculine life plans that takes unexpected turns.

But before examining Soyinka's play in further detail, certain theoretical assumptions need to be clarified. In her important study *The Gender of the Gift*, Marilyn Strathern argues in favour of the following notion of gender:

> By gender I mean those categorisation of persons, artefacts, events and sequences [...] which draw upon sexual imagery [and] make concrete people's ideas about the nature of social relationships. (ix)

This means that neither the character of sexual imagery nor the relation to social experience are fixed or universal. It implies that the local setting and the point of view of those who use sexual imagery have to be taken into account. In the case of Soyinka, one has to analyse the cultural requisites for an individual of the male/female sex to be considered a man/a woman in the Yoruba context.

The Yoruba cosmology[2] as articulated in the oral heritage of Ifa divination and in Yoruba writings shows gender relations as being hierarchical rather than egalitarian: though not rigidly authoritarian, the gender relations structure gives the impression of power radiating from a central male-oriented, male-dominated source, with a distinct separa-

---

2   H. Trabelsi employs the term "Yoruba cosmogony" to refer to "the values inherent in the creation and sustainment of the Yoruba universe and the consequent social and mental basis of the apprehension of reality" (109).

tion of spheres (cf. Newell).[3] Not only can one distinguish predominantly male from female spheres; in Soyinka's play, maleness is attributed to specific places, such as the odan tree or the silk-cotton tree.

Furthermore, because some of the requisites that govern the male/female dichotomy are corporeal, one has to look for interpretations of the body that are activated for a discourse on gender. These can fruitfully be complemented by theories of performance, closely tied to the study of ritual because these make vital contributions to embodiment.[4] Indeed, performance theories focus on the experiencing body, situated in time, space, and history, and regard it as a locus of ideological struggle. Moreover, the requisites that govern gendering are also built into the verbal language, and both pervade all aspects of social life, such as family life, work, status, class, and age. This all links up to an interpretation of gender as a system of symbols and meanings that influence and are influenced by cultural practices and experiences. An area of gender-relevant issues is mapped up by such a method "considering local discourses of agency, causation, personhood and identity" (Cornwall and Lindisfarne 40).

In addition to this gender-relevant cultural map, there has, over the last few years, been a rise of interest in the study of men and masculinity. Of special interest here are R.W. Connell's insights in his groundbreaking work *Masculinities* (1995), in which he proposes to think of those ideologies which privilege some men by associating them with a particular form of power and designating them as "hegemonic masculinities," which can be understood as follows:

> Hegemonic masculinity is far more complex than the accounts of essences in the masculinity books would suggest [...]. It is, rather, a question of how particular groups of men inhabit positions of power and wealth and how they legitimate and reproduce the social relationships that generate their dominance. (Carrigan et al. 92)

Following T. Carrigan, R. W. Connell, and J. Lee, privileged forms of masculinity could also be considered as "hegemonic masculinities" in a Yoruba context. Such dominant constructions, which are seen as a current "ideal," establish the standards against which other masculinities are classified. The latter will be referred to as "subordinate masculinities".

---

[3]   R. Sethuraman emphasises the role that Soyinka's women characters play in the maintenance of the Yoruba cosmic balance, as they prefer to replace the antagonistic dichotomy by a male-female principle as a single cohesive unit (222).

[4]   In Balme's words: "A ritual is a complete entity comprising beliefs, a performative structure, and discrete cultural texts such as music, movement, verbal texts and culturally precribed communal involment" (213).

Like the notion of gender, the notion of masculinity should be conceived of as fluid and situational. Therefore, it is necessary to examine the various ways in which people understand masculinity within the particular setting of *The Lion and the Jewel*. In the process, this essay will also in part explore how different masculinities are defined and redefined in social interaction. Our approach of Soyinka's comedy will seek to address some of the following questions: in *The Lion and the Jewel*, how do individuals display and cope with a gendered identity? How and why are particular images and behaviours given gendered identities (cf. Cornwall and Lindisfarne 3)? Are masculinities linked to particular places in the play? Or, are special activities and occupations, such as teaching and wrestling, gendered in *The Lion and the Jewel*? In connection with our borrowed concept of "hegemonic masculinity," it might also be interesting to understand how relations of power and powerlessness are gendered in Soyinka's plays and how attributions of masculinity are assumed or imposed in particular settings within his work. Or, to put it differently, if in the West being male is often associated with the power to dominate others, how are ideas of power linked to maleness in the Yoruba microcosm which Soyinka describes in *The Lion and the Jewel*?

With these various questions in mind, let us now turn to the dramatic text itself and examine some of the forms that "hegemonic" and "subordinate" masculinities take in it. Physical prowess is definitely one of the attributes through which these are respectively imposed or displayed in *The Lion and the Jewel*. The personality of Baroka, the hero of the play, dominates the action, although he is not present on stage until towards the end of the first part ('Morning') and has left the stage well before the end of the last one ('Night'). Even before the chief of the village makes his first appearance, the audience/the readers may already catch a glimpse of him through the village school teacher's point of view, who characterizes Baroka as "an ignorant old man who grabs a girl young enough to be his grand-daughter from the educated young man who loves and wants to marry her" (Erapu 24). But the audience/the readers will find out very soon that this view has no basis: the chief and the teacher are in a sexual battle, being suitors after the same girl. Consequently, virility has to be paraded.

The chief is given a number of praise-names: "the Lion of Ilujinle," "the Fox of the Undergrowth," "the living god among men" (12), "the panther of the trees" (25), "the fearless rake," "the thoughtful guardian of the village health" (44), and others. Baroka has no problem using these names himself (cf. 25, 27, 38, 44). He seems to live up to his reputation, even at the age of sixty-two. In a series of rhetorical questions, he praises his own heroic deeds:

Did I not, at the festival of Rain,/Defeat the men in the log-tossing match?/Do I not still with the most fearless ones,/Hunt the leopard and the boa at night/And save the farmers' goats from further harm?/[...]/Did I not, to pronounce the Harmattan,/Climb to the top of the silk-cotton tree,/Break the first pod, and scatter tasselled seeds/To the four winds—and this but yesterday? (27)

Baroka, moreover, demonstrates physical prowess when he performs the tree-climbing ritual and flaunts his great shape as an elderly man. One might argue whether Baroka's victory in the log-tossing competition or his muscular superiority over a wrestler in a later scene constitute real displays of physical strength. In any case, Sidi, the village beauty, feels full of admiration for Baroka when, in the middle of a wrestling match, he explains to her the absolute necessity to pit his strength against somebody who is anything else but a weakling. The chief knows that he must win against "this son of [...] a python for a mother, [...] fathered beyond doubt/By a blubber-bottomed baboon" (these words are compliments to the wrestler, of course). Perhaps, in order to dispel doubt that the wrestler may have been tutored to lose the match (cf. Tripathi 89), Baroka adds: "Only yesterday, he nearly/Ploughed my tongue with my front teeth" (39).

Conversely, Lakunle is not exactly remarkable for his physical prowess. When Sidi asks him to perform the dance of the lost Traveller, he refuses to do so: "I won't take part. [...] No, no. I won't" (14). It does not help much, though: Lakunle is dragged towards a platform and forcibly seated on it—not by a blubber-bottomed baboon, but by four girls. However, Lakunle still considers himself a member of the stronger sex. Earlier in the play, he states that women are called the weaker sex, because they "have a smaller brain" than men (5). By contrast, and in conformity with modern Western ideology, he considers that his intellectual work as a school teacher expresses his superior manhood. It is the study as well as the possession of books ("The scientists have proved it. It's in my books"[6]) which enable Lakunle to feel like a man ("I obey my books" [55]). He thinks that he behaves in a manly fashion when he can show off his erudition about life in the West and when he quotes from the Bible like a vicar in the pulpit. A man of the world like him knows about eating with knives and forks, dancing the waltz and the foxtrot, or kissing in the way "all educated men kiss their wives" (10). The teacher opposes this kind of manliness to the ignorance of the "bush minds" (7), the "race of savages" (5). He wants to win Sidi's love so that he can civilise the ignorant "bush-girl" through marriage.[5] Lakunle resorts to "barren, borrowed and bombastic rhetoric" (Gibbs

---

5   "Lakunle desires Sidi more with his head than with his heart," while Baroka is a "past-master in the practical arts of wooing" (Jones 29).

49), which he deems appropriate for an educated man. However, his alien Western imagery and Biblical phraseology only cause confusion and further reduce his chances to arouse Sidi's interest in marrying him. In the last analysis, Lakunle ironically fails to have any individual power over this woman, whom he supposes to be deviant, owing to his particular male mind-set (cf. Newell 163).

Added to which, in *The Jewel and the Lion*, the intellectual enterprise symbolized by Lakunle is also associated with the social inferiority of femininity in a strange inversion of the rational/emotional dichotomy. It is an open secret that the members of his community do not really feel compelled to respect Lakunle, as Sidi tells the audience very early in the play: "the whole world knows of the madman/Of Ilujinle, who calls himself a teacher!" (5). Even the children regard him a fool. Sadiku, the chief's head wife, has a laughing fit when she thinks of Lakunle's manliness: "You a man? Is Baroka [whom she believes to be impotent at this stage of the play] not more of a man than you?" (32) Later, when Sidi has lost her virginity to Baroka and is packing her things to move to his palace, Sadiku makes fun of Lakunle (who does not realize that Sidi is preparing to become Baroka's wife, not his): "It serves you right. It all comes of your teaching" (55). What Lakunle has always defined as an expression of his superior manhood—his education—is completely rejected by Sidi in the final scene: "Out of my way, book-nourished shrimp" (57).

Is Baroka then an example of "hegemonic masculinity" and does Lakunle meet the criteria of "subordinate masculinity"? Let us look at instances in which males are metonymically linked to might and control through association with images or instruments of power (Cornwall and Lindisfarne 21). In his home, Baroka surrounds himself with weapons: "There are heads and skins of leopards/Hung around his council room." But Sidi drops the remark that "the market is also/Full of them" (42). A particularly impressive image of power is the "carved figure of the Bale, naked and in full detail," the full detail of an enormous and permanent erection, suggesting sexual vigour and stamina, as Sadiku "takes a good look at it" and Sidi "stares in utter amazement" (30). Baroka likes to make his masculine domination "obvious": his still healthy body exudes "affirmation," "strength," "activity" and "verticality" as innate masculine virtues.

Baroka's rival cannot match such a performance. He does not indulge in physical training, nor does he excel in an activity in which men without a wrestler's physique could effortlessly participate: drinking! Indeed, Lakunle cannot take alcohol. During the Dance of the Traveller, Lakunle "tries the local brew" (17), first with scepticism, later appearing to relish it and imbibing it profusely. The result: he is sick and rushes out with his hand held to his mouth, passing Sidi, who makes fun of him, because he is such a good impersonation of the white Traveller.

Another instrument that can be regarded as empowering in the Yoruba context and which frightens men in particular is Baroka's bull-roarer. A new railway line is to be built, and the surveyor's team has already been deployed. Lakunle rejoices at the thought that the railway line will bring "Trade,/Progress, adventure, success, civilisation,/Fame" to Ilunjinle (24). But the Bale manages to protect his land disrupting the work of the surveyor's team. He scares off the prison gang working as the surveyor's labourers by frightening them out of their wits with the menacing and weird sound of the bull-roarer, a simple device that, whirled around the head of the operator, produces a pulsating whine and is used to "warn off uninitiates from secret rituals" (Erapu 17; see also Brian). By resorting to the sound of a bull, Baroka invokes many elements of gender ideology. The symbolism of the bull itself is called upon and linked up with him. The bull symbolizes wild nature, virility, noble manliness, fertility, courage, and aggression. Its phallic horns are forcefully reminiscent of the idea of penetration.

Metonymic associations often expose the kind of "commodity logic" (See Strathern 338) which characterizes capitalist formations. In this logic, masculine identities may be found via possessions, which can be acquired or lost. Baroka owns dogs, horses, wives, and concubines (this is the order in which they are listed in the play). But the most obviously coveted "commodity" is Sidi, whom both Baroka and Lakunle wish to possess—Baroka in order "to teach this unfledged birdling" about sex ("I also change my wives/When I have learnt to tire them" [39]), Lakunle to have a "life-companion" and to kiss her only in the way of "civilised romance" (10), i.e. within the restraints befitting an educated man. From Sidi's perspective, such a male comes close to a eunuch. In fact, at the end of the play, she says that Lakunle fades into "a watered-down/A beardless version of unripened man" (57)—an imagery suggesting that Lakunle is, at best, only a boy parading as a man.

Let us now investigate the way in which Baroka turns Sidi into a woman. He does so in terms of particular idioms and in a language which defines his "hegemonic masculinity" as opposed to Lakunle's "subordinate" one. The teacher proves unable to effect such an apparently magical feat. (We have already hinted at his role as a clownesque outsider in the village community.) Using the "mask of impotence" (Tripathi 85), the chief has gained access to a formerly unwilling young woman: Sidi had declined an earlier invitation to the palace, but is now reassured that a meal with him would be harmless and, at the same time, satisfy her curiosity. The initiative seems to be in her camp, but Baroka has taken precautions. The chief pretends that he is reluctantly following the teacher's progressiveness and has arranged for a *tête-à-tête* that will not be disturbed:

> Prompted by the school teacher, my servants/Were prevailed upon to form something they call/The Palace Workers' Union. And in keeping/With the habits—I am told—of modern towns,/This is their day off. (35)

Having claimed similarity with the teacher and his ideas of modernity and progress, Baroka does not fail to ridicule the Western intellectuality of his rival in the wooing competition. When Sidi, knowing about Baroka's alleged impotence, asks a seemingly naive question about any possible dissatisfaction of the harem's head wife with the Bale ("Was the Favourite ... in some way ... / Dissatisfied ... with her lord and husband?" [38]), the chief not only straightens out aliens ideas like Lakunle's conception of monogamy and a certain emancipation of women, but also like the one that a polygamist such as him could care about the whims of one of his harem wives:

> Now that/Is a question which I never thought to hear/Except from a school teacher. Do you think/The Lion has such leisure that he asks/The whys and wherefores of a woman's/Squint? (38)

Using the indefinite article with "school teacher," he shows up Lakunle's "subordinate masculinity" without attacking him personally. In the course of the seduction process, which R. McDougall interprets as the enactment of "a kind of ritual process for social purification, exorcising unbalanced alien powers and confirming social stability" (112), the Bale makes it clear that he adheres to traditional male-female role allocation:

> I lose my patience/Only when I meet with/The new immodesty with women./Now, my Sidi, you have not caught/This new and strange disease, I hope. (44-45)

Critics disagree on the ups and downs of the "verbal wrestling" (McDougall 114) between Sidi and Baroka, but there is unanimity on one point: his speech on progress marks "the climax of the Bale's verbal assault on her" (Tripathi 94), by the end of which Sidi is entirely under his spell, as she "is capable only of a bewildered nod" (48). Baroka's approach to and use of language absolutely differ from the teacher's. Carefully handling words and "delighting in their individual qualities" (Gibbs 50), the chief plays upon Sidi's vanity by suggesting that the future postal stamps of the village should picture her:

> [....] Can you see it, Sidi?/Tens of thousands of these dainty prints/And each one with this legend of Sidi./The village goddess, reaching out/Towards the sun, her love. (46)

The passage of his speech which is directed against the sameness that comes with progress, captures the simple girl and makes her fall into an erotic trap. Its language is "rich and sentimental, overwhelming Sidi with its exoticism" (Banham 10):

> Below the humming birds which/Smoke the face of Sango, dispenser of/The snake-tongue lightning; between this moment/And the reckless broom that will be wielded/In these years to come, we must leave/Virgin plots of lives, rich decay/And the tang of vapour rising from/Forgotten heaps of compost, lying/Undisturbed ... (47)

The Bale's technique of outmanoeuvering Sidi by using lush imagery and sexual connotations in his words sharply contrasts with Lakunle's courting, full of banality:

> I want to walk beside you in the street,/Side by side and arm in arm/Just like the Lagos couples I have seen/High-heeled shoes for the lady, red paint/On her lips. And her hair is stretched/Like a magazine photo. I will teach you/The waltz and we'll both learn the foxtrot. (9-10)

As already indicated earlier, *The Lion and the Jewel* switches between specific settings in which masculinities are performed or enacted—the teacher's school on the one hand, the Bale's bedroom on the other hand. The odan tree offers another example of this theatrical strategy. An "immense" odan tree (3) dominates the village centre of Ilujinle, and it is definitely not by accident that Baroka, the Bale, enters the stage "from behind the tree" (16). The tree symbolizes traditional life, just like Baroka, "the champion of tradition" (Erapu 35).[6] Moreover, this strong, giant odan tree makes the teacher's bush school look like a dwarf. In the final scene of the play, Lakunle, who is getting a nuisance to Sidi ("I shall not let you./I shall protect you from yourself"), is given a shove "that sits him down again, hard against the tree base" (57). He has to face the facts: the Bale and his ideas on tradition and progress, on masculinity and love will continue to influence the community of Ilujinle.

In this essay, we have sought to outline several new perspectives for the study of gender and portrayals of masculinity/ies, applying them to a literary depiction of a specific postcolonial rural setting in Western Nigeria. As Cornwall and Lindisfarne point out in their important study *Dislocating Masculinity* (1994), "the contexts and criteria in terms of which men are differentiated from each other is [still] an area which has been neglected [...] in much of the men's studies of literature" (19). Therefore, we want to conclude our essay with some questions that might serve to extend our provisional interpretive framework to broader examinations of literary representations of masculinities.

---

[6] Also see Jones (6-7) on the role of some trees in Yoruba sacred festivals.

In British colonial discourse, patriarchal masculinity and the pre-
dominance of men function as a gendered institutional practice. So, it is
generally interesting to find out how this is translated in the social
reality of the occupied country. With Soyinka's *The Lion and the Jewel*,
could we not consider that colonial/postcolonial textuality has emerged
out of a network of "multiple encounters and negotiations of differential
meanings" (Bhabha 173)? Does this not somehow anticipate the web of
indeterminacies characterizing "the-Empire-writes-back" literatures and
globalization writings of today?

"The old must flow into the new." In saying so, Baroka, the Moslem
harem owner, alludes to a well-known saying from St Mark's Gospel, in
the crucial seduction scene of the play (49). Could we therefore regard
Ilujinle as the place of a crucible of cultures? *The Lion and the Jewel*
stands "at the confluence of two traditions." It thus appeals to an audience that is familiar with either of the two, "the Yoruba masque and the
European satirical musical" (Gibbs 53). Along the lines of the crucible
of cultures theme of this book, scholars should seek to point out those
instances where the traditional, gendered cultural identity is affected by
the gendered identity of the colonial power. Furthermore, researchers
will need to examine the material culture used in a text—a point which
may be particularly important for the study of drama, where objects are
presented concretely on the stage. Are there objects/artefacts exclusively
employed in male or female spaces? Or, are there any objects celebrated
as markers of masculinities? Scholars should analyze the various gen-
der-specific languages used in a text. Are gender identities associated
with a particular language?

We are convinced that constructions of masculinities in different cultures constitute a relevant and legitimate topic in the study of postcolonial drama. This is especially true if one understands theatre, as the
editors of this volume do, as a place where the "many-faceted societal
and aesthetic changes that mark the beginning of the new millennium"
are translated into innovative idioms.

Works Cited

Balme, Christopher. "Syncretic Theatre: The Semiotics of Postcolonial Drama
    and Wole Soyinka's *Death and the King's Horsemen*." *New Theatre in
    Francophone and Anglophone Africa: A Selection of Papers Held at a Con-
    ference in Mandelieu, 23-26 June, 1995*. Ed. Anne Fuchs. Amsterdam: Ro-
    dopi, 1999. 209-28.
Banham, Martin. *Wole Soyinka. The Lion and the Jewel: A Critical View*. Ed.
    Yolande Cantù. London: Rex Collings/The British Council, 1981.

Bhabha, Homi K. *The Location of Culture.* London/New York: Routledge, 1994.

Brians, Paul. "Wole Soyinka Study Guide." 4 Feb. 1999. Http: //www.wsu.edu/~brians/angophone/soyinka.htm.

Carrigan, Tim, Robert W. Connell, and John Lee, "Toward a New Sociology of Masculinity." *Theory and Society* 14.5 (1985): 551-604.

Connell, Robert W. *Masculinities.* Berkeley: U of California P, 1995.

Cornwall, Andrea, and Nancy Lindisfarne. "Introduction." *Dislocating Masculinity: Comparative Ethnographies.* London/New York: Routledge, 1994. 1-10.

_____. "Dislocating Masculinity: Gender, Power and Anthropology." *Dislocating Masculinity: Comparative Ethnographies.* London/New York: Routledge, 1994. 11-47.

Erapu, Laban. *Notes on Wole Soyinka's The Lion and the Jewel.* Nairobi: Heinemann, 1975.

Gibbs, James. *Wole Soyinka.* Basingstoke/London: Macmillan, 1986.

Jones, Eldred Durosimi. *The Writing of Wole Soyinka.* London/Ibadan: Heinemann, 1973.

Hughes, Claire W. D. "Soyinka and the Literary Canon." 10 Dec. 2000. Http: //landow.stg.brown.edu/post/soyinka/wscanon2.html.

McDougall, Russell. "The Snapshot Image and the Body of Tradition: Stage Imagery in *The Lion and the Jewel*" *New Literatures Review* 19 (1990): 102-18.

Newell, Stephanie. "Petrified Masculinities? Contemporary Nigerian Popular Literatures by Men.*" Journal of Popular Culture* 30.4 (1997): 161-82.

Sethuraman, R. "The Role of Women in the Plays of Wole Soyinka." *World Literature Written in English* 25.2 (1985): 222-27.

Soyinka, Wole. "Introduction." *Six Plays.* London: Methuen, 1984.xi-xxi.

_____. *The Lion and the Jewel.* 1963. Soyinka, *Collected Plays.* Vol. 2. Oxford/New York: Oxford UP, 1974. 1-58.

Strathern, M. *The Gender of the Gift.* Berkeley: U of California P, 1988.

Trabelsi, Hechmi. "The Place of Tradition in the Plays of Wole Soyinka." *Les Cahiers de Tunisie* 46 (1993): 105-24.

Tripathi, P. D. "The Lion and the Jewel: A Comparative and Thematic Study." *Ba Shiru* 11.1 (1980): 82-101.

"The Critical and the Dissident, the Irreverent and the Playful" Drama in the New South Africa

Geoffrey V. DAVIS

Aachen University of Technology

> I'm sick of all the gloom and doom.
> Theatre has always struggled.
> Go ask Shakespeare.
> (Greig Coetzee, quoted in Sherrifs 54)

During April and May 2001, a festival was held in London to "Celebrate South Africa." The Zulu version of *Macbeth—Umabatha*—opened the year's Shakespeare season at the rebuilt Globe; *Suip!*,[1] a play about Cape Town winos written in Afrikaans and English, took the stage at the Tricycle Theatre in Kilburn; a festival of new South African movies ran at the National Film Theatre; the great South African diva Sibongile Khumalo and the legendary jazz trumpeter Hugh Masekela regaled the audience at the Royal Festival Hall; and Nelson Mandela attended a Freedom Day Concert in Trafalgar Square, where his effigy is soon to join that of the venerable Lord, his namesake, on a pedestal in front of South Africa House.

Why, then, one may wonder, should one of South Africa's foremost theatre critics, Robert Greig, have called for a boycott of such a prestigious occasion put on to mark the seventh anniversary of his country's first democratic elections (see "Artists should boycott")? On the face of it, it would seem quite perverse for South African artists to wish to impose a cultural boycott in reverse—particularly on a festival whose purpose it was in part to celebrate the lifting of the very cultural boycott under which they had themselves suffered for so long. The answer lies

---

[1] *Suip!* by Heinrich Reisenhofer and Oscar Petersen is one of the plays to emerge from the Baxter Theatre Centre's New Writing Programme and has recently been published by the Baxter Theatre Centre at the University of Cape Town in *2+2 Plays* (Cape Town: comPress, 2000).

in the crass divide that the critic perceives between the manifest desire of the Department of Arts, Culture, Science and Technology to "position South African arts globally"[2] and the dire current situation of the arts inside the country itself. For Greig, such an overseas extravaganza was a public relations charade, a costly marketing exercise, serving only to divert much-needed funding from the more urgent purpose of sustaining the cash-strapped arts at home.

The social and political changes of the 1990s in South Africa have brought tumultuous times for all the arts, not least the theatre. An instructive example of how difficult things had become in the immediate post-apartheid phase was provided by the production of *Titus Androni-cus* directed at the Market Theatre, Johannesburg, in 1995 by Gregory Doran from the UK and starring the London-based South African actor Antony —now *Sir* Antony—Sher in the lead role. This was certainly the kind of performance that London audiences would, and in fact later did, rush to see. The picture that emerges from the account Sher and Doran give of the experience in their book *Woza Shakespeare!* is not a happy one. Here was the major theatre in South Africa operating without a subsidy, and, to the great frustration of its somewhat impatient visiting artists, with all of its departments understaffed and apparently unable to "deliver the goods" (152): no publicity, no marketing, and thus, of course, no bookings (154). Brilliantly acted shows that had garnered rave reviews were playing to houses of 60 or 70—in a theatre which seats 450 (154). Even Barney Simon's own production of *Hedda Gabler* was playing before audiences of only 30 people. No wonder Sher thought the Market looked "a bit lost in the New South Africa" (44).

When their own show, *Titus Andronicus*, also had very poor houses, critic Barry Ronge in the *Star* berated Johannesburg audiences for their lack of discernment, warning them that South African theatre was "on the verge of extinction," and that they would soon rue the day when the Market, the Civic and the Alhambra had all vanished from the scene (quoted in Sher and Doran 222). Some of the explanations offered for the fate of this particular production might have been expected —*Titus* was hardly a text for schools and, apparently, nobody in the country had ever heard of Sher—but others seemed more ominous, as when they were told that "security fears" were turning "Jo'burg, the murder capital, into a ghost town on Saturday and Sunday nights" (207), or when Janet Suzman attributed the lack of interest to the long-term effects of the cultural boycott: "People have lost their sense of curiosity," she suggested. "They were deprived of outside culture for so long that they've

---

[2]   This phrase is taken from the irritated response to Greig from the director general of the Dept. of Arts, Culture, Science and Technology (Rob Adam).

got to the point where they say, 'What we can't have, we won't want'" (218).[3]

In view of such depressing conclusions, it is with some relief that one reads of how the locally cast South African performers (including Sello Maake ka Ncube) embarked on rehearsals with all the enthusiasm and acting skill befitting such a unique opportunity; of how the visitors somewhat belatedly recognised—after having heard a moving account of the history of Market by its co-founder Barney Simon—that being invited to work in such a place constituted more of a privilege than a burden; and of how the Minister for the Arts chose—at last!—to announce the award of an annual state grant to the Market on the opening night of the show (Sher and Doran 200).

The social and political transformation underway in South Africa has required major changes at all levels of theatrical activity. New institutional structures have been put in place in an effort to redress the balance between those sections of the arts—largely white-run—which were long subsidised by the state, and those—many of them black-initiated—which endeavoured to survive on the margins. Theatres have set about redefining their function to serve a different kind of society; formerly white-dominated institutions have been reconstituted. It has all proved a very complex process indeed.

The first official attempt to address the fraught issue of transformation in the arts was the government *White Paper on Arts Culture and Heritage*, entitled *All our Legacies, All our Futures*. "Distilled" from numerous sources, prime among them the voluminous *Draft Report prepared by the Arts and Culture Task Group for the Ministry of Arts, Culture, Science and Technology*, the *White Paper* frankly acknowledged from the outset that it was dealing with "one of the most emotive matters to face the new government" (1.11). It recognised that hitherto, under apartheid, cultural expression had been "stifled" and "distorted" (2.2), since some art forms had been entirely neglected (it specifically named "oratory, praise poetry, story telling, dance, and ritual"), while others had been privileged (it spoke of the "European classics," opera, and ballet). It recognised, too, that the distribution of funds, infrastructure and skills had likewise reflected "significant bias in favour of a highly selective slice of artistic expression," and that government was now seeking to ensure both that "the full diversity of our people [...] be expressed in a framework of equity which is committed to redressing

---

[3]   In an article entitled "Spinning out the present: narrative, gender, and the politics of South African theatre," Dennis Walder wonders, appositely enough, why critics "enthuse over consciously local versions" of European classics such as *Titus* and *Woyzeck:*, "but to what end, in the new dispensation" (219).

past imbalances and facilitating the development of all of its people," and that its resources be equitably distributed (2.7).

The largest stumbling block in this process was the previous (apartheid) government's funding practices: under their terms, the lion's share of the arts budget had gone to the four provincial Performing Arts Councils, which traditionally served middle-class white audiences and were located in city centres where they maintained large and luxurious theatres. Stephen Gray once dubbed them "concrete bunkers," and one only had to look at the Nico in Cape Town or the State Theatre in Pretoria to see what he meant. The figures which the *White Paper* revealed were startling enough. 46% of the Department's whole budget was continuing to be absorbed by the PACs, whose opera and ballet performances were consuming some 30% of their government grants and whose box office receipts represented only 18% of income, not even enough to cover administration costs. It is hardly surprising that the authors of the *White Paper* came to the conclusion that "government is subsidising expensive art forms and infrastructure for a small audience at an unaffordable level" (4.19) and that to continue to do so would hardly contribute to its Reconstruction and Development programme.

The *White Paper*, therefore, proposed radical reform. In order to spread more widely what it conceded were "limited public resources" (4.24)—and here we must bear in mind that in present-day South Africa education, health, and housing are seen to represent much more urgent priorities than culture, or as one commentator succinctly put it: "drains come before art" (Sherrifs 55)—the Performing Arts Councils grants would be progressively reduced over a three-year period, beginning with an immediate cut in subsidy of 22%, and at the same time the theatres would be transformed through a process designated by the awful neologism "rightsizing" into commercially run playhouses. Henceforth, only running costs for the buildings would be met from government subsidy. An unspecified proportion of the amount thus saved would be channelled to "a wider variety of artists, cultural groups and art disciplines" (4.24). In its concern to broaden appreciation of and access to the arts in South Africa, the *White Paper* also proposed that arts infrastructure be moved "close to where people live" (4.59). Indeed, we need to bear in mind that one of the obstacles placed in the way of theatregoing for the majority of the population by apartheid legislation took the shape of the Group Areas Act, which had decreed where people were permitted to live and had thus determined audience composition. Therefore, it was hoped that by setting up community arts centres where there had been no theatres at all before, this state of affairs would finally be overcome and new audiences be reached.

The issue at the heart of the transformation of South African theatres is, of course, their financial viability, their ability to survive under changed circumstances. If, as critic Adrienne Sichel has recently suggested, "keeping track of South African arts funding is a lot like writing a thriller" (Sichel, "Arts Whodunit"), it is rapidly turning out to be one abounding in multiple twists of plot, cliff-hanger endings, sudden death, and unexpected reprieves. In the light of recent government measures, it hardly appears surprising that one of the country's foremost ballet dancers—Timothy le Roux—should have transformed "The Dying Swan" into a critique of the current glaring imbalance between arts patronage and corporate sports sponsorship, and should have given the performance the sardonic title "I should have been a rugby fly-half" (Sichel, "Dancing" 54). For it has not been the theatre alone, but the arts as a whole which have suffered badly. Orchestras, opera and ballet companies have endured a series of what has somewhat euphemistically been termed "structural readjustments" (Sachs). Thus, the National Symphony Orchestra has closed (see de Beer, "The State of the Theatre"), the Cape Town Philharmonic has gone into liquidation (see Anstey), and the KwaZulu Natal Philharmonic now survives as the country's only permanent orchestra. Funding for the Port Elizabeth Opera House has been "slashed" (Gray). Meanwhile, Sachs remains confident that these institutions will "re-emerge and flourish, more firmly rooted in our cultural and economic reality" (17); on the other hand, some have chosen to regard the Minister for the Arts' recent expression of opinion that "all of these art forms are regarded as South African" (Macliam, "The buck stops") as somehow reassuring.

The survival of several theatres was endangered through savage budget cuts. The Johannesburg Civic, saddled like the PACs with heavy long-term debts, had its budget reduced by 36%, the City Council announcing that henceforth the theatre would have to become "multi-purpose" and look to more "private-sector use with conferences to fund it." The artistic programme would, they added, "concentrate more on popular entertainment to make money" (Greig, "City fights"). By October 2000, the Civic had been privatised (see Myers). Recognition that, in the absence of government largesse, theatres would, henceforth, have to function as business enterprises became widespread. Even John Kani, director of the Market—which was managing to fill the house only when it offered such sensational fare as *Shopping and Fucking*—was faced, notwithstanding its new R6 million annual grant, with the need for major staff cuts, and had to concede that "we cannot continue to budget according to a wished-for income that we might raise overseas. The Market has to function as a business" (quoted in Anstey).[4]

---

[4]   Mannie Manim suggested that most of their income had been spent on staff earnings, leaving nothing for productions ("So Many Questions. Mannie Manim." *Sunday*

The Windybrow Centre for the Arts had likewise to live under constant threat. Ironically, it was one of the first theatres where black artists had begun to find employment in key positions and whose director, Walter Chakela, had, on his appointment, stated that he regarded this as "an opportunity to give space and expression to the culture of the people of the Transvaal and possibly, in the process, to stumble across a new way to deal with culture in a democratic society" (33). In February 2000, critic Garalt Macliam reported that the Windybrow, "a theatre which also happens to be a national monument goes forever dark next month, its staff of 25 having already received notices of retrenchment" ("Wind out of the Sail"). Fortunately, however, he was eventually proved wrong, when the city and the national Department of the Arts granted the theatre a last-minute stay of execution (see Mokoena, "Windybrow"), and a subsidy of R1.8 million was later approved (see Sichel, "Arts Whodunit").

There were closures, too—and not only in the theatre itself. At the University of Durban-Westville, for instance, the Drama Department fell victim to the process of downsizing and merging of university departments (see Lakhani and Suter respectively). On June 15, 2000,[5] the most high-profile theatrical closure of all was announced when—in the wake of major financial scandal—no less an institution than the hitherto highly prestigious State Theatre in Pretoria was mothballed by ministerial decree. The press expressed much sympathy for redundant company members (see de Beer, "More tears" and Accone, "Cultural cryogenics"). The institution, but not the company, was given an unexpected reprieve from what seemed an inevitable fate: in October, an organisation called Maestro Entertainment Holdings proposed to revive the theatre's fortunes with a summer season of ballet, concerts, and drama, which included Mbongeni Ngema's blockbuster *The Zulu*, billed as "fresh from a sell-out success in Germany." But, by December, planned productions were already being cancelled and the chairman of Maestro was taking the by-now-familiar line that "they would have to focus on commercially successful productions, and forget about 'high art'" (Cillie and Greig 17). Although the Advisory Board created to recommend a rescue package for the State Theatre has now reported, its final fate does not yet seem to have been decided (see Macliam, "Ngubane").[6] In the press, accusations flew that all of this was not so much the product of

---

Times, July 23, 2000: 16). In August 2000, the Market obtained a R2 million grant from Japan.

[5]   Critic Darryl Accone, writing in *The Star*'s Tonight section (23 June 2000: 9), dismissed the announcement as "a mealie-mouthed piece of Governmentspeak."

[6]   In November 2001 the State was hosting performances of *Suip!* and *Glass Roots* by the Baxter Theatre, Cape Town.

social transformation as of ministerial vacillation (Sichel, "Arts Who-dunit").

The financial problems which plagued theatre managements resulted not only from organisational upheaval, but also from dwindling audiences. The situation at the Market has already been referred to—but the problem was apparently being duplicated all over the country. A 1998 report on the year's theatre in Durban, for instance, concluded that "theatre attendance must have hit an all-time low," the reason advanced for this being that a "culture of attending live theatre" was no longer being created (Greer 10). In Cape Town, a high-profile show like *The Elephant Man* at the Baxter had "very poor" audiences (Willoughby), as did Reza de Wet's *Yelena* at the State Theatre in Pretoria. Examples are legion. As we have seen in the case of the Market, some of this was put down to the problem of security. "Some of the country's best theatres," it was said, "are in areas where people are reluctant to drive to at night" (Sherriffs 53). The director of Performing Arts Promotions at the Cape complained that what they really needed was transport: the crucial issue for community theatre was not so much audiences' tastes in theatre, but their security, the question of "how to get them back home safely, with crime rife and train and bus services practically non-existent after dark" (Fletcher). Even if, as some suggested, the crime problem was being hyped in the press (see Accone, "Stop wringing your hands"), would other theatres have to emulate the Market and launch an "adopt a cop programme, that has a police caravan stationed in the theatre precinct and the presence of plain-clothes policemen on the hoof" (see Accone, "Stop wringing your hands")?

Is it any wonder then, that in the face of mounting evidence, theatre critics frequently bewailed what they termed "the bewildering absence of theatre in Johannesburg" (Greig, "Sachs"), or wrote resignedly that "drama is not dead in KwaZulu-Natal. It just seems that way sometimes" (Tyler). The frequent recourse of some theatres to European and American musicals was dismissed by one critic, Robert Greig, as a "sure sign of managerial disarray" ("Musical Overkill"), while the "umpteen one-man, one-woman shows" seemed to another more a ploy to save money than to advance the cause of drama (Wilson). (Two of the latest Cape Town offerings in this genre are *At Home ... with William Plomer: a Play about Letters and Loves* at the Nico,[7] and Moira Lister's reminiscences of working with Noël Coward at the Theatre on the Bay).

And yet, if I may take as my text for the day the title of an article of critic Darryl Accone's "Stop wringing your hands, leave the comfort zone and get your bum on a theatre seat," there are many signs of theatre

---

[7]   Written and directed by Roy Sargeant, with Ralph Lawson as Plomer, performed at the Nico Arena in March 2001.

fighting back against the innumerable threats that currently besiege it. Four widely differing examples will provide some idea of the range of options being pursued. As a first instance, TV soap star Thoko Ntshinga took Zakes Mda's play *And the Girls in their Sunday Dresses* to squatter camps and townships not only to conscientise women, but also in an effort to gain new audiences. Commenting on the project, the actress said: "We're hoping to say to people in the townships who are hooked on television, 'OK, you've got your soaps, but you've also got your theatre. Don't let it die'" (Sichel, "Girls"). Second, some gambling casinos have begun to offer theatrical performances, a rather curious innovation welcomed by theatre practitioners largely as a means of job creation. One of Johannesburg's major casinos, for example, Gold Reef City, recently mounted the highly successful musical *African Footprint* at its own Globe Theatre (see Mokoena, "Actors hit"); the show later transferred to the London Old Vic where the publicity described it as "an explosive stampede of song and dance fresh from South Africa"—I fear we've been there before! A third example is provided by a community youth theatre—the Cape Town Theatre Laboratory—which has been established in the suburb of Woodstock, riven as it is by gangster-ism and drug-use, with the aim of "remedying" social problems through working with youth and "bringing to life" the many stories out there in the community (van Dyk). Finally, shows have also been relocated to one or another of the growing number of arts festivals which are now held throughout the country (quoted in Greig, "Moving beyond"),[8] this in an effort to escape the problems of inner-city locations, where, as arts consultant Mike von Graan pointed out some time ago, theatre "is all but dead"—a conclusion anyone attending the annual Grahamstown Festival 900km from Johannesburg would hardly be likely to reach.

By now, it seems to have been recognised that the White Paper "hasn't worked, transformation has not taken place and revisions are necessary to 'articulate a new vision guided by the realities of the day'" (Macliam, "New Policy"). Garalt Macliam has recently reported on a new action policy contained in an arts discussion paper, which envisages the creation of a Performing Arts Corporation of South Africa, as well as four bodies responsible for opera, orchestral music, dance and theatre, and folk and traditional music. These are to be respectively based at Artscape (the renamed PAC, Cape Town), the State Theatre (Pretoria), the Market Theatre (Johannesburg), and the Playhouse (Durban), a proposal Macliam feels would entail "much wailing and gnashing of teeth in the arts community when its prescriptions become public knowledge" (Macliam, "New Policy").

---

[8]   Sherriffs quotes a figure of 130 festivals.

What do theatre practitioners, who are most nearly affected by all of this, think about what has been going on? Interestingly, Mark Fleishman, Malcolm Purkey, Zakes Mda, and Janet Suzman, all of them much involved in current theatre activity, have recently made known their feelings on changes in the theatre, and much of what they have to say, of course, reflects back on their own practice as theatre artists.

Mark Fleishman, writing very much from a Western Cape point of view, is wary of what he perceives as the desire of Gauteng province to maintain its hegemony in the world of theatre and of the rise of a new theatre élite out of what he calls "the Market stable." He asks whether the "new dynamics in South African culture and art," evident from about 1990 in a concern with social issues of immediate relevance, with cultural history and with the intercultural, have been sustained through the decade (Fleishman, "Unspeaking the Centre" 91). His concern that institutional changes should be "translated into theatre practice itself" (94) is allayed by the evidence of the programmes of the annual Grahamstown theatre festival, which has registered a healthy increase in the number of new South African plays being performed there. Fleishman sees "a collection of multiple voices" (98) replacing the earlier single voice of protest, "a theatre of smaller narratives [...] more reflective of the ambiguities and contradictions which are at the heart of our new society" (98), supplanting the grand narrative of apartheid, a multiplicity of "personal and cultural identities" (113) reflecting the complexity of the new South Africa on stage. His own recent show *Voices Made Night* bears witness to this.

Malcolm Purkey, whose views are informed by his experience as a founder member and director of the Junction Avenue Theatre Company, starts from the—commonly held—position that "with the demise of apartheid South African theater's role in society has disintegrated" (Steinberg and Purkey, "South African Theater" 32) and that, since then, "theatre-makers have [...] been unable to find new forms and ideas to give expression to our times" (24). Conscious of the continuities in the history of South African theatre, he believes that some aspects of crisis "like the struggle for audiences and funding" (26) have been around for years, and that they are not simply a product of transformation. No doubt with Junction Avenue in mind, he asserts that some of the "constituent principles [of anti-apartheid theatre]—most notably the determination to represent and engage with popular experience— [...] are vital to the sustenance of a new theatre" (26) as well, and he later specifies further what these are: "to use the language of ordinary people, to draw on indigenous performance traditions, and to locate agency in the lives of the masses" (32). His recent work on *Love, Crime and Johannesburg*, Junction Avenue's first new production in ten years, demonstrates these kinds of continuity.

Zakes Mda, who spent many years in exile in Lesotho where he worked in theatre for development, and many of whose plays have only recently been performed in South Africa, makes a good case for the argument that "the South African context is richer and more varied than the theatre has hitherto attempted to depict" (Mda, "Introduction" ix). Under apartheid, playwrights had, for instance, told the story of those who went to jail for their political beliefs or laboured in the mines, but they had "forgotten to tell the story of those who did not follow them to jail or to the mines—the women and children who stayed at home and struggled to make the stubborn and barren soil yield" (ix). They had created a theatre which was "basically an urban and male one" (ix), ignoring peasants and rural dwellers and, as he puts it, "(shying) away from depicting social and class conflicts among the oppressed themselves" (ix). Now that "the post-apartheid era has freed the imagination of the theatre practitioner," new opportunity beckons; "a new post-apartheid theatre [can be seen] gradually emerging" (xx) —witness the plays in an anthology Mda himself recently edited, which include Fatima Dike's hugely successful and "not overtly political [...] domestic comedy" (xxii) *So What's New* together with his own *The Nun's Romantic Story*, which, as he explains, allows him "to explore subjects and themes that are beyond the borders of South Africa, but that are still relevant to this new society here" (xxiii). For Mda, in the post-apartheid phase, theatre has lost nothing of its social mandate. Against the background of harrowing personal experience of violence, he movingly reasserts the political function of theatre demanding that it "examine our society and its values" ("Theater and Reconciliation" 44), "resensitize us to violence and its effects on individuals and families"(44), and "contribute to the process of healing" (45).

Janet Suzman, writing in the introduction to her play *The Free State*, which is a transposition of Chekhov's *Cherry Orchard* to the South African context, elucidates the history of a project which was first suggested to her by Barney Simon back in the 1970s, but which did not come to fruition until the mid-1990s, under a different political dispensation. "Intended," in the words of its author, "to celebrate the year 1994" and "the Mandelian dream of a multiethinic concord," the play "urges reconciliation" and exudes what she describes as "benign, even amiable, hope" (Suzman, *The Free State* xxi). That Chekhov's play lends itself to such treatment need not be doubted in spite of the optimistic ideology it is made to bear. For what more "perfect image for the dying throes of apartheid" could one imagine than a cherry orchard which no longer bears fruit? And as Suzman tells us: "To a South African sensibility, where the air you breathe is political, [*The Cherry Orchard*] becomes a play specifically about a new order taking over from the old" (xxiii).

Suzman offers a fascinating account of the rationale for each of the changes she has made to the original: why Lopakhin had to become a representative of the new black middle class; why Afrikaners had to be given a role; why the play had to be set in the Eastern Free State (it is the only area in South Africa where cherries can be grown!); how it came about that Pitso (Chekhov's Trofimov) could quote Chekhov in the original (because he had trained in Russia with the ANC), and so on. As she explained to Dennis Walder, "It's all in the detail" ("God" 266). Suzman believes that "it's terribly crucial that South Africa looks at its own stories and stops importing" (254), and, thus, she modestly sees the plays she has chosen to adapt to South African conditions (previously Brecht's *Good Woman of Sezuan* as *The Good Woman of Sharkville*, and now *The Cherry Orchard* as *The Free State*) as "a sort of interim measure [...] a sort of stop-gap" (256), while theatre finds its feet in a transitional society and playwrights identify new social issues to write about. Which is just what seems to be happening.

To judge from my press clippings, critics have been greatly given to bandying about phrases such as " theatre drought" (Greig, "Musical Overkill"), "dry white season" (Dikeni), or "state of inertia" (Macliam, "The future") to describe the current state of theatre, and to lamenting that in South Africa drama is becoming a "fast-dying theatrical form" (Greig, "Musical Overkill"). But this no longer quite seems to suit the case. For, as Robert Greig has pointed out, "While theatre funding falls apart"—a phenomenon which he attributes to failed state policies and managerial incompetence—"South African theatre is experiencing a renaissance. New playwrights are emerging and experienced actors are writing new plays" (Greig, "Local playwrights"). Mannie Manim, the new director of the Baxter in Cape Town, agrees: as far as new plays are concerned, theatre appears to be "in reasonable health" (Manim). They are both thinking of people like Paul Slabolepszy (with *Mooi St. Moves*), Brett Bailey (with *iMumbo Jumbo* and *Ipi Zombi*), Greig Coetzee (with *White Men with Weapons*), Sello Maake kaNcube (with *Komeng*), Aubrey Sekhabi (with *Homegirls* and *Not without my Gun*), Heinrich Reisenhofer and Oscar Petersen (with *Suip!*), and Fiona Coyne (with *Glass Roots*), some of whom have come to the fore through the Baxter Theatre's New Writing programme or the Grahamstown Festival. So, there does seem to be a host of new names to conjure up, a new generation of younger writers. The satirist Greig Coetzee was surely speaking for all of them when he said: "I'm sick of all the gloom and doom. Theatre has always struggled. Go ask Shakespeare. Yes, it's tough as hell, but this place is also a dream for any artist. It's bursting with stories and images that are begging to be put on stage" (Sherriffs 54). Since I cannot discuss all of them here, let me briefly review just three

productions seen recently to give at least some notion of the directions
in which some writers are trying to go.

The Magnet Theatre production *Voices Made Night* premiered at the
Nico in Cape Town in March 2001. Directed by Mark Fleishman and
Jennie Reznek, it is the result of an innovative project undertaken to
explore the possibility of adapting African writing from neighbouring
countries for the stage by using the resources and methods of physical
theatre. The texts chosen for this unusual experiment were the short
stories of Mia Couto, a writer from Mozambique. Uniquely, perhaps, for
a South African show, the production involved the cast in travelling to
Mozambique, where the show was researched, workshopped, and
initially performed, and where much interaction took place both with the
author and with local theatre groups. Visually evocative, fragmentary in
form and fluid in movement, the performance abounds in arresting
stories of the psychology of poverty cast in resonant imagery—the
woman who falls in love with statues of the former colonists, for instance, or the old man digging a grave for his aged wife, who resolutely
refuses to die. The production provides ample proof that the exploration
of African literature from the rest of the continent, especially such
formally experimental texts as those presented here, could provide an
abundant source of material for fertile, cross-cultural theatrical innovation in South Africa.

Suip! by Heinrich Reisenhofer and Oscar Petersen, hugely successful
in South Africa itself and recently seen at festivals in Australia and
England, is, as one critic appositely put it, a "vision of South Africa's
cultural and socio-political history [...] seen through a brandy bottle"
("A sip of pure joy"). And a vision of local history too, of course,
because this is very much a Cape Town play. Inspired by the story of a
family of "bergies" or winos living in the streets of Cape Town—in
Kloofnek St. to be precise, across from Reisenhofer's own house—it
traces their ancestry back to the arrival at the Cape of the first whites,
who promptly set about producing VOC brandy and for centuries paid
their vineyard workers according to the "dop" system—in wine. The
effects of alcoholism and the plight of the homeless are the twin foci of
the play, which finally holds out little hope of improvement, as we
witness through the figure of Boy the initiation of the next generation of
"bergies" into a career of drink. Performed before a vast pile of South
African Brewery beer crates stacked in the shape of Table Mountain, the
play employs minimal props with great versatility: the inevitable super-
market trolley does service as ox wagon, tractor, police van, prison cell,
and court dock.

The play accurately captures the life of the streets: beginning as
street theatre in St. George's Mall, where in the spirit of free enterprise
of the new South Africa, the bergies hope to earn some paltry income,

the audience function as the passing tourists when the cast pass among them begging for coins or are given the chance, on one hilarious occasion, to partake of what looks like a quite lethal brew that Sofia has concocted on stage. Taking us through the personal histories of each of the characters in turn, the performance relies heavily for its characterisations and wit on the dialectal richness of the Afrikaans of the Cape, which had to be partly rewritten for the Australian and English audiences, who would otherwise have been quite defeated, not least by the deluge of expletives. Whether, as one character suggests, bottles of liquor have indeed become the cultural weapons of the new SA, it is not for me to judge, but *Suip!* is certainly both a highly entertaining and a deeply thought-provoking confrontation with an aspect of South African reality which many have hitherto preferred to ignore.

Fiona Coyne's *Glass Roots,* which in 2001 carried off a number of *Fleur du Cap* theatre awards, is a very funny domestic comedy, firmly set in the "new" South Africa, full of witty repartee, in-jokes, and contemporary references to life in a country caught up in transition. Indeed, its very conception relies on the transition from the old society to the new, with all the contradictions, identity problems and lost illusions that that entails. Set in an upmarket Cape Town loft apartment, so minimally furnished that it looks as though it has been burgled, the play juxtaposes members of two generations—the "old" and the "new." The former is represented by two women, the one a talkative, rum-sipping, and outrageously racist white, who thinks the great virtue of the Nationalists was to have done "a damn good job of keeping the blacks hidden" (Coyne 150)—but now claims to vote ANC; the other woman is a worldly-wise coloured, "lived-in rather than old" (132), who works for Pick 'n Pay, but votes for the National Party, and who peppers the dialogue with the fruit of her wisdom in the form of lines such as "the meek will inherit the earth, but not the mineral rights thereof..." (171). The "new" generation are performed by a young and attractive, cocaine-snorting, would-be advertising executive and her business partner and would-be lover, an up-and-coming member of the new black élite, a genuine and sympathetic young man. These two have embarked on a joint business enterprise, the setting-up of an advertising agency which is about to make its first commercial.

To do so—and this is where the play takes off—they need the services of a "quintessential South African" (140) to advertise the product in question, which turns out to be "the only beer that captures the spirit of the new South Africa, the drink that'll unite the nation" (160), a notion which generates the pun—the bad pun—of the play's title, for "the roots of the nation are in a glass." The person they come up with, of course, is not the stereotypical, middle-aged white male of audience expectation, but the aging coloured woman. A glorious satire on the search for a new South African identity, the play does not disguise the very real problems of the country—the violence of the Cape Flats, for example, or the difficulties of poverty, unemployment, and retrenchment in the wake of apartheid—and it has a good deal to tell us about the need to revise values and change attitudes in a new society. Through its particular constellation of characters and the manner in which they resolve their problems, this highly successful play has its finger on the pulse of the nation and points—optimistically—to the future.

Taken together, the plays which I have very briefly reviewed perhaps offer—in spite of the admittedly very real difficulties facing theatre practitioners working in a society caught in the travails of major social transition—some confirmation of the remark of Malcolm Purkey and Carol Steinberg from which I have borrowed my title: "In the context of the extraordinary achievement of the 'new' South Africa, we are granted a wonderful freedom to be critical, to be dissident, to be irreverent, to be playful" ("Introduction" xiv).

Works Cited

"A sip of pure joy" (unsigned). *The Star* 7 July 1999, Tonight section: 2.
Accone, Darryl. "Cultural cryogenics ice the State." *The Star* 23 June 2000, Tonight section: 9.
_____. "Stop wringing your hands, leave the comfort zone and get your bum on a theatre seat." *Sunday Independent* 6 September 1998: 12.
Adam, Rob. "Critic overlooks role of culture in the economy." *Sunday Independent* 4 March 2001: 11.
Anstey, Gillian. "The state of the play in South African theatre." *Sunday Times* (SA) 30 July 2000: 27.
Chakela, Walter. *Weekly Mail and Guardian* 19 February 1993: 33.
Cillie, Helene, and Robert Greig. "Plug pulled from two State theatre productions amid allegations of large-scale theft." *Sunday Independent* 24 December 2000: 17.
Coyne, Fiona. *Glass Roots. 2+2 Plays.* Cape Town: comPress, 2000. 131-216.
de Beer, Diane. "More tears, and yet a glimmer of hope." *Pretoria News* 4 July 2000: 4-5.
_____. "The State of the Theatre. Diane de Beer talks to Jerry Mofokeng." *The Star* 16 February 16, 2000, Tonight section: 8.
Dikeni, Sandile. "Severance, a cut above the rest." *Cape Times* 22 January 1999: 16.
Draft Report prepared by the Arts and Culture Task Group for the Ministry of Arts, Culture, Science and Technology. Pretoria: April 1995.

Draft White Paper on Arts, Culture and Heritage. All our Legacies, All our Futures. Pretoria: Dept. of Arts, Culture, Science and Technology, 4 June 1996.

Fleishman, Mark. "Unspeaking the Centre: Emergent Trend in South African Theatre in the 1990s." *Culture in the New South Africa. After Apartheid.* Ed. Robert Kriger and Abebe Zegeye. Vol. I. Cape Town: Kwela Books and SA History Online, 2001. 91-115.

_____. *Voices Made Night.* Unpublished.

Fletcher, Jill. "Actors going places." *Cape Times* 15 December 1998: 12.

Gray, Ian. "Beware! The Phantom looks." *Eastern Province Herald* 16 January 2001: 4.

Greer, Graham. "Theatre: Some highs and a lot of lows." *Sunday Tribune* 27 December 1998, The Other Mag section: 10.

Greig, Robert. "Artists should boycott London festival and tell UK press why they are doing so." *Sunday Independent* (SA) 11 February 2001.

_____. "City fights to keep the lights on." *The Star* 2 December 1998, Tonight section: 2.

_____. "Local playwrights defy collapse of theatre." *Sunday Independent* 23 July 2000: 10.

_____. "Moving beyond the theatre of declamation." *Sunday Independent* 18 July 1999: 10.

_____. "Musical Overkill." *The Star* 10 March 1999, Tonight section: 2.

_____. "Sachs gives arts a standing ovation where a hiss would be deserved." *Sunday Independent* 22 October 2000: 10.

Lakhani, Kefan. "UDW Drama dept. faces closure" *Daily News* 8 September 1999, Tonight section: 7.

Macliam, Garalt. "Ngubane addresses state of the 'State.'" *The Star* 12 February 2001: 9.

_____. "New Policy mooted for SA arts." *Cape Argus,* 3 March 2000, Tonight section: 12.

_____. "The buck stops with the minister." *The Star* 7 April 2000, Tonight section: 3.

_____. "The future beckons." *The Star* 6 January 1999, Tonight section: 2.

_____. "Wind out of the Sail." *The Star* 23 February 2000, Tonight section: 2.

Manim, Mannie. "So Many Questions. Mannie Manim." *Sunday Times* 23 July 2000: 16.

Mda, Zakes. "Introduction: An Overview of Theatre in South Africa." *Four Plays.* Compiled and introduced by Zakes Mda. Florida Hills: Vivlia, 1996. vi-xxvi.

_____. "Theater and Reconciliation in South Africa." *Theater* 25.3 (1995): 38-45.

Mokoena, Eddie. "Actors hit the casino jackpot." *Sowetan* 9 February 2001, Education: 12.

_____. "Windybrow is given last-minute reprieve" *Sowetan* 6 April 2000: 16.

Myers, Gaenor. "Civic puts itself on show for survival." *Sunday Times* (SA) 1 October 2000, Business Times: 5.

Purkey, Malcolm, and Carol Steinberg. "Introduction" to *Love, Crime and Johannesburg*. By Junction Avenue Theatre Company. Johannesburg: Witwatersrand UP, 2000): vii-xiv.

Reisenhofer, Heinrich, and Oscar Petersen. *Suip! 2+2 Plays*. Cape Town: comPress, 2000. 75-129.

Sachs, Albie. "Beauty and the politically correct beast." *Sunday Times* (SA) 15 October 2000: 17.

Sher, Antony, and Greg Doran. *Woza Shakespeare!* Titus Andronicus *in South Africa*. London: Methuen, 1996.

Sherriffs, Pam. "Theatre fights back." *Fair Lady* 30 September 1998: 50-55.

Sichel, Adrienne. "Arts Whodunit." *The Star* 4 December 2000, Tonight section: 4.

_____. "Dancing as fast as they can." *Sawubona* (in-flight magazine of South African Airways) March 2001: 52-58.

_____. "Girls getting out there." *The Star* 4 August 1999, Tonight section: 2.

Steinberg, Carol, and Malcolm Purkey. "South African Theater in Crisis." *Theater* 25. 3 (1995): 24-37.

Suter, Billy. "Axe hangs over Varsity drama department." *The Mercury* 3 September 1999, The Good Life section: 2.

Suzman, Janet. "'God is in the Details': An Interview with Janet Suzman by Dennis Walder." *South African Theatre As/And Intervention*. Ed. Marcia Blumberg and Dennis Walder. Amsterdam/Atlanta, GA: Rodopi, 1999. 253-266.

_____. *The Free State. A South African Response to Chekhov's* The Cherry Orchard. London: Methuen, 2000.

Tyler, Humphrey. "Dismal year for drama in Durban." *Sunday Tribune* 27 December 1998: 10.

van Dyk, Gary. "Working wonders in Woodstock." Interview with Royston Stoffels. *Cape Argus* 7 December 1998, Tonight section: 5.

Walder, Dennis. "Spinning Out the Present: Narrative, Gender, and the Politics of South African Theatre." *Writing South Africa. Literature, Apartheid, and Democracy, 1970-95*. Ed. Derek Attridge and Rosemary Jolly. Cambridge UP, 1998. 204-220.

Willoughby, Guy. "Life an art form in the new South Africa." *The Star* 24 August 1998, Tonight section: 3.

Wilson, Derek. "Tonight theatre." *Cape Argus* 30 January 1998: 4-5.

Mapping Counter Truths and Reconciliations: Staging Testimony in Contemporary South Africa

Marcia BLUMBERG

The Open University

> Nothing like the final truth exists, as truth is contextual, contingent and historical. It is precisely the apartheid regime's appeal to truth which made it such a dangerous ideology. (Cornel du Toit 119)

> After 18 months of victim hearings no one in SA could ever again be able to say, "I did not know" and hope to be believed. (Desmond Tutu, *No Future* 120)

> This Truth Commission thing is useless—it wastes hard-earned money to listen to a bunch of crooks. Only literature can perform the miracle of reconciliation. (Adam Small, quoted in Krog 18)

These epigraphs trace the trajectory of my essay, which examines crucial and complex issues of truth-telling, reconciliation, and the staging of memory in "post-apartheid" South Africa. In focusing upon two different kinds of theatre, I briefly outline some of the positions adopted with regard to the performance of truth-telling at the Truth and Reconciliation Commission (TRC), and give more extensive attention to these very issues as they relate to two theatrical productions: *Ubu and the Truth Commission* and *The Story I'm about to Tell*. What unites my readings of the national theatre of the TRC and these specific drama pieces is the central role of testimony. The theatrical productions afford spectators a nuanced and ethical understanding of testimony as a dynamic force operating between political representation and a representation particular to the theatre of performance, a force that disallows any apprehension of testimony as yielding to transparent, self-evident Truth. By yoking both types of theatre together—the national theatre of the TRC and the dramaturgical productions that take for their theme the TRC—a form of testimony emerges that seeks to bring an impossible justice to the people of a nation brutally oppressed by a regime's recourse to Truth, one that was anything but contextual, contingent, and historical.

I utilize the term "post-apartheid" as a stage following apartheid—not in the sense of completion but rather as another phase that has continued since the watershed democratic elections of 1994. While marked juridical changes and a new constitution promise greater equity for all and prohibit discrimination on grounds of race, gender, religion, and sexual orientation, material conditions have become more onerous for millions. Archbishop Emeritus Desmond Tutu foregrounds this problem: "The huge gap between the haves and have-nots, which was largely created and maintained by racism and apartheid, poses the greatest threat to reconciliation and stability in our country" (*No Future* 273-4). The spotlight was turned on the disastrous ramifications of apartheid when recent history was painfully remembered in the proceedings of the Truth and Reconciliation Commission, which provided a forum to hear testimony about "'the causes, nature and extent of gross violations of human rights' committed against *all* the people of South Africa between 1 March 1960 and 5 December 1993" (quoted in Maja-Pearce 51). While nothing can reverse the egregious acts revealed at the TRC, the voicing of these injustices renders audible and brings into the public domain the pain and grief previously often borne in relative silence and anonymity by victims and their families. Although these hearings have made an impact on all spheres of South African life, this essay will address the performance of the TRC's catalytic role on the national stage and in two theatrical productions.

The Truth and Reconciliation Commission can be contextualized as a drama of national proportions; from February 1996 onwards, public sessions have been staged in many towns and on regular televised programs. Lesley Marx categorizes the live event in theatrical terms:

> The Truth Commission offers theatre of a very specific kind, analogous in some ways to the Medieval Mystery Cycles. Like the Cycles, the actors in this drama move around the country re-enacting a Christian allegory of birth, pain, passion, death and hoped-for resurrection, to which the audience gives its heart and its faith. (213)

Notwithstanding the abstraction of "audience" Marx acknowledges the linkage of theatrical and Christian attributes that characterize a commission led by Desmond Tutu, who instituted prayer rituals and ensured that the tone of the proceedings emphasized forgiveness and charity instead of vengeance. Yet, the event was neither a court hearing nor a confessional. It was rather a hybrid of two systems that Advocate Johnny de Lange, a TRC commissioner, categorized as a restorative justice model as opposed to a retributive justice system.[1] Russell H. Botman and Robin M. Peterson insist that "Reconciliation replaces the culture of revenge, not the culture of justice" (11); they thereby assume that reconciliation is a necessary and logical outcome.

Michael Ignatieff challenges the Commission's founding premise, which states that the TRC's objective is "to assist in the healing of a traumatized, divided, wounded, polarized people" (Tutu, "Healing a Nation" 39). He questions certain assumptions positing "that a nation has one psyche, not many; that the truth is one, not many; that the truth is certain, not contestable; and that when it is known by all it has the capacity to heal and reconcile: [that] the truth is one and if we know it, it will make us free" (Ignatieff 111). Ignatieff considers it imperative to "distinguish between factual truth and moral truth, between narratives that tell what happened and narratives that attempt to explain why things happened and who is responsible" (111). Speaking in socio-political terms of "false reconciliation," he brings to mind what the German theologian, Dietrich Bonhoeffer, called "cheap grace": "the acceptance of the offer of forgiveness and reconciliation without any reciprocal owning of responsibility and action" (Petersen 57).

Mahmood Mamdani interrogates another complexity arising out of what he deems too narrow a focus: "If reconciliation is to be durable, would it not need to be aimed at society (beneficiaries and victims) and not simply at the fractured political elite (perpetrators and victims)?" (5). Understanding that systemic injustice includes ramifications of economic oppression, Mamdani asks for more complex reconciliation than exposing a putative truth. Who has reaped benefits at whose expense? How have conditions improved or do they remain inequitable?

While many agree that the TRC constitutes a significant step in the potential healing of deep wounds in the body politic, some fear that reconciliation will become synonymous with amnesia. Furthermore, truth-telling and the staging of memory, so integral to the TRC, are vitally affected by positionality. How does a victim, a perpetrator, or an unaffected or perhaps even indifferent spectator regard these issues, and how varied are the demands on each? In addressing an African perspective that interprets memory from another viewpoint, Mr. Koka argues that

> the guilt of the oppressor and the oppressed shall never be the same and shall never be faced from the same angle. [...] This disparity in memorial discourses of oppressor and oppressed establishes an understanding of memory in opposition to reconciliation, memory as fragmented rather than whole, as warning and witness rather than redemptive and reconcilable. (quoted in Grunebaum 148)

---

[1] Cited in a lecture given at the Osgoode Law School in Toronto on Oct.1, 1997.

Koka considers memory as much invested in the present as in the past. He also differentiates between claims by the oppressed and the oppressor about these traumatic events, and problematizes the certainty of reconciliation.

In the final analysis, no process can adequately redress the massive wrongs or satisfy the historic needs that have resulted from apartheid, no commission can fully solve the problems inherited from such a regime or provide compensation for its horrors. Yet, the stagings of truth-telling at the TRC have contributed to what Justice Albie Sachs terms "a profound time of self-examination for many South Africans. Judges don't cry, Tutu did."[2] It is also imperative to attend to Tutu's *caveat*: "To accept national amnesia [...] would in effect be to victimize the victims of apartheid a second time" (*No Future* 29).

The TRC proceedings form a dialogue with the two theatrical productions which this essay examines. Their differing methodologies were strikingly evident in June 1999, when they were staged at the Tricycle Theatre one week apart during LIFT (London International Festival of Theatre). *Ubu and the Truth Commission* (1997) is a collaborative effort by artist and film maker, William Kentridge, writer, Jane Taylor, and Handspring Trust puppeteers, Basil Jones and Adrian Kohler. This multimedia theatrical production acknowledges and at the same time radically disrupts generic, cultural, political, artistic, and historical categories to occupy an in-between space during what Homi Bhabha terms an "interstitial time" (204).

Staged a century after Alfred Jarry's *Ubu Trilogy* shocked audiences in France, *Ubu and the Truth Commission* addresses the networks of power and political oppression under the brutal apartheid regime, the varying effects on victims and perpetrators, and the indelible scarring of the social fabric. After its world premiere at the Kunstfest in Weimar in June 1997, the production immediately transferred to the National Arts Festival at Grahamstown. The revisioning offered by *Ubu and the Truth Commission* places a white Afrikaner Pa Ubu and a black Ma Ubu in the South African post-election period—specifically within the ongoing hearings of the TRC. Disavowing the bravado of Jarry's Ubu, who carries his conscience in a suitcase, Jane Taylor explains the central premise of the production: "to take the Ubu-character out of the burlesque [Jarryesque] context and place him within a domain in which actions do have consequences" (iv). The necessity for truth-telling, accountability, and reconciliation, which are non-issues in the Jarry text, claim prominence in the contemporary debate and make it imperative for spectators to acknowledge the manifold acts of injustice and brutality made audible and visible onstage.

---

[2]   Cited in a lecture at the University of Toronto in October 1999.

The Ubu actors are juxtaposed with witness rod-puppets operated by manipulators. These puppets constitute mouthpieces to utter poignant testimony (taken directly from TRC transcripts) about atrocities and their effects. The pained facial expression, emotive voice, and unbroken focus of the puppeteer on the heavily carved puppet endows the latter with poignancy without appropriating his/her story. Furthermore, an actor in a glass booth delivers an English translation of the Xhosa or Sotho testimony [3] in a flat monotone, never taking ownership of the narrative that is at once so personal and proves concomitantly metonymic of systemic national violence.

Charles Spencer offers a reductive misreading of this process: "it seems to me insulting to have the appalling evidence delivered by wooden dolls. Surely the whole point is that the hideous [...] brutality happened to people, not inanimate objects" (*Daily Telegraph*). In contrast, Megan Lewis emphasizes the effectiveness of the witness puppets: the "tension created between the humanized object, the puppet, and the dehumanized translation by an actor sent shivers through the audience" (105). In the dynamic relationship "between the 'conviction' of the puppeteer and the willingness of the audience," the puppet is brought to life (quoted in Taylor xvii). This very procedure Lesley Marx considers an "analogy for the process of the Truth Commission itself, where witnesses, who for decades have literally been denied life, mobility and expression, are given a space in which to perform with the help of the conviction of the Commission and the willingness of the audience" (216). The TRC thus operates as a putative space of empowerment for victims, no matter what more distanced observers and others may offer as a valid critique.

Throughout *Ubu and the Truth Commission* Ma and Pa Ubu engage in a fraught domestic relationship, in which verbal sparring and physical blows enacted in stylized sequences keep the Ubus' interaction true to their Jarryesque forebears. Conforming to the stereotype of patriarchal structures, Pa's address to the audience emphasizes the elevation of male-gendered values within the power differential: Pa performs his important secret work while a suspicious Ma is wracked with jealousy. Other aspects complicate this apparently simple gender divide. Unlike Jarry's bloated Pa Ubu, this skinny Pa is clad throughout in vest and underpants. Compared to Ma's lavish pink satin dressing gown, his clothing, particularly in the eyes of male Afrikaner spectators, spells humiliation, which is exacerbated when a cowardly Pa cringes and hides.

---

[3] These African languages constitute two of the eleven official languages of South Africa. Testimony was given in the witness's mother tongue.

Pa's nightly ablutions enacted in the glass booth/shower stall are rendered more sinister when images on a large screen incorporate bits of body parts washed away after his nightly torture sessions. The repetition of Kentridge's drawings, a huge eye and a tripod with camera that transforms into a skeleton, emphasizes the covert nature of Pa's barbaric actions and reminds spectators of oppressive state structures in which surveillance, and the selective recording or obliteration of data are routinely deployed as control mechanisms. Don Cameron foregrounds this dynamic in Kentridge's short video, *Ubu tells the Truth*, segments of which are incorporated into the play: "a camera on a tripod, sees everything and then uses its knowledge to try to wipe out non-corroborating witnesses. [...] [T]he camera is crucial, because it clearly implicates the witness as an active agent in the carrying out of atrocities" (Cameron 79). By extension, audience members watching this spectacle have witnessed disturbing revelations that demand attention.

In the revelation scene, Pa performs two testimonial narratives: one in Afrikaans explains methods of torture in the "witness" mode; the other story in English, evoking his perpetrator role, focuses upon victims: "the burning of a body to ashes takes about seven hours [...] we were drinking and even having a braai next to the fire" (45). Kentridge explicates the disjuncture between the languages of victims and perpetrators: the latter "seem incapable of imagining the effect of their actions on others. Their surprise that their behavior is inappropriate marks a failure of a moral imagination."[4] Ma's provocative response to the incriminating evidence she found stuffed into Niles[5] reminds us of the complex individual perspectives operative in South Africa:

> I had no idea Pa was so important. All along, I thought he was betraying me and here he was, hard at work, protecting me from the Swart Gevaar [Black Danger]. (*Wipes her eyes sentimentally. Change of mood*). Still, this is my chance. A girl can't be too careful. Who can she turn to once her charms begin to fade? (45)

Her pride in his activities also stems from relief at her misguided fears of Pa's infidelity. The quick decision to betray Pa and sell the damning material foregrounds the question of expediency associated with revela-

---

4   Cited in a lecture delivered at the National Arts Festival, Grahamstown, on 10 July 1997.

5   Niles is a crocodile with carved tail and large carved head, whose mouth opens wide enough to be able to swallow documents, vidoes, and other incriminating objects. His body, an old army kit bag, forms a repository for these objects. The resonances are even more significant for a South African audience who would associate his Afrikaans name, die Groot Krokodil (the big crocodile) with former President P. W. Botha, who refused to testify at the TRC or utter an apology for the brutal apartheid activities carried out during his leadership but instead remained silent and metaphorically "swallowed" his knowledge of dirty deeds.

tions in the TRC process, an expediency which generates the sense of false reconciliation rather than the one of a genuine desire to acknowledge responsibility and build a new understanding.

On a darkened stage, Pa ascends a podium and testifies in the glare of a spotlight. Deploying the personal pronoun, he denies wrongdoing: "I am not a monster. I am an honest citizen and would never break the law [...]. These things, they were done by those above me; those below me; those beside me. I too have been betrayed" (67). Significantly changing mode from the personal to the collective, Pa speaks proudly as a good soldier and patriot to justify *their* activities in the light of international conspiracies. In another shift Pa reads a statement admitting remorse for all "the corpses that I will have to drag with me to my grave" (69). Breaking out into a hymn, Pa is wheeled offstage to the singing of a massed chorus while a video montage includes documentary footage.

Jarry's ending is replicated in the final scene when the Ubus sail into the sunset. A table serves as a boat as they escape at "miraculous speed" from the disturbing events and contemplate their future. Ma's assessment—"What we need is a fresh start" (71)—is uncharacteristically in harmony with Pa's sentiments: "A bright future" (73). If the actual events of the TRC have engendered ambivalent responses, this production incorporates the absurd and the familiarly real, and "ricochets between contending forms of reality" (Cooke 44). Spectators neither gain solutions nor receive comfort from this complex theatrical event. Despite many outstanding critical reviews, performances in local venues were regularly marked by a few walkouts—possibly by those ashamed of the figure of the Afrikaner protagonist or still in denial about apartheid practices. Since these performances began early in the mandate of the TRC, they proved far more disturbing for local audiences, but also varied in shock value according to the timing. The initial production provoked outrage from some spectators who, in the opening stages of the TRC, fervently desired the process to change decades of systemic discrimination and injustice. They regarded Ubuesque dynamics within the TRC as unwanted cynicism, especially the finale.[6] In 1997 empha-

---

[6] The mainly negative reviews of the LIFT performances by the London critics in June 1999 are atypical of the acclaim accorded the production in venues as varied as South Africa, Europe, and North America. The unsuitability of the Tricycle theatre's small stage and intimate audience area caused the multimedia effects to overwhelm spectators when combined with the burlesque antics of the Ubu actors. Although the show initially constituted what some felt to be an inappropriate response to the excellent intentions and high moral ground of the TRC, by 1999 factual events had followed fictional flights of fantasy: what was fresh and shocking in 1997 seemed more mundane to these critics who mentioned the greater effectiveness of the recent

sizing the difference between the play and the commission, a South
African critic, Daryl Accone, considered "Ubu a searing shorthand of
the evils of the apartheid state. [The production] does what the real-life
TRC explicitly does not: condemn those murderous and expedient
amnesty seekers" (1997). The theatre piece also raises painfully difficult
issues, as well as new and often threatening awareness.

Another TRC-related theatrical event eschews the multimedia mode
of Ubu and instead deploys poor theatre to powerful effect. *The Story
I'm about to Tell*—conceived at the Market Theatre Laboratory in 1996
by cultural activist, Bobby Rodwell, and director, Robert Colman, with
writings from Lesego Rampolokeng—constitutes a theatrical event for
three actors from the Mehlo players in collaboration with three members
of the Khulumani Support Group for survivors of human rights abuses.
The pretext for the staging is a minibus taxi ride to Sharpeville, a journey during which the driver/narrator engages in dialogue with his pas-
sengers: three "real" people, as they are categorized in the opening
remarks, and two other actors. The narrator explains: "We came together
to make a play about 'reconciliation.' A bit like trying to push a camel
through the eye of a needle. Reconciliation is an explosive and sensitive
issue. [...] let's see what happens" (2).[7] Despite the workshop-style
staging and sparse set (a few chairs on a bare stage), the play leaves an
indelible impression.

Combining the humorous, angry commentary of the actors with the
poignant stories of harsh injustice, this theatre enacts the ramifications
of issues arising out of the TRC as well as those of the wider politics of
the new democracy. The young black actor K.K. warns that Afrikaners
are unfairly playing on the African capacity to forgive: "Ask me for my
forgiveness, don't demand it" (9). He refutes the facile notion of a "post-
apartheid" era that implies a reversal of onerous conditions:

> "I am sick of hearing of the miracle of South Africa [...] Liberation didn't
> fall like manna from heaven [...] in fact it was people who fell into the
> grave [...] from hunger, from disease, from human rights abuses of illiteracy
> [...] who talks about that?" (11).

He also vents anger at liberals who are apparently shocked at the revelations and react with revulsion, yet seemingly experience a catharsis that
clears their consciences. His expletive "rainbow nation *se gat* (asshole)"
(7) challenges the simplistic elisions inherent in the term or the upbeat
assessments of the new democracy which exclude the myriad problems.

---

simpler stagings of the Stephen Lawrence Inquiry and the Nuremberg trials at the
same theatre.

[7]   The pages number of this and following citations refer to the manuscript of "The
Story I am about to Tell" (1996) which was kindly provided by Bobby Rodwell.

The actors change configuration when the three who have testified leave the "taxi" locale and sit alone centre-stage to perform truth-telling. Mam Catherine speaks about her son's assassination when a walkman and headphones sent as a 'gift' by the hit squad exploded on contact: "When I looked at him, his blood was splashed on the ground and on the wall and his head was in pieces" (14). The death of this young human rights lawyer, Bheki Mlangeni, has meant the loss of her child as well as the sole breadwinner for her and his four children.

The second storyteller is Thandi Shezi, who initially refuses to testify at the TRC, certain that it will not lessen the pain of repeated rape by four white police officers. She explains the degradation suffered in response to her severe injuries: "they took me to the district surgeon and told him that I am a prostitute and I injured myself trying to run away. You do not survive this, you just carry on living" (18). Operating from gendered and racial privilege, the police brutality casts her into a state of abjection, which exacerbates the trauma long after the physical wounds have healed. Thandi explicates the Commission's severe limitations: "They will talk about reconciliation and forgiveness. How can I reconcile and forgive whilst I am no longer a woman? [...] [I]nside I am dead. And it is them that did it" (16). Her experiences in the play and as a field worker led her to testify at special Women's hearings of the TRC, convinced that this action might encourage others with stories to tell.

Finally, a member of the Sharpeville Six, Duma Khumalo, who spent seven years in jail, three on Death Row, implores that "the truth must come out. They must take this rope off my neck" (18). As Duma explains poignant rituals enacted by fellow inmates condemned to die, his quiet dignity heightens the barbarism of the authorities. Instead of outrage, he expresses an urgency to set the record straight:

Today my contemporaries are teachers, which is what I wanted to be. I want dignity restored. The case should be reopened and my innocence declared. Otherwise this rope is around my neck for the rest of my life. (23)

Dhuma's lack of embitteredness contrasts markedly with the rage of the young black actor, KK, whose fierce verbal attack virtually explodes into physical blows against Dan, the white Afrikaans actor/passenger. KK's taunts provoke Dan's complex declaration of confusion and vulnerability:

For you white means no guilt, no shame, no soul, just white. Do you think I don't feel shame when I see perpetrators on TV suffering from selective amnesia? [...] Ja, I was 21 when I did my 2 years compulsory national service in the SADF. [...] [E]ither go to the army, leave the country or go to jail for six years. [...] You go straight from being schoolboys to killing machines [...] [then we] were told it was all a big mistake. [...] It fucks up your mind. Do you know how many white kids [...] committed suicide? (25)

Dan's truth-telling invokes KK's dismissive reply, which he turns into a paean of pain:

> It's words about broken bodies, words spoken but they planted bombs in the soul of my brain [...] shots fired right into my mind [...]. They talk like there was pain sometime ago [...] I'll need my heart cut off and replaced with an artificial one so I can learn to love again even if it is with plastic feelings. [...] The distance of the past has become a blade sharpened every time each day dawns and it strikes right into my being. (26)

This closing monologue of the play elaborates the plight of one young black man, yet the exponential effect of voices such as his reminds spectators of the varied positionings in the new society, and of the impossibility of the TRC being a putative national balm to cure all ills.

The importance of truth-telling, the desire to disclose previously unknowable experiences, and perhaps most importantly, the urgent need to provoke greater awareness and a sense of responsibility for a range of behaviors that have run the gamut from inaction and complacency to torture and other grotesque acts, have dictated what the collective felt was an integral part of each performance. The half-hour post-show talk built into the advertised length of the presentation elicits questions and comments from spectators and further explanations, especially from the three testifiers, who affirm the role of story-telling.[8] Dori Laub argues that "repossessing one's life story through giving testimony is itself a form of action, of change, which [one] has to actually pass through, in order to continue and complete the process of survival" (85). The process validates them, in their words, as "wounded survivors," and reinforces their knowledge that people are learning from what may be marginal to the lives of some spectators, but remains a central traumatic event that structures theirs. A facilitator from the Khulumani Support Group joins the six for this segment of the performance to contextualize the event in broader terms. This powerful presentation stages the vastly differing perspectives within and between subject positions, and the constant negotiation between potentially incendiary situations and the desire to acknowledge the past, while making a supreme effort to heal in order to envision a future.

The inclusion of stories by the actual protagonists raises questions about survivor testimony, ones that strongly challenge the notion of

---

[8]   In private conversations after performances in London and South Africa in 1999, the three TRC witnesses acknowledged the emotional difficulty of repeating the truth-tellings, but were more concerned about the trauma associated with silence, amnesia, and virtual erasure when the play finally closes.

what some critics have called "victim art." Thomas Keenan describes testimony in directly apposite terms when thinking of the South African production:

> testimony is an address, which means that it is a provocation to a response. And that's what [the uninvolved] don't want to give. They don't want to respond to the person who has called—for responsibility. (542)

In this instance, response demands attention to many difficult aspects. The three survivors emphasize the therapeutic value of truth-telling, which not only provides a license for spectators to listen actively rather than consume voyeuristically, but also makes it imperative for them to pay attention with responsibility and effortfulness. While these stories teach people with similar horrific experiences about the potential for healing, the personal narratives provide visceral lessons about abuses of power, which each teller hopes will never be repeated.

Another question concerns the danger of commodifying or exoticizing the victim testimony within the spectacle of performance. There is no doubt that the Handspring production constitutes a theatrical spectacle, in which a multimedia collage envelops the Ubu's domestic drama and the TRC narratives. The Brechtian distancing that foregrounds the various removes from the actual transcripts of TRC testimony—through the ventriloquized voices of the puppet manipulators to the flat recitation of the translation—situates spectators in a position thrice removed from the actual testifiers. Contradictory dynamics operate since the puppet testimony, while poignant and unforgettable in an overall assessment of the piece, engages the spectators' compassion only transiently, since Pa's bombastic interactions with Ma or his cynical and disturbing performances of testimony at the TRC interrupt the dynamics of empathy and oblige audience members to grapple with the complexity of the issues. In *The Story I'm about to Tell*, the graphic pain of factual story-telling occurs within a verbally and physically charged fictional frame. Since the performed personal experiences alternate with acting roles, those poignant moments are juxtaposed with angry banter or humorous dialogue, thus making it imperative for listeners to interrogate a range of situations. Most importantly, the post-show question and answer session challenges spectators to engage with the ramifications of different kinds of spectacle, be they the egregious socio-political structures known as apartheid, or the differing spectacles presented in the TRC's theatre of testimony or dramaturgical productions, which incorporate other theatrical antecedents or factual events.

These productions constitute varied theatrical and ideological interventions in the vital engagement with the complex processes of truth-telling and the difficult steps towards possible reconciliation. Integral to these tenuous negotiations is the staging of memory, a process clearly dependent on individual positioning. Cornel du Toit argues insightfully that we "deal with the past from a situation where we suffer the consequences of the past" (119):

> To face the past means to face the person whom you have injured. We must stop speaking about one another and start speaking to each other by jointly discussing our experiences and feelings of hate, anger, guilt, sorrow [...]. It is not only what we remember, but also how we remember, how we interact with memory that co-determines our identity. (122; 124)

These truth-tellings, stagings of personal memory, and rememberings of history offer varied but thought-provoking vehicles in the performance of a drama of and for a democratic South Africa. They speak powerfully to the potential for testimonial theatre to play a significant role in renegotiating structures and dynamics of national importance.[9]

Works Cited

Accone, Daryl. "Ipi Tombi's grisly reminder of white feelgood attitudes recedes in the face of some remarkable new theatre." *Sunday Independent* July 1997: n.p.

Bhabha, Homi K. "Unpacking My Library [...] Again." *The Post-colonial Question: Common Skies, Divided Horizons*. Eds. Iain Chambers and Lidia Curti. London: Routledge, 1996. 199-211.

Botman, H. Russel and Robin M. Petersen. "Introduction." *To Remember and To Heal: Theological and Psychological Reflections on Truth and Reconciliation*. Cape Town: Human & Rousseau, 1996. 9-14.

Cameron, Dan. "A Procession of the Dispossessed." *William Kentridge*. London: Phaidon, 1999. 38-81.

Caruth, Cathy & Keenan, Thomas. "'The AIDS crisis Is Not Over': A Conversation with Gregg Bordowitz, Douglas Crimp, and Laura Pinsky." *American Imago* 48.4 (1991): 539-556.

Cooke, Lynne. "Mundus Inversus, Mundus Perversus." *William Kentridge*. New York: Harry N. Abrams, 2001: 39-57.

du Toit, Cornel. "Dealing with the Past." *To Remember and To Heal: Theological and Psychological Reflections on Truth and Reconciliation*. Ed. H. Russel Botman and Robin M. Petersen. Cape Town: Human & Rousseau, 1996. 118-28.

---

[9] A very warm debt of gratitude to Basil Jones and Adrian Kohler for their rich dialogue and generosity in providing me with a range of material. Sincere thanks to Miki Flockemann for sending TRC information and to Bobby Rodwell for providing material and discussing the project. Immense appreciation to Stephen Barber for his ongoing engagement with my work.

Grunebaum-Ralph, Heidi Steir, and Oren Steir. "The Question (of) Remains: Remembering Shoah, Forgetting Reconciliation." *Facing the Truth: South African Faith Communities and the Truth & Reconciliation Commission.* Ed. James Cochrane, John de Gruchy, and Stephen Martin. Cape Town: David Philip, 1999. 142-52.

Ignatieff, Michael. "Articles of Faith." *Index on Censorship: Wounded Nations Broken Lives—Truth Commissions and War Tribunals.* 25:5 (Sept./Oct.1996). Issue 172: 110-22.

Krog, Antjie. *Country of My Skull.* Johannesburg: Random House, 1998.

Laub, Dori. "An Event Without a Witness." *Testimony: Crises of Witnessing in Literature, Psychoanalysis, and History.* Eds. Shoshana Felman and Dori Laub. New York: Routledge, 1992. 75-92.

Lewis, Megan. "Standard Bank National Arts Festival, Grahamstown, South Africa, 1997." *Theatre Journal* 50.1 (March 1998): 105-7.

Maja-Pearce, Adewale. "Binding the Wounds." *Index on Censorship: Wounded Nations Broken Lives—Truth Commissions and War Tribunals.* 25:5 (Sept./Oct.1996). Issue 172: 48-53.

Mamdani, Mahmood. "Reconciliation Without Justice." *Southern African Review of Books* 46 (Nov./Dec. 1996): 5.

Marx, Lesley. "Slouching Towards Bethlehem: *Ubu and the Truth Commission.*" *African Studies* 57.2: 209-20.

Petersen, Robin. "The Politics of Grace and the Truth and Reconciliation Commission." *To Remember and To Heal: Theological and Psychological Reflections on Truth and Reconciliation.* Ed. H. Russel Botman and Robin M. Petersen. Cape Town: Human & Rousseau, 1996. 57-69.

Rodwell, Bobby, Robert Colman, and Lesego Rampolokeng. *The Story I'm about to Tell.* Unpublished ms. 1996.

Spencer, Charles. "LIFT kept firmly earthbound by modern Ubu." *The Daily Telegraph* 14 June 1999: npn.

Taylor, Jane. *Ubu and the Truth Commission.* Cape Town: University of Cape Town Press, 1998.

Tutu, Desmond. "Healing a Nation." *Index on Censorship: Wounded Nations Broken Lives—Truth Commissions and War Tribunals.* 25:5 (Sept./ Oct. 1996). Issue 172: 38-43.

_____. *No Future Without Forgiveness.* New York: Doubleday, 1999.

Jane Harrison's *Stolen* and the International Postcolonial Context

Marc MAUFORT

Université Libre de Bruxelles

At the turn of the millennium, Australian drama has definitely moved beyond the limitations of parochialism. *Stolen*, the first play by Aboriginal dramatist Jane Harrison, perfectly illustrates this remarkable development. Harrison's poignant drama deals with the painful consequences of the white Australian government adoption policy of Aboriginal children. As such, it is concerned with the issues of Aboriginal identity in a racist context. Premiered by the Playbox Theatre in Melbourne in the 1998 season, *Stolen* can be studied alongside the growing body of Aboriginal writing for the theatre in Australia, inaugurated by the seminal plays of Jack Davis produced in the 1980s, namely *The Dreamers*, *No Sugar*, and *Smell the Wind*. Like her contemporaries Wesley Enoch, Roger Bennett, and John Harding, Harrison further refines the themes introduced by Jack Davis, most importantly the implications of the Aboriginal crisis of identity in a dominantly white society. The hybrid vision of the self dramatized in *Stolen* echoes a recurrent postcolonial theme, manifest in the works of novelists and dramatists so diverse as Salman Rushdie, Caryl Phillips, Michael Ondaatje, Tomson Highway, and Guillermo Verdecchia.

The thematic "inbetweenness" of *Stolen* is reflected in its concept of dramatic form. It clearly refashions Western stage realism through the use of abstraction, abandoning linear forms of presentation. I wish to argue here that Jane Harrison devises such a strategy to revision the polymorphous legacy of Empire. As Homi K. Bhabha suggests in *The Location of Culture* (85-92; 102-22), she resorts to mimicry/hybridity to unsettle the artistic domination of the Western canon. Harrison's use of mimicry is ostensibly subversive: far from signalling cultural cringe, it creates a "third hybrid space" which de-stabilizes the rigid artistic categories of the West. *Stolen*'s mimicry reveals a kinship with Australian Aboriginal novelist Mudrooroo's definition of "Aboriginal realism" as a form apparently predicated on the same modes of referentiality as those of Western, Euro-American stage realism, but which subverts them through subtle reminders of the oppressed culture such as the use of myth, abstraction, transformations, story-telling and special sound effects (Mudrooroo 17). These palimpsests of a colonized culture foreground a hybrid magical realism pervasive in postcolonial literatures, which radically questions Western modes of rational perception and challenges colonial readings of history. This theatrical version of "Aboriginal realism" dialogizes, to borrow M. M. Bakhtin's phrase (263), two antithetical discursive patterns: *Stolen* relies both on Western and non-Western traditions, implying a measure of undecidability. Further, subversive mimicry enables the critic to recast *Stolen* in a wider international cross-cultural context. Indian Canadian dramatist Drew Hayden Taylor's hybrid realism offers a representative instance of such intertextual connections, as his play *Someday* deals with the tragic identity problems caused by the Canadian adoption policy of native children.

Stolen challenges essentialist notions of identity, by focusing on a group of children who feel neither black nor white as a result of a racially-biased historical social policy: the Australian government's decision to integrate Aboriginal children into white society by taking them away from their families. Not only does the play dramatize the intricacies of postcolonial hybridity, i.e. the duality of being experienced by the postcolonial subject; it also develops the concomitant themes of loss of home and belonging, which constitute a common trope of postcolonial literatures. A sense of spiritual displacement, then, stands at the core of this powerful drama, which clearly formulates the political hope that Australia's First Nations will never tolerate such a form of internal colonization and oppression again. The very title of the play yields manifest metaphorical resonances: while it refers first and foremost to the historical theft of adopted children, it also points to the ensuing symbolic loss of their Aboriginal identity.

The play, in a somewhat filmic style, gives us insights into the psychological evolution of several of these displaced children, Jimmy, Sandy, Anne, and Ruby. It likewise portrays a mother figure, Shirley, who by the end of the drama, experiences her first true sense of motherhood, after becoming a grandmother. Harrison sheds light on these children's plight during and after their stay in a foster home, away from their Aboriginal families. First, the play's indirect narratives underscore the unfairness of the system that removed these children: the ironically named welfare workers, Harrison shows, often took poverty as a pretext for their drastic measures, inevitably leading to uprootedness. Despite the mother's pleas to retrieve her son Jimmy once her husband has found a decent form of employment, the authorities remain silent (28). As evoked in the vignette entitled "A Can of Peas," Sandy is taken away when the welfare officers declare his mother unfit, after finding in the house a single can of pea past its use-by-date: "The Bloody Welfare! Who gave us the rotten can in the first place" (22). Another vignette strikingly re-enacts Sandy's grotesque dream of the Englishwoman who treats him like a dog: "A pompous Englishwoman stomps over to Sandy [...] she makes an elaborate gesture of putting a dog tag around his neck. ENGLISHWOMAN: It's important to let them know who's boss right from the start [...] heel, you black dog! [...] Now beg, beg I said [...]" (15-16). The scene points to the slave-master relationship between the white and black communities of Australia, with the suggestion that the dog/Aboriginal subject must mimic the master and behave like a (white) human. This grotesque distortion, an analogue of the loss of cultural identity, replicates the polarity of colonized/colonizer. Its implications are even further reminiscent of Homi Bhabha's mimicry: the identification of the slave with the master inevitably contains an element of potential danger, as the dog has been known to bite its owner. Thus, the play possesses a dialogic aspect: it challenges the dominant discourse of white supremacy while giving a voice to the minority. The suggestion that the children are subjected to physical abuse by the white people who invite them into their home for the week-end offers a further condemnation of the legacy of Empire. Similarly, as an adolescent maid, Ruby is sexually harassed. These images of sexual violence evoke the metaphorical rape of black culture and identity by white society. Another instance of Harrison's challenge of Western beliefs and ethics consists in Sandy's parodic depiction of his many Christmas holidays spent away from his family. Harrison subverts the symbol of peacefulness traditionally associated with the religious connotations of Christmas: "MAN: On your way home for Christmas? SANDY: Not likely. Never spent Christmas in the same town twice" (27). These ironic undertones echo Drew Taylor's bleak dramatization of the same Christian celebration in *Someday*. Further, Harrison obliquely indicts the complicit role of Christianity in the tragedy of Aboriginal dispossession.

Harrison gives her theme of the loss of roots, family and home a Bakhtinian polyphonic expression, which manifests itself in multiple ways in the different behaviour of each child. Anne, who has been adopted by white parents, feels moreover entrapped in a no-man's land as the play draws to a close:

> ANNE: S'pose you want a happy ending from me. You blackfellas want me to be reunited with my family, learn to love them, and move back home, all of us living happily ever after. You whitefellas want my adopted parents to become loving and tolerant of my black family and invite them around for Sunday roast [...] I don't know where I belong anymore ... it's Mother's day [...] I got Mum some milk chocolates ... And I got my *mother* some dark chocolates [...] If you close your eyes they still taste the same, but. (37)

This interior monologue skilfully translates Anne's experience of hybridity into a concrete theatrical image—the difference in the kinds of chocolates. Far from offering a total sense of reconciliation, this confession leaves one with a bitter aftertaste: Anne feels deprived of emotional stability. Jimmy's fate proves even less palatable. He eventually commits suicide in a prison cell to achieve a final reunion with his mother in the afterlife. Ruby, on her part, wastes her life away as a servant to rich white people, which leaves her no possibility of founding her own family. For her, this painful lack of cultural belonging results in utter madness: "RUBY stands centre front stage and wipes at her body obsessively" (27). On a more cheerful note, Sandy journeys back to the desert where he feels he belongs, like his ancestors: "Back to me place. That bit of red desert. I still remember it. The sand must have seeped into me brain [...]" (37). The key to retrieving a home lies in the rediscovery of cultural roots, Harrison implies. Shirley's destiny, first as a mother and later as a grandmother, likewise provides a somewhat more optimistic ending. However, in the early scenes, Shirley's predicament epitomizes the psychological fragmentation plaguing all of Harrison's characters:

> SHIRLEY, as a child, clutches the one remaining physical link to her family —an old sepia photo of her as a toddler with her smiling parents and siblings ... A shadow of the matron falls on the projected image and we hear the sound of the photo being ripped and see it fragmenting into little pieces [...] The pieces fall like snow all over the stage and she runs to collect them and tries to put them together [...] the other children enter with their brooms and sweep away the pieces of Shirley's childhood while she is frantically trying to keep them. (18)

In addition, Harrison theatrically emphasizes the negative influence of the matron, a representative of white society, in the progressive destruction of Shirley's identity. However, at the end of the play, Shirley finds it in her to give to a grandchild the affection of which her children were deprived. In this gesture of love and solidarity lies hope for future generations, the dramatist suggests:

> SHIRLEY stands in a beam of light at the front of the stage while someone brings her baby granddaughter to her [...]
>
> JIMMY: Don't let it happen again. Don't let it happen again.
>
> SHIRLEY [...] We won't let it happen again, Willy.
>
> The others are standing in line [...] and as the baby is handed to each of them, a single beam of light illuminates them individually. They are symbolically "reclaiming" their child that was stolen from them. (38)

The playwright thus metaphorically equates the image of the child with cultural inheritance. The play ends on an invitation for black people to re-possess or, to borrow Toni Morrison's phrase, to "re-memory" the wealth of their cultural legacy. Only by becoming aware of the nature of these roots will they be reborn into a new spiritual life. This last scene projects a sense of epiphanic revelation reminiscent of the modernist techniques of novelists such as Virginia Woolf or James Joyce.

Thus, *Stolen* can be understood as a historiographic work, a re-writing of official history from the perspective of the margins, shedding light on an all-too tragic aspect of Australian life. In this sense, *Stolen* echoes the historical concerns manifest in postmodern and postcolonial literature, both in fiction and in drama: one need simply give the example of Joy Kogawa's *Obasan*, which unveils the terrible predicament of Japanese Canadians during the second world war; Caryl Phillips' *Crossing the River*, and Toni Morrison's *Beloved*, which both offer an inside view of the throes of slavery; closer to home, Harrison's play positions itself within the historiographic tradition initiated by Jack Davis in *Kullark*. Other examples in postcolonial drama abound: the plays of Daniel David Moses in Canada, those of Metsemela Manaka in South Africa, or those of Hone Kouka in New Zealand.

The hybridity, indeed fragmentation, characterizing the lives of the children resurges in the non-linear structure of the play, which constitutes perhaps its most innovative feature. *Stolen* apparently belongs to the Western tradition of poetic realism; witness thereof is its blend of naturalism and subtle scenic symbolism. It nevertheless redraws the limits of its Euro-American model. First, it relies on a distortion of chronological time, freely moving to and from the childhood, adolescence, and adulthood of the characters in a non-sequential order. Harrison consistently relies on the devices of projected images and voice-over. Moreover, she only sketches her characters: they seem so interchangeable that they resemble mere types whose dreams we discover on the stage. These techniques, it is true, were already used by European Expressionists at the beginning of the twentieth-century. Further, the play's fluid structure recalls the novelistic stream-of-consciousness of modernists like Virginia Woolf and Katherine Mansfield. Indeed, the script is interspersed with explorations into the minds of the characters, such as the dream sequence involving an Englishwoman and a dog referred to earlier. These narrative vignettes function as interior or confessional monologues, making transparent the protagonists' inner turmoil. More importantly, the "exploded" structure of the play made up of a series of loosely related short scenes can be decoded as an analogue of the fragmentation that afflicts the characters' lives. The play's overall structure resembles the torn photograph that Shirley desperately seeks to reconstruct. *Stolen* depicts a broken world, in which the characters embark on a futile quest for the unity of the self. Finally, the work's most striking departure from the conventions of Western realism resides in its story-telling, which conjures up Aboriginal culture. Thus, a collage of various narratives—sometimes antithetical ones—enables Harrison to reconfigure Aboriginal history through a polyphonic story-telling design. As a story-teller, Sandy performs a pivotal role. Shaped as interior monologue-like reflections, his narratives allow the world of Aboriginal magic to invade the rationalism of white culture. The intrusion of myth and legends signals a magical realist reconfiguration of the colonizer's world view. The very concept of magical realism has proved elusive, even difficult to define. Jeanne Delbaere's recent work on the subject clarifies this theoretical crux. Magical realism often expresses a reaction against the centre, against hegemonic society. It serves to designate a "fracture in the real," a sense of crisis. Delbaere defines three variants of magical realism. In what she terms "psychic realism," the "magic" is "almost always a reification of the hero's inner conflict" (251). Second, she suggests that "grotesque realism" be used "for any sort of hyperbolic distortion that creates a sense of strangeness through the confusion or interpenetration of different realms like animate/inanimate or human/animal" (256). A third sub-category, which Delbaere terms "mythic realism," emanates from the supernatural features of the environment itself rather than from the character's psyche (252-53). *Stolen* offers a typical instance of Delbaere's third sub-category, in its theatricalization of legends from the Dreamtime. Mythic magical realism emanates from Sandy's first story, which explains how the monster Mungee—under cover of darkness—came to steal tribal children:

> SANDY: The yurringa—that's the sun—shone all the time, day, and what we now call night [...] Until the Mungee came along. The Mungee was an outcast from the mob and he was mean and he was huge [...] The Mungee got so hungry that he came and snuck into his people's camp and stole one of the children! Then he ate him up! [...] The next day the elders waited for the Mungee, and when they sensed his presence they threw magic powdered bone all over him [...] The Mungee was turned into a pale skin and that was his punishment. He would never be able to sneak into the camp to steal the children because he would be seen. And the people would know. And the people would never forget. (11)

This story ironically describes the white man as a grotesque monster, as the victim of a curse. However, the end of the monologue contains a double ironical twist: Sandy suggests that because they have lost touch with the world of their Dreaming, Aboriginals have now forgotten this legend. They have again let the white man penetrate into their camp to steal children away. A further instance of mythic magical realism resurges in Sandy's efforts to comfort Ruby. Sandy again alludes to the Aboriginal Dreaming in connection to the creation myth of the desert. In an attempt to show off to their neighbours, Sandy's ancestors once built a supposedly magic place out of red rocks:

SANDY: But then the Banga—the Old Wind [...] high up in the sky was blowing by and he saw what my people had done to fool their neighbours and he laughed and laughed at them. He laughed and he roared around the rocks and they all crumbled into sand and blew all over, until the land, he was covered in red sand [...] That's how the desert sands were created [...] My Mum [...] used to say that when you walk on the sand, the wind can blow away your footsteps, like you had never made them, and the earth would become pure again. The sand could heal itself. (24)

Ironically, the magic of the sand, which gave its name to the protagonist, Sandy, was unable to protect Aboriginal women and culture. Nor could it spare Sandy any of the hardships he had to endure. And yet, at the end of the play, Sandy feels closest to home in the desert, where his deep cultural allegiances lie. Thus, the intrusion of the supernatural into the drabness of everyday reality reveals Harrison's desire to reshape Western realism along the lines of Jack Davis, whose allusions to the Dreamtime in *The First Born* trilogy immediately come to mind. She achieves a perfect blend of Western and Aboriginal techniques in a markedly syncretic style. Mudrooroo has himself brilliantly developed this form of polysemic "Aboriginal realism" in his groundbreaking novel *Wild Cat Falling*, when in an epiphanic moment of revelation, his protagonist re-possesses the Dreamworld of his ancestors. Harrison's extension of the conventional boundaries of poetic realism underscores her sense of subversive mimicry and hybridity.

A specific instance of the international appeal of *Stolen* is foregrounded by a comparison with native Canadian dramatist Drew Hayden Taylor's *Someday*, produced in November 1991 by the De-ba-jeh-mu-jig Theatre Group on Manitoulin Island. Taylor's play evokes the "scoop-up" period in Canadian history in a moving rendition of a Native family's renewed sense of bereavement around Christmas time. While *Stolen* takes a general view of the Australian equivalent political issue, Taylor's play could be regarded as an amplification of one vignette of *Stolen*, "Am I Black or White?" In this short scene, as she revisits her Aboriginal family, Ann feels rejected by her relatives. As a result, she undergoes a profound existential crisis. In Taylor's play, an identical theme receives a more detailed dramatization. Although *Someday*'s plot appears simple on the surface, it resonates with subtle symbolic overtones. Rodney, who filters the action through the prism of his memory, shares with the audience painful reminiscences of a recent Christmas celebration. In this play as in *Stolen*, the occasion functions as a false symbol of family reunion. In *Someday*, Anne Wabung wins a lottery ticket a few days before Christmas. She then prays that this recent material happiness be matched by a more spiritual one. Somewhat strangely, she fosters the hope that the child taken away from her thirty-five years ago will return home in time for Christmas. Because these hopes eventually prove illusory, the religious festival loses its connotations of symbolic rebirth, as in *Stolen*. Even though she won the lottery ticket, Anne will never be reunited with her lost daughter. Unexpectedly, the latter, Grace, suddenly calls the family and announces that she will come back to visit them. She has become a rich lawyer in Toronto, who has now completely forgotten the values of her native ancestry. She is presented as a false Messiah, dressed in a white and expensive fur coat, the symbol of her corruption through the Western values of materialism. Her old name Grace is obviously meant ironically: she fails to offer the family spiritual regeneration. Her new name, Janice Wirth, likewise underscores her materialistic personality: the "worth" she may possess hardly transcends the mundane. Her ephemeral reunion with her real mother testifies to her whimsical desire to observe Aboriginal people from a distance without seeking to understand her own roots. As the near-farcical red-stain episode demonstrates, she displays a characteristic white bourgeois obsession with cleanliness:

> JANICE. I can't believe it!—they're [the shoes] Italian leather and the dye is running! [...] I hope they won't stain your floor [...] Oh I'm so sorry. Look at your floor.
>
> *Janice takes them off and turns around quickly, accidentally bumping Rodney with the shoes, leaving a red stain on his shirt [...] Janice is horrified at what she's done and covers her mouth with her hand in shock [...] She grabs a dishtowel from the table to wipe off Rodney's stain [...] The once magnificent Janice is now like the rest of them.* (44)

Moreover, the reservation-made moccasins that her mother gives her hardly fit. Before she returns to Toronto, she feels relieved "to take them off" (75). Thus, this failed Christmas party bespeaks, as in *Stolen*, the lack of home and identity shared by all the members of a displaced family. Like *Stolen*, *Someday* is a historiographic work that revisions the true causes of the scoop-up from the perspective of the victims. Taylor's technique of revelation differs somewhat from Harrison's: once Rodney has established the memory framework, the plot line remains more chronological than in *Stolen*. The truth progressively surfaces in the course of Act Two through several confessional monologues inspired, as in *Stolen*, by old family pictures. Like Anne, Barb Wabung, the sister, vehemently indicts the white system that deprived them of a family member. Ironically, the child was taken away because the father had enlisted in the Canadian army:

> BARB: [...] the Indian agent became suspicious of a single mother living on the reserve and not on welfare. He called the Children's Aid and they sent an investigator who didn't find the home life ...

ANNE: ... suitable. My home wasn't suitable. What the heck do they know about what makes a home? I clothed you. I fed you. I loved you. Out here that was suitable ... (73)

Shocked by this manifestation of the cruelty of white Canadian society, Janice paradoxically dissociates herself from her biological mother, perhaps out of some obscure sense of guilt. She returns to the city, where she definitely belongs, although she promises to come back "someday." The spectator could hardly miss the irony inherent in this concluding line: the gulf between the cultural background of the adopted children and their real parents will never be bridged. More than Ann in *Stolen*, Janice wishes to obliterate the Aboriginal part of herself. Consequently, *Someday* ends on a somewhat sadder note than Harrison's play, on a bitter restatement of the false values conjured up by Christmas:

RODNEY: When do you think you'll be back? [...]

JANICE: Oh, someday, I suppose. Goodbye, Rodney. And Merry Christmas [...]

RODNEY: God, I hate Christmas. (80)

The cross-cultural similarities between Taylor's and Harrison's works indicate that the Australian play finds echoes well beyond the confines of the Southern continent. Like *Stolen*, Taylor's *Someday* epitomizes the notion of displaced and distorted identity so characteristic of the postcolonial ending of the twentieth-century. Like Harrison, Taylor extends the limits of poetic realism: although he does not resort to magical realism in this particular play—as he previously did in his acclaimed *Toronto at Dreamer's Rock*—his play nonetheless dialogizes Western and non-Western modes of expression. His subversive mimicry reveals itself in a parody of traditionally happy Christmas tales and Christian myths of spiritual regeneration. Like Harrison, Taylor further subverts Woolfian or Joycean modernist epiphanies, pointing to the impossibility of enlightenment in the postcolonial world. Combined with the play's nostalgic mood derived from Euro-American stage realism, the ironic undertones of *Someday* recall Homi Bhabha's third space of hybridity.

Harrison's *Stolen* should not be reserved to black audiences. Its historical revisionism will undoubtedly strike responsive chords with mainstream audiences in Australia and abroad, as it partakes of what Linda Hutcheon has termed the postmodern notion of the "ex-centric." It clearly gives expression to the voice of an oppressed minority, while articulating universal themes such as the human quest for home and identity. The emotional intensity of this work will enthrall Aboriginal and white audiences alike, not only throughout the postcolonial world, as the connection with Taylor's play suggests, but also beyond the margins of the Commonwealth.

Works Cited

Bakhtin, M. M. *The Dialogic Imagination. Four Essays*. Ed. and trans. Caryl Emerson and Michael Holquist. Austin: U of Texas P, 1981.

Bhabha, Homi K. *The Location of Culture*. London: Routledge, 1994.

Delbaere, Jeanne. "Psychic Realism, Mythic Realism, Grotesque Realism: Variations on Magic Realism in Contemporary Literature in English." *Magical Realism. Theory, History, Community*. Ed. Lois Parkinson & Wendy B. Faris. Durham & London: Duke UP, 1995. 249-63.

Harrisson, Jane. *Stolen*. Sydney: Currency Press, 1998.

Hutcheon, Linda. *A Poetics of Postmodernism. History, Theory, Fiction*. London: Routledge, 1988.

Mudrooroo. "Towards a New Black Theatre." *New Theatre Australia* (March-April 1989): 16-17.

Taylor, Drew Hayden. *Someday*. Saskatoon: Fifth House, 1993.

Multicultural Arts,
Ethnicised Identities?

Tom BURVILL

Macquarie University

> "[...] in the midst of the postmodern flux of no-
> madic subjectivities, we need to recognise the
> operation continuous and continuing of 'fixing'
> performed by the categories of race and ethnic-
> ity [...] on the formation of identity." (Ang, "On
> Not Speaking Chinese" 5)

This article focuses on two original theatre pieces produced over the last
couple of years in Sydney, under the sign of multicultural arts. I am
interested in the way in which these two works relate to issues of ethnicity and representation in the current stage of Australian multiculturalism. I also wish to examine how these theatrical productions interact
with the cultural processes of "ethnicising," which I take to be an aspect
of that recalcitrant fixing of identity to which Ang refers in the epigraph
above. Each of the shows worked with memory—including both personal and family memories—and with what it may be appropriate to call
"community memories," particularly as embodied in stories and images.
The various roles of narrative and performance in relation to memory
and ethnicity are highlighted by the different places which they occupy
in these formally and culturally contrasting performance events. The two
shows which will be discussed here are *Burying Mother* and *The
Wound, or anyone can be ordinary, but it takes a very special person to
be Greek* (hereafter *The Wound*). *Burying Mother*, a solo performance
work by Meme Thorne, was presented at the Belvoir Street Theatre as
part of the 1997 Asian Theatre Festival "Variasians." As such, it was
partly funded by the Australia Council's Community Cultural Development Fund and the Council's national policy "Arts for A Multicultural
Australia." *The Wound* was presented in July 1999 as part of Carnivale,
the annual Multicultural Arts Festival sponsored by the New South
Wales State Government Ministry for the Arts. Both were new works
made by the participants. *Burying Mother* was devised, written, and

performed by Meme Thorne, a Sydney-based Malaysian-born British-Chinese-Australian performer and choreographer. Created by a group of Greek-Australian actors, *The Wound* was based on texts by several specifically commissioned Greek-Australian writers and developed out of an idea by Lex Marinos, a well-known theatre and television actor and—at the time—director of Carnivale, who conceived and produced the work.

The Wound—Memory, Migration and Nostalgia

Both shows benefited from important contributions from other artists. These included a music/sound environment by composer Peter Wells in the case of *Burying Mother*, and an audio-visual "track" in the form of projected video and sound in *The Wound*. The track in question was composed and collated by video-maker Michael Karris, from materials comprising his own video footage, music by Tom Kazas, a photocollage by Peter Lyssiotis, and individual photographs by Effie Alexakis. These were pictures of individuals from the *In Their Own Image* photo-documentation project on the lives of Greek-Australians. Much of Karris' video footage was also taken from interviews video-recorded for the same project and presents grabs of responses from a range of primarily first-generation Greek-Australians. Their "live" answers to interview questions and their accounts of the various experiences of migration and post-migration life are recorded in local and domestic settings.

Each of these performance pieces worked with a combination of acting, image, movement, and narration. They each included sections presented as monologue, as personal testimony addressed directly to the audience. The nature of these monologues reflected the two shows' variations in artistic approach to the material of family, personal history, and cultural specificity which they explored. In *The Wound*, the backdrop of projected video images acted as publicly reproduced communal memories of recent family histories of migration, bringing brief excerpts of actual recorded migrant life-stories into juxtaposition with the more fictionalised stories acted out on the stage. Other images which included references to classical Greece (such as artefacts, masks) appeared in the video-collage too. Michael Karris mentioned the Greek Orthodox Church as one of the central elements of modern Greek identity in Australia. It is for this reason that he incorporated Orthodox religious imagery in his video composition, as well as because of the spiritual undertones in the music of composer Tom Kazas, which formed part of the sound track for his collage. The church received a rather more everyday and less reverent treatment in at least one of the acted scenes, which focused on its social function as a meeting place for teenagers.

This contrast illustrates the internal diversity of the image of the Greek-Australian experience folded into this multi-layered performance text.

Many of the acted scenes in *The Wound* dramatised post-migration family life, largely from the children's point of view. Some stories were entirely presented in monologue, with the relationship of the speaker to the story ranging from the reflectively personal, as in the sequence "Letter to the Dead," to the more humorous observations of family pathologies, as in "Asphyxia." The latter story—perhaps the most humorous one in the show and also the least documentary in content—was performed entirely by one actress and without video background. "Asphyxia" conveyed a vision of inner-city migrant life as seen from the youth sub-culture space of drugs, dance-parties, and dream workshops. It built a picture of an obsessive set of surreal family relationships, as if recalled from a trip or a series of dreams.

Lex Marinos gave the first line from a poem by George Seferis as the thematic stimulus to his chosen group of writers. The line, "Where ever I go, Greece wounds me" (Lex Marinos' unpublished translation) becomes an emblem of the pain of the Greek diaspora, as it invokes the melancholy of that alienation and distance from the land felt to be home. As I read it in translation, the Seferis poem, "In the Manner of G. S." (See Seferis), develops the trope that all the parts of Greece "wound" him as he travels around it. Greece wounds him especially with the past, a past which is still in evidence at particular sites of historical or mythic events, events magnified, canonised by time, giving a weighted naming to everything. "In the Manner of G. S." is about Greece as a country itself weighted with historic pain. And parallel to Seferis' poem, the sense of the relation to home conveyed in part from this performance of *The Wound* is that the Greek past remains present and in (another) place, a place one can either personally remember or have heard about from parents, where family connections are still embodied in villages, property, living relatives, but which exists above all in memory and thus as past.

Most of the stories recreated as images in *The Wound* deal with private everyday family events, recorded in family photo albums. It was this memory-material, indeed, which the *In Their Own Image* documentation project set out to discover and recover, so as to set it alongside newly-taken photo-images of the present. Many of the project respondents provided treasured family photographs, which appear in the exhibition next to the more recent images taken in Australia of their owners—who are sometimes also their subjects. Each photograph is accompanied by a short text, including quotations from their subjects and/or owners. The archive, which also tours as an exhibition, sets out to be a kind of visual history, dedicated to the empirical recording (and therefore "fixing," perhaps too) of a period of migrant life and identity conceived of as being in danger of getting lost. So, like the stories, the pictures from *In Their Own Image* become part of in *The Wound* and are already imbued with melancholy, with that sense of simultaneous presence and disappearance which photographs as such can distinctively suggest. In this sense, melancholy is inscribed as essential or intrinsic to ethnicity itself.

The *Wound* drew on a documentation project about a migration community informed by a need to "capture" a passing moment of memory, as well as on the writings of a range of second generation migrant authors invited by the invocation of the Seferis poem to express the pain of migrant "Greekness." Like *Burying Mother*, however, the show was performed in English, with only occasional returns to the mother tongue of the country of origin. In *The Wound*, these rare occurrences of the Greek language may have marked moments of recognition and identification, but may also have highlighted the majority use of English in preference to Greek. This was significant given that *The Wound* appeared to be intended for "the Greek community." It was played in an inner-suburban theatre associated with "ethnic" shows, owned by a Greek family. But the majority use of English and the lack of a translation made few concessions to the fact that the English language would still be foreign to and difficult for the older, first-generation migration members of its audience. At least some of these older people in the audience found parts of the show uncongenial in any case, especially those scenes of family conflict which included some naturalistic "bad language." The show's implicitly favoured audience appeared to be young second-generation Greek-Australians, at home both in the context of the Greek community and of the Australian English-language environment.

In performing *Burying Mother*, Meme Thorne was aware that at least some of her audience would know more of "Chinese-ness"—and certainly of the Chinese language—than herself. The fact that she had been brought up not speaking Chinese at all forms a part of the underlying material of this work. Even the titles of the two shows indicate this crucial difference between them. *Burying Mother* refers to a gender problematic (especially once you know the gender of the "author"), and in that sense to a situation or condition not ethnically specific. It connects to particular aspects of the passive obedience expected of girl children in Chinese cultural tradition, but tends not to label that as a "cultural" issue, but rather as a psychological one. I shall discuss later the way in which Meme Thorne and her show were, however, ethnicised as Asian and Chinese before, after, and around the event of the production of *Burying Mother*. In particular, I shall examine how this ethnicisation was generated by social and cultural processes—including aspects of the "Variasians" festival itself. For instance, the circulation of visual publicity material turned the poster image for the show into an iconic image for the Festival as a whole. Moreover, the federal funding body, the Australia Council, appropriated the event as firstly "multi-cultural art" and secondly as Chinese (without even resorting to the usual hyphenation, as in Chinese-Australian). We might call these processes instances of the social "technologies of ethnicity," to adapt Teresa de Lauretis' phrase "technologies of gender" (vi). This over-ethnicised reading was not only a misconstruction of Meme Thorne's work, but also of her personal origins and cultural identity.

In both *Burying Mother* and *The Wound*, the telling of the particular person's story involves some sort of coming to terms with their parents. In a sense, because of migration, the past is compressed into the immediate past generation, i.e. into the immediate family, especially mother and father. This seems obvious in the case of some of these artists, because that past generation represents the one which actually migrated and made the crucial physical break with the country of origin; yet, paradoxically enough, it is also the same generation which, because of its reasons for migrating, did not break or feel the need to break with the norms and culture of their first homeland. In the case of *The Wound*, the overwhelming role of nostalgia is also balanced by the actual difficulties of the second generation (the children of the actual migrating generation) in dealing with the emotional demands of their parents. In some of the scenes, we see that these are often manipulative, sometimes even violent, and strongly express a possessive variety of family love. In other parts of *The Wound*, as the character played by Jen Apostolu says in the monologue "Asphyxia," the house where her aunt Despina lived in Stanmore was an "ethnic temple to diminished love" (40). The character speaking here appears in some obscure way to be the victim of that diminishedness. She refers to spending time in some sort of therapy facility, the "high dependency unit" (39), which itself almost seems like an analogy to or metaphor for the intensity of the relationships involved in apparently obsessively difficult family relationships.

One of the theatre critics reviewing the show commented that, judging from it, Greek-Australians have a high proportion of dysfunctional families. In a way, this judgement may be just a misconstruction of a cultural habit of vigorous interaction, including within the family unit itself, where relations which look like a mere domination/subordination game to the Anglo-Saxon sensibility may certainly exemplify strong contestation of authority, but cannot simply be reduced to oppressive/resistant interactions. On the other hand, the critics' interpretation may be totally missing the point that these families are functioning under different conditions, ones which happen to be stressed in the performance, because some of the well-known structural dimensions of migration themselves mean that many relationships in families—

particularly authority relations—have to be re-invented. The stories in *The Wound* are stories told from the point of view of the young adult looking back on the experience of growing up in Greek-Australian homes. There is a certain amount of getting even in retrospect or of more general recollection of the difficulties inherent in separation, identity formation and rebellion, given the pressures of growing up in a culture with different assumptions about youth, sexuality, and the importance of religious belief.

One of the most interesting sections in *The Wound* is that called "Letter to the Dead," in which the unnamed character tells of his imagined writing to his dead father from his present perspective as a young adult. In the process, the son re-evaluates him with new respect as a father, a husband to a "difficult" mother, a man who migrated and later "went home." The question is whether this narrative strategy represents an advance on "telling your own story" (which might be more individualistic and somehow involves a kind of heroism), or whether it constitutes a new stage of investigation into identity in the odd in-between state of migrant time. Maybe this has more to do with interrogating a given identity than with "expressing" it against a cultural repression. In "Letter to the Dead" at least, there is a hint of that kind of nostalgia which might partly be about desire for some added sense of authenticity as a subject. The nature of this nostalgia is influenced, however, by the productive tensions between the sound and image track and the acted language. The monologue begins in voice-over, as if coming from outside the character, and is taken up by him as his own words and continued. The main theme of the text is a melancholy celebration of the man who was the protagonist's father, as if re-discovering what was brave and rather tragic in his life. This also becomes a search for the meaning of that life, with the realisation that the son had taken it for granted, that it had more to teach him than he had, almost too late, begun to realise. Nikos Papastergiadis has written positively about the radical possibilities of nostalgia:

> Nostalgia is usually understood as the rebounding away from the threatening aspects of the present and the search for safer grounds in the past, but implicit in this very manoeuvre is an attention to the unnamed aspects of the present. It is this element of nostalgia which can yield critical insight, and paradoxically work towards naming the present. (167)

Burying Mother ... Asian and/or Theatre?

The definitive identification of this piece as firmly "Chinese" is one of the first things challenged or at least made problematic by the performance itself in *Burying Mother*. Meme Thorne told me in interview that part of her motivation in making this show, only her second major solo work in a more than twenty-year performance career, stemmed from two levels of insecurity. One was about her ability to show other sides of her personal performance skills—to work with language and narrative as well as movement. The other insecurity revolved around her identity. Her mother is Chinese, she was born and lived until age fourteen in Malaysia, and her father was British. Thorne never learnt to speak Chinese, as her mother thought it would be more to her children's advantage to speak English and not identify themselves as Chinese. For this reason also, Thorne and her siblings were sent to Australia to be educated there as teenagers. For many audiences, however, and significantly for funding bodies, Thorne is an "Asian" artist (the Australia Council indeed declares her "Chinese" on its web-site).

As I have suggested, the show itself foregrounds the provisional nature of her Chinese-ness as well as the intimate connection between that identity and Thorne's association of it with her mother, which renders the identification doubly problematic. This foregrounding is achieved by a number of intriguing devices. Thorne appears to the audience dressed in layers of white and near white material; she also wears a white fabric headdress, which gives her a generally "priestlike" appearance. She is seen burning in an iron bowl Chinese paper "Hell Bank notes," the kind which you can buy quite cheaply in China Town supermarkets and which have been available to the audience to pick up as they came in. She also burns other paper shapes, cut-outs of objects mentioned in the ensuing voice-over. She kneels, concentrating intently as she ignites the objects, carefully handling each one to make sure it is fully consumed. The sight of real fire on stage, very close to both her costume and the audience in the very small theatre, adds to the ritual air of the actions at this point. Simultaneously, a recorded female voice-over, which we may recognise as Thorne's, addresses us quietly and matter-of-factly with these words:

> Apparently, as soon as someone dies, the family cat is given to the neighbours to be taken care of, to prevent pussy from leaping or walking over the death bed, causing the corpse to sit up. (1)

Not only does the content of this information sound somewhat startling in its mixture of irreverence and detachment, but the voice appears notably more cultivated in diction and accent than the "average" Australian voice. There is also little trace of any stereotyped "Asian-Australian" inflection. The tone, moreover, sounds surprising. If these are the thoughts of the woman we see on stage and if she is speaking even indirectly of funeral rites for her mother, she is very composed.

There is an explanation of the Envelope of the Soul and the nature of the burnt offerings—paper imitation clothing, money for the journey etc. However, the information offered about Chinese burial customs is foregrounded as provisional, even superficial, learned rather than known. The voice-over begins with the provisional "Apparently [...]," which distances the information. It continues punctuated with hesitant "ums" and "ers," as if the speaker often felt unsure of how to put it or how to pronounce obviously Chinese terms and names for things. As Jacqueline Lo argues, "Not only is the protagonist unsure about her ability to translate for her audience, doubts are also cast on her suitability as a source of 'native' knowledge" (68). Meme Thorne had in fact researched the beliefs about funerary rituals and the cultural meanings of particular colours, and she does not try to hide this synthetic relation to tradition in the performance itself. Indeed, the major texts used are credited in the theatre programme.

A moment later, we realise from the dialogue that her mother is not yet dead. She moves to a make-up table in front of a small mirror, and begins to put on make-up and a bouffant black wig. As she transforms into an image of her mother as a 1950s film star beauty the performer explains:

> Her name is Rose. She lives in Adelaide. She smokes. She knits. She crochets.
>
> She is very clever with her hands. She sits on the sofa. She watches TV. Alone, eating her peanuts.
>
> She often told me I looked just like her. I was the one—blessed—with her looks, her abilities. People said she was beautiful. Just like Elizabeth Taylor. (4)

We also witness the re-experience of events from childhood, when her mother threatened to commit suicide—and actually began to do so with the gas oven—in front of the assembled children in the kitchen. We witness the way Thorne can transform performatively into that figure, but still only partly rid herself of the psychologically wounding power of her emotional force, to which Thorne's attachment is part trauma, part fascination or fixation.

Perhaps the bravest and most frightful sequence of all is a striking movement sequence which follows soon afterwards: half-squatting almost as if to give birth, but also swaying as if in a trance, Thorne cradles a small worn and much-cuddled children's stuffed toy dog. She coos and "mothers" it like a baby, but gradually moves into a manic rhythm, harshly swinging the toy, only to end by tearing open its stomach and disgorging handfuls of peanuts in a mad rage. In many ways, this scene is the heart of the piece, as it gives the frightening sense that the angry mother and the scared child are both still and always part of the individual we see before us.

Burying Mother was informed by both Asian and European performance styles and disciplines, but also by feminist psycho-analytic theory. However, the mis-construction and simplification effected by the way in which the multicultural rhetoric of cultural diversity and its associated discourse of the ethnic appropriated the show readily transpire from the supposition made in some of the publicity material that in her performance Meme is mourning the literal death of her mother. To continue to read the opening of the piece as literal funeral rites is to miss the point. A correct perception of what the performance was attempting to convey may have been rendered more difficult by quasi-anthropological, exoticising assumptions about authenticity which can go with the reception of ethnic, multicultural arts. Ironical use of ritual is not apparently compatible with ethnic authenticity. At the same time as "burying" and exorcising the bad mother who still oppressed her in her mind, Meme Thorne was trying to perform—and therefore somehow to discover—what part of her mother lived in herself, and through that, what her own "Chineseness" might mean—her Chinese self was presented as a set of partial and provisional knowledges.

For the "Asian" woman artist, there may, moreover, be further specific issues. The popular cultural image of "Asia" which circulates in Australia is often a feminised one, constructed in an exoticising Orientalist vein, particularly in the visual imagery of tourism. Suvendrini Perera has discussed some pointedly symptomatic instances in television and advertising (Perera). This discourse is re-iterated—in order to be confronted—in the imagery of the public poster for *Burying Mother*. In this poster, Thorne is shown buried in peanuts up to her collar bones and thighs inside a large wicker basket. Her bare legs and arms hang over the sides of the basket. She looks straight at the camera, her face dramatically whitened, like a mask which reminds us of geisha faces or aristocratic Chinese women in traditional watercolours. Her eyes have a striking butterfly wing make-up treatment. Her hair is short, modern, her lips dark red and pursed in a rosebud shape, emphasising the firmness of her expression. She may have just fallen into the peanuts, she may be about to get out. The image does not represent any scene in the show. It asks questions, rather than telling a clear story. Thorne and her photographer Heidrun Lohr intended the image to invite speculation about the show's relation to both Chinese tradition and modernity. Meme Thorne told me in interview that the intent of the image was to suggest the idea of the child's vulnerability—a baby in a basket—with some humour, so as to leaven any impression that the show was angst-ridden and full of painful experiences. The image was also meant to cheekily combine the contemporary and the traditional, as the eye make-up provided a reference to female make-up in traditional Chinese Opera. Intention or coding of course does not control reading or decoding, particularly when the image is appropriated into more generalised circulation and less ironically aware ethnicising contexts.

After having seen the show, we know the precise significance of the peanuts in the story of Meme's childhood. Before that, however, they can only be intriguing, incongruous, enigmatic. Thereby, the image perhaps co-operates with a general ambient Orientalist discourse of Asian "inscrutability." Similarly, if we do not manage to read the eye make-up as Chinese Opera, it becomes part of an imagery of sexy/daring/demonic otherness. On Meme Thorne's invitation cards for the show, sent out to the theatre mailing list, this image also appears, but set alongside a family snap of a little girl who is recognisably Thorne at the age of three or four, paddling at the water's edge of what resembles the seaside, wearing a frilly swimsuit, and smiling somewhat uncertainly at the camera. We can imagine that the photo was probably being taken by a parent, at whom Meme is looking behind the camera. In this context, the pictures together ask for answers about the life-story in which the character evolved from the tentative child to this confronting woman, but they at least equally suggest that this is a story also involving the re-visiting of childhood. In this juxtaposition of photographs, the basket image is framed differently, more as part of a life-story, less as an exotic spectacle.

The snapshot of Thorne in the basket became the poster image not only for *Burying Mother* itself, but for the "Variasians" festival as a whole. It was pasted up on billboards all over Sydney and appeared in the newspaper advertisements. Most strikingly, the image has been taken over by the Australia Council: it is published in full colour on the multicultural arts section of the Council website and on the cover of their printed brochures as an emblem of the "Asian" in multicultural arts. Meme Thorne is referred to as a "Chinese" artist in Australia Council publications. Circulating in advance of the show as the emblem of the "Variasians" festival and after it as the funding bodies' emblem of multicultural arts, the image appears to have become one of those certified signifiers of ethnicity, an officially circulated signifier of "Asianness."

Conclusion

Ethnicised public identities in a multi-immigrant society like Australia are positions for identification, for modes of subjectivity made available by the circulating discourses of the ethnic other at a given time. For the subject interpellated by some multiculturalist discourses, the expression of "ethnic identity" can become an imperative in recognisable ways— ways recognisable from time to time as appropriate, as a sign of possession or retention of identity. Given that this is so, ethnicised cultural identity can become both a voice and a cage. This means that identity can become a kind of mimicry, one that purveys "ethnicity as masquerade."

State multiculturalism represents one of the conditions of production of Australian "multicultural arts" —or of arts as multicultural—and is in a sense constitutive of that category. This form of multiculturalism requires the cultural production of identifiable "ethnicities," as much as racism requires the credibility of identifiable "races." The idea of multiculturalism and accompanying ideas of ethnicity and cultural diversity certainly operate as a major force in the general reception of productions by artists marked as "ethnic." The arts occupy a privileged place amongst the accepted signs of what constitutes multiculturalism, inasmuch as Australian multiculturalism is often presented as a spectacle of colourful diversity, of acceptable and intelligible difference ostended. Through the state-multiculturalist "sponsoring" of expression of particular identities and the funding of ethnicised cultural production in the name of diversity, the "fixing" of identities referred to by Ang finds perhaps one of its most seductive social technologies.

Works Cited

Ang, Ien. "On Not Speaking Chinese—Postmodern Ethnicity and the Politics of Diaspora." *New Formations* 24 (Winter 1994): 1-18.

De Lauretis, Teresa, ed. *Technologies of Gender: Essays on Theory, Film, and Fiction*. Bloomington: Indiana University Press, 1987.

Lo, Jacqueline. "Dis/orientations: Contemporary Asian-Australian Theatre." *Our Australian Theatre in the 1990s*. Ed. Veronica Kelly. Amsterdam & Atlanta, GA: Rodopi, 1999. 53-70.

Marinos, Lex et al. *The Wound, or anyone can be ordinary, but it takes a very special person to be Greek.* Unpublished script. Performed Sydney, 1999.

Papastergiardis, Nikos. *Modernity as Exile.* Manchester: Manchester UP, 1993.

Perera, Suvendrini. "Representation Wars: Malaysia, *Embassy* and Australia's Corps Diplomatique." *Australian Cultural Studies—A Reader*. Eds. John Frow and Meaghan Morris. Sydney: Allen and Unwin, 1993. 15-29.

Stratton, Jon and Ien. "Multicultural Imagined Communities: Cultural Difference and National Identity in Australia and the United States." *Continuum, The Australian Journal of Media and Culture* 8.2 (1994): 124-158.

Seferis, George. "In the Manner of G. S." Keeley, Edmund and Philip Sherrard. Trans. and ed. *George Seferis. Collected Poems*. Princeton: Princeton University Press, 1967. 107-111.

Thorne, Meme. *Burying Mother*. Unpublished script. Performed Sydney, 1966.

Pacific Overtures and Asian Encounters: New Zealand Theatre and the Bi-Cultural Paradigm[1]

Christopher BALME

Johannes Gutenberg-Universität, Mainz

Introduction

The coat-of-arms on my New Zealand passport conveys a clear icono-graphical message. The British crown presides over a country in the South Seas dependent on the export by ship of sheep, alive and dead, as well as grain, wealth accumulated by hard labour. The population is divided into two discrete groups: citizens of European descent versus those of Maori ancestry. The former are represented by a blond young woman, Zealandia, clad in a low-cut white nightgown and bearing the national flag. She stands in opposition to a male Maori chief wearing ceremonial regalia consisting of feathered cloak and *taiaha*, the spear-club. Like most coats-of-arms, this one is structured around a set of binary oppositions: female-male; white-brown; Europe-Polynesia. This sign represents what may be termed the cultural and political consensus of the last one hundred years: one country, two peoples. At the end of the nineteenth century, visiting dignitaries to New Zealand were already being greeted by Maori warriors in feather cloaks and brandishing *taiaha*. Even while New Zealand was still a British colony, the indige-

---

[1] This essay is based on a paper which was first presented at the "Crucible of Cultures" conference, organized by the Université Libre de Bruxelles and held in Brussels from 16 to 19 May 2001. It was subsequently presented at the Department of Theatre and Film, Victoria University of Wellington, and at the School of Performing and Screen Arts, UNITEC, Auckland. My thanks go to Marc Maufort, David Carnegie, and Bridget Marsh for inviting me to discuss the paper. I particularly benefited from the discussions in New Zealand, and have tried to incorporate some of the suggestions made there into this revised version of the original paper.

nous culture was already an important part of official protocol and ceremonial display. This coat-of-arms was in fact introduced in 1911, exactly ninety years ago. It provides, in the words of the historian Keith Sinclair, "a guide to the symbolic state of the New Zealand psyche at that time" (Sinclair 190). What I have described is my third passport. The important addition to this one, issued in 1998, is the *bilingual* text. The previous ones were exclusively written in English.

While New Zealand passports figure identity formation in binary terms—one country, two peoples—and all official discourse today reiterates the same formula, it is questionable whether the cultural make-up of the country can be contained within a bicultural framework. New Zealand theatre has also moved from a *mono*cultural to a *bi*cultural model in keeping with resurgence of Maori political and cultural aspirations. Only in very recent years have we seen evidence of multicultural theatre. These newest tendencies are the focus of my interest today.

My considerations on this topic will be divided in four parts. I shall begin with general comments on the development of New Zealand theatre from a *mono-* to a *bi*cultural self-image. In a second section of my argument, I shall provide my first concrete example of the burgeoning theatre experiments by Pacific Islanders. I shall look at the co-production between the Christchurch-based group Pacific Underground and an Australian community theatre group, Zeal. The production is called *Tatau*. Further examples of the bicultural trends on New Zealand stages will be given in a third part, which in fact groups two mono-dramas: *Krishnan's Dairy*, written and performed by Jacob Rajan; and *Ka-Shue (Letters Home)* by Lynda Chanwai-Earle, also written and performed by the author. The authors are of Indian and Chinese origin respectively. The fourth section of this essay will be devoted to a last example which stretches the notion of the theatrical to encompass a cultural performance. In this final part, I shall examine a ceremonial encounter of a political kind that was enacted in 1999 during the APEC meeting in New Zealand.

From Bi- to Multiculturalism

The title of my essay requires a degree of explanation. The word "overture" has two quite different meanings. Its primary meaning is of course musical, as the term alludes to the instrumental opening to an opera, in which leitmotifs of the work are usually performed in concentrated abbreviation. An overture, in this sense, always implies something preparatory and anticipatory, indicating things to come. Applied to the context of theatre, we could say that the entrenchment of multicultural theatre is still in its infancy. An overture also signifies an approach, often of an amorous or intimate kind, or sometimes in a political sense. This latter connotation of overture suggests the tentative nature of these developments.[2] The title of this essay refers both metaphorically and associatively to the process of tentative approaches and changes in New Zealand theatre, a process which—via a notion of biculturalism—has seen a shift from the imitative manufacture of eurocentric copies to uncertain models of multiculturalism.

Turning now to drama and theatre in New Zealand, we can identify a clear succession of paradigms. Until the 1980s, the medium was securely situated in a *mono*cultural one: the dominant questions, as they had been for art and literature since the 1930s, were figured within a family conflict, with the white *sons* intent on breaking away from the British mother and establishing aesthetic independence in the new country. The most frequently invoked metaphor was that of identity, the creation of a new homogeneous cultural unity. The Maori warrior had a part to play in this oedipal conflict—mainly on the level of supernumerary, but even occasionally as a major player, as reflected in the Maori plays of Bruce Mason. Within this model, however, the Maori acted as an ambivalent index of cultural vitality, one to be held up to the ailing parent, while he himself gained dramatic status only through sacrifice. I quote from the foreword to Mason's second Maori play *Awatea*: "Sometimes I saw a bardic Maori bursting joyously through the narrow straits of pakeha feelings and emotions, finding his true image and stature only in death" (Mason 287). Located somewhere between images of Greek and Celtic oratory, the Maori fulfils the usual function within the economy of exoticism by exhibiting preternatural vitality while at the same time redeeming the European through the native's timely demise. Despite the ennobling tragic function apportioned to the Maori, Mason's view remains pessimistic. He frequently speaks of a broken culture, of fragmentation and alienation. This pessimism is grounded in a basically Rousseauian perspective. While his Maori characters are by no means noble savages, it is clear that he does glorify pre-colonial Maori society, mainly as a distorted mirror to a white "culture," a word he only ever uses in inverted commas when talking about his fellow countrymen and women of European descent.

---

[2] A third association can be added, which links the theatrical with the geopolitical. *Pacific Overtures* is the title of one of Steven Sondheim's less successful musicals. It deals with Admiral Perry's famous expedition to Japan in 1853, America's early contribution to gunboat diplomacy. Using the conventions of Kabuki theatre, he tells the story of an intercultural encounter using the theatrical languages and conventions of both cultures.

The first major challenge to the monocultural model in theatre came in the late 1980s, as Maori artists began to discover the stage as a medium for writing and performing. The first institutional milestone was the renaming of the Depot theatre in Wellington as Taki-Rua Depot, with an explicit mandate to perform Maori and indigenous work. These developments towards a bicultural understanding of theatre have attracted a growing body of research and shall not be enumerated again.[3] It is, however, important to stress the wider political and economic climate in which Maori playwriting flourished. Spurred on by a ground swell of political discontent which culminated in the famous 1975 land march, a Maori cultural renaissance slowly gathered momentum in the 1980s. Its major achievement was the reintroduction of the Maori language and its establishment, finally, as the country's second official language. Today the Maori language enjoys a high presence in education and broadcasting. On a political level, the decision in the late 1990s to award Maori tribes compensation for confiscated land in the nineteenth century was truly a momentous one. The slogan "one country, two peoples" now corresponds to a cultural and political reality.

Before we bathe in the reflected glory of a utopia attained, we must realize that New Zealand, like most countries, is not composed of just two cultures or ethnic groups, but of many. The New Zealand population is already showing clear signs of substantial shifts. The most recent official figures from the 1996 census give the following breakdown: the European/Pakeha and the New Zealand Maori respectively represent 79.6% and 14.5% of the population; Pacific Islanders account for 5.6% of it; the Chinese total 2.2%, and the Indians 1.2%. The new 2001 census will certainly produce different percentages, particularly for the last three groups. The European group will most certainly fall below its present level, whereas the figures for all other groups will certainly rise.

Although the figures indicate a development towards multiculturalism, the official discourse has not moved with it. In comparison with other settler societies such as Canada or Australia, however, the term multiculturalism is, if not *tapu*, at least not current in official documents. To illustrate this, I may digress briefly to mention Te Papa, New Zealand's new national museum, which opened in 1998. I quote from the recent official government briefing paper:

> Te Papa has made a commitment to being a bicultural organisation—the importance of the Treaty of Waitangi and the partnership which is implicit

---

[3]   For the historical development of Maori theatre, see Christopher B. Balme's "New Maori Theatre in New Zealand" (1989/90) and "Between Separation and Integration: Intercultural strategies in contemporary Maori Theatre" (1996).

in the Treaty is acknowledged. Te Papa's bicultural policy is designed to ensure the development of a strong operational partnership between Maori and Pakeha that is active throughout the organisation and at the governance level. (http://www.tepapa.govt.nz/briefingpapper/BriefingPaper.html#Introduction Last visit 1.5.2001

The term bicultural is enshrined in all official discourse pertaining to the Museum, whereas the few references to the country's multi-ethnic composition are very vaguely worded to the tune of New Zealand's "place in the Pacific and the World" etc. In the museum itself, however, there are permanent exhibitions reflecting the country's different immigrant groups, particularly Pacific Islanders. We find, therefore, a curious discrepancy between discourse and reality, as though political language seemed unwilling or constrained to go beyond the bicultural paradigm.

Pacific Island Theatre

In 1992, I published an article in German under a similar title to this one, in which I looked at intercultural tendencies in New Zealand theatre. Its focus was, not surprisingly, mainly on the Maori theatre movement. It proved interesting for me to reread the final paragraphs, which I shall quote here, for they contain a kind of prophecy which in fact did come true.

> Finally we should glance at a further important dimension of New Zealand's Pacific identity, the many ethnic groups from the Pacific islands. The inhabitants of Samoa, Tonga, the Cook Islands and Niue who have settled in New Zealand are now an integral part of New Zealand's cultural life. Until now they have not yet used theatre to give expression to their experiences in New Zealand's major cities. There is, however, a growing body of literature in English written by South Pacific people. [...] Although there have been few attempts to create a Polynesian theatre, it is certainly only a question of time until, analogous to Maori theatre, a syncretic theatre culture emerges based on the indigenous Polynesian performance culture. (Balme, "Pacific Overtures" 258)

Developments in the past decade have indeed borne out the portent. Within a short period, a young generation of writers, performers, and directors has emerged and established itself as a major force. In 1996, one of the few commissioned works for the International New Zealand Arts Festival, *When the Frigate Bird Sings*, was co-written by Oscar Kightley and David Fane, and directed by Nathaniel Lees, all of Samoan descent. Kightley and Fane are co-founders of the Christchurch-based group Pacific Underground. Founded in 1992, Pacific Underground terms itself a "Polynesian theatre and music company [...] specialising in telling the stories of Pacific Islanders who live in Aotearoa" (Unpublished mission statement, Balme and Carstensen, 46, n. 23).[4] The play deals with the *fa'afafine*, the now famous Samoan transvestites—boys raised as girls from an early age. Their place in New Zealand society remains an ambivalent one as the play shows. The evocative production by Lees was one of the major successes of the festival (see Besnier).

The Human Canvas

Some of these artists came together again for the play *Tatau—Rites of Passage*. Created in 1996 as a co-production between Pacific Underground and Zeal Theatre, companies from New Zealand and Australia respectively, this work was performed to high acclaim in both countries. The action of the "play" is framed by a tattooing ceremony with which the performance commences and which is carried out throughout the performance backstage.

In a succession of short scenes, the play *Tatau* tells the story of a family of Samoan immigrants to New Zealand. It closely relates the actual historical situation between the 1940s and the 1990s: the parents meeting to the rhythms of 1940s swing music, the son Floyd's discrimination at school, the mother's incomprehension when he is expelled, his time in borstal. After his release and return home, he is beaten by other family members who cannot comprehend his failed integration. The family disintegrates: the daughter becomes pregnant and Floyd joins a youth gang, who even rob their own families and tattoo themselves as a sign of their group identity. Only at this point does the family as a whole realize its disastrous state of loneliness and alienation, so that the process of reintegration can begin. The play ends as Floyd prepares himself for the *pe'a*, the tattooing ritual for Samoan men, the prerequisite for full integration into Samoan society.

The public exhibition of the tattooing ceremony in the frame of a play was criticized by older Samoans in New Zealand. It was not until

---

[4]   Its mission statement reads: "Pacific Underground's aims and objectives include: to use the entertainment industry to tell the stories of Pacific Islanders who live here, to create an awareness of issues facing them, to promote the talents of young Polynesian artists, and to develop Polynesian Theatre which is accessible to the whole community, Polynesian and non-Polynesian" (quotedin Balme and Carstensen 46, n.23). Since 1992 Pacific Underground has produced theatre in education shows as well as acclaimed mainbills such as *Fresh Off The Boat, Sons* and *A Frigate Bird Sings*. Zeal Theatre is a theatre company founded in 1988, which devises original productions dealing with relevant social issues for a cross-section of Australian society.

the production team secured the participation of a respected tattoo artist, the *Tafuga*, Su'a Paolo Suluape II, a member of an acknowledged tattooing family in Samoa going back four generations and which has done much to preserve the tradition itself—that the New Zealand Samoan community could accept the public performance of the ritual. At the end of the evening, the "human canvas," the tattooed person, addressed the audience:

> This is getting towards our last night and we are full of thoughts about what can happen to families that are in culture shock, in misunderstandings, double standards. Like Floyd in the play, that's real life experience for me. This *pe'a*, it grows on me and will be completed tonight. It's had a profound effect and I have gone through all sorts of emotions and I am finding myself again, that's it. [...] It has been a real life experience for me. I am not an actor I am just the canvas. [...] I wanted some changes in my own personal life. More than that. You've not only got to talk the talk, but walk the walk as well. And it's a heavy decision for me. But I have walked the other way and it is time to walk the other way. This *pe'a* is the other way. Thank you for coming tonight. (*He hobbles off the stage assisted by the tattooer and his assistants*).[5]

In this speech, the "human canvas" establishes an analogy between himself and the character of the son in the play, who at the end is ready for initiation by tattooing.[6] Although the son is already marked by other tattoos—a result of his involvement with street gangs and imprisonment—these signs single him out as a social outsider. The Samoan initiation ritual, on the other hand, has precisely the opposite function. It enables an individual to be fully socially integrated. Applied to the situation of the Samoan diaspora in New Zealand, it means that the son is prepared to assume responsibility for himself and Samoans in New Zealand. It symbolizes the assumption of responsibility for the *communitas* in the diaspora.

The integration of a tattooing ceremony into a theatrical performance posed a number of controversial questions, involving as it did a redefinition of "frames" in Erving Goffman's terms. The ritual ceremony, which is normally performed in a semi-private space, is transported into the public arena of the theatre; conversely, the theatrical frame, which is

---

[5] The speech is a transcript from a videotape of the Auckland production (premiered at the Herald Theatre on 1st February 1996) kindly provided by Pacific Underground.

[6] The tattooing on stage occupies only a fraction of the time which the whole process requires. During the two-week performance season, the body is decorated throughout the day, so that by the end of the run the ritual can be completed. In this way, the spectator becomes witness to a genuine "work in progress."

determined by its capacity to fictionalize all elements within clearly
defined special and temporal parameters, is destabilized by the presence
of an actual ceremony. The scenes at the beginning and the end of the
evening are marked by actual events, real pain and non-actors. Those
involved in the ceremony—the tattooer and his "human canvas"—are
not actors, although certainly performers in a broader sense. Whereas
Goffman assumes that switching or confusing frames results in a negative experience for the participants, the performance of *Tatau* produced
precisely the opposite.[7] The tension generated by the authentic ceremony has an undeniable effect on the "subjunctive" frame of the theatrical performance. The wooden tapping of the tattooing instruments
provides an audible "drum beat" throughout the evening, so that its
rhythm becomes an important structuring element of the play, even
though it has no direct bearing on the diegetic level. In a certain sense,
the tattooing ceremony can be said to "authenticate" the fictional story
presented on stage, as it provides a frame of a different kind for the
events depicted. In the original Auckland production, further authenticity was added by the fact that the "body canvas," Vic Tamati, had
supplied much of the material for the fictional story being enacted. He in
effect listened to his story each night while being tattooed.

New Immigrants

An additional force to be reckoned with today are young artists from
Asia, particularly Indians and Chinese. Indian immigrants to New
Zealand have traditionally come from the Fiji Islands with its large
Indian population. Recently, there have been increasing numbers of
immigrants arriving directly from the Indian subcontinent without the
diversion via Fiji. The Chinese community is similarly divided—in
temporal terms at least. Some Chinese New Zealanders have roots going
back to the nineteenth century, others immigrated immediately after the
Second World War, and the most recent group, mainly from Taiwan and
Hong Kong, have arrived over the past ten years.

    These experiences have found theatrical expression in two highly ac-
claimed monodramas—from an international perspective perhaps New
Zealand's most effective form of theatre, hinging as it does on fine
writing and performative skills. Since 1997, New Zealand monodramas
have each year picked up major awards at the Edinburgh Fringe Festival.

---

[7]   Goffman notes: "Expecting to take up a position in a well-framed realm, he finds that
      no particular frame is immediately applicable, or the frame that he thought was appli-
      cable no longer seems to be. [...] He loses command over the formulation of viable
      response. He flounders." (378 f.)

In 1999, Jacob Rajan's *Krishnan's Dairy* received a coveted Fringe First award, after its sell-out seasons in New Zealand. I quote from the advertising blurb:

Gobi and Zina Krishnan have travelled from India to set up a corner shop in the farthest corner of the world—New Zealand—and they keep their dreams stacked on the shelves of their struggling business: Krishnan's Dairy. The Taj Mahal, love, obsession, magic, live music, high comedy and profound tragedy in an enchanting story of two ordinary people and a legendary love.[8]

Using *Commedia dell'arte* style half-masks, Rajan, Malaysian-born of South Indian parents, intertwines two stories. The play depicts the quotidian struggle of Gobi and Zina in their attempt to "make a go" of the corner dairy, retail outlets which in New Zealand today are predominantly run by Indians. Gobi's less than professional approach to business is considerably hampered by his wife Zina, who not only eats the sweets out of the stock, but is desperately homesick for India. In intercutting scenes, Zina tells her baby the story of the Emperor Sha Jahan, who built the Taj Mahal, a tale of great love and extreme cruelty. Rajan performs all the characters, in the quotidian as well as the mythohistorical worlds. The play is heavily bilingual as Rajan switches deftly not only between characters, but also between different registers of English and Hindi. The play also merges both tragedy and happy end: tragedy insofar as Gobi is shot dead by a burglar; a happy end insofar as the final scene shows Zina hard at work in the now thriving business, in the company of her son Apu who is a student of architecture:

Zina: Just a minute. Oh, hello, Gill how are you, how's the baby? Oh, good. Is that all? OK. That's ... $126, all right, can I have your card please. That's fine. Do you want a bag for that? OK Gill ... pardon, no, yes, I know, we usually do but I'm sorry we're sold out. There was another funeral at Davies St this morning. Big funeral, they all wanted flowers, hundreds of people just like in India, I think they were Maoris. No, I asked one of the women buying flowers, it was just a young boy, my son Apu's age, I know, terrible, terrible. Motor cycle accident, I know, I know, terrible, terrible. Apu went through a phase of wanting a motor cycle, I said nothing doing, motor cycle shmotor cycle, if you want to impress a girl, be nice to your mother. Oh, he's fine, it's the University holidays now, but he's studying hard for his exams. Architecture, no, I don't know ... well, his great uncle Regu was an architect, famous architect, he designed the ... what do you call the place where they race the bicycles ... no, no ... just a moment ... Apu, monee, bicycle *[Apu, son, the place* orditchure, athenda pera, ... *where they race the bicycles, what's that called?]*

Apu: Velodrome

---

8   Unpublished publicity material.

Zina: Velodrome, that's right. He designed the velodrome for the Olympic
games. Yah, I don't know it must be in the blood. OK, Jill, OK, cheerio ...
pardo ... oh really. No, I'm sure we do. Just a moment. *Apu, monee, ladder
keeri, 1.5 kilogram bag whole-meal flour onda norku ...slowly, [Apu, son,
get up the ladder and see if we've got a 1.5 kilogram bag of whole meal
flour] careful, sooshika, sooshika, pethika po [careful, careful, slow down]*

Apu: Mum, I'm O.K. Hi, Mrs Johnson, cold isn't it? (16)[9]

This ending deserves closer examination. On a thematic level, it neatly
ties together the motifs of the two narrative strands. Apu as a student of
architecture becomes associated with the great architect of the Taj
Mahal. The flourishing business in funereal flowers is a direct result of
Gobi's prescience in an earlier scene. On an ideological level, however,
the unequivocally affirmative ending throws several issues into relief.
The first one to be highlighted is, of course, the strong family bond, as
the previously uncooperative and as a storekeeper hapless Zina master-
fully handles all activities, aided by her obedient son. Here we are
confronted with one of a number of clichés and stereotypes which the
play unashamedly parades.[10] These, like all stereotypes, are ultimately
grounded somewhere in "real life," otherwise they would not have
sedimented into the popular experience and imagination. More unsettling, however, is the brief allusion to Maori culture. Put bluntly, the
Indian family is profiting from the Maori as they purchase large quanti-
ties of flowers ("hundreds of people just like in India") for a teenage son
killed in a motorcycle accident. In comparison with the family bonds
exerted by the Maori, Zina has her son firmly under control. Here we
find, albeit not stated explicitly, a form of inter-minority comparison
endemic to all multicultural societies. While Zina voices no explicit
criticism of the Maori (pity is more in order here), she nevertheless
makes an implicit assumption of superiority in the happy end scene.

Letters Home

Family bonds of a less secure nature link together the characters in *Ka
Shue: (Letters home)*, a monodrama by Lynda Chanwai-Earle, a fourth
generation Eurasian New Zealander. Unashamedly autobiographical, the
play connects the experiences of three generations:

> In writing *Ka-Shue (Letters Home)* I have focused on the personal and do-
> mestic lives of three generations of a Chinese family. *Ka-Shue* spans the
> cultures of New Zealand and China, encompassing a broad sweep of the po-

---

[9] My thanks go to the author for kindly providing me with access to his unpublished
script.

[10] In a less than ecstatic review, the New Zealand reviewer Tessa Laird articles a whole
series of stereotypes; see www.physicsroom.org.nz/2cents/dairy.htm, 28 June 1998.

litical events of this Century between the two countries as a backdrop for the personal dramas of the characters. (n. p.)

The published version comes with the usual and some unusual accoutrements of promotion: amongst the usual ones, one finds the biographical information and accolades by the press; the unusual accoutrements are the personal family photographs included. This dramatic work features many similarities to *Krishnan's Dairy*, with *Ka-Shue* in fact predating the Indian play by about a year. Apart from the family focus, we have bilingualism on the level of print rather than speech. All Chinese words are followed by their pictographs. The action also moves between the present, the past, and the world of the spirits. Involved in the action is a ghost figure, Lady Li, a concubine. Her "movements are loosely based on the performance style of the Peking Opera and should be graceful and surreal, as if she is the link between the living and the dead" ("Production Notes" n. p.). The three central figures are, however, women: Jackie Leung-Taylor, a student in her early twenties and, like the author, a Eurasian and fourth generation New Zealander; her mother, Abbie Leung, born in China and divorced from a New Zealander; Paw Paw, Abbie's stepmother, who runs the family greengrocer store in Wellington. Like *Krishnan's Dairy*, the involvement in business, for better or worse, constitutes a central motif in the play. The one male character, Gung Gung, the grandfather, is an addicted mah-jong gambler.

Rather than interpret the play myself, I shall quote at some length a response by a young New Zealand critic, Vanessa Jack, published in the online arts review *The Physics Room*:

she asked if i wanted to be involved. a review of a play. it was so exciting ... so exciting 'cos it's you ... i keep forgetting. a solo performance by lynda chanwai earle. called ka shue, letters home. music by karen hunter. directed by jim moriarty. supported by asia 2000, creative New Zealand, christchurch arts festival. the system approves. and it seemed logical for me to be interested in a half-caste artist. and I felt nervous and excited cos it matters. and i got dressed up, and i carried a pen and notebook, and I wore my silk brocade jacket and checked my chineseness in the mirror. my eyes looked squintier with my hat on. the intensity of her beginning alienated me. alone, yelling. energy projectiles, vigorous, propelled across the theatre. alienated by some stuck up idea that was instilled in me when i was too young to know, michael. about being obedient and inoffensive and humble [...]. i was alarmed by how well i knew this story. between feminist studies and amy tan it's all covered. let them feel secure in their knowledge. repetition makes things true. chinese for beginners. first chinese play from New Zealand. teach them. affirm what they know. inscrutable dog eaters. [...] across a taiwanese street, in a different lifetime, a boy recited to me at the top of his lungs the english he knew. Hello. I love you. Fuck you. tiananmen square.

bok choy. concubines. is this what it is to be chinese? culture clash. half-caste. this is why i was asked to write. 'cos we're the same. her and i. half castes [...] i enjoyed her schizophrenia, her multiplicity. pulling me in. jarring me. being many, contrary. capricious. the evening post sensibly noted that "the different attitudes and concerns of the women are vividly portrayed." déja vu. three generations of women. the wall was half-built already, i could feel my eyes roll. jesus. is there no more than this? three generations of women, the chinese version. what does it mean? all the stories we know? shadows on the wall death puppet show. HELLO? I love you. Fuck you. (wwww.physicsroom.org.nz/log/archive/2chch2.htm)

Vanessa Jack being too of Eurasian descent, her highly subjective and ambivalent reaction to the performance reflects the contradictory dynamics of the piece. The difficulty for the reviewer to find a position of "disinterested observation"—the one normally expected of theatre criticism—suggests that with plays such as these—which are themselves unashamedly autobiographical—it becomes difficult for spectators with a similar background to find a position "outside" the work.

Asia in the Pacific

These considerations would not be complete without a few words about Asia in the Pacific today, from a more explicitly political perspective. As it is only from the point of view of performance that I can speak about these matters with any kind of scholarly competence, I have selected a very recent cultural performance with which to conclude my analysis and with which to interrogate the question of New Zealand's *bi-* or *multi*cultural identity. The cultural performance in question is the ceremonial welcome given to Chinese president Zhiang Zemin upon his arrival on 11 August 1999 in Auckland, New Zealand for the recent APEC meeting.[11]

The following is a transcription of the television commentary accompanying the broadcast.

COMMENTATOR 1: John, can you hear me now?

COMM 2: I can indeed, thank goodness. The Pacific Island group is now approaching the aeroplane and now laying down the *tapa* cloth as you can see. That *tapa* cloth is very important. It was made in a Tongan village and is normally only used for Royalty and very high ranking chiefs. The equivalent basically of our red carpet.

[...]

COMM 1: Any sign of him, John?

---

[11] The following account and analysis are based on a video-recording of the event.

COMM 2: Yes, he's just emerged right now, Richard. President Zhiang Zemin of China with Madame Zhiang beside him. [...] They've just started coming down the steps and the challenge rings out from the Maori warriors who are lined up to give him an informal welcome here at the airport.

COMM 1: This of course will be quite an experience. I mean, China is a very different country from most of the rest of the world. They are coming here to an Anglo-Saxon country which also has a Maori part of the population. He will have never seen anything quite like this before. The best of us find it intimidating to be confronted by a *kapa haka* party. It will be interesting to hear, if we do hear, how the President has reacted to this challenge.

COMM 1: Prof. Clark, the President looks interested and impressed. Would you agree?

PROF. CLARK: As John Stewart said. I don't think he's seen anything like this before. He is a man who is aware of cultural difference, the importance of cultural difference. He has probably been briefed on the indigenous peoples of New Zealand and the Pacific island population of New Zealand, so he is seeing it now: in the flesh, so to speak.

COMM 1:But it also has to be said that for many Chinese they wouldn't be so positive about this sort of welcome.

PROF. CLARK: Some Chinese might regard this as a little dubious or a little uncivilized. Many Chinese people are aware of 5000 years of Chinese civilization. Zhiang Zemin himself and people of education in China recognize that different countries have different cultural traditions and it was obvious on the face of the President that this was a source of great delight.

COMM 1: Let's go back now to this marvelous welcome by the Polynesian communities of Auckland.[12]

Welcome ceremonies are elaborately staged, carefully prepared cultural performances with a high degree of semantic explicitness. One can speak of a semiotically controlled environment where nothing is left to chance: each step, each televisual image has been clinically tested. From a media point of view, political ceremonies of this kind are multi-use, as the images are transported not just to New Zealanders, but to viewers around the world, including of course China.[13] We have here an explicit double perspective: that of the television viewers and that of Zhiang himself as he exits the plane and surveys the scene beneath him. It is this perspective which interests the television commentators, who have at

---

[12] Transcript of a videotape recorded on 11 August 1999.

[13] The importance of this controlled media environment can be seen from the fact that Zhiang boycotted a state dinner in his honour in Christchurch later the same week until a handful of protesters on Tibet were removed or at least screened from his view. Police blocked off the protesters with vehicles until they were invisible both to his sight and, more importantly, to cameras.

their disposal an "expert," a professor of Chinese studies from Auckland University, to provide insight into it. Prof. Paul Clark officiates as the cultural broker or Oriental mind-reader for the New Zealand television audience. What Zhiang surveys is culturally speaking a mixed bag indeed: a motley array of New Zealand politicians in suits led by the then Prime Minister Jenny Shipley; a Maori kapa haka party with painted tattoos and whose intimidating dance of welcome appears designed to persuade the visiting Chinese dignitary to return whence he has come; the red carpet, international symbol of welcome, has been overlaid by a Tongan *tapa* cloth of great ceremonial significance. After having survived the *haka*, Zhiang is greeted by a pan-Pacific performance. Different island groups—Samoans, Cook Islanders, Tongans, Fijians, Tokelauns, and Niue islanders—provide a kind of Polynesian potpourri. As the camera cuts from group to group, the television commentators—not one ethnomusicologist among them—are hard put to distinguish one island group from the other. Ultimately, it does not matter, because in this case, the medium is indeed the message. In live performance, the age-old moment of first encounter that the first explorers to the Pacific recounted in such detail is being used again to welcome an Asian guest this time. In the carefully staged and choreographed steps of this encounter, there are, however, new as well as old agendas which lead us back to our area of inquiry: "Pacific Overtures and Asian Encounters." At the end of the twentieth century, the coordinates have indeed been shifted and rearranged. The Asians have reappeared on the gangway of a 747 of Air China to attend the most important meeting of Asian and Pacific trading partners. So what statement is being made here? There are of course as many answers as viewing perspectives. For the *pakeha* New Zealander viewer, the most striking element of the welcoming performance appears to be the inclusion of Pacific Islanders, albeit in a generic mix. This offers the clearest demonstration that the political rhetoric of New Zealand as a Pacific nation is given concrete form—it also demonstrates a decisive shift in the country's perception of itself as a bicultural nation. But where may we ask are New Zealand's many Asian immigrants? The large Chinese and Indian communities? They remain conspicuously absent, even for a visitor from China. It would seem that the performance is designed to expand the notion of the bicultural to encompass the Pacific immigrants rather than to attempt a genuine performance of multiculturalism. Even the commentators find it difficult to speak outside the bicultural paradigm.

Conclusion

There is another perspective on the question of *bi-* versus *multi*cultural-ism which I have not tried to elaborate in any detail: the Maori perspective. Whether one proceeds from the principles laid out in the Treaty of Waitangi or from the fundamental semantics of *marae* Protocol, then the great *bi-* versus *multi*cultural debate may in fact be a non-issue. If questions of encounter, of local versus foreign, or visitors and guests are viewed along the basic division of *tangata whenua* (local people) and *manuhiri* (guests), then the need to create ever increasing numbers of ethnic subdivisions can be regarded as a eurocentric problem arising from a European epistemology. Yet, when surveying other settler societies and postcolonial countries, the recognition of biculturalism in so many aspects of New Zealand life represents a significant achievement. We may therefore argue that the success of Pacific Island and other immigrant groups in the theatre is in fact a direct result of this bicultural model which can include so many forms of cultural diversity.

No matter what cultural perspective we apply, there is no doubt that New Zealand is realigning itself within coordinates defined not just by Europe, but also by Asia and the Pacific basin. These perceptual realignments, however, constitute difficult processes that cannot be effected just by staging folkloric performances for visiting dignitaries, although such performances are important indicators of wider paradigmatic shifts. One nation, two peoples: the equation no longer holds demographically. It remains to be seen if and when official discourse evolves to take cognizance of this. In the theatre, the move is already afoot, as we have seen, fraught with all the necessary conflicts and contradictions attendant on cultural performances in a multiethnic context. I wonder what my next passport will look like.

Works Cited

Balme, Christopher B. "New Maori Theatre in New Zealand." *Australasian Drama Studies* 15/16 (1989/90): 149-66.

_____. "Pacific Overtures: Interkulturelle Tendenzen im zeitgenössischen Theater Neuseelands." *Pazifik-Forum* 3 (1992): 211-26.

_____. "Between Separation and Integration: Intercultural Strategies in Contemporary Maori Theatre." *The Intercultural Performance Reader.* Ed. Patrice Pavis. London: Routledge 1996. 179-87.

_____ and Astrid Carstensen. "Homes Fires: Creating a Pacific Theatre in the Diaspora." *Theatre Research International* 26:1 (2001): 35-46.

Besnier, Niko. "Crossing the Boundaries: Niko Besnier looks at the dramatization of Fa'afafine in *A Frigate Bird Sings*." *Illusions* (Wellington) 25 (Winter 1996): 18.

Chanwai-Earle, Lynda. *Ka-Shue: Letters Home.* Wellington: The Women's Play Press, 1998.

Goffman, Erving. *Frame Analysis: An Essay on the Organisation of Experience.* Cambridge, Mass.: Harvard UP, 1974.

Http://www.tepapa.govt.nz/briefingpaper/BriefingPaper.html#Introduction. Last visit 1.5.2001.

Jack, Vanessa. *The Physics Room.* http://wwww.physicsroom.org.nz/log/archive/2chch2.htm.

Laird, Tessa. http://www.physicsroom.org.nz/2cents/dairy.htm

Mason, Bruce. *The Healing Arch: Five Plays on Maori Themes.* Wellington: Victoria UP, 1987.

Rajan, Jacob. *Krishnan's Dairy.* Unpublished manuscript, 1997.

Sinclair, Keith. *A Destiny Apart: New Zealand's Search for National Identity.* Wellington: Allen & Unwin, 1986.

Tatau – Rites of Passage. Videotape of the Auckland production. Premiered at the Herald Theatre on 1st February 1996.

Embodied Knowledges:
Technologies of Representation
in a Postcolonial Classroom[1]

Helen GILBERT

University of Queensland

To speak about postcolonial pedagogy from the vantage point of the Western academy is inevitably to engage with very personal and some-times confronting questions about how we, as individuals, are situated in relation to the material we bring to the classroom. For me, as an Austra-lian teacher of postcolonial theatre studies, such questions must begin with the possible uses of Aboriginal performance texts in university and school curricula. This focus on the local stems less from an assumption of familiarity with home-grown (as opposed to foreign) texts than from a conviction that in contemporary Australia, in the new millennium, the postcolonial classroom should be understood, with urgency, as a place for the work of reconciliation between indigenous and non-indigenous communities. Such urgency results in part from the stalling of the official reconciliation process[2] under our current conservative govern-ment, whose reign has overseen a general backlash against multicultur-alism on the part of white Australians and, in some sectors, more spe-cific resentment about the very gradual—and still very partial—empowerment of various Aboriginal groups. A fiercely debated issue in this political landscape is our prime minister's continued refusal to apologise or offer compensation to survivors of what has been termed the Stolen Generations, those thousands of Aboriginals (mostly of mixed ancestry) forcibly removed from their parents as children during

---

[1] I wish to thank Gillian Whitlock for her invaluable feedback on an early draft of this essay and to acknowledge her work on memoir and the Stolen Generations' testimo-nials as starting points for my research.

[2] A Commonwealth Government act established the Council for Aboriginal Recon-ciliation in 1991. Its task was "to promote a process of reconciliation between Ab-original and Torres Strait Islanders and the wider Australian community based on appreciation of Aboriginal and Torres Strait Islander cultures and achievements" (quoted in Casey 55).

an era of government-mandated assimilation lasting from early in the twentieth century until the 1970s.[3] Since the tabling five years ago of the *Bringing Them Home* report, which registers testimony gathered by the Australian Human Rights Commission from hundreds of Aboriginals segregated from their families and communities and often subjected to physical, sexual, and psychological abuse in their new homes, the "stealing" of Aboriginal children has become our most publicly discussed atrocity and, for many intellectuals on both sides of the racial divide, a kind of flash-point signalling the ongoing crisis in cross-cultural relations.

Australia's troubled progress towards a reckoning with injustices inflicted upon indigenous peoples is by no means unique. As Gillian Whitlock notes, "Discourses of reconciliation have emerged in the past decade as one of the most powerful scripts for interracial negotiation in states which struggle with the legacies of Eurocolonialism" (210). Her contention that reconciliation is now a key word/concept in ideoscapes of democracy in "widely dispersed though not disconnected locations" such as Australia, Canada, and South Africa (210), suggests the potential force of a comparative analysis within this field, even though that exercise also has its perils. In particular, recent scholarship warns of two opposing tendencies as crucial pitfalls in postcolonial teaching: the tendency to draw all texts into an incorporating universalism that seeks equivalents—in experience, in outlook, in essence—as a way of understanding other cultures; and, equally limiting, the tendency towards a cultural relativism that positions other cultures as *so* different that there can be no criteria for real engagement. By taking this latter approach, as Satya Mohanty argues, "we may avoid making ethnocentric errors, but we also, by the same logic, ignore the possibility that [other cultures] will ever have anything to teach us" and so "gain only an overly general and abstract kind of tolerance" divorced from understanding or empathy (112).

With these pitfalls in mind, I hope to illustrate the immense pedagogical value of using performative processes such as workshopping, improvisation, and rehearsal as strategies for interpreting (and responding to) both local and foreign plays within a postcolonial classroom. The ensuing analysis is not designed to address more general debates about the effectiveness of performance as a form of pedagogy within academically based drama or theatre programmes; it appears well established by now that performing a text can and does work to produce valid and

---

[3]   In contrast, the Canadian government has formally apologised for similar policies during what is often termed the "scoop-up period," which roughly corresponds to the assimilation era in Australia.

valuable forms of knowledge.[4] My focus is much more specific, hinging on processes of embodiment that might be situated as part of a classroom agenda of cross-cultural engagement. The classroom discussed here remains a hypothetical one, but by no means one conceived as politically or culturally neutral. It is modelled on what I know of postcolonial theatre teaching in Australia, which happens mostly in academic, liberal arts programmes rather than in profession-based actor training facilities, and which supposes that students will be predominantly Anglo-Australian and mainly middle-class. I am not presuming that most classrooms will necessarily approximate mine, though I hope to elicit productive resonances or, perhaps even more crucially, productive dissonances across a range of teaching situations.

To insist upon a place for performance within classrooms where students are asked to confront texts by and about their racial or cultural others, is to bring issues of embodiment into focus in a particularly fraught way, necessarily raising questions about authenticity, respect, and agency, as it becomes clear that the performing body can never be reduced to a sign of free connotation. In this respect, Jon Erikson explains theatrical embodiment as follows:

> the problem of the body in performance is a two-fold one: when the intention is to present the body itself as flesh, as corporeality [...] it remains a sign nonetheless [...] not *enough* of a pure corpus. When the intention is to present the performer's body as primarily a sign, idea, or representation, corporeality always intervenes, and it is *too much* of a body." (242)

What this implies is that body-based categories such as race can be read, paradoxically, as both *pre*-formed and *per*formed,[5] as historically conditioned, but often anchored in biology. In performance, the tension between the body as sign and the body as corpus manifests or recedes according to the various technologies of representation through which the body is brought into visibility. By technologies of representation, I mean the intentional, mechanical processes used within a culturally inflected context to present an image of the body on stage, whether those processes involve fleshy embodiment, puppetry, multimedia, or even virtual simulation. This yields a Foucaultian notion of body technologies, which suggests that performance entails the enactment of all sorts of power relations, not only among actors, and between actors and their audiences, but also between actors, audiences, and broader systems of ritual practice.

---

4   See Dolan (1996), Knowles (1995) and Bennett (1995) for discussions of the ways in which debates about performance as pedagogy have unfolded in the United States and Canada.

5   This terminology is borrowed from Melissa Western's work on the performance of race and ethnicity in recent Australian theatre (2000).

To think about such issues in a pedagogical context, we might first examine the various body technologies embedded in particular teaching texts, researching historical and/or cultural data where necessary. This strategy is designed to allow for meaningful articulations between the performative templates suggested by the script and the body-based exercises developed in response. I am not claiming here that characters constructed according to certain conventions—be they naturalistic, ritualistic, Brechtian, operatic, carnivalesque, or whatever—should only be played in those styles, but rather that we need to identify the representational devices used to depict the body and assess their possible implications, both in their original cultural contexts and in the classroom situation. In this way, my pedagogy aims to combine conventional processes of interpretation with an investigation of performance as a possible site of intercultural engagement.

While various postcolonial plays could be brought into dialogue around specific aspects of representation, space limits my current discussion to just two recent texts: Jane Harrison's *Stolen* (1998) and Jane Taylor's *Ubu and the Truth Commission* (1997), both of which deal with issues of testimony and reconciliation following state-sanctioned atrocities, but in different national arenas: Australia and South Africa respectively.[6] My first example, *Stolen*, speaks directly to Australia's current debate about the Stolen Generations. Although Harrison's play premiered just months after the *Bringing Them Home* report was tabled, the project had begun some five years earlier with a commission by the Ilbijerri Aboriginal and Torres Strait Islander Theatre in Melbourne. Harrison, as writer, worked with a researcher and, during the later stages of the project, with a number of other Aboriginal theatre practitioners to produce a gripping text that draws from real life stories but, for the most part, does not re-enact testimonial as such. Instead, narratives of pain and loss are conveyed through an almost dizzying progression of non-chronological vignettes that sketch the experiences of five Aboriginals stolen from their families as children. Further fragmenting the individual character portraits are occasional dream/nightmare sequences, short sections of documentary footage, and two storytelling scenes that allegorise the figure of the white body snatcher within an Aboriginal oral history/mythology. As Marc Maufort notes, this "exploded" structure, reiterated visually in a poignant moment when one of the children

---

6   In each nation, these texts form part of a larger body of "reconciliation theatre," versions of which include Deborah Mailman and Wesley Enoch's *The Seven Stages of Grieving* (1995), Deborah Cheetham's *White Baptist Abba Fan* (1998), and, in South Africa, the Khulamani Support Group's 1997 play, *Indaba Engizoyixoxa (The Story I Am About To Tell)*. In the latter text, designed to spread awareness of issues raised by the Truth and Reconciliation Commission hearings, actual victims of apartheid play themselves.

attempts to reconstruct a photo that has been torn to pieces, functions as an "analogue of the fragmentation that afflicts the characters' lives" (4). Five old iron institutional beds arranged across the stage establish the main setting as a children's home, which, with the aid of a few functional props easily morphs into other spaces: a prison cell, a mental institution, a girl's bedroom (Harrison n.p.). At the very end of the play, the stage is repositioned as a place for formal witnessing when the Aboriginal actors step out of their roles and speak directly to the audience, giving personal responses to the stories of the Stolen Generation.

At first glance, the corporeal technologies employed in this play seem relatively straightforward: in what *we* might categorise as a Brechtian aesthetic, five adult actors demonstrate rather than fully impersonate their characters, moving easily between roles as children, adults, chorus members, white authority figures, and off-stage voices. Except for the fact that the actors themselves are Aboriginal—and need to be so within the cultural, political, and theatrical contexts of a public production—the performance text demonstrates a "radical flexibility"[7] in its use of body-based signifiers. Hence categories such as physical type, age, gender, and even race are brought into representation across bodies that do not always allow a seamless fit, thereby making visible their position within ideology. This kind of dramaturgy models the transformative body that postcolonial theorists often valorise.

But, crucially, there is another kind of body embedded in this text, an essentialised, racialised body brought into sharp relief when the institutionalised children assemble for inspection by a white couple who will choose just one to take home for the weekend. In the stage directions, the scene is described as follows:

> A bell rings and the children line up centre stage, front. Then, they look at the person next to them and realise that they are not in the right order of lightest to darkest. They rearrange the line-up and stand expectantly, straightening their clothes and looking eager. (4)

Subsequently, in what becomes a potent visual motif, the children periodically repeat the line-up routine, rapidly learning their ascribed places in the racial hierarchy. Since this careful choreography is never explained in the dialogue, it achieves its full effect only if the actors themselves can be lined up in a similar "light-to-dark" formation. Here, despite the demand that each actor's skin colour must be seen to fit his or her role quite precisely, I would hesitate to classify the representation of race at work as naturalistic, because it seems that something much more strategic is happening. The recurrent line-up routines create a

---

[7]   The term is Richard Schechner's (6), though the practices to which he refers are relatively common outside the realm of Western naturalism.

spectacle of the actors' and the characters' apparent racial differences—
from each other and from non-Aboriginal audience members—to the
extent that the Aboriginal body begins to signal its historical status as
over-determined, over-classified, which in turn upsets the very dynamics on which the scene hinges. In this respect, the line-up motif might be
seen as a performative rendition of Gayatry Spivak's notion of "strategic
essentialism," the deliberate foregrounding of particular markers of
"pure" difference as part of a "scrupulously visible political interest"
(205). The line-ups also crystallise opposing "surface-versus-depth"
interpretations of race insofar as the children initially experience Aboriginality as fully embodied (in this case through experiences of loss
and trauma), but quickly learn how surface markers of Aboriginal
identity (shades of skin) are made to mean.[8]

   The strategically racialised body in *Stolen* also functions as the
means through which narratives of trauma are enacted as history. Without this specific body technology, generally operating in tension with
the flexibly raced, transformative body as outlined earlier, many of the
vignettes could be dislodged from their specific historical referents. In
particular, the children's games and cleaning routines, which form a
central part of the text, are anchored to the Stolen Generations testimonials via corporeal markers of Aboriginality inscribed in/on the actors'
bodies. Let me briefly illustrate how this works by describing "Cleaning
Routine 2," a particularly resonant scene for Australian audiences. An
authority figure, in voice-over, asks the Aboriginal children what they
are going to be when they grow up; then, as each child in turn calls out
"nurse," "fireman," "circus performer," "doctor," and so forth in a long
list, the voice shouts an adamant "no!" Only menial domestic roles or
manual labour get a thumbs-up response. Disappointed, the children
dance around singing a song about what kinds of work they will and will
not be allowed to do, appropriating the tune of "We're Happy Little
Vegemites" in a moment of piquant irony. (For the uninitiated, vegemite, a black yeast-based spread represents something of an Australian
icon; the song is an advertising jingle originally sung by emphatically
white children, who, apparently, would be able to do anything provided
they ate their vegemite.) More sombre moments at which the Aboriginal
body specifically functions to historicise narratives of trauma are scattered throughout the text. One early scene shows a youth, Jimmy, being
beaten while a letter written by his mother but intercepted by the white
authorities is projected over his face. Equally disturbing is a series of

---

[8]   The surface-versus-depth debate about race seems to depend on pitting Foucaultian
      notions of an inscribed body against phenomenological notions of a lived body. For
      further discussion of this issue, see Nick Crossley (1996), who argues persuasively
      that the distinction between the two cannot be maintained.

"unspoken abuse scenes" in which a patty-cake game with its simple refrain of "I promised not to tell" reveals, elliptically, that two of the children have been sexually violated while visiting white homes.

The dialectic between transformative and essentialised body modalities that I have outlined in relation to *Stolen* models a real-world politics of identity that comes into focus at the very end of the performance text, when cast members shed their roles to speak directly to the audience in what might be interpreted as another kind of line-up scene. The actors talk about their own lives, about their ancestry, about the children they have had or will have. One, Pauline Whyman, reveals that she and ten of her fourteen siblings were all stolen. In what constitutes a fairly representative response from reviewers, Jo Litson, writing for *The Australian*, describes this moment as a "blow to the solar plexus," when "your heart goes out to her while guilt curdles your stomach" (16). What I think is happening here is a complex moment of witnessing which fulfils Harrison's claim that her play works towards "healing the rift between black and white Australia" (quoted in Hart 67). The actor, as an Aboriginal stolen from her family, bears the physical inscription (the past) of that trauma—conveyed to the audience though memory—at the same time as she is fully embodied in the performative present. Her role(playing) as the character Shirley and her real-life testimonial as Pauline Whyman are both witnessed as authentic in this finale, although perhaps in different ways. The reviewer appears ideally positioned at this point to become the "second person" implied in all testimonial transactions. In Whitlock's formulation, the second person, the addressee, "is called upon to witness her own complicity and implication in the loss and suffering which is finally being spoken" (209). This forms a necessary part of the process of reconciliation which "demands from the second person an ethical performance of civic virtue that is cast in a particular discursive framework, and which is understood to be an engagement with emotion, and a recognition of shame" (Whitlock 210). Litson's review manifests exactly this response, and I imagine it speaks for much of the wider audience, despite the fact that, in Harrison's words, "there was a lot of sorrow [in the play] but not a lot of blame" (quoted in Hart 67).

If *Stolen* depends so crucially on its Aboriginal actors for both aesthetic and political effect, if it functions so specifically within a testimonial contract between Aboriginal and non-Aboriginal Australians—a contract that becomes more urgent with our government's continued refusal to witness the testimonies of the Stolen Generation in any ethical way—how can we take this text into a pedagogical context that would seem to strip away much of its performative power? If scenes are workshopped using a colour-blind casting model, what are the possible politics of embodiment for non-Aboriginal students—or for Aboriginal students, if there are any in the class? Can white actors understand aspects of Aboriginality through an empathetic performance of roles marked specifically as outside their racial/cultural experience? Perhaps. But I would suggest that the more valuable task here would be a corporeal exploration of race itself as an ideologically loaded category. Enacting scenes using the transformative body technologies that the play itself incorporates might produce credible Brechtian-style performances of Aboriginal stories (alienating assumed signifiers of alterity in ways that could be analysed intellectually), but I wonder whether this really constitutes a praxis of embodiment. Moreover, because so much of *Stolen* dramatises the characters' experiences as children, their specificity as Aboriginals is easily elided in a broader narrative of childhood that positions them as inherently at risk, inherently disempowered in the face of adult cruelty. Such elisions can be understood in terms of Joanne Wallace's proposition that the child's uncertain ontological status lends itself to appropriation within colonial discourse. She argues that the category of "the child," while highly visible, is never fully marked with the signs of culture: the child "remains caught in tension between what one might call the empty and the full, between lack (of personality, attributes, and history) and excess (full natural presence)" (291). He or she is therefore a site of anxiety, a presence without agency. This could explain why the trope of the stolen child figures so prominently in fables about childhood across diverse cultures.[9]

If the discursive purchase of childhood as a co-optative framework allows an easy *entrée* into *Stolen*, my strategy of interference would focus on ways to unsettle that dynamic, possibly by workshopping the line-up sequences in which Harrison's other body technology comes into play so forcefully. One workshop scenario might go as follows:

a) with 8–10 students, I imagine that we have been instructed to arrange ourselves in a line according to physical manifestations of whiteness, most white at one end, least at the other; we must do this in silence, without consultation or argument;

b) then we are told to reassemble because the order is incorrect, so we repeat the exercise, perhaps several times;

c) eventually, when the onlookers (the rest of the class) agree that the line-up is satisfactory, we go ahead and finish the short scene as written.

---

[9] In *Stolen*, the Mungee is explicitly troped as a body-snatcher, a mythologised outcast who steals and eats children from the Aboriginal camp. He is made visible when the elders throw magic powdered bone over him, thereby turning him into a pale skin—a metaphor for the white authorities responsible for removing the children from their families.

Of course, there are perils embedded in such an exercise, but, in theory, it brings whiteness into focus as a racial category, an embodied "something" that has to be identified—and even defended—as we establish our position in the line. Richard Dyer's pioneering work on whiteness suggests the import of this kind of cognition: "As long as race is something only applied to non-white peoples, as long as white people are not racially seen and named, they/we function as a human norm" (1). This, in turn, allows white hegemony to reproduce itself, "regardless of intention, power differences and goodwill" (10). The line-up exercise might also raise the issue of Aboriginality that is not necessarily marked by visible racial difference, for instance among students who look white but identify as Aboriginal. The difficulty in categorising such students also works to destabilise hegemonic power relations, because, in Dyer's terms, the power of whiteness as a racial category relies on its exclusive ability to reproduce itself as white (25). In terms of the reconciliation work that *Stolen* aims to perform, I would argue that to dislodge the centrality of whiteness while acknowledging our own position(s) in relation to its constructed parameters—these will vary across historical periods and cultural groups—is to prepare ourselves to choose that second person position, to become witnesses to our own complicity in the theft of Aboriginality that the narratives of the Stolen Generations so poignantly convey.

More fully aware of their whiteness as a privileged though not uncontentious identity, students might productively workshop another scene, titled "Racial Insults," in which Jimmy and an unseen white antagonist hurl offensive epithets at each other, until the action segues to a prison cell where Jimmy hangs himself after writing a final letter to the mother he so desperately wanted to find. My purpose in this particular exercise is to set up a situation through which non-Aboriginal students might experience in more complex ways what it means to be absolutely unable to pass across the technologies of race instantiated at that particular moment in the play. Following Rebecca Schneider's work, I see this moment as one of heightened embodiment, as a fragment of history "passes across a body that cannot pass" to produce an "ontology of error" (11). This error, evidence of a performance that is relentlessly citational, fosters respect for difference—at least theoretically. In this rather counter-intuitive assertion, my thinking is influenced by Spivak's argument that, whatever the "political necessity" for predicating knowledge on identification, and "whatever the advisability of attempting to 'identify' (with) the other as subject in order to know her, knowledge is made possible and is sustained by irreducible difference, not identity" (254). In the scenario I have described from *Stolen*, the embodied narrative of not passing also encapsulates precisely the irony of Australia's assimilationist practices: light-skinned children were removed from their families, apparently "rescued from their blackness," because they stood "a chance of passing as white" (Frow 358), which in turn was diminished by their very entry into white society. As one witness states in the *Bringing Them Home* report: "They tried to make us act like white kids but at the same time we had to give up our seat for a whitefella because an Aboriginal never sits down when a white person is present" (quoted in Frow 358-59).

Taking my second limit text, *Ubu and the Truth Commission*, into an Australian classroom involves a different set of dynamics, for at least two reasons: on the one hand, the text is likely to be understood as foreign to our particular experiences; on the other, it uses very different body technologies, presenting the performing body in a complex dialectic between the animate, the inanimate, and the animated. In broad terms, this multimedia tour de force, written by Jane Taylor in collaboration with visual artist William Kentridge and the Handspring Puppet Company, investigates issues of truth, reconciliation, and culpability in post-apartheid South Africa. The play's project, according to its author, was/is to examine the ambiguities inherent in the official reconciliation process—"the disjuncture between the testimony of those looking for amnesty and those seeking reparation" (Taylor iv). Different modes of expression register this disjuncture. A chilling vision of apartheid's perpetrators and tacit supporters is dramatised through the politicised reworking of Alfred Jarry's Ubu plays, so that Ubu and his wife are lifted out of their original burlesque world and into a domain where rampant greed and violence are shown to have recognisable, indeed catastrophic, consequences (Taylor iv). Two animal puppets feature within this domain, enabling the presentation of symbolic acts and/or concepts that would be somewhat difficult to achieve with human actors. Ubu's canine henchman, Brutus, figured as a dog puppet with three heads, is a potent reminder of the dogs trained to victimise black South Africans during the apartheid era. Niles, Ubu's advisor and cover-up man, takes the form of a crocodile puppet whose capacious mouth functions metaphorically as a shredding machine, an image Kentridge associates with a society asked to confront its crimes (viii). Projected archival film footage together with Kentridge's crude, Jarry-esque animations punctuate the perpetrator narrative, variously suggesting the extent of Ubu's crimes, the perversity of his desires, and the depths of his self-deception. Interpolated into the narrative of Ma and Pa Ubu's exploits, several scenes reveal the stories of apartheid's victims by using humanoid puppets through whom witness testimony drawn from the Truth and Reconciliation Commission hearings is staged. The play's animations and documentary clips, while seldom used during the spare, sombre witness scenes, nonetheless expand the latter's resonances, often demonstrating what is unspoken—or unspeakable—within the testimonies.

In terms of body technologies, *Ubu and the Truth Commission* provides a surfeit of possible models. While Ma and Pa Ubu, as played by human actors, are fully bodied, they are also paradoxically disembodied by the burlesque performance style and, in particular, by their recurrent representation in (or in relation to) mediatised forms. As Geoffrey Davis notes, "It is primarily the Kentridge animations that determine the characteristic visual language of the production" (69). Pa Ubu takes on some of the physical qualities of his screen double, becoming a cartoon-like figure with exaggerated movements and facial expressions and with a limited repertoire of emotional responses. At times, he almost seems to merge with the bizarre world depicted by the animations. Ubu's embodiment as a character is also modified by his interaction with Brutus, particularly during an early song-and-dance routine in which a composite figure is created by the combination of actor and puppet in various poses, including one that features a dog's head and over-long neck as Ubu's giant phallus. Another image of Ubu with his tail apparently wagging gives visual emphasis to his line: "We are the tail that wags the dog" (7). For her part, Ma also appears as something of a shape-shifter, seeming physically inflated—or what might be termed "over-embodied"—in many of her interactions with Ubu, merely human in her roles as translator and sometime puppeteer during the witness testimonials, and then disembodied when she presents herself, in video projection, as a giant, apparently free-floating head for the rendition of her television interview.

The various puppets in the play comprise a different sort of body technology. In an effort to explain the workings of puppetry as a mode of representation, Steve Tillis describes the puppet as "a theatrical figure, perceived by an audience to be an object, that is given design, movement, and frequently, speech, so that it fulfils the audience's desire to imagine it as having life" (65). For my purposes, there are two important aspects to this definition: that the puppet is always already theatricalised—because it exists only as a particular process of performance—and that it creates a paradoxical double vision as both inanimate and animated, provoking doubt as to its ontological status. We might argue, then, that the puppet occupies a space between embodiment and disembodiment, between perception and imagination. The puppets featured in *Ubu and the Truth Commission* are designed to exploit such ambiguities to various degrees. For instance, the witness puppets, according to Kentridge, were developed as a practical solution to the ethical question of how material drawn from real-life testimonials could be staged:

> There seemed to be an awkwardness in getting an actor to play the witness—the audience being caught halfway between having to believe in the actor for the sake of the story and also not believe in the actor for the sake of the actual witness who existed out there but was not the actor. Using a pup-

pet made this contradiction palpable. There is no attempt to make the audience think the wooden puppet or its manipulator is the actual witness. The
puppet becomes the medium through which the testimony can be heard. (xi)

Put in a slightly different way, we could say that the puppet functions as
an embodied space in and through which the viewer—the one who takes
responsibility for investing the puppet with life—fulfils his or her part in
the testimonial transaction by becoming the "second person" as discussed earlier in relation to *Stolen*, the responsive listener, the necessary
complement to the first person narrator in the generic form of testimony
(see Whitlock 199-200).

As a way of exploring Kentridge's dramaturgy in the classroom
situation, I want to imagine workshopping the puppet scene excerpted
below (the witness testimony is given in italics, the translation in plain
type as per Taylor's text):

Lomlungu wesikhafu esibomuu, wadubula lomntwana ngompu.

This white man with a red scarf, he shot at the child with his rifle.

Ndambona eruqa umntwana wam u Scholar.

I saw him dragging my child, Scholar.

U Scholar Wayeseswekekile.

Scholar was already dead.

Wayemtsala ngemilenze njengenja njengenja ecunyuzwe endleleni.

He was dragging him by the legs, like a dog, like a dog that is crushed in the
road.

Ndambona esimba umgodi wokufaka ubuchopo buka Scholar.

I saw him digging a hole—for Scholar's brains—

*Ilanga lalithe nka kodwa suke kwabamnyama xa ndimbona elele apho eli
linxeba elingasoze liphele.*

The sun was bright but it went dark when I saw him lying there. It's an ever-
lasting pain.

Andiqondi ukuba iyakuze iphele entliziyweni yam.

I do not think that it will ever stop in my heart. (47)

Various renditions of the scene could be attempted:

a) dispense with the puppet figure and have an actor perform the role of
witness with another actor translating his/her testimony;

b) keep the puppet concept but have this role performed by an actor
with expressionless face plus movements, manipulated by one or two
others who also deliver and translate the testimony;

c) have the actors assemble and animate a makeshift puppet, using
available materials and play the scene essentially as described in the
text.

Assuming that students are able to play these variant scenarios in a committed way, a number of generative issues might arise. Most obviously, performing the scene highlights the idea of mediated testimony, whereas reading it (in English) allows us to imagine that the witness character is speaking directly to a comprehending audience, particularly since the language is so powerful. In all three workshopped versions of the text, students are asked to voice—and listen to—an unfamiliar language, one that, in all likelihood, they have simply skipped over when reading the text. Such performative encounters with the foreign language (Xhosa) prove valuable insofar as they produce, at least theoretically, a sensory, embodied experience of alterity that helps to establish the distance between the words and the actor who now voices them as a cultural gap. In this manner, difference is maintained in the process of engagement. Even though the witness testimony is subsequently translated into English, notions of the "infinite transmissibility"[10] of meaning become problematic. For the actor playing the role of witness in the first (puppet-free) scenario, the cultural gap likely widens, since he/she is being asked to give expression to text that is not understood except when rendered comprehensible by another voice, that of the translator. This particular situation might be examined in reference to Kentridge's point about the awkwardness—and ultimately the ethics—of staging real-life testimonials. It might also raise questions about the relative ways in which the live actor and the puppet lend themselves to metaphor.

Different kinds of issues should emerge for the students using puppets to stage the witness testimony. As they physically manipulate their puppets, the puppeteers have opportunities to develop a corporeal awareness of mechanisms of control, of their own power as mediators, and, hopefully, of the responsibilities that it carries. Juxtaposed to such empowerment is the likely helplessness and voicelessness—the disempowerment—experienced by the actor who plays the role of a puppet. For the group with the makeshift puppet, there may be a developing experiential knowledge of possible connections between animate and inanimate objects as the puppeteers try out ways in which their puppet can be made to signify a particular kind of humanity. Can the puppet technology still function when there is no black puppeteer acting as metonym for the witness as in the original production directed by Kentridge? When comparing all three scenarios, in what ways are the politics of the situation worked out through different citations of the text?

---

[10]   This concept, drawn from Bill Ashcroft's work on postcolonial language, is more fully discussed in my book, *Sightlines*, but in reference to orality in Aboriginal theatre (Gilbert 85).

Rather than simply transferring knowledge, the pedagogical process sketched here aims to produce, in the moment of embodiment, acts of cognition.[11] Of course there is no guarantee that this will happen, nor is the exercise without its pitfalls. The student attempting to enact the witness might simply become disengaged if unable to find ways of negotiating the cultural gaps manifest in the task. The student playing the puppet may baulk at crossing the ontological gap between human and object. In the hands of inexperienced animators, the strategy of using puppets to represent our cultural others could suggest white ventriloquism at its most basic level. A similar risk applies to the play itself, but is minimised in Kentridge's production by an insistence on theatrical (and political) transparency during all the witness scenes; thus the puppeteers remain highly visible, while the role of the translator is also foregrounded. In this way, the play seems to fulfil its creators' brief to "capture the complex relations of testimony, translation and docu-mentation apparent in the processes of the [Truth and Reconciliation] Commission itself" (Taylor vii).

The experiments outlined are not intended to lead towards authentic renditions of the texts;[12] as David Moody has argued, that would be both impossible to achieve and "an act of critical bad faith to the plays them-selves and to their own postcolonial contexts and interventionist agen-das" (140). In this respect, I remain mindful of Alan Filewod's warning about the risks of taking a play out of its interproductive field—"the matrix of texts, performances and audiences [that] constitutes a dis-course of material practice, and which therefore can absorb and synthe-size contradictions" (372). But, I suppose, I *am* claiming the classroom as a privileged space, where protocols of response and established interpretive repertoires[13] might allow us to confront the risks inherent in exploring the vexed politics of theatrical embodiment. By bringing *Stolen* and *Ubu and the Truth Commission* into this classroom within a broadly comparative framework, my aim is to seek echoes, not rigid symmetries. That project is made easier by the fact that these plays have participated quite visibly in the transnational discourse of reconciliation

---

11   In this respect, my approach is based on Paulo Freire's contention that "education consists in acts of cognition, not transferrals of information" (53).

12   Nor is my approach designed to produce vicarious experiences of otherness that are not critically interrogated.

13   The concept of "interpretive repertoires," borrowed from discourse analysis, refers to "systems of terms used for characterizing and evaluating actions, events and other phenomena" (Potter and Wetherell 149). In the classroom situation discussed here, a repertoire would be organised around a recognisable range of verbal, physical, and emotional expressions/gestures that are typically used for interpreting texts. Obvi-ously, the repertoires would depend to some extent on the kind of framework set up for the study of particular courses.

discussed earlier, both having been staged outside their countries of origin to great critical acclaim. Their portability reminds us that in an increasingly globalised world the politics of reconciliation, while intensely localised, are not wholly determined within national domains (Whitlock 201). To bring the performing body into this transnational discourse at the very personal level of teaching is to draw attention to the fissures running through postcolonialism as an academic formation, but also—I hope—to realign knowledge viscerally, as well as intellectually.

Works Cited

Bennett, Susan. "Academic Trouble: A Response to 'This Discipline Which Is Not One'." *Theatre Research in Canada* 16.1/2 (1995): 92–94.

Casey, Maryrose. "Siting Themselves: Indigenous Australian Theatre Companies." *Siting the Other: Revisions of Marginality in Australian and English-Canadian Drama.* Ed. Marc Maufort and Franca Bellarsi. Brussels: P.I.E.-Peter Lang, 2001. 53–68.

Crossley, Nick. "Body-Subject/Body-Power: Agency, Inscription and Control in Foucault and Merleau-Ponty." *Body and Society* 2.2 (1996): 99–116.

Davis, Geoffrey. "Addressing the Silences of the Past: Truth and Reconciliation in Post-Apartheid Theatre." *South African Theatre Journal* 13.1/2 (2000): 59–72.

Dolan, Jill. "Producing Knowledges That Matter: Practicing Performance Studies Through Theatre Studies." *TDR* 40.4 (1996): 9–19.

Dyer, Richard. *White.* London: Routledge, 1997.

Erikson, John. "The Body as Object of Modern Performance." *Journal of Dramatic Theory and Criticism* 5.1 (1990): 231–43.

Filewod, Alan. "Receiving Aboriginality: Tomson Highway and the Crisis of Cultural Authenticity." *Theatre Journal* 46 (1994): 363–73.

Freire, Paulo. *Pedagogy of the Oppressed.* Trans. Myra Bergman Ramos. London: Penguin, 1972.

Frow, John. "A Politics of Stolen Time." *Meanjin* 57.2 (1998): 351–68.

Gilbert, Helen. *Sightlines: Race, Gender, and Nation in Contemporary Australian Theatre.* Ann Arbor: U of Michigan P, 1998.

Harrison, Jane. *Stolen.* Sydney: Currency, 1998.

Hart, Jonathan. "Act of Healing." *The Advertiser* (31 March 2000): 67.

Kentridge, William. "Director's Note." *Ubu and the Truth Commission.* By Jane Taylor. Capetown: U of Capetown P, 1998. vii–xv.

Knowles, Richard Paul. "This Discipline Which Is Not One." *Theatre Research in Canada* 16.1/2 (1995): 82–91.

Litson, Jo. "White Heat Black Stories." *The Australian* (20 May 2000): R16.

Maufort, Marc. "Jane Harrison's *Stolen* and the International Post-Colonial Context." Paper delivered at the Playing Australia Conference, London, November 1999.

Mohanty, Satya. "Colonial Legacies, Multicultural Futures: Relativism, Objectivity, and the Challenge of Otherness." *PMLA* 110 (1995): 108–18.

Moody, David. "Different Stages: Post-colonial Performance as Frictional Methodology." *(Post)Colonial Stages: Critical and Creative Views on Drama, Theatre and Performance.* Ed. Helen Gilbert. Hebden Bridge: Dangaroo, 1998. 136–45.

Potter, Jonathan, and Margaret Wetherell. *Discourse and Social Psychology.* London: SAGE Publications, 1987.

Schechner, Richard. "Race-Free, Gender-Free, Body-Type Free, Age Free Casting." *TDR* 33.1 (1989): 4–12.

Schneider, Rebecca. "Flesh Memory and the Logic of the Archive." Paper delivered at the Australasian Drama Studies Association Conference, Newcastle, July 2000.

Spivak, Gayatri. *In Other Worlds: Essays in Cultural Politics.* New York: Routledge, 1988.

Taylor, Jane. *Ubu and The Truth Commission.* Capetown: U of Capetown P, 1998.

Tillis, Steve. *Toward an Aesthetics of the Puppet: Puppetry as Theatrical Art.* New York: Greenwood, 1992.

Wallace, Jo-ann. "Technologies of 'The Child': Towards a Theory of the Child Subject." *Textual Practice* 9.2 (1995): 285–302.

Western, Melissa. "*Per*fomed or *Pre*-formed: An Interrogation of the 'Racially Marked Subject' as Seen on Contemporary Brisbane Stages." Paper delivered in the English Department Thesis Prospectus Seminar Series, University of Queensland, July 1999.

Whitlock, Gillian. "In the Second Person: Narrative Transactions in Stolen Generations Testimony." *Biography* 24.1 (2001): 197–214.

Notes on Contributors

Erol Acar studied English, history, educational theory and Romance languages and literature at the University of Bielefeld. He was a language teacher at secondary schools in Britain and France and a lecturer at the Goethe-Institut Helsinki and the Helsinki School of Economics and Business Administration. He is currently teaching at Janusz Korczak Comprehensive School in Gütersloh, Germany.

Robert Appleford teaches Native literatures and Canadian Drama at the University of Alberta in Edmonton. He has published numerous articles on Native Canadian performance and contributed to the volume *Native America: Portrait of the Peoples* (1994). Currently, he is at work on a monograph entitled *The Indian 'Act': Tactics of Performance in Native Canadian Theatre*.

Valérie Bada took her B.A. in German language and literature (1995) and her M.A. in English Studies in 1996. In 1996/97, she received a fellowship from the Belgian American Educational Foundation to spend a year at Harvard University. She has been a junior assistant with the Belgian Research Foundation at Liège University, where she is writing a Ph.D. thesis on African American and Caribbean theatre. She is currently working as a researcher at the Interdisciplinary Centre for Applied Poetics (CIPA) at Liège University.

Christopher Balme was born and educated in New Zealand. He has lived and worked in Germany since 1985. At present he holds the Chair in Theatre Studies at the University of Mainz. He has published widely on German theatre. He is Associate Editor of *Theatre Research International*. His most recent publication is *Decolonizing the Stage: Theatrical Syncretism and Post-Colonial Drama* (Clarendon Press, 1999). His current research project focuses on theatricality and cross-cultural performative encounters in the Pacific.

Franca Bellarsi is an instructor in English and American Literature at the Université Libre de Bruxelles. She has been associate editor for *Siting the Other. Re-visions of Marginality in Australian and English-Canadian Drama* (2001). She is currently finalizing her doctoral thesis devoted to a Buddhist reading of Allen Ginsberg's work and has contributed several articles on Beat mysticism and literature. Her book *Understanding Allen Ginsberg* will be published in late 2003 by the University of South Carolina Press.

Marcia Blumberg is Visiting Research Fellow at the Open University in England and Course Director for Drama Studies and English courses at Glendon College, York University in Toronto. Her doctoral thesis focussed on contemporary South African theatre; her postdoctoral work in England explored Theatrical Representations of AIDS. Specializing in contemporary theatre, she has presented numerous papers at international conferences, published many articles, and co-edited a book with Professor Dennis Walder, *South African Theatre As/And Intervention*.

Tom Burvill heads the Department of Critical and Cultural Studies at Macquarie University, Sydney. He has written extensively on Australian community and radical theatre and alternative performance forms, as well as co-published with John Tulloch on the production and reception of Anton Chekhov in English-speaking cultures. He maintains a close association with Sidetrack Performance Group, based in Marrickville in Sydney, with which he has collaborated as *dramaturg* and co-writer.

Geoffrey V. Davis teaches English at the University of Aachen in Germany. He read Modern Languages at Oxford, wrote his doctorate on German literature and recently received the degree of Dr. habil. for a thesis on South African writing during and after apartheid from the University of Essen. He is co-editor of the African Studies journal *Matatu* and of the series *Cross/Cultures: Readings in the Post/Colonial Literatures in English* for Rodopi.

Jozef De Vos studied Germanic Philology at the University of Ghent, where he also took his Ph.D. with a dissertation on the reception of Shakespeare in Flanders. He has published articles on the reception of Shakespeare and Shakespeare in performance in *Theatre Research International, Shakespeare Quarterly, Shakespeare Jahrbuch*. He is the editor of *Documenta*, a journal of theatre studies published in Dutch. He currently teaches English literature and theatre history at the University of Ghent.

Thierry Dubost is Professor of English, Dean of the Distance Learning Center and Director of the Groupe de Recherches en Etudes Irlandaises at the University of Caen (France). He is the author of two books: *Struggle, Defeat or Rebirth: Eugene O'Neill's Vision of Humanity* (Jefferson: McFarland, 1997), and *Le théâtre de Thomas Kilroy* (Caen: Presses Universitaires de Caen, 2001) and coeditor of three books: *La Femme Noire américaine, aspects d'une crise d'identité* (1997), *George Bernard Shaw, un dramaturge engagé* (1998), *Du Dire à l'Etre. Tensions identitaires dans la littérature nord-américaine* (2000), all published by Presses Universitaires de Caen.

Harry J. Elam, Jr is Robert and Ruth Halperin University Fellow, Professor of Drama, Director of Graduates Studies in Drama and Director of the Committee on Black Performing Arts at Stanford University. He is author of *Taking It to the Streets: The Social Protest Theater of Luis Valdez and Amiri Baraka* , coeditor of *African American Performance and Theater History: A Critical Reader* and co-editor of *Colored Contradictions: An Anthology of Contemporary African American Drama* and *The Fire This Time: African American Plays for the New Millennium*. He has just finished a book entitled, *(W)Righting History: The Past as Present in the Drama of August Wilson*.

Alan Filewod is Professor of Drama in the School of Literatures and Performance Studies in English at the University of Guelph. His books include *Performing "Canada": The Nation Enacted in the Imagined Theatre* (forthcoming in 2002 by *Textual Studies in Canada*), *Workers' Playtime: Theatre and the Labour Movement since 1970* (with David Watt,

Currency Press, 2001), *Collective Encounters: Documentary Theatre in English Canada*. (U Toronto P, 1987) and several edited anthologies of Canadia drama. He is an editor of *Canadian Theatre Review* and has served as president of the Association for Canadian Theatre research.

Helen Gilbert teaches drama and theatre studies at the University of Queensland where she also directs experimental performance work. Her books include the award-winning *Sightlines: Race, Gender, and Nation in Contemporary Australian Theatre* (1998), *Post-colonial Drama: Theory, Practice, Politics* (co-authored with Joanne Tompkins 1996), and the edited anthology, *Postcolonial Plays* (2001). She is currently working with Jacqueline Lo on a study of Asian influences in Australian performing arts.

Eriko Hara is Associate Professor of International Communication at Tokyo Kasei University. Her teaching and research fields include American Literature, particularly modern American drama and feminist criticism. She has published articles on African American and Asian American women's drama. She is the translator of Gayle Austin's *Feminist Theories for Dramatic Criticism*. As an editor, she is currently completing a book on Gender and American Literature, which will be published in Japan in 2002.

Ric Knowles is Professor of Drama and founding member of the Centre for Cultural Studies at the University of Guelph. He is also a member of Faculty of the Graduate Centre for the Study of Drama, University of Toronto. He is editor of *Modern Drama*, editor of *Canadian Theatre Review* and author of *The Theatre of Form and The Production of Meaning: Contemporary Canadian Dramaturgies* (ECW Press, 1999).

Amelia Howe Kritzer currently serves as associate professor and chair of the Department of Theater at the University of St. Thomas in St. Paul, Minnesota. She is the author of *The Plays of Caryl Churchill: Theatre of Empowerment* (Macmillan, London, and St. Martin's Press, 1991). Her essays have appeared in a wide range of journals and edited collections, and she also edited *Plays by Early American Women, 1775-1850* (University of Michigan Press, 1995). As a specialist in women dramatists, she has directed plays by Caryl Churchill, Tina Howe, and other female playwrights. She has previously taught at West Virginia University and Indiana University.

Marc Maufort is a professor of English, American and postcolonial literature at the Université Libre de Bruxelles (Belgium). He is the author of *Songs of American Experience: The Vision of O'Neill and Melville* (1990), as well as the editor or co-editor of *Eugene O'Neill and the Emergence of American Drama* (1989), *Staging Difference. Cultural Pluralism in American Theatre and Drama* (1995) and *Siting the Other: Re-visions of Marginality in Australian and English-Canadian Drama* (2001). His current research concentrates on contemporary Canadian, Australian and New Zealand drama.

Drew Milne is the Judith E. Wilson Lecturer in Drama and Poetry at Cambridge University. He works on drama, poetry and critical theory with an emphasis on modernism and contemporary writing, especially Samuel Beckett. He is also interested in aspects of Elizabethan and Jacobean drama. He edited

Marxist Literary Theory: A Reader (Blackwell, 1996) with Terry Eagleton and edits the journal *Parataxis: Modernism and Modern Writing*. He has published several books of poetry, including *Sheet Mettle* (1994), *Bench Marks* (1998) and *The Gates of Gaza* (2000).

Anne Nothof is a professor of English at Athabasca University, Alberta, Canada, where she has developed distance education courses on theatre history, Canadian and British drama, feminist and post-colonial literature. Her essays on Canadian and British playwrights appear in *Modern Drama, Mosaic, TRIC, The International Journal of Canadian Studies, David Hare: A Casebook*, and *Siting the Other* (2001). For Guernica Press, she has edited a collection of essays on Sharon Pollock, and for NeWest Press, a new edition of Pollock's *Blood Relations and Other Plays*. She is a board member for NeWest Press, and president of the Association for Canadian Theatre Research/Association de la recherche théâtrale au Canada.

Robert Nunn was, until his recent retirement, a professor in the Theatre and Dramatic Literature Programme of the Department of Fine Arts, Brock University, St. Catharines, Canada. He is the author of a number of articles on Canadian drama and dramatists. From 1993 to 1996 he was co-editor of *Theatre Research in Canada /Recherches théâtrales au Canada*. He is on the editorial board of that journal and of *Essays in Theatre /Etudes théâtrales*.

Barbara Ozieblo teaches American Literature at the University of Malaga, Spain, where she has been Head of the Department of English and Dean of the Facultad de Filosofia y Letras; her fields of research are Women's Studies and theatre. In 2000, the University of North Carolina Press published her biography of *Susan Glaspell: A Critical Biography*. Barbara Ozieblo is the coordinator of a research team at the University of Málaga, which concentrates on women in the American theatre.

Alain Piette is Professor of English and Director of the American Studies Center at the University of Mons-Hainaut, as well as Visiting Lecturer at the Catholic University of Louvain, Belgium. He is the author of numerous essays and of books on drama, cinema, translation, and education published in the United States and Canada, Asia, and Europe. A former Fulbright Scholar at the University of Michigan (Ann Arbor), he holds M.F.A. and D.F.A. degrees from the Yale School of Drama, where he studied as a CRB-Hoover Fellow of the Belgian-American Educational Foundation.

Maya Roth is a lecturer in drama at UC Berkeley, where she recently completed her Ph.D. Her specializations include contemporary women playwrights, modern drama, and creative revisionings of theatrical and civic space. She has presented extensively on the plays of Timberlake Wertenbaker. A former graduate coordinator of the inter/national Jane Chambers Playwriting Contest, Roth now serves as Associate Editor for the *Women and Theater* newsletter. She is also an accomplished performer, director and *dramaturg*.

Donna Soto-Morettini is Director of Drama for the Royal Scottish Academy of Music and Drama. She previously served as Head of Acting for the Central School of Speech and Drama in London and Head of Acting for the

Liverpool Institute for Performing Arts. Born in California, she has taught at the University of California, Irvine, and at Orange Coast College before completing her Ph.D. at Oxford in 1988, under the supervision of Terry Eagleton. Prior to this she worked as a professional actress, vocalist and studio singer, performing throughout the Western United States and Canada. Her work has been published in *Theatre Journal, Kreatief,* and *The Journal of Dramatic Theory and Criticism,* and her book *Slipping into Something Comfortable: Identity and Popular Culture* was published by LIPA Press.

Martina Stange holds a doctorate in American Studies. She studied financial law, English, comparative literature, history and theology in Sigmaringen, Bielefeld and Paderborn. She is the author of *"Modernism and the Individual Talent": Djuna Barnes' Romane* Ryder *und* Nightwood (1999) and has co-edited *Sammeln—Ausstellen—Wegwerfen: Kulturwissenschaftliche Gender Studies 2* (2001). Since July 1999 she has held a postdoctoral scholarship for her project "The poetics of collecting" at the University of Paderborn.

Drew Hayden Taylor is a Dora Mavor Moore and Chalmer's award winning playwright, author, journalist, and film maker. He has recently celebrated the launch of his eleventh book and the release of a documentary he directed for the National Film Board of Canada on Native-Indian Humour, titled *Redskins, Tricksters and Puppy Stew.* He is Ojibway from the Curve Lake Reserve in Ontario, Canada.

Bob Vorlicky is Associate Professor of Drama, and Coordinator of the Honors Program at the Tisch School of the Arts, New York University. He is the current President of the American Theatre and Drama Society and the author of *Act like a Man: Challenging Masculinities in American Drama* (1995). He is the editor of two books: *Tony Kushner in Conversation* (1998) and *From Inner Lives to Outer Space: The Multimedia Solo Performances of Dan Kwong* (2001). He has been the recipient of fellowships from such Institutions as the National Endowment for the Humanities and the Fulbright Foundation.

Jerry Wassermann is Professor of English and Theatre at the University of British Columbia in Vancouver, specializing in modern drama and theatre, and African American literature. He is editor of *Modern Canadian Plays,* now in its 4th edition, and has published widely on Canadian drama, modern fiction and blues literature. He is also an actor with many stage and screen credits including *The X-Files, Beggars & Choosers* and *Alive.*

Timberlake Wertenbaker is the celebrated author of such plays as *Our Country's Good,* winner of the Laurence Olivier Play of the Year Award in 1988 and New York Drama Critics' Circle Award for Best New Foreign Play in 1991, *The Love of the Nightingale* (1989), *Three Birds Alighting on a Field* (1992), *The Break of Day* (1995), and *After Darwin* (1998).

Dramaturgies
Texts, Cultures and Performances

This series series presents innovative research work in the field of twentieth-century dramaturgy, primarily in the anglophone and francophone worlds. Its main purpose is to re-assess the complex relationship between textual studies, cultural and/or performance aspects at the dawn of this new multicultural millennium. The series offers discussions of the link between drama and multiculturalism (studies of minority playwrights—ethnic, aboriginal, gay and lesbian), reconsiderations of established playwrights in the light of contemporary critical theories, studies of the interface between theatre practice and textual analysis, studies of marginalized theatrical practices (circus, vaudeville etc.), explorations of the emerging postcolonial drama, research into new modes of dramatic expressions and comparative or theoretical drama studies.

The Series Editor, **Marc MAUFORT**, is Professor of English literature and drama at the *Université Libre de Bruxelles*.

Series Titles

No.12– Malgorzata BARTULA & Stefan SCHROER, *On Improvisation. Nine Conversations with Roberto Ciulli*, Brussels, P.I.E.-Peter Lang, 2003, ISBN 90-5201-185-0.

No.11– Peter ECKERSALL, Naoto MORIYAMA & Tadashi UCHINO (eds.), *Alternatives* (provisional title), Brussels, P.I.E.-Peter Lang (forthcoming), ISBN 90-5201-175-3.

No.10– Rob BAUM, *Female Absence. Women, Theatre and Others Metaphors* (provisional title), Brussels, P.I.E.-Peter Lang (forthcoming 2003), ISBN 90-5201-172-9.

No.9– Marc MAUFORT, *Transgressive Itineraries. Postcolonial Hybridizations of Dramatic Realism*, Brussels, P.I.E.-Peter Lang, 2003, ISBN 90-5201-990-8.

No.8– Ric KNOWLES, *Shakespeare and Canada: Essays* (provisional title), Brussels, P.I.E.-Peter Lang (forthcoming 2003), ISBN 90-5201-989-4.

No.7– Barbara OZIEBLO & Miriam LÓPEZ-RODRIGUEZ, *Staging a Cultural Paradigm. The Political and the Personal in American Drama*, Brussels, P.I.E.-Peter Lang, 2002, ISBN 90-5201-990-8.